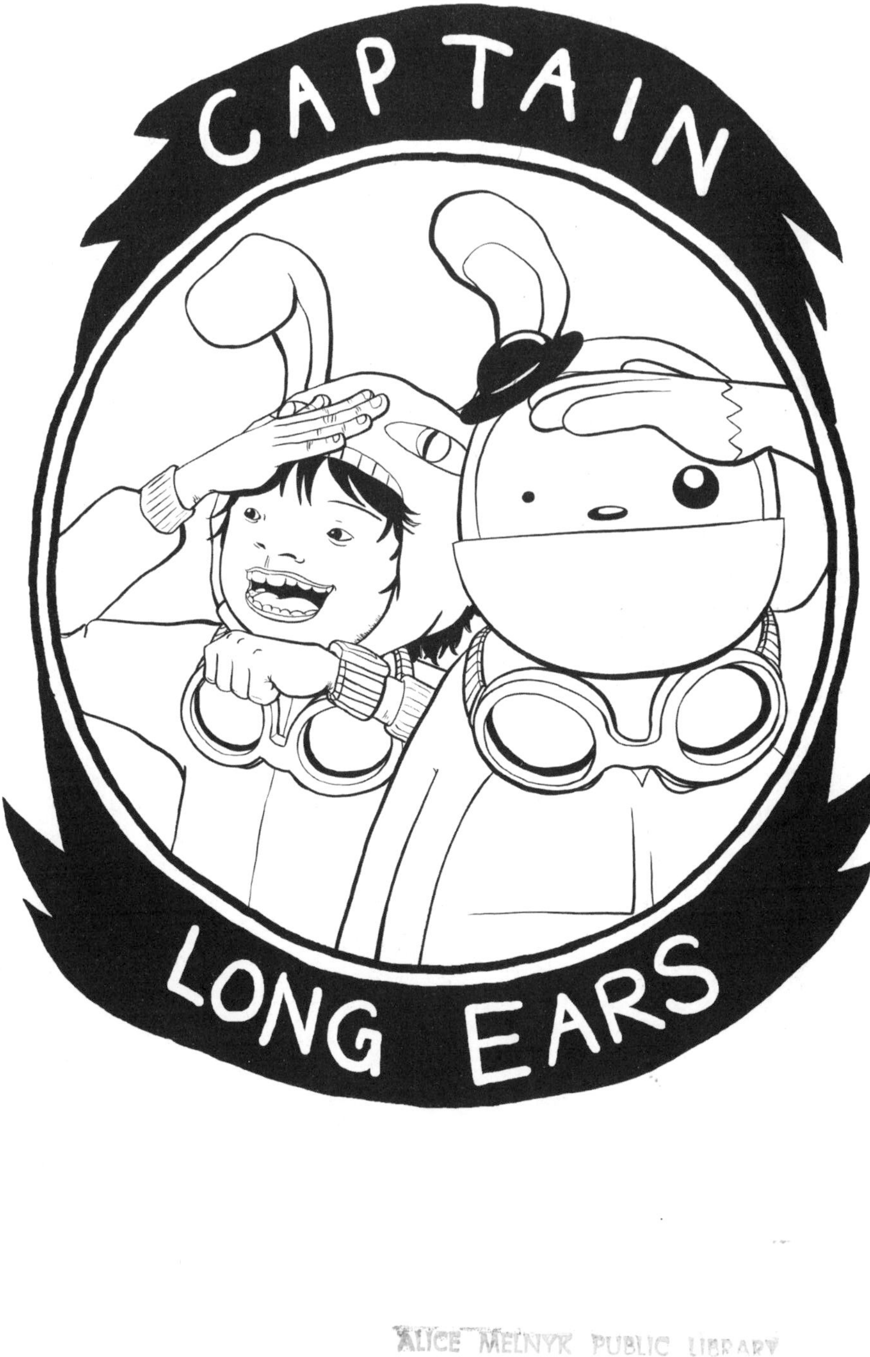
CAPTAIN
LONG EARS

Written and Illustrated by
Diana Thung

Published by
SLG Publishing
P.O. Box 26427
San Jose, CA 95159

www.slgcomic.com
www.dianathung.com

President and Publisher
Dan Vado

Editor-in-Chief
Jennifer de Guzman

First Printing: May 2010
ISBN: 1-59362-187-6
ISBN-13: 978-1-59362-187-2

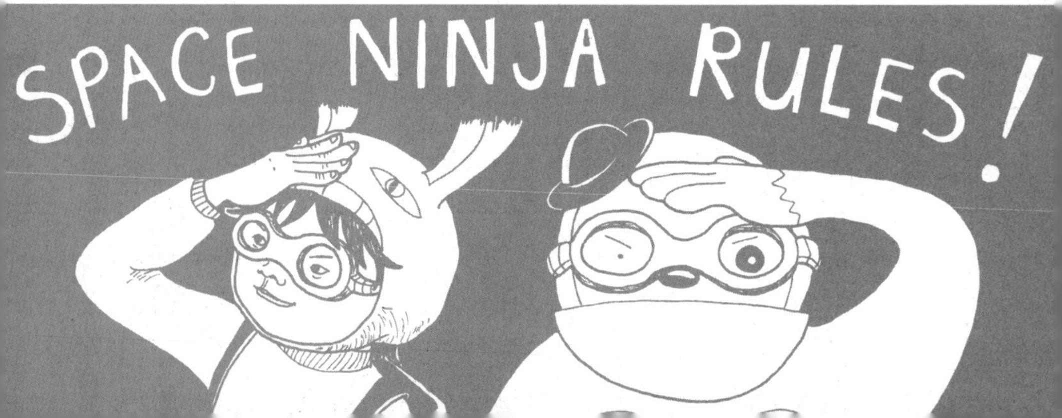
SPACE NINJA RULES!

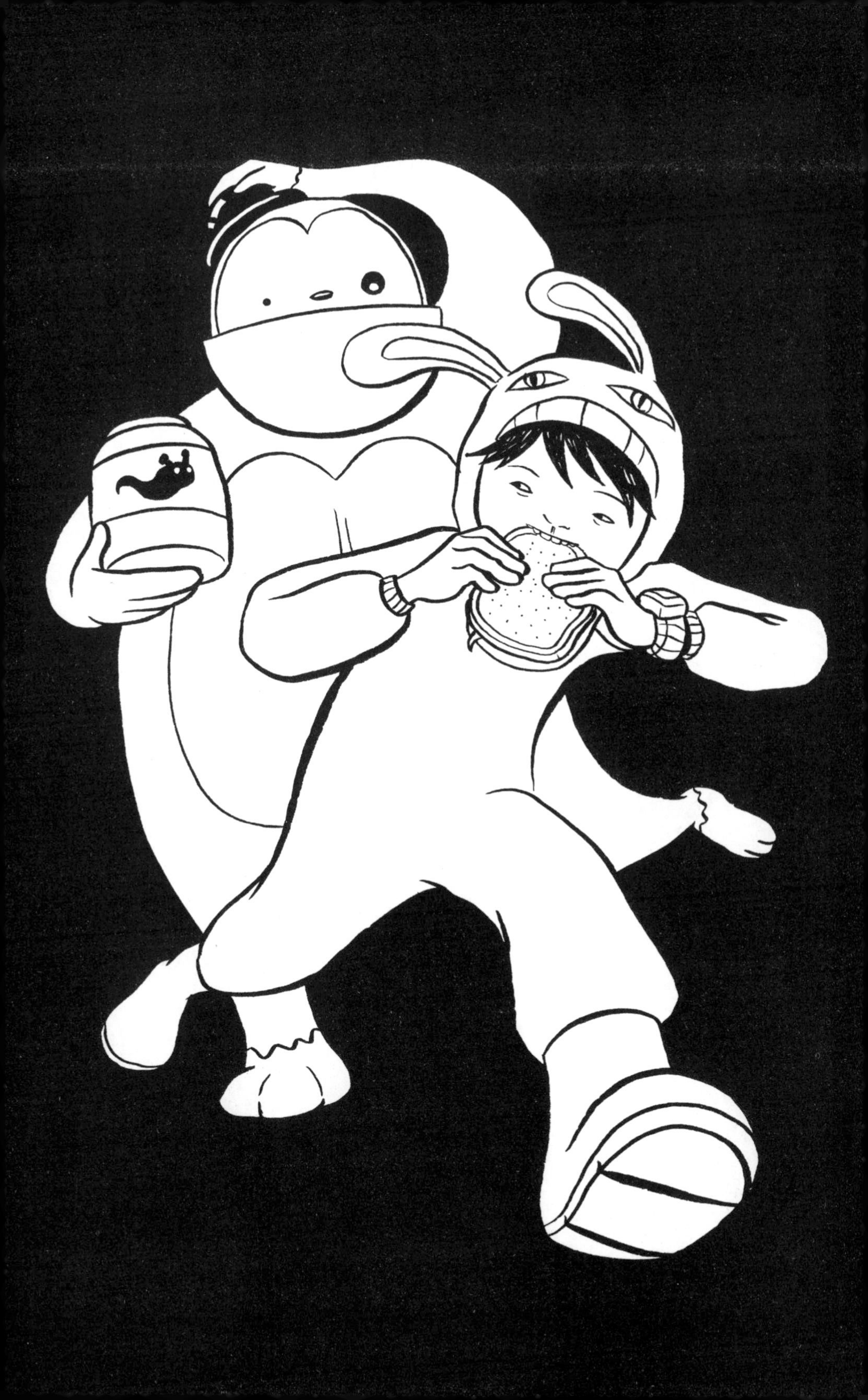

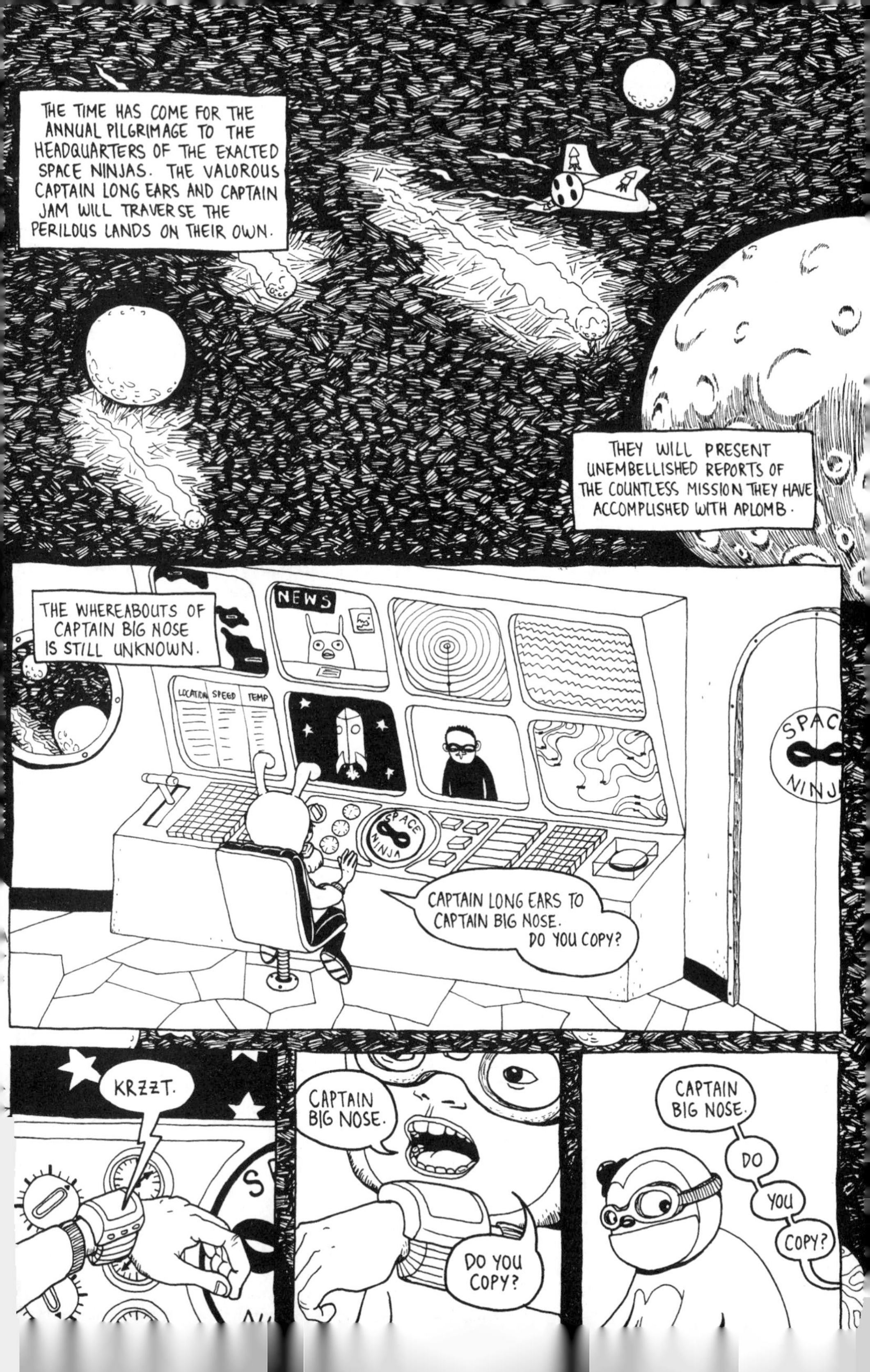
THE TIME HAS COME FOR THE ANNUAL PILGRIMAGE TO THE HEADQUARTERS OF THE EXALTED SPACE NINJAS. THE VALOROUS CAPTAIN LONG EARS AND CAPTAIN JAM WILL TRAVERSE THE PERILOUS LANDS ON THEIR OWN.
THEY WILL PRESENT UNEMBELLISHED REPORTS OF THE COUNTLESS MISSION THEY HAVE ACCOMPLISHED WITH APLOMB.
THE WHEREABOUTS OF CAPTAIN BIG NOSE IS STILL UNKNOWN.
NEWS
LOCATION
SPEED
TEMP
SPACE NINJA
CAPTAIN LONG EARS TO CAPTAIN BIG NOSE. DO YOU COPY?
KRZZT.
CAPTAIN BIG NOSE.
DO YOU COPY?
CAPTAIN BIG NOSE.
DO
YOU
COPY?

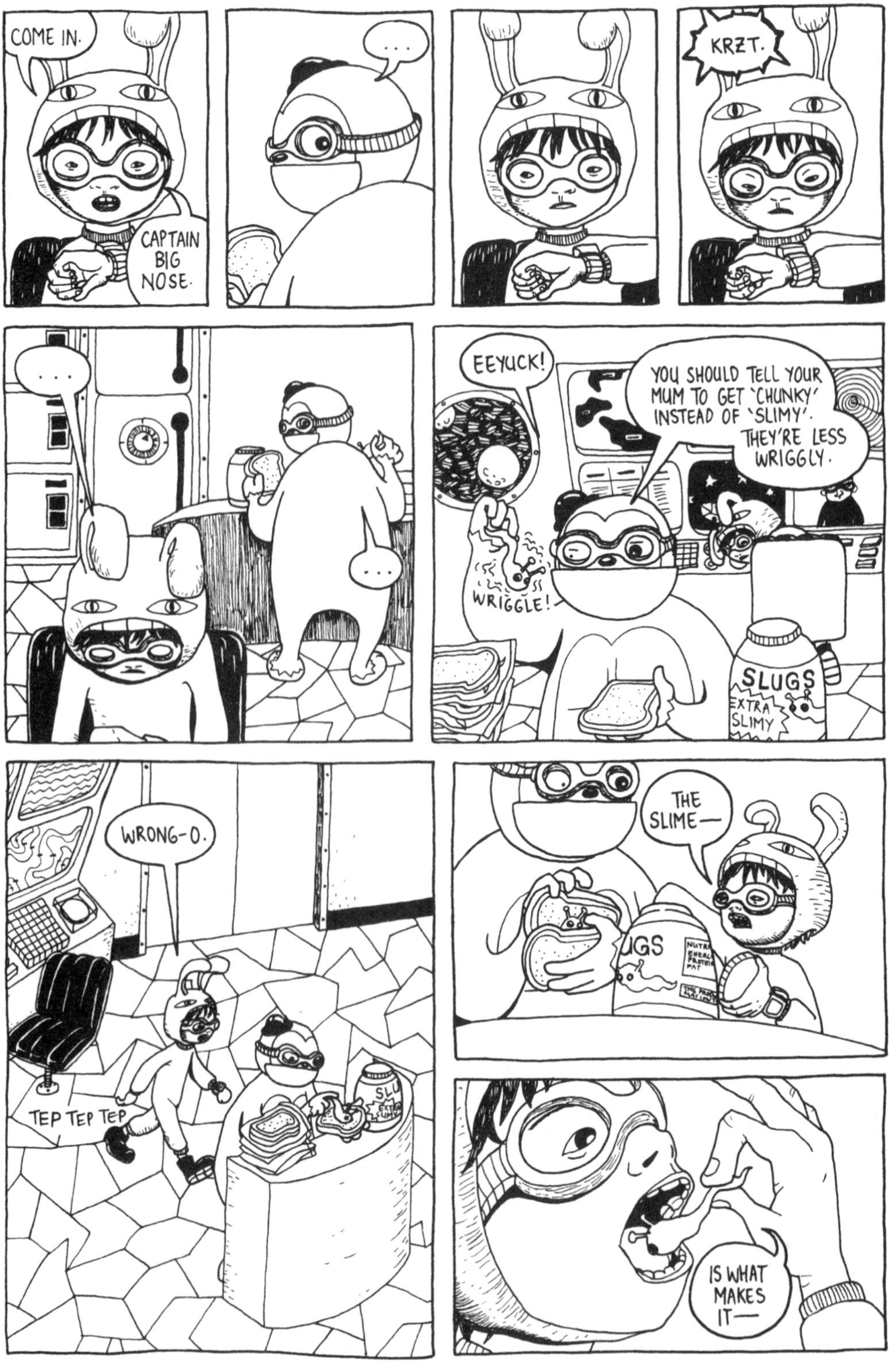
COME IN.
CAPTAIN BIG NOSE.
...
KRZT.
...
...
EEYUCK!
WRIGGLE!
YOU SHOULD TELL YOUR MUM TO GET 'CHUNKY' INSTEAD OF 'SLIMY'.
THEY'RE LESS WRIGGLY.
SLUGS
EXTRA SLIMY
WRONG-O.
TEP TEP TEP
THE SLIME—
IS WHAT MAKES IT—

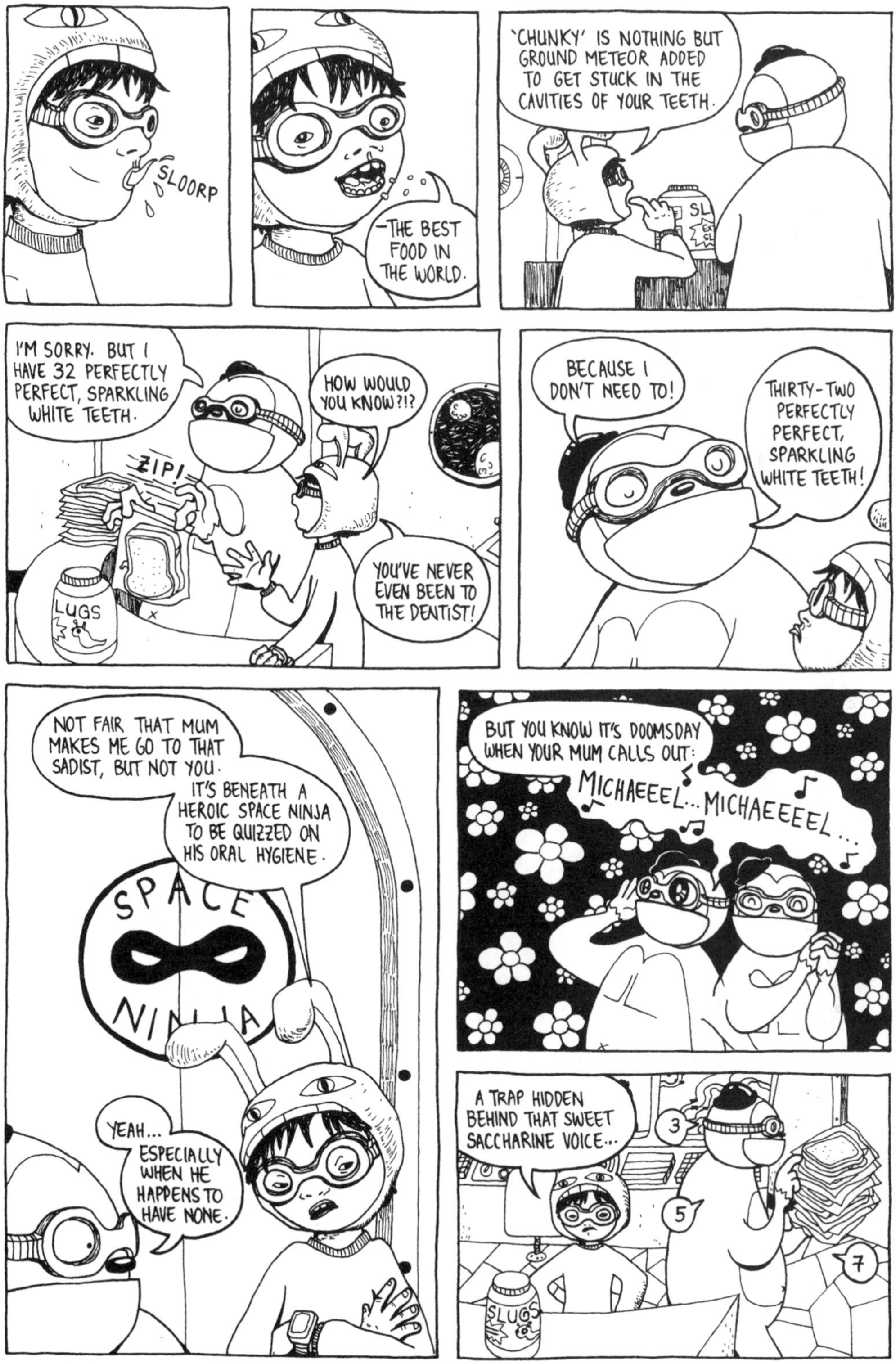
SLOORP
-THE BEST FOOD IN THE WORLD.
`CHUNKY' IS NOTHING BUT GROUND METEOR ADDED TO GET STUCK IN THE CAVITIES OF YOUR TEETH.
I'M SORRY. BUT I HAVE 32 PERFECTLY PERFECT, SPARKLING WHITE TEETH.
ZIP!
HOW WOULD YOU KNOW?!?
YOU'VE NEVER EVEN BEEN TO THE DENTIST!
LUGS
BECAUSE I DON'T NEED TO!
THIRTY-TWO PERFECTLY PERFECT, SPARKLING WHITE TEETH!
NOT FAIR THAT MUM MAKES ME GO TO THAT SADIST, BUT NOT YOU.
IT'S BENEATH A HEROIC SPACE NINJA TO BE QUIZZED ON HIS ORAL HYGIENE.
SPACE NINJA
YEAH... ESPECIALLY WHEN HE HAPPENS TO HAVE NONE.
BUT YOU KNOW IT'S DOOMSDAY WHEN YOUR MUM CALLS OUT:
MICHAEEEL... MICHAEEEEL...
A TRAP HIDDEN BEHIND THAT SWEET SACCHARINE VOICE...
3
5
7
SLUGS

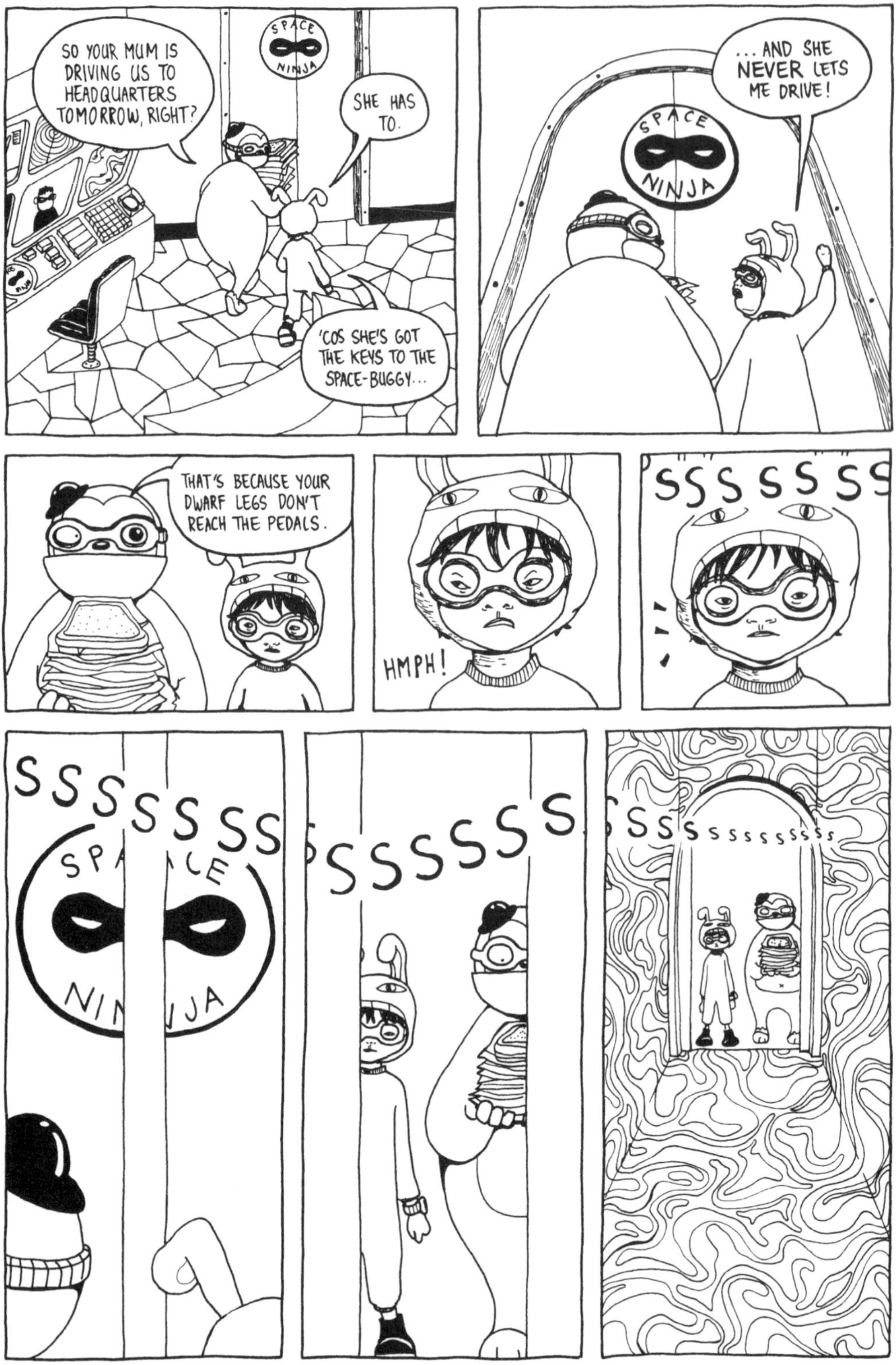
SPACE NINJA
SO YOUR MUM IS DRIVING US TO HEADQUARTERS TOMORROW, RIGHT?
SHE HAS TO.
'COS SHE'S GOT THE KEYS TO THE SPACE-BUGGY...
SPACE NINJA
...AND SHE NEVER LETS ME DRIVE!
THAT'S BECAUSE YOUR DWARF LEGS DON'T REACH THE PEDALS.
HMPH!
SSSSSSS
SSSSSSSS
SPACE NINJA
SSSSSSSSS
SSSSSSSSSSSSS

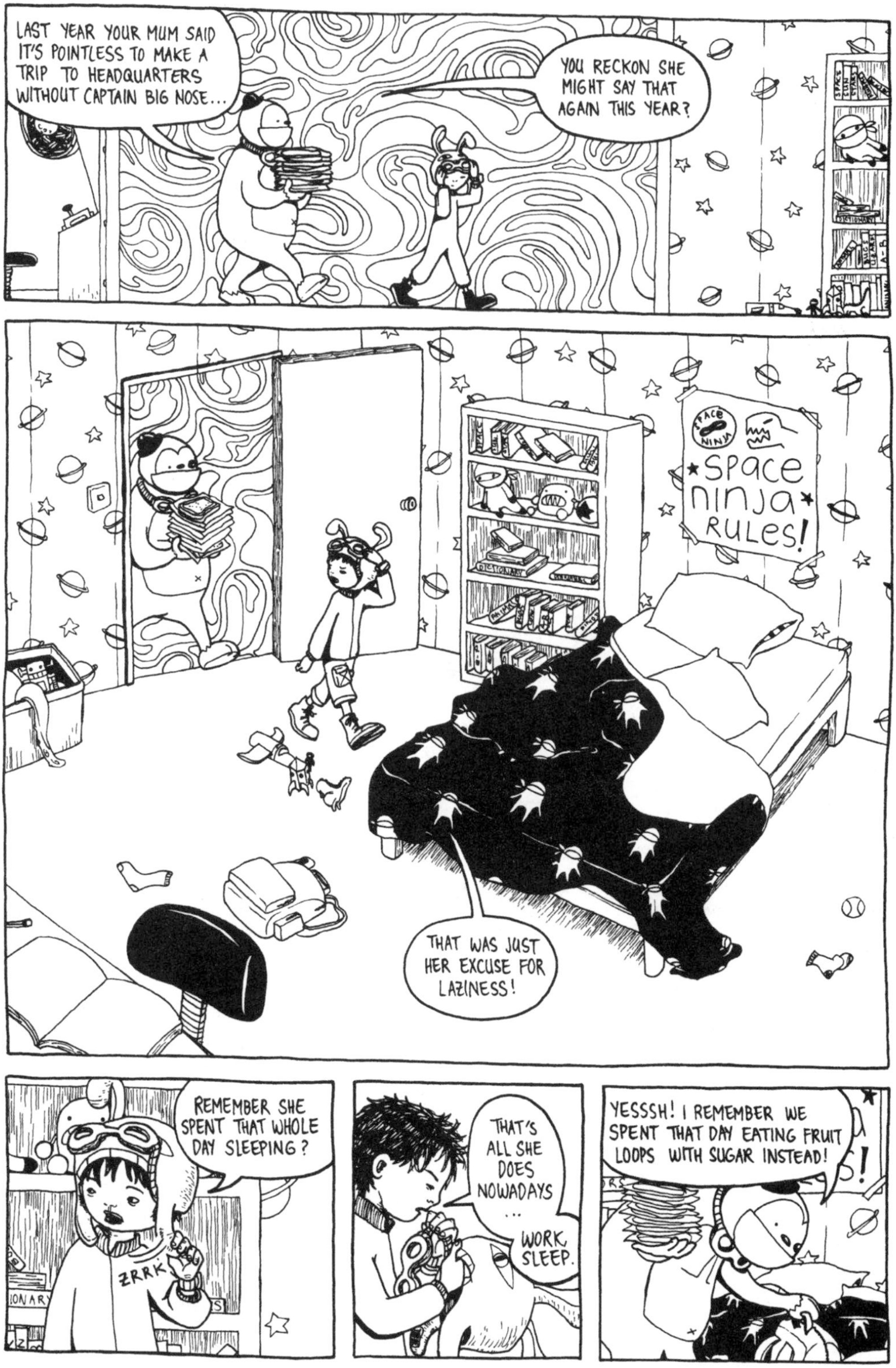
LAST YEAR YOUR MUM SAID IT'S POINTLESS TO MAKE A TRIP TO HEADQUARTERS WITHOUT CAPTAIN BIG NOSE...
YOU RECKON SHE MIGHT SAY THAT AGAIN THIS YEAR?
SPACE NINJA
SPACE NINJA RULES!
DICTIONARY
THAT WAS JUST HER EXCUSE FOR LAZINESS!
REMEMBER SHE SPENT THAT WHOLE DAY SLEEPING?
ZRRK
THAT'S ALL SHE DOES NOWADAYS ... WORK, SLEEP.
YESSSH! I REMEMBER WE SPENT THAT DAY EATING FRUIT LOOPS WITH SUGAR INSTEAD!

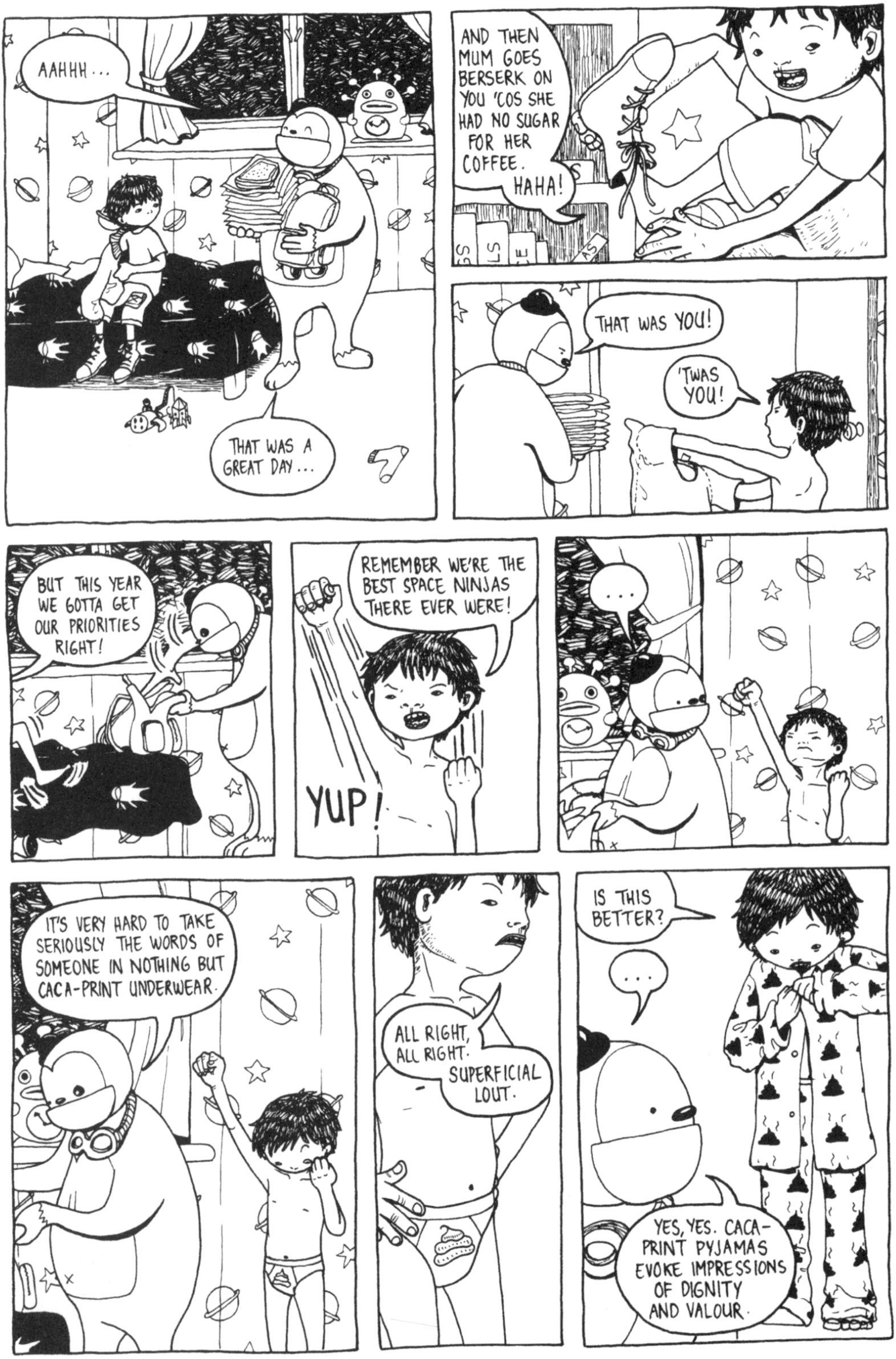

AAHHH...
THAT WAS A GREAT DAY...
AND THEN MUM GOES BERSERK ON YOU 'COS SHE HAD NO SUGAR FOR HER COFFEE.
HAHA!
THAT WAS YOU!
'TWAS YOU!
BUT THIS YEAR WE GOTTA GET OUR PRIORITIES RIGHT!
REMEMBER WE'RE THE BEST SPACE NINJAS THERE EVER WERE!
YUP!
...
IT'S VERY HARD TO TAKE SERIOUSLY THE WORDS OF SOMEONE IN NOTHING BUT CACA-PRINT UNDERWEAR.
ALL RIGHT, ALL RIGHT.
SUPERFICIAL LOUT.
IS THIS BETTER?
...
YES, YES. CACA-PRINT PYJAMAS EVOKE IMPRESSIONS OF DIGNITY AND VALOUR.

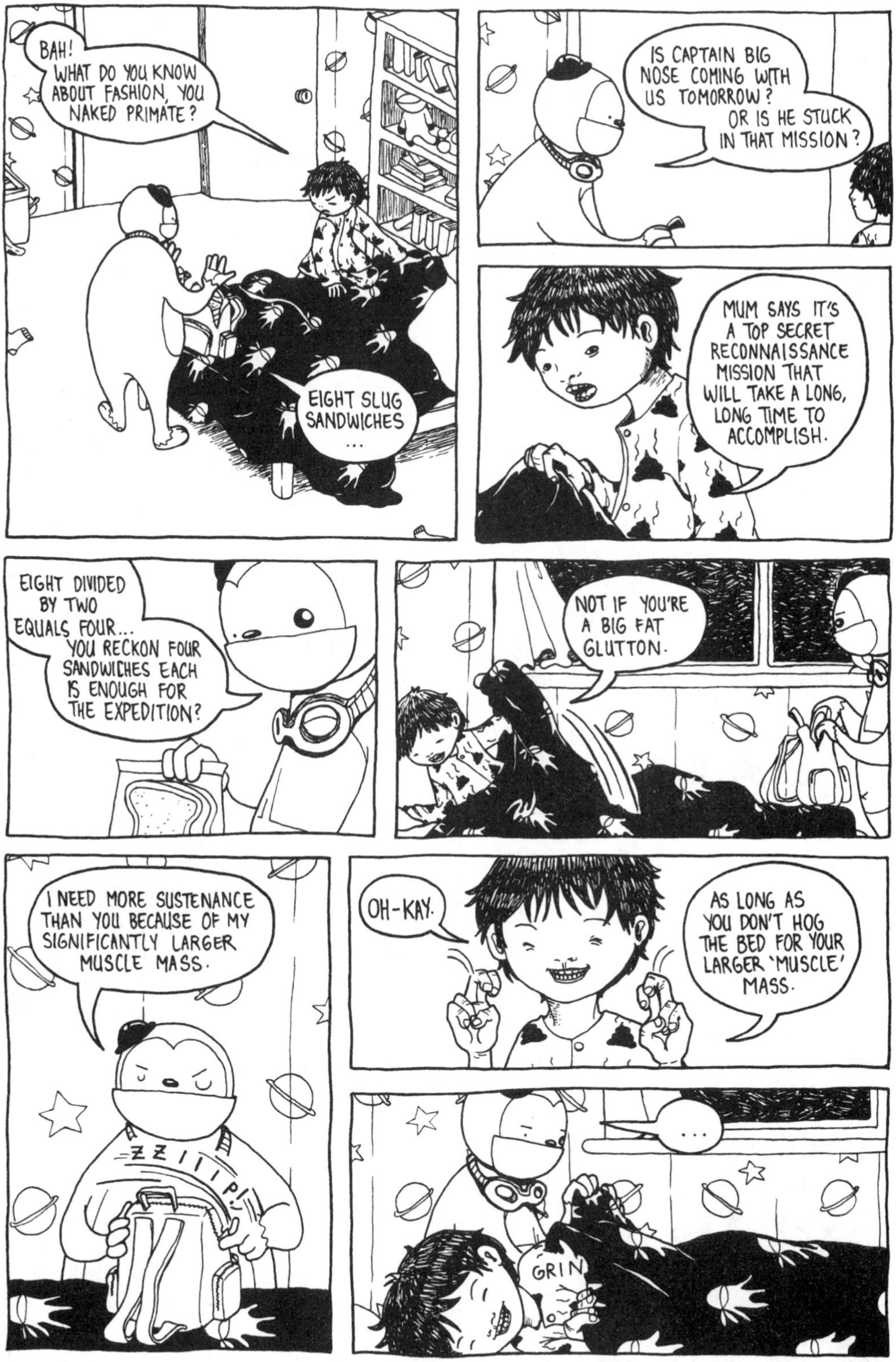
BAH! WHAT DO YOU KNOW ABOUT FASHION, YOU NAKED PRIMATE?
EIGHT SLUG SANDWICHES ...
IS CAPTAIN BIG NOSE COMING WITH US TOMORROW? OR IS HE STUCK IN THAT MISSION?
MUM SAYS IT'S A TOP SECRET RECONNAISSANCE MISSION THAT WILL TAKE A LONG, LONG TIME TO ACCOMPLISH.
EIGHT DIVIDED BY TWO EQUALS FOUR... YOU RECKON FOUR SANDWICHES EACH IS ENOUGH FOR THE EXPEDITION?
NOT IF YOU'RE A BIG FAT GLUTTON.
I NEED MORE SUSTENANCE THAN YOU BECAUSE OF MY SIGNIFICANTLY LARGER MUSCLE MASS.
ZZIIIP!
OH-KAY.
AS LONG AS YOU DON'T HOG THE BED FOR YOUR LARGER 'MUSCLE' MASS.
...
GRIN

ninja RULES!
OOOH...
DON'T WORRY ABOUT MY HOGGING THE BED...
POOOOOOT
HEY!
TOXIC GORILLA BUTT FUMES!
GROSS!
GOOD NIGHT, CAPTAIN JAM!
GOOD NIGHT, CAPTAIN LONG EARS!
TWEET
TWEET
TWEET

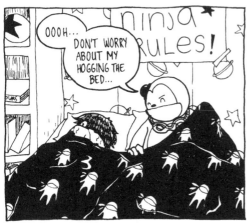

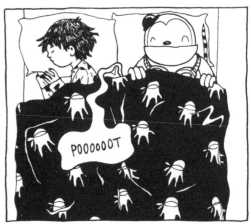

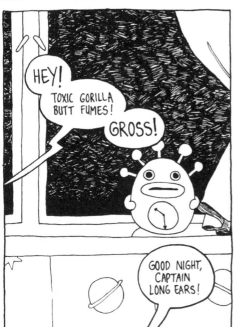

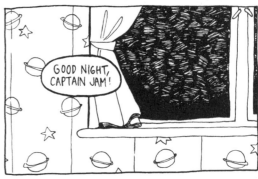

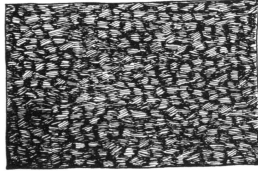

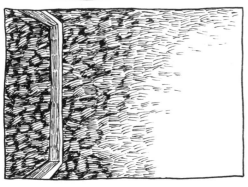

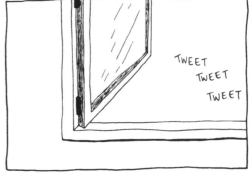

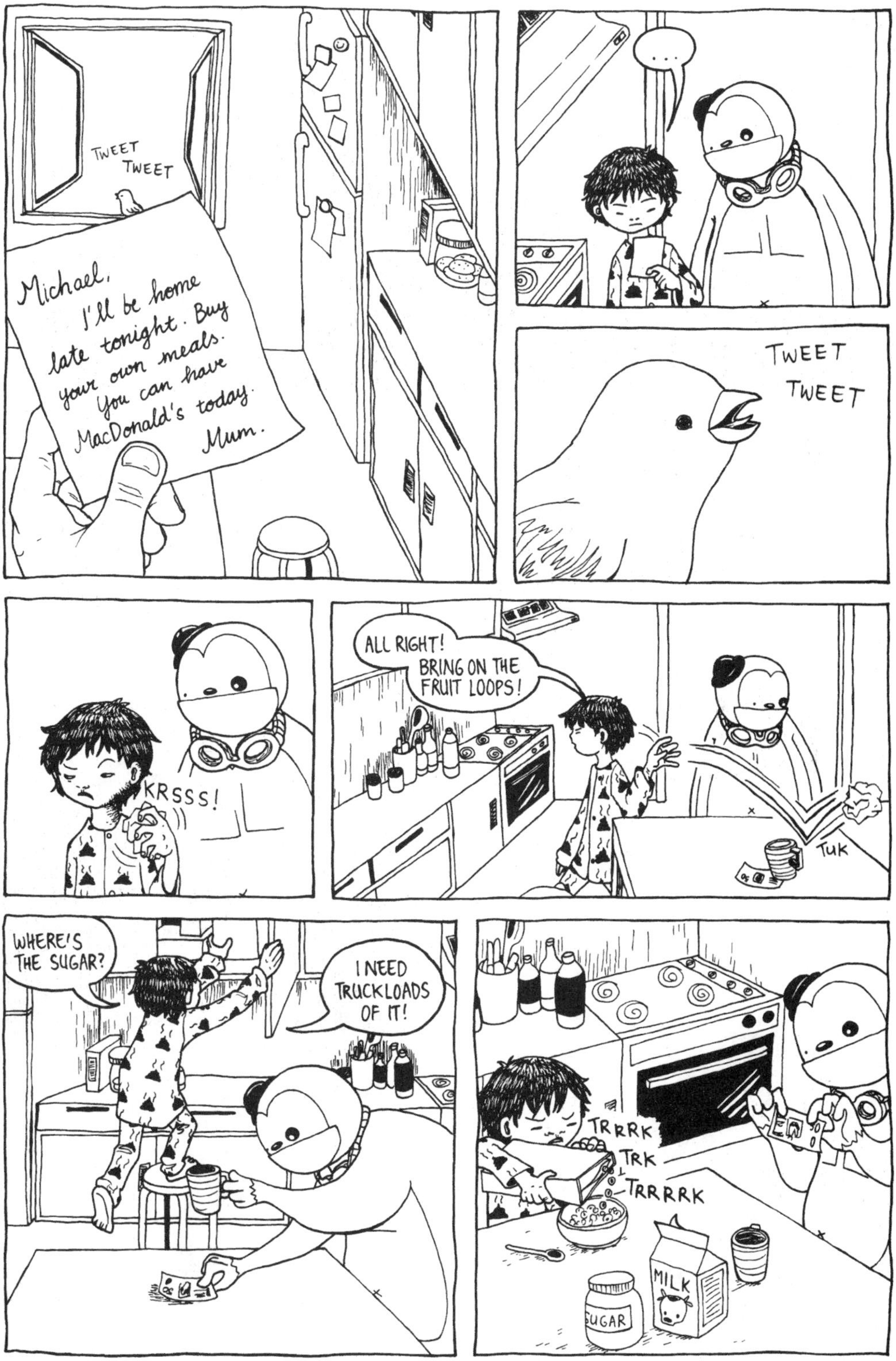

TWEET TWEET
Michael,
I'll be home late tonight. Buy your own meals. You can have MacDonald's today.
Mum.
...
TWEET TWEET
KRSSS!
ALL RIGHT! BRING ON THE FRUIT LOOPS!
TUK
WHERE'S THE SUGAR?
I NEED TRUCKLOADS OF IT!
TRRRK
TRK
TRRRRK
MILK
SUGAR

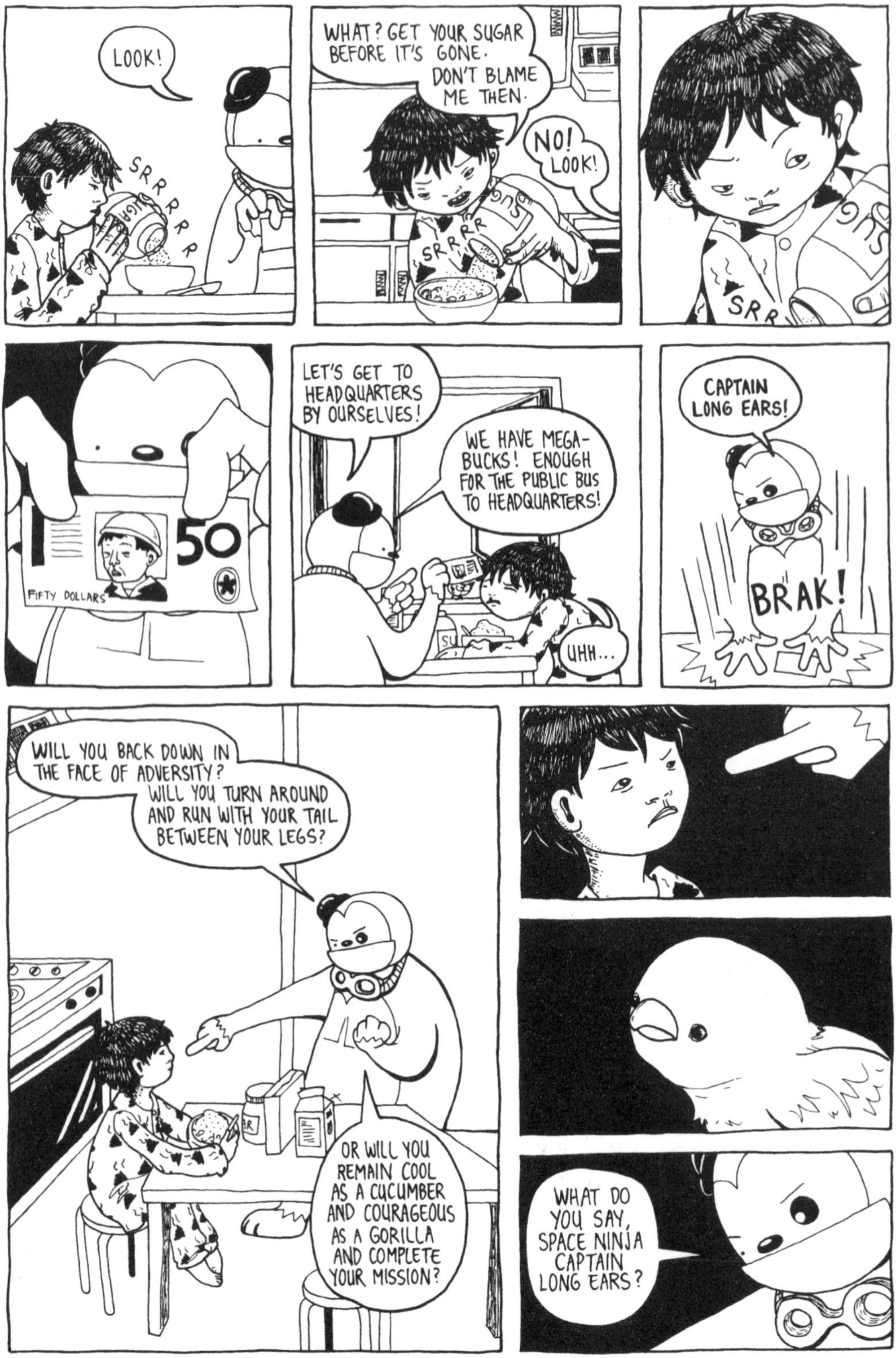
LOOK!
SRRRRRR
WHAT? GET YOUR SUGAR BEFORE IT'S GONE.
DON'T BLAME ME THEN.
NO! LOOK!
SRRRR
SRR
FIFTY DOLLARS
50
LET'S GET TO HEADQUARTERS BY OURSELVES!
WE HAVE MEGA-BUCKS! ENOUGH FOR THE PUBLIC BUS TO HEADQUARTERS!
UHH...
CAPTAIN LONG EARS!
BRAK!
WILL YOU BACK DOWN IN THE FACE OF ADVERSITY?
WILL YOU TURN AROUND AND RUN WITH YOUR TAIL BETWEEN YOUR LEGS?
OR WILL YOU REMAIN COOL AS A CUCUMBER AND COURAGEOUS AS A GORILLA AND COMPLETE YOUR MISSION?
WHAT DO YOU SAY, SPACE NINJA CAPTAIN LONG EARS?

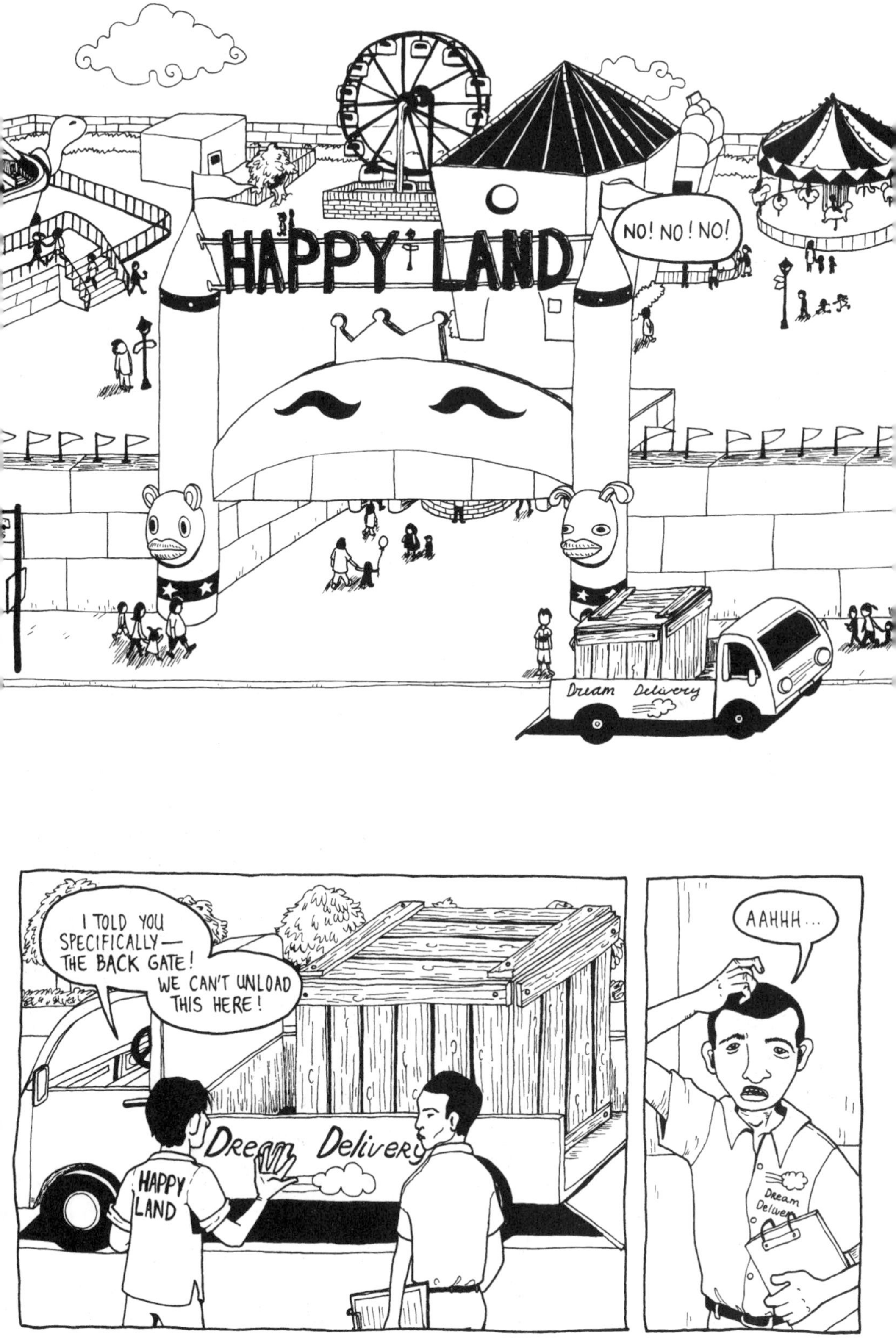
HAPPY LAND
NO! NO! NO!
Dream Delivery
I TOLD YOU SPECIFICALLY— THE BACK GATE!
WE CAN'T UNLOAD THIS HERE!
HAPPY LAND
Dream Delivery
AAHHH...

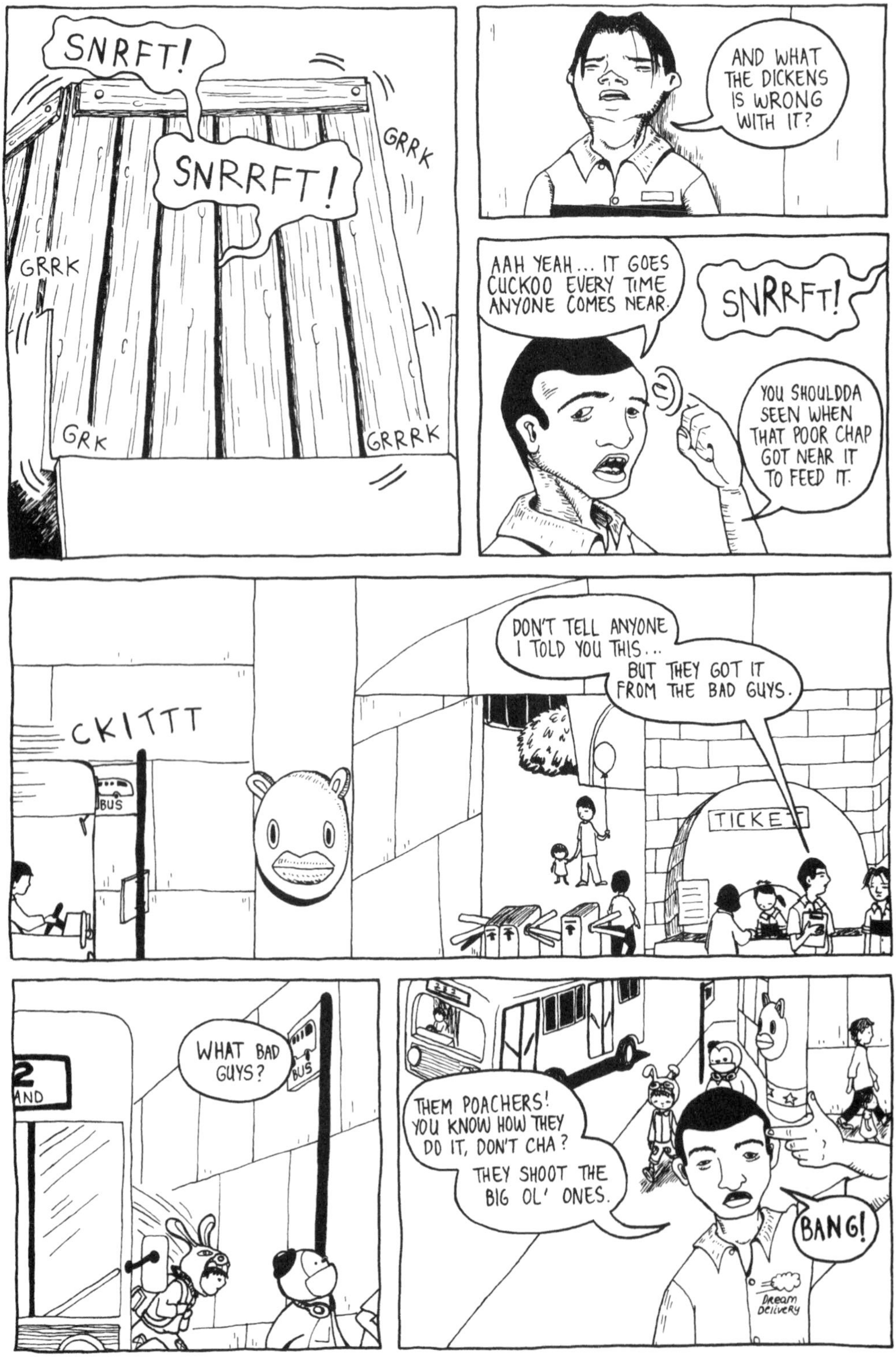
SNRFT!
SNRRFT!
GRRK
GRRK
GRK
GRRRK
AND WHAT THE DICKENS IS WRONG WITH IT?
AAH YEAH... IT GOES CUCKOO EVERY TIME ANYONE COMES NEAR.
SNRRFT!
YOU SHOULDDA SEEN WHEN THAT POOR CHAP GOT NEAR IT TO FEED IT.
CKITTT
BUS
DON'T TELL ANYONE I TOLD YOU THIS...
BUT THEY GOT IT FROM THE BAD GUYS.
TICKET
WHAT BAD GUYS?
BUS
THEM POACHERS! YOU KNOW HOW THEY DO IT, DON'T CHA?
THEY SHOOT THE BIG OL' ONES.
BANG!
Dream Delivery

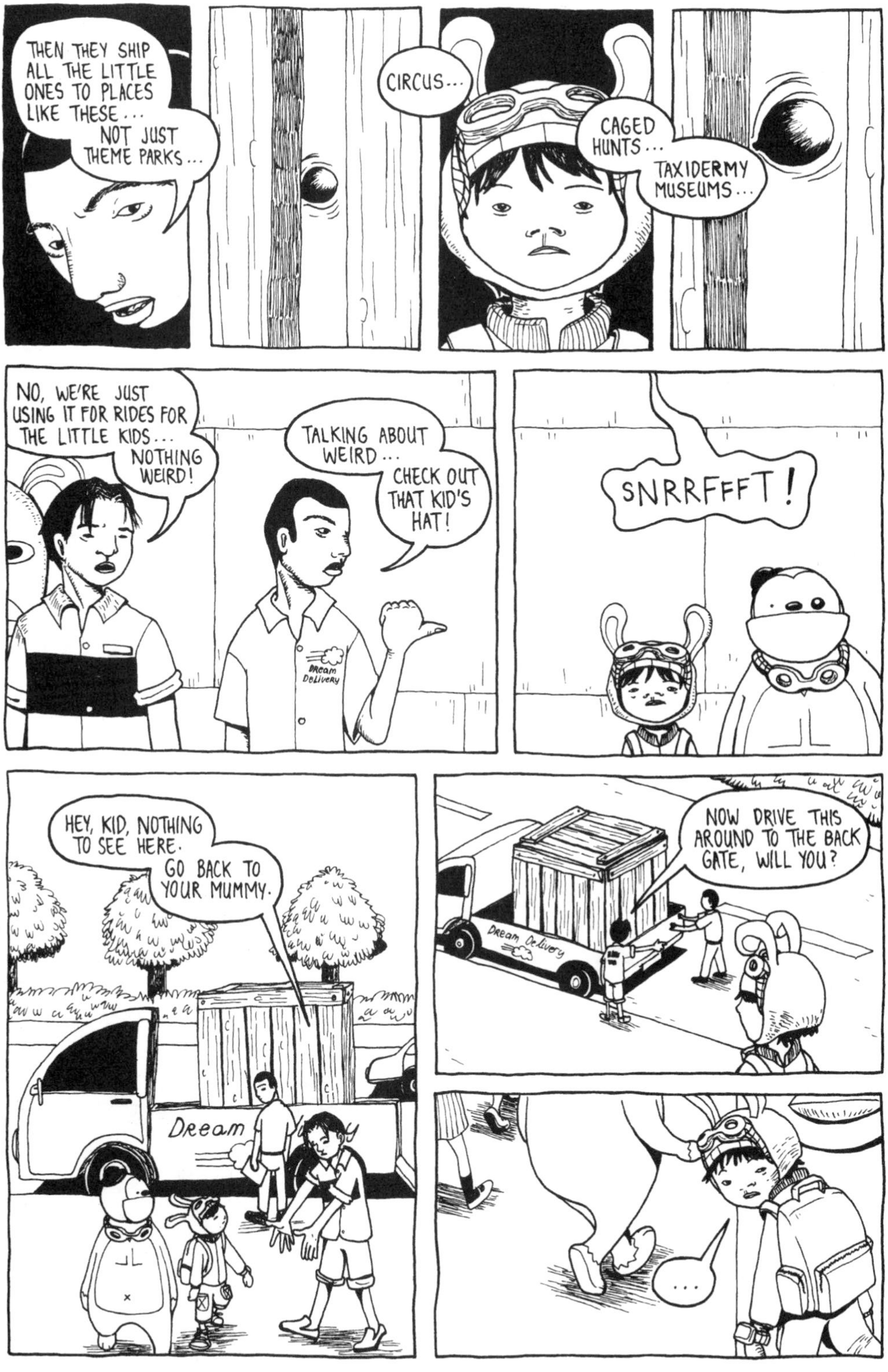
THEN THEY SHIP ALL THE LITTLE ONES TO PLACES LIKE THESE...
NOT JUST THEME PARKS...
CIRCUS...
CAGED HUNTS...
TAXIDERMY MUSEUMS...
NO, WE'RE JUST USING IT FOR RIDES FOR THE LITTLE KIDS...
NOTHING WEIRD!
TALKING ABOUT WEIRD...
CHECK OUT THAT KID'S HAT!
Dream Delivery
SNRRFFFT!
HEY, KID, NOTHING TO SEE HERE.
GO BACK TO YOUR MUMMY.
Dream
NOW DRIVE THIS AROUND TO THE BACK GATE, WILL YOU?
Dream Delivery
...

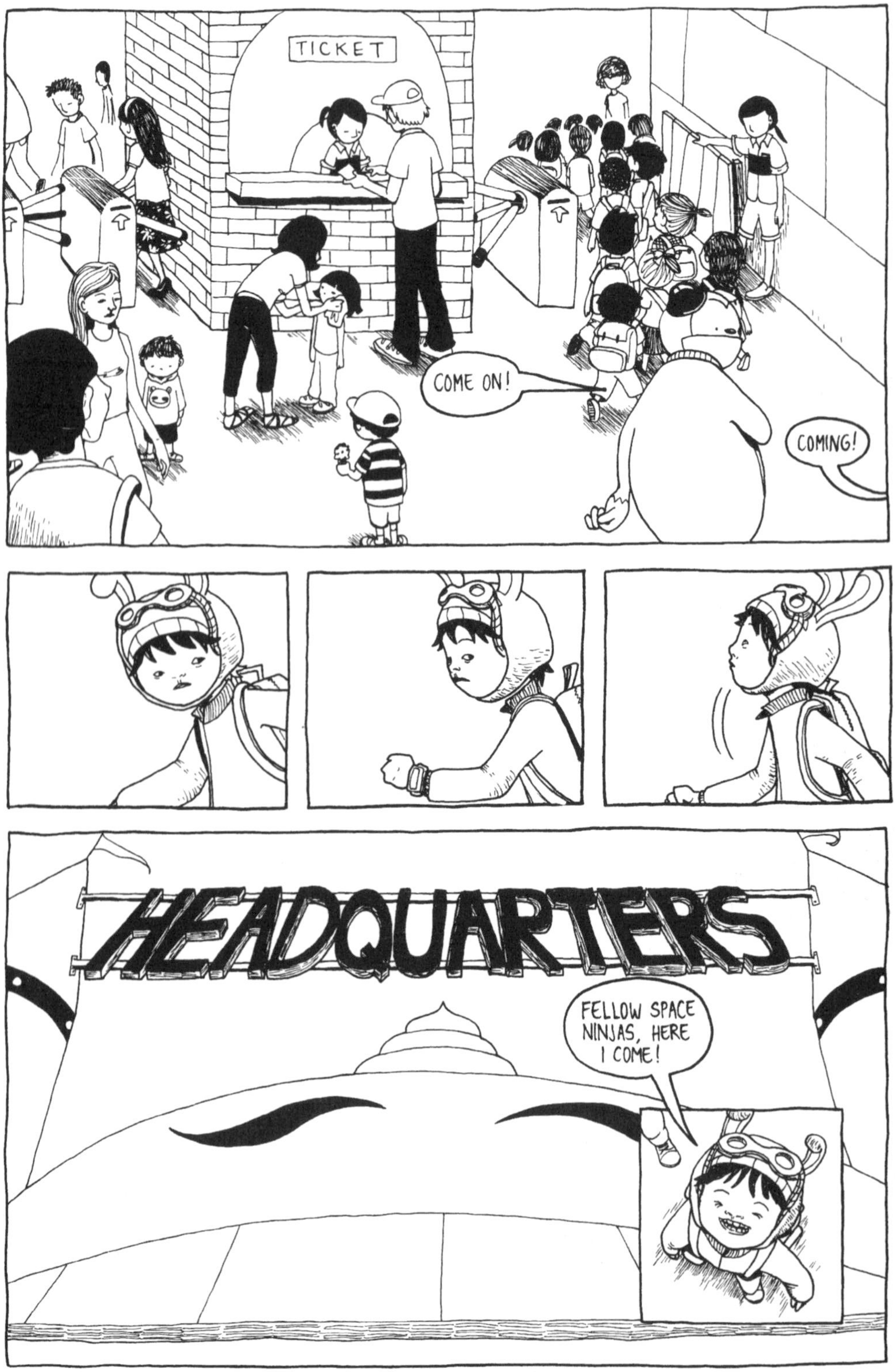
TICKET
COME ON!
COMING!
HEADQUARTERS
FELLOW SPACE NINJAS, HERE I COME!

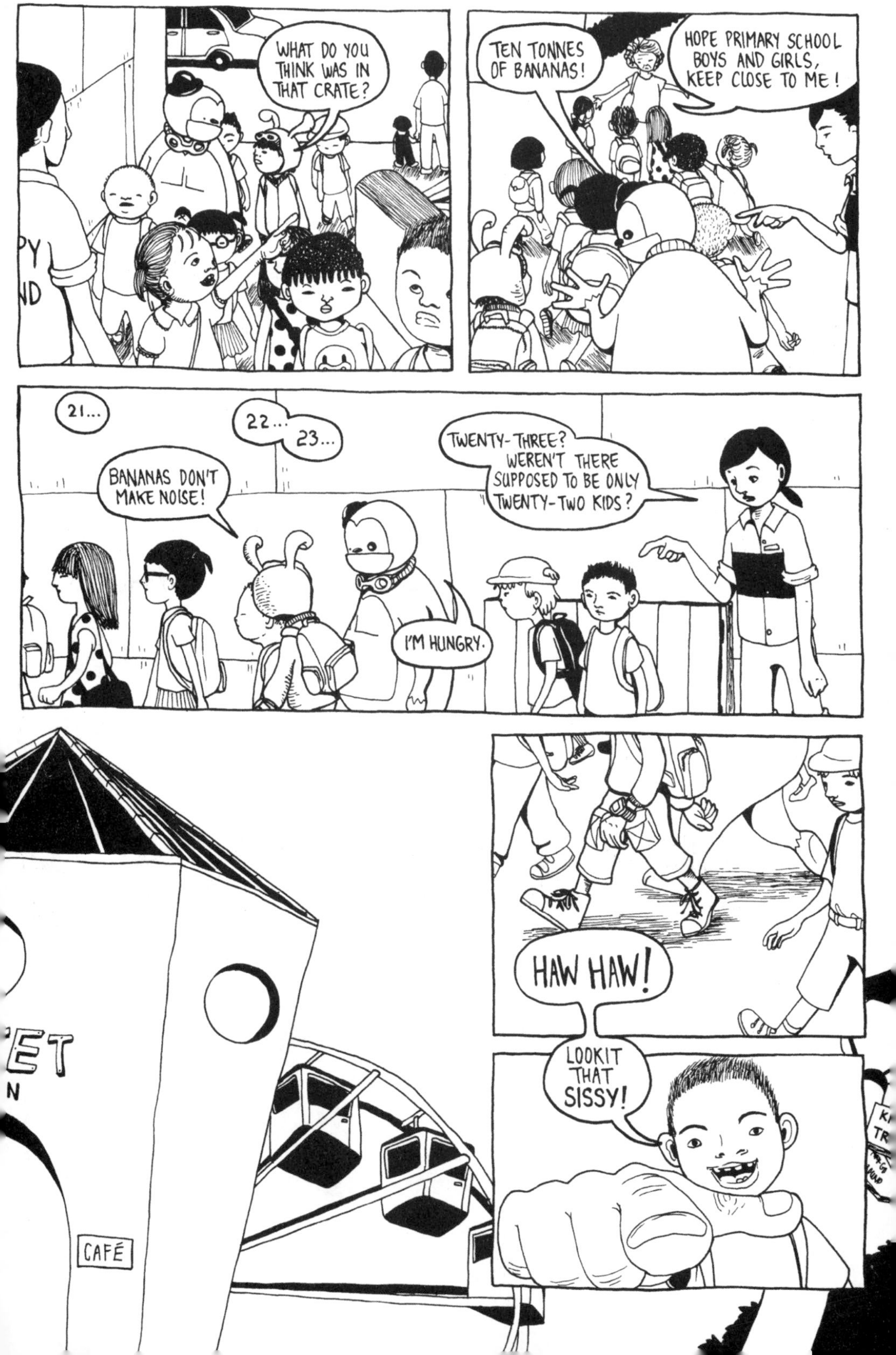
WHAT DO YOU THINK WAS IN THAT CRATE?
TEN TONNES OF BANANAS!
HOPE PRIMARY SCHOOL BOYS AND GIRLS, KEEP CLOSE TO ME!
21...
22...
23...
BANANAS DON'T MAKE NOISE!
TWENTY-THREE? WEREN'T THERE SUPPOSED TO BE ONLY TWENTY-TWO KIDS?
I'M HUNGRY.
CAFÉ
HAW HAW!
LOOKIT THAT SISSY!

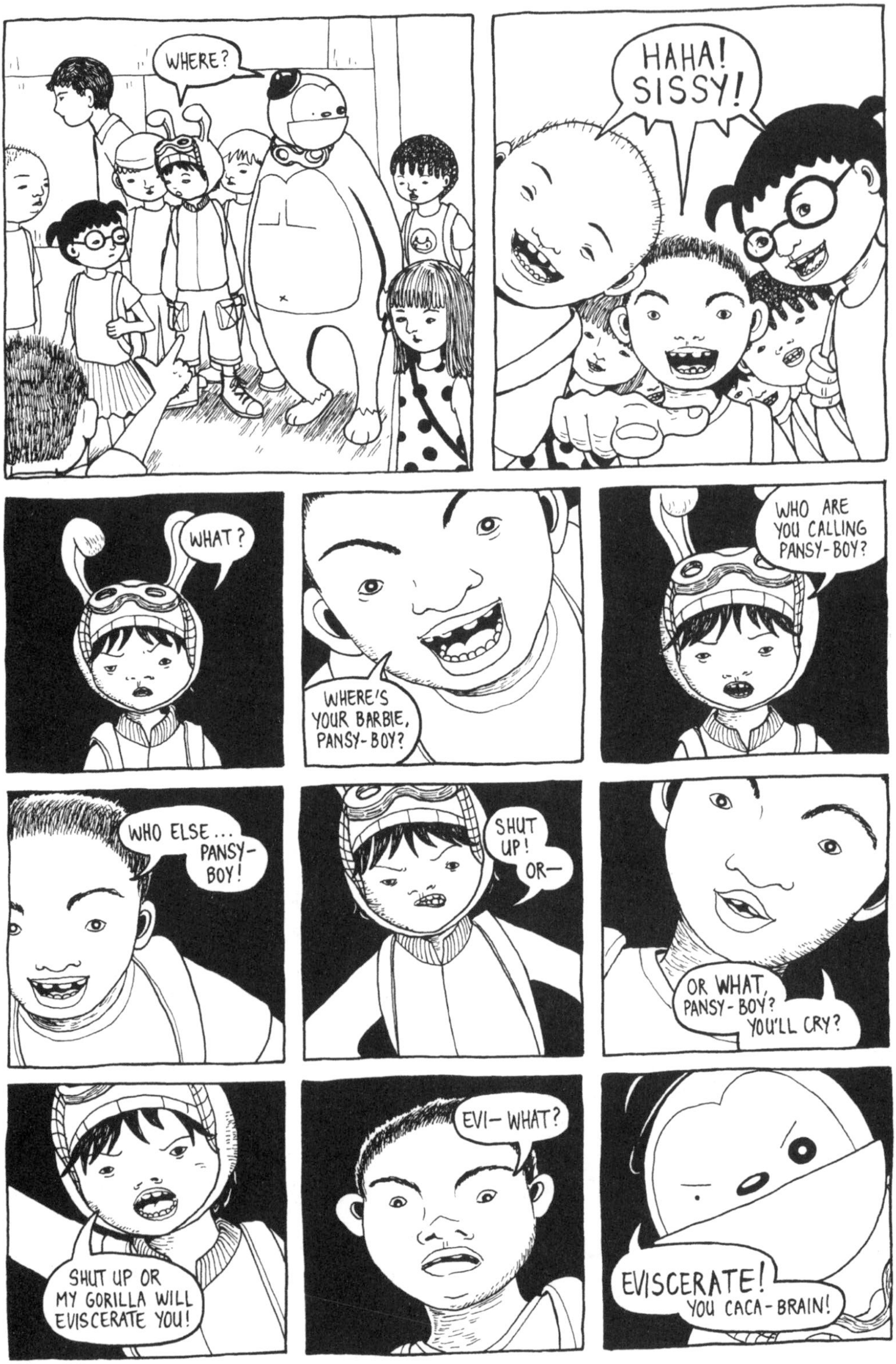
WHERE?
HAHA! SISSY!
WHAT?
WHERE'S YOUR BARBIE, PANSY-BOY?
WHO ARE YOU CALLING PANSY-BOY?
WHO ELSE... PANSY-BOY!
SHUT UP! OR—
OR WHAT, PANSY-BOY? YOU'LL CRY?
SHUT UP OR MY GORILLA WILL EVISCERATE YOU!
EVI-WHAT?
EVISCERATE! YOU CACA-BRAIN!

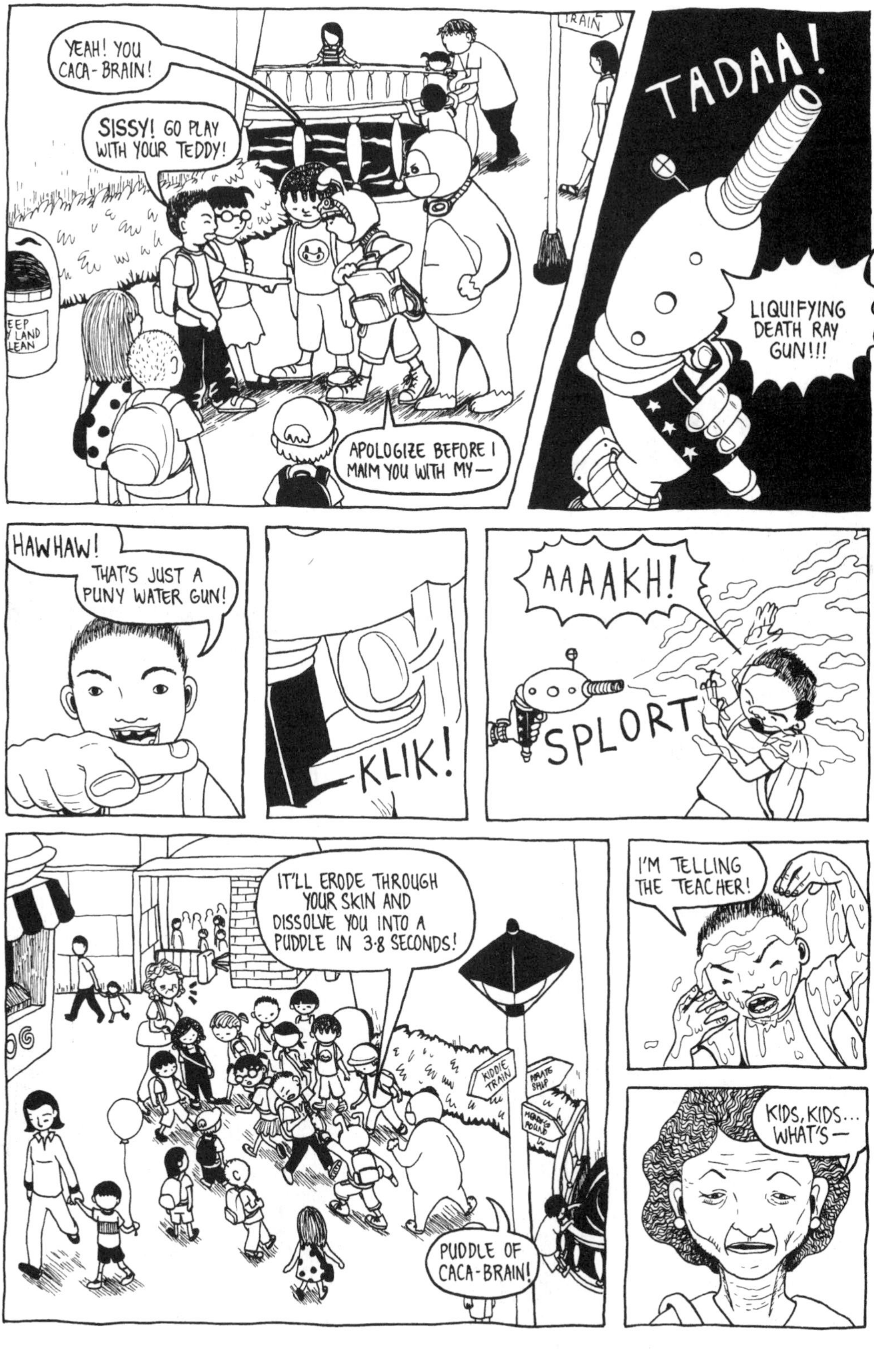

YEAH! YOU CACA-BRAIN!
SISSY! GO PLAY WITH YOUR TEDDY!
APOLOGIZE BEFORE I MAIM YOU WITH MY—
TADAA!
LIQUIFYING DEATH RAY GUN!!!
HAWHAW!
THAT'S JUST A PUNY WATER GUN!
KLIK!
AAAAKH!
SPLORT
IT'LL ERODE THROUGH YOUR SKIN AND DISSOLVE YOU INTO A PUDDLE IN 3·8 SECONDS!
PUDDLE OF CACA-BRAIN!
I'M TELLING THE TEACHER!
KIDS, KIDS... WHAT'S—

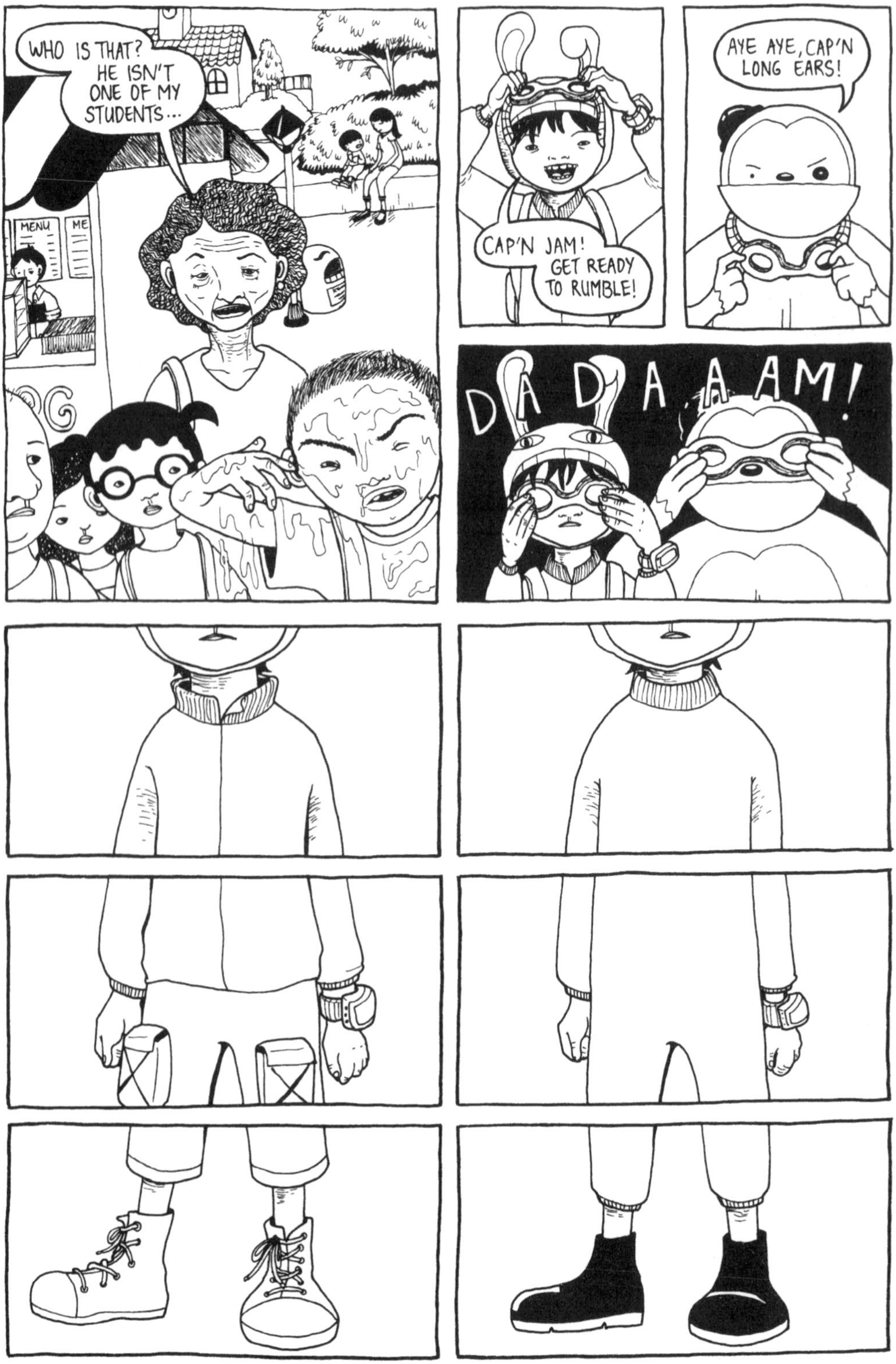
WHO IS THAT? HE ISN'T ONE OF MY STUDENTS...
MENU
CAP'N JAM! GET READY TO RUMBLE!
AYE AYE, CAP'N LONG EARS!
DADAAAAM!

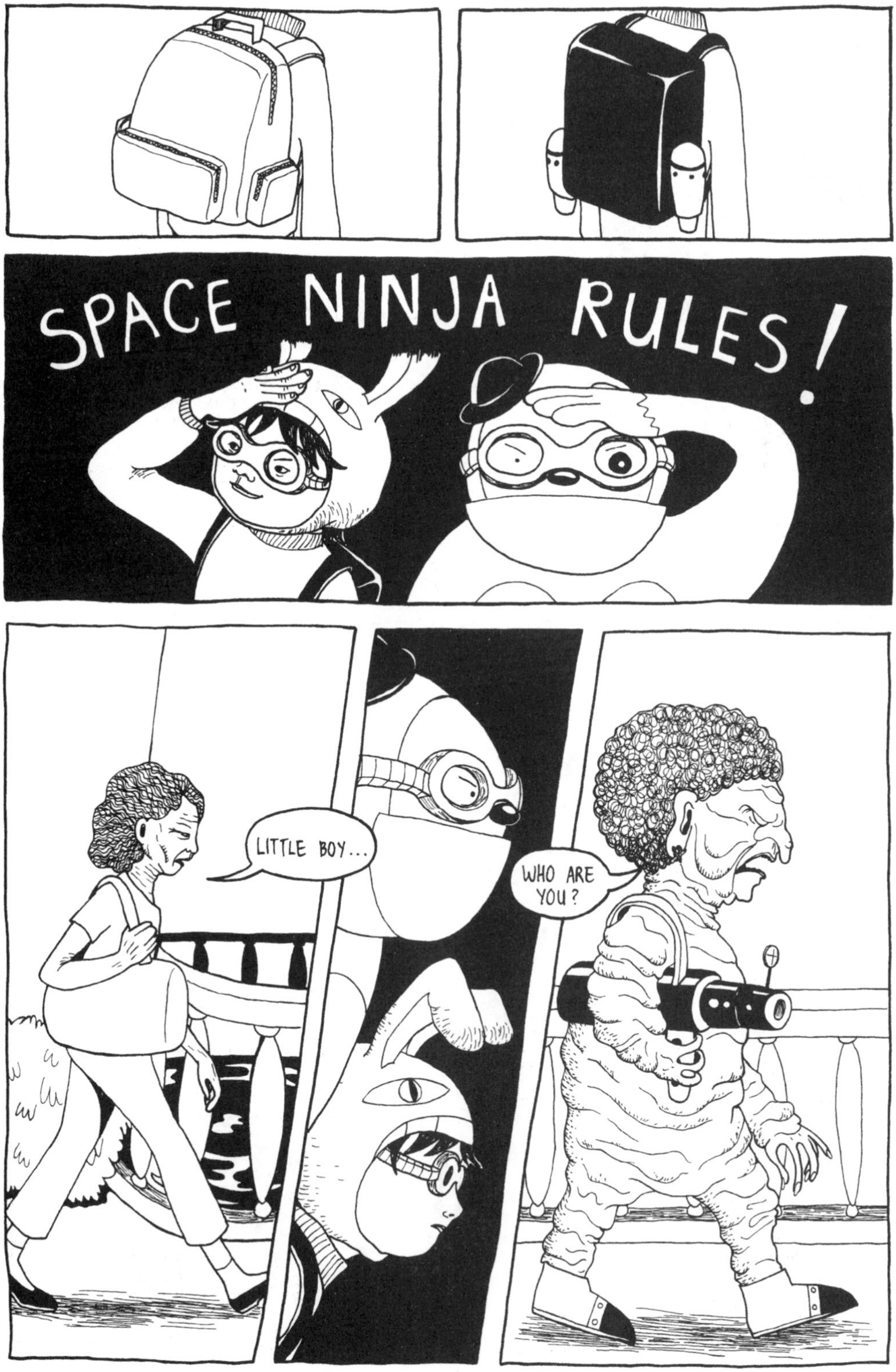
SPACE NINJA RULES!
LITTLE BOY...
WHO ARE YOU?

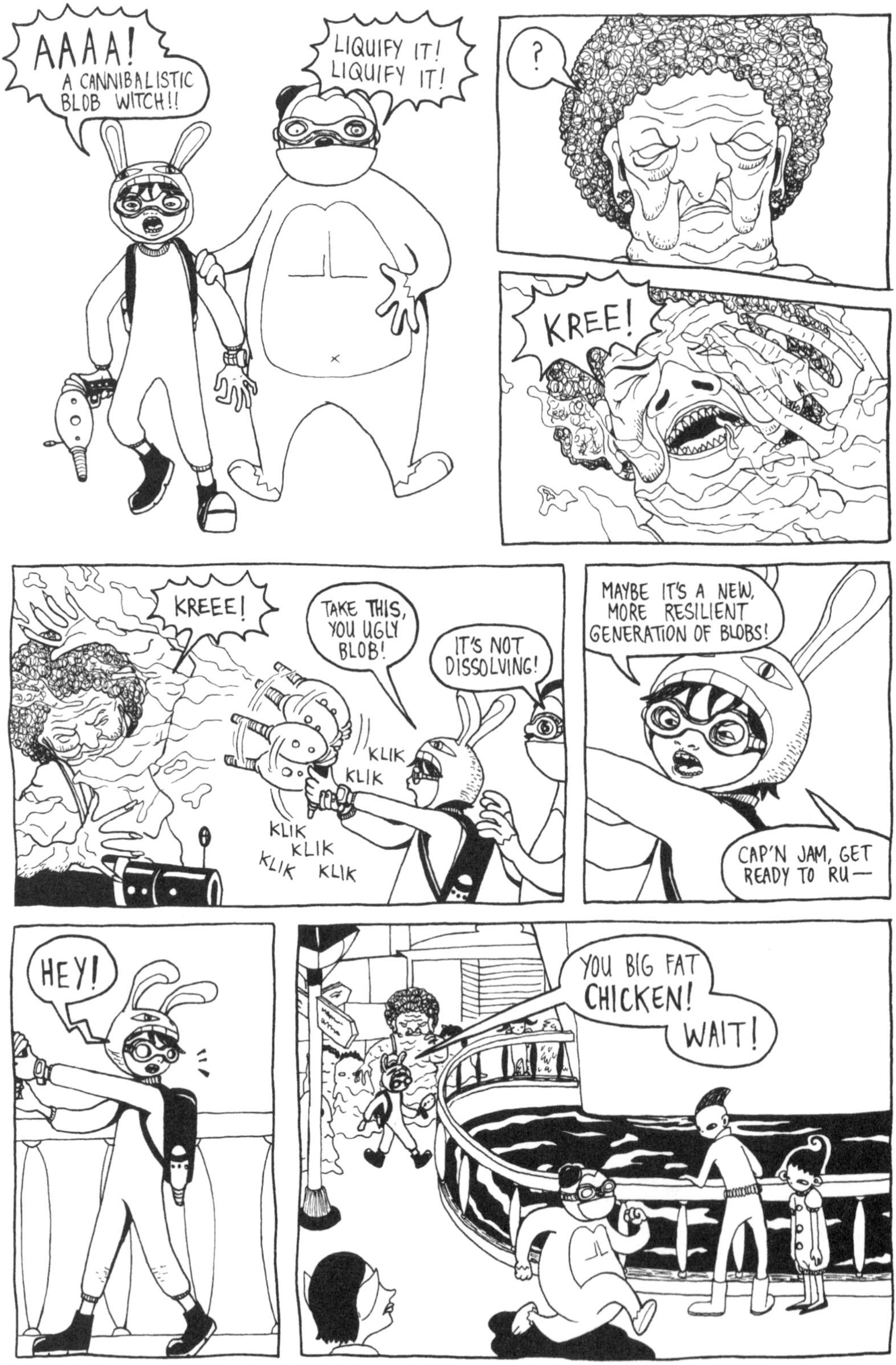
AAAA! A CANNIBALISTIC BLOB WITCH!!
LIQUIFY IT! LIQUIFY IT!
?
KREE!
KREEE!
TAKE THIS, YOU UGLY BLOB!
IT'S NOT DISSOLVING!
KLIK
KLIK
KLIK
KLIK
KLIK
KLIK
MAYBE IT'S A NEW, MORE RESILIENT GENERATION OF BLOBS!
CAP'N JAM, GET READY TO RU—
HEY!
YOU BIG FAT CHICKEN!
WAIT!

DRIP

DRIP

???

DRIP

WHAT A STRANGE KID...

WHO IS HE SHOUTING AT?

IS HE TALKING TO HIS FAT TEDDY BEAR?!?

SQUIRT

YES, CAP'N JAM!

KOI GARDEN

OF COURSE I NOTICED THE VENOMOUS, SLIMY WRINKLES!

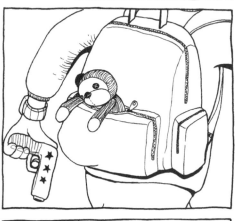

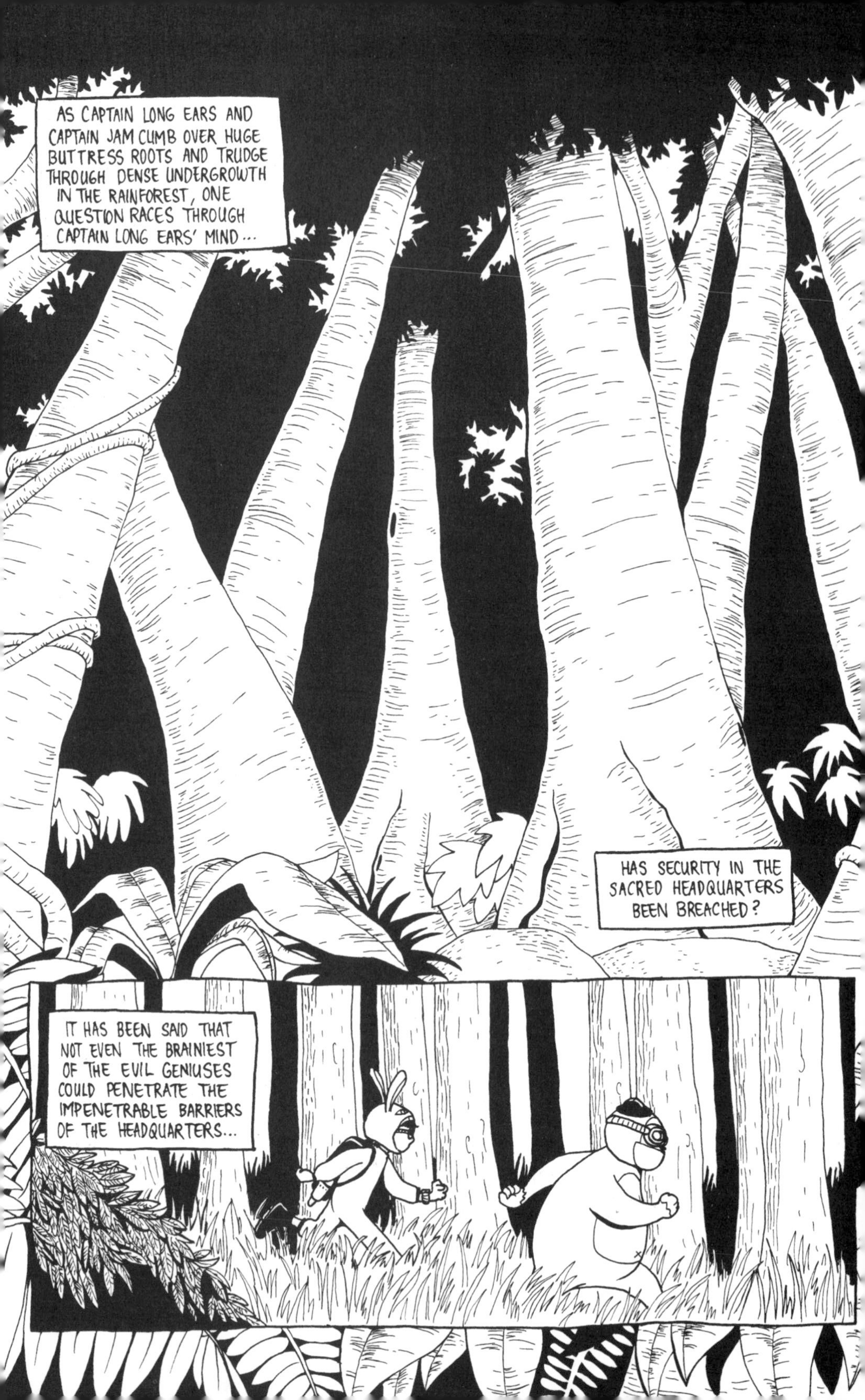
AS CAPTAIN LONG EARS AND CAPTAIN JAM CLIMB OVER HUGE BUTTRESS ROOTS AND TRUDGE THROUGH DENSE UNDERGROWTH IN THE RAINFOREST, ONE QUESTION RACES THROUGH CAPTAIN LONG EARS' MIND...
HAS SECURITY IN THE SACRED HEADQUARTERS BEEN BREACHED?
IT HAS BEEN SAID THAT NOT EVEN THE BRAINIEST OF THE EVIL GENIUSES COULD PENETRATE THE IMPENETRABLE BARRIERS OF THE HEADQUARTERS...

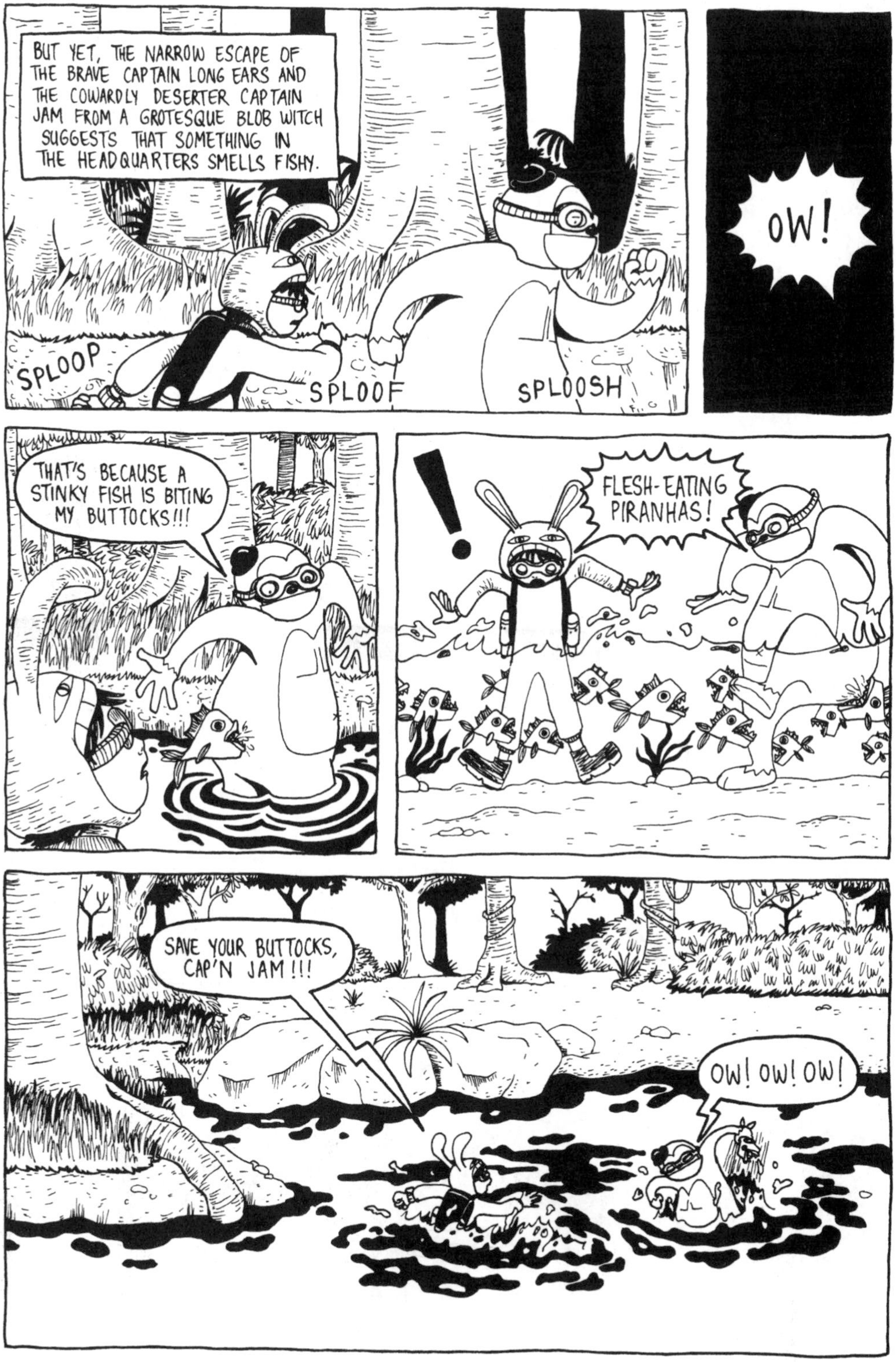
BUT YET, THE NARROW ESCAPE OF THE BRAVE CAPTAIN LONG EARS AND THE COWARDLY DESERTER CAPTAIN JAM FROM A GROTESQUE BLOB WITCH SUGGESTS THAT SOMETHING IN THE HEADQUARTERS SMELLS FISHY.
SPLOOP
SPLOOF
SPLOOSH
OW!
THAT'S BECAUSE A STINKY FISH IS BITING MY BUTTOCKS!!!
!
FLESH-EATING PIRANHAS!
SAVE YOUR BUTTOCKS, CAP'N JAM!!!
OW! OW! OW!

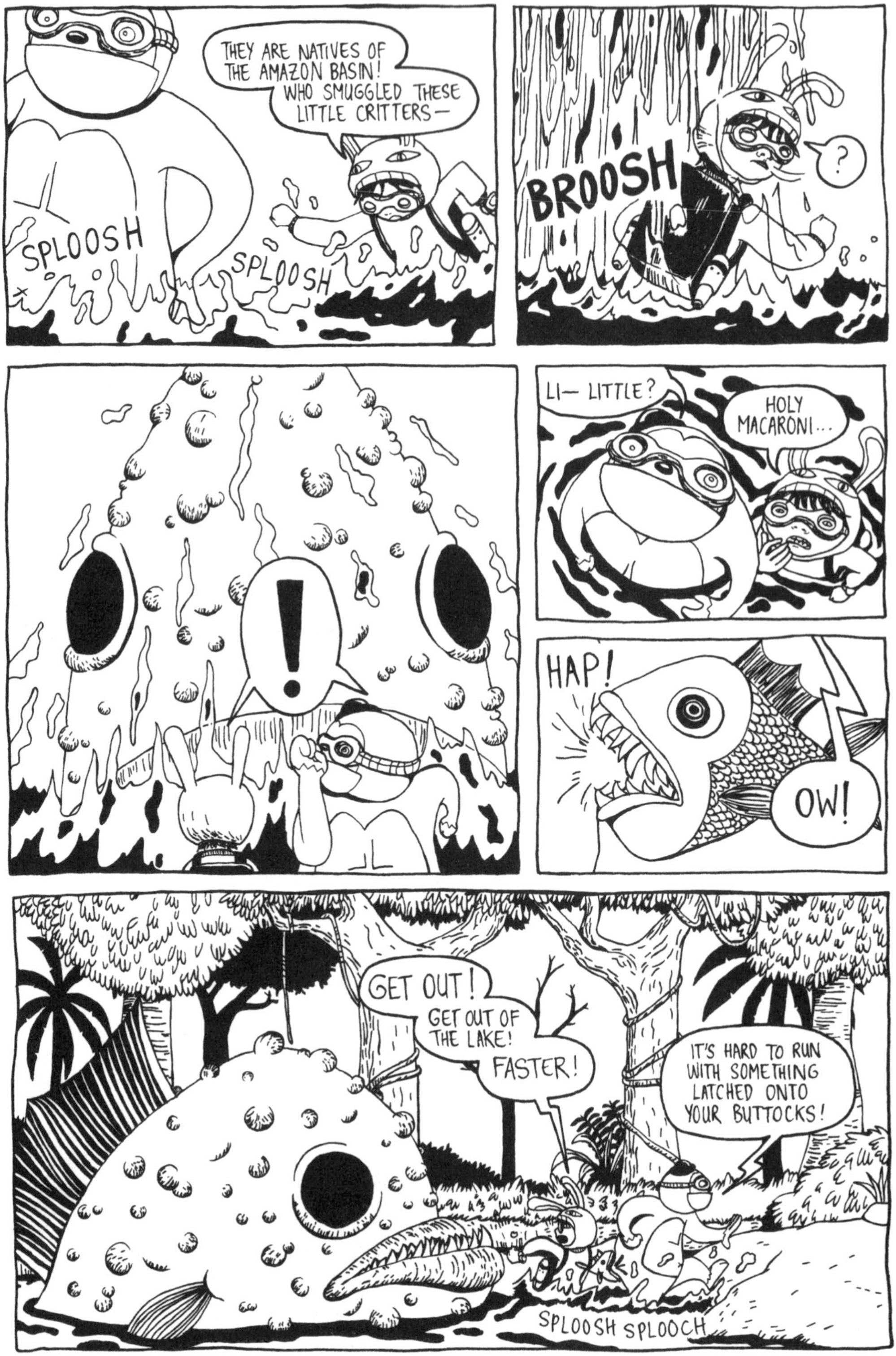
THEY ARE NATIVES OF THE AMAZON BASIN!
WHO SMUGGLED THESE LITTLE CRITTERS—
SPLOOSH
SPLOOSH
BROOSH
?
!
LI— LITTLE?
HOLY MACARONI...
HAP!
OW!
GET OUT!
GET OUT OF THE LAKE!
FASTER!
IT'S HARD TO RUN WITH SOMETHING LATCHED ONTO YOUR BUTTOCKS!
SPLOOSH SPLOOCH

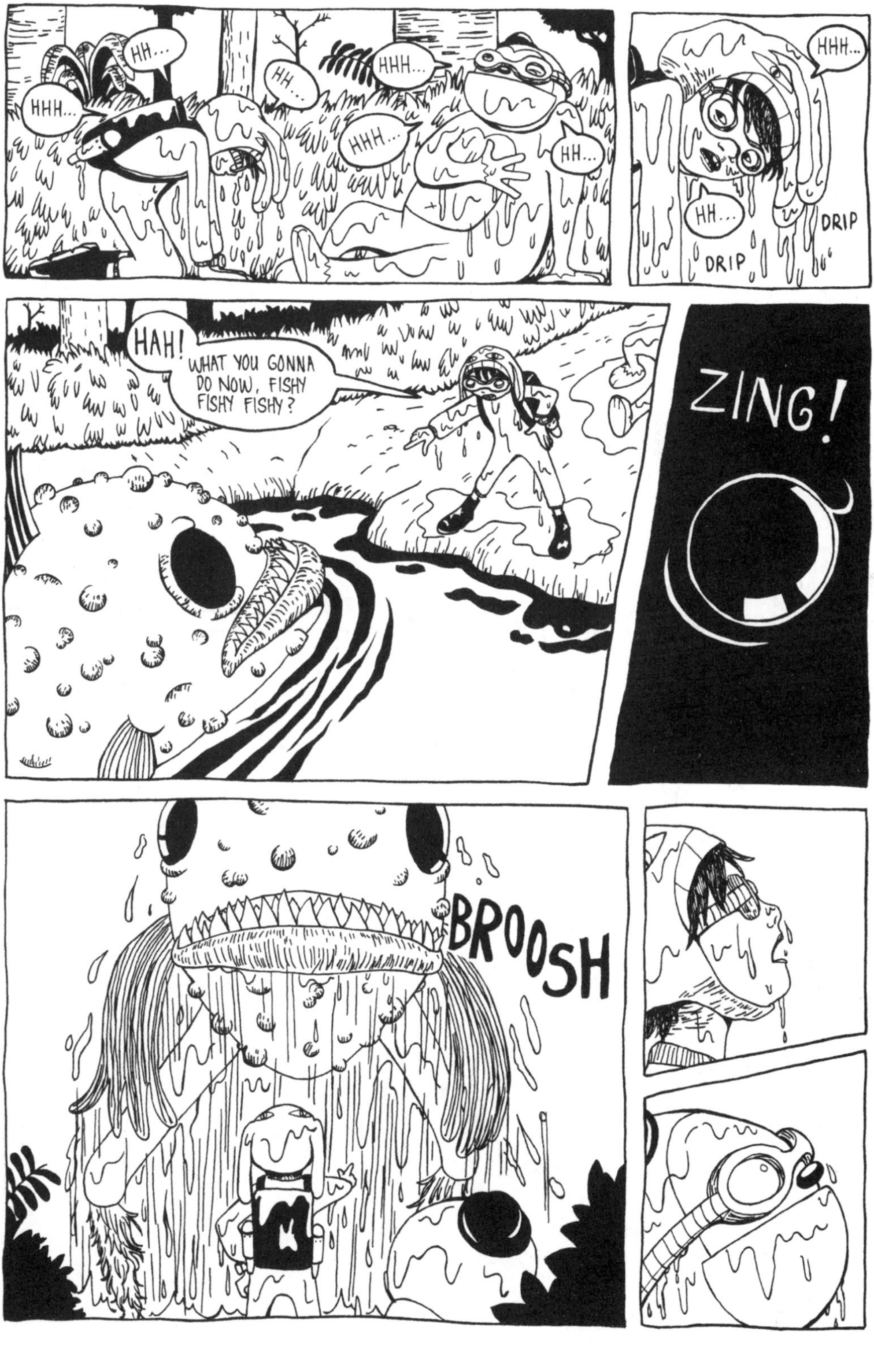

HHH...
HH...
HH...
HHH...
HHH...
HH...
HHH...
HH...
DRIP
DRIP
HAH!
WHAT YOU GONNA DO NOW, FISHY FISHY FISHY?
ZING!
BROOSH

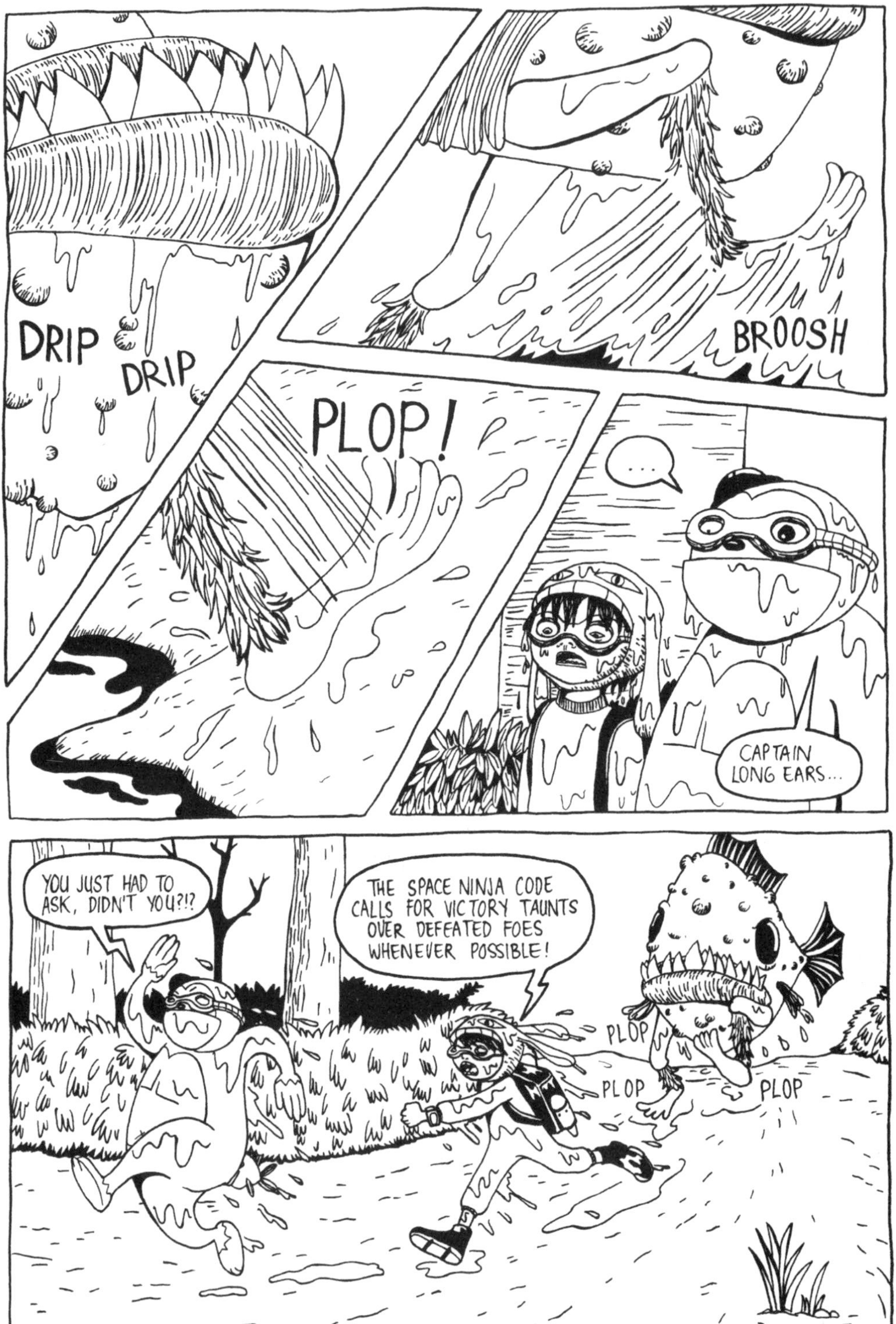
DRIP
DRIP
BROOSH
PLOP!
...
CAPTAIN LONG EARS...
YOU JUST HAD TO ASK, DIDN'T YOU?!?
THE SPACE NINJA CODE CALLS FOR VICTORY TAUNTS OVER DEFEATED FOES WHENEVER POSSIBLE!
PLOP
PLOP
PLOP

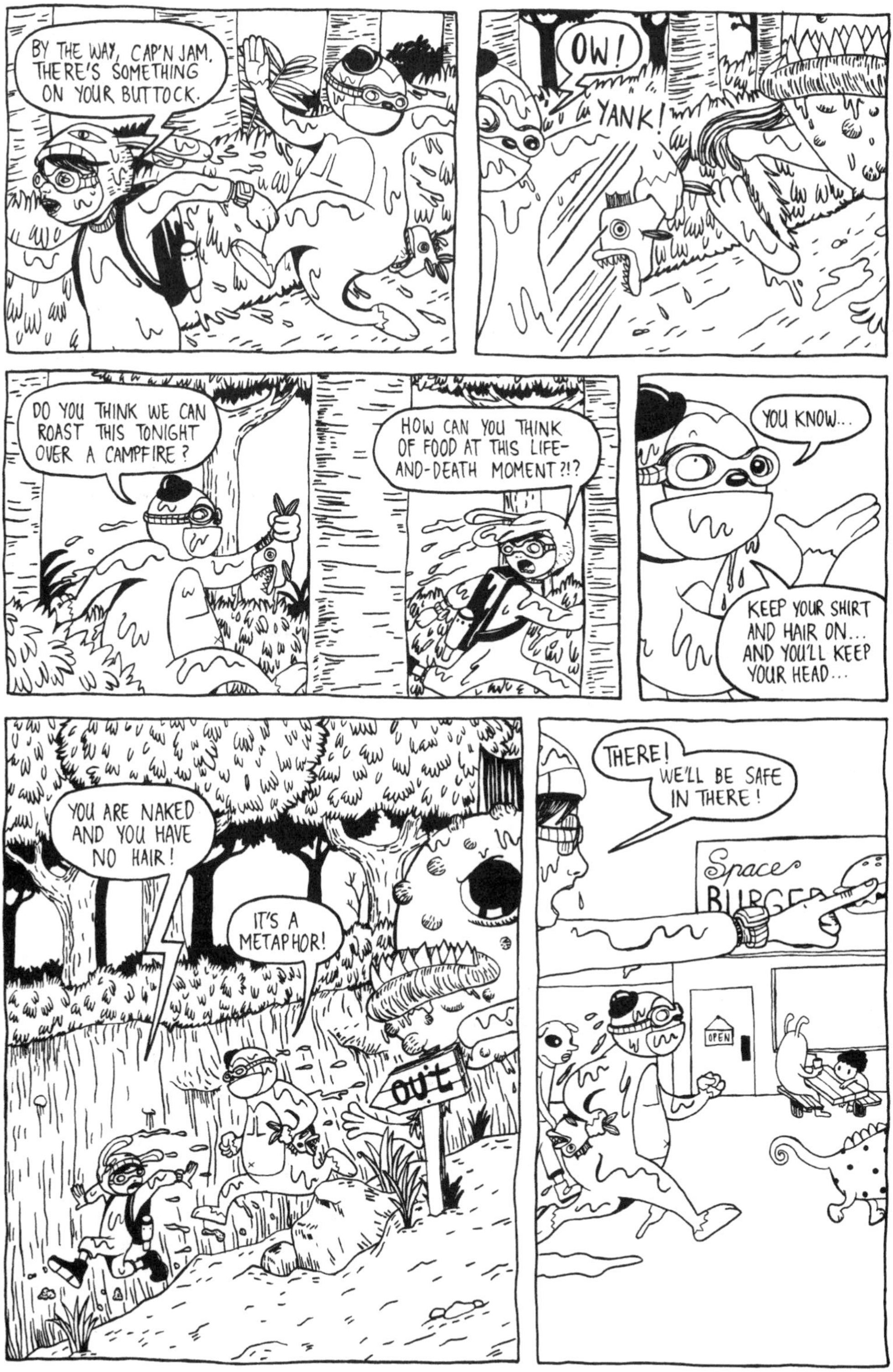
BY THE WAY, CAP'N JAM. THERE'S SOMETHING ON YOUR BUTTOCK.
OW!
YANK!
DO YOU THINK WE CAN ROAST THIS TONIGHT OVER A CAMPFIRE?
HOW CAN YOU THINK OF FOOD AT THIS LIFE-AND-DEATH MOMENT?!?
YOU KNOW...
KEEP YOUR SHIRT AND HAIR ON... AND YOU'LL KEEP YOUR HEAD...
YOU ARE NAKED AND YOU HAVE NO HAIR!
IT'S A METAPHOR!
OUT
THERE! WE'LL BE SAFE IN THERE!
Space BURGE
OPEN

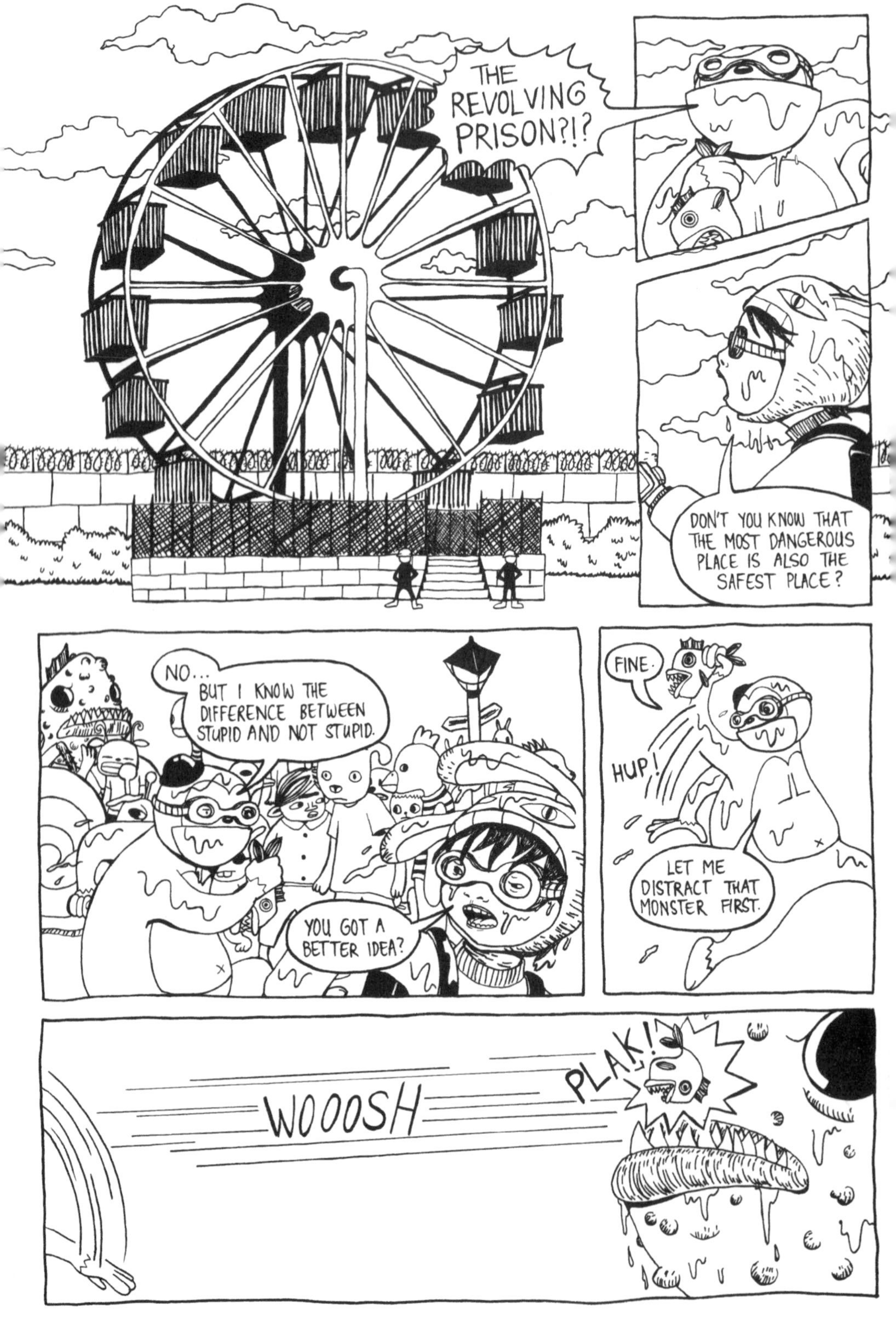
THE REVOLVING PRISON?!?
DON'T YOU KNOW THAT THE MOST DANGEROUS PLACE IS ALSO THE SAFEST PLACE?
NO...
BUT I KNOW THE DIFFERENCE BETWEEN STUPID AND NOT STUPID.
YOU GOT A BETTER IDEA?
FINE.
HUP!
LET ME DISTRACT THAT MONSTER FIRST.
WOOOSH
PLAK!

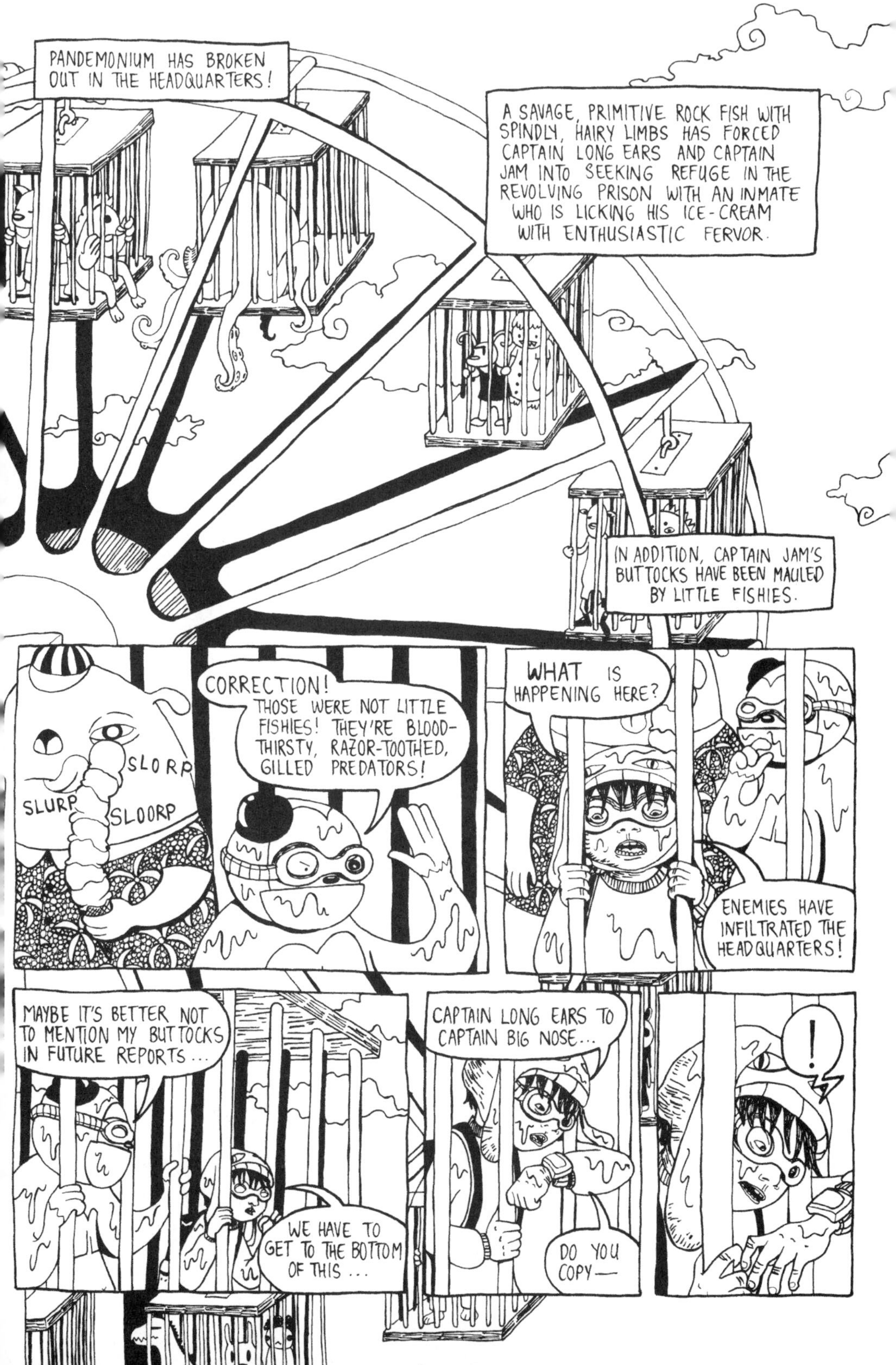
PANDEMONIUM HAS BROKEN OUT IN THE HEADQUARTERS!
A SAVAGE, PRIMITIVE ROCK FISH WITH SPINDLY, HAIRY LIMBS HAS FORCED CAPTAIN LONG EARS AND CAPTAIN JAM INTO SEEKING REFUGE IN THE REVOLVING PRISON WITH AN INMATE WHO IS LICKING HIS ICE-CREAM WITH ENTHUSIASTIC FERVOR.
IN ADDITION, CAPTAIN JAM'S BUTTOCKS HAVE BEEN MAULED BY LITTLE FISHIES.
SLORP
SLURP
SLOORP
CORRECTION! THOSE WERE NOT LITTLE FISHIES! THEY'RE BLOOD-THIRSTY, RAZOR-TOOTHED, GILLED PREDATORS!
WHAT IS HAPPENING HERE?
ENEMIES HAVE INFILTRATED THE HEADQUARTERS!
MAYBE IT'S BETTER NOT TO MENTION MY BUTTOCKS IN FUTURE REPORTS...
WE HAVE TO GET TO THE BOTTOM OF THIS...
CAPTAIN LONG EARS TO CAPTAIN BIG NOSE...
DO YOU COPY—
!

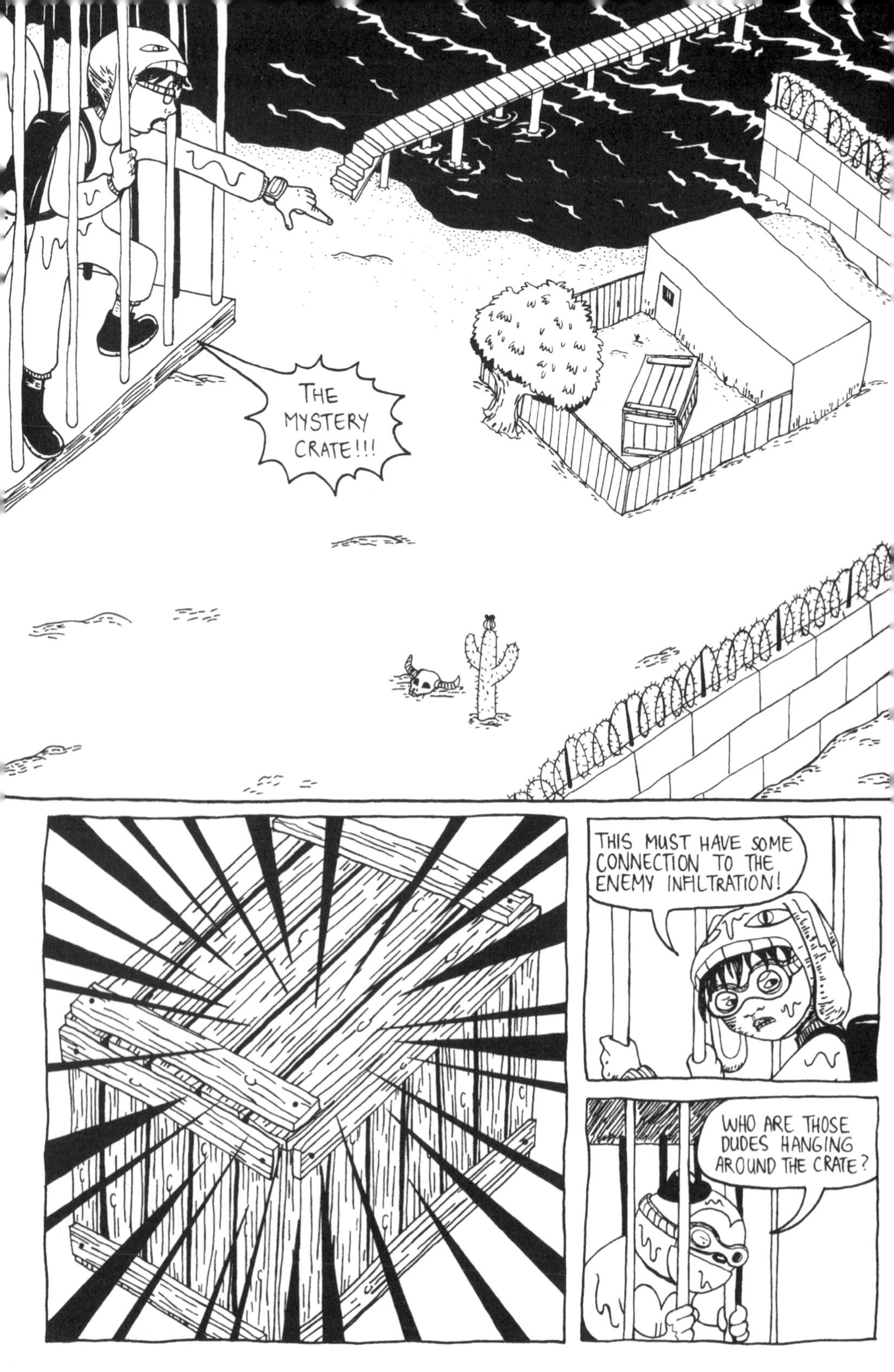
THE MYSTERY CRATE!!!
THIS MUST HAVE SOME CONNECTION TO THE ENEMY INFILTRATION!
WHO ARE THOSE DUDES HANGING AROUND THE CRATE?

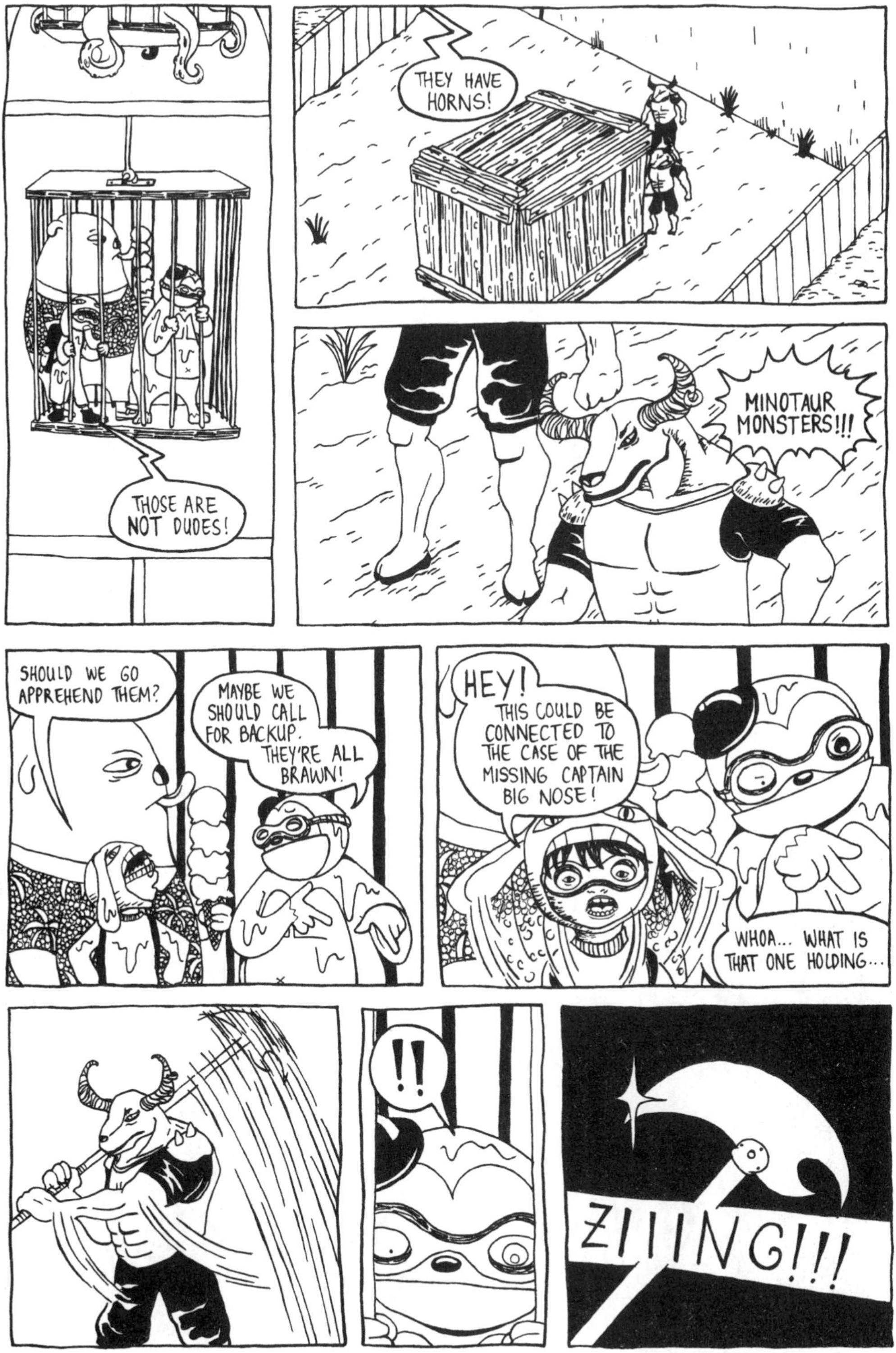
THOSE ARE NOT DUDES!
THEY HAVE HORNS!
MINOTAUR MONSTERS!!!
SHOULD WE GO APPREHEND THEM?
MAYBE WE SHOULD CALL FOR BACKUP.
THEY'RE ALL BRAWN!
HEY!
THIS COULD BE CONNECTED TO THE CASE OF THE MISSING CAPTAIN BIG NOSE!
WHOA... WHAT IS THAT ONE HOLDING...
!!
ZIIING!!!

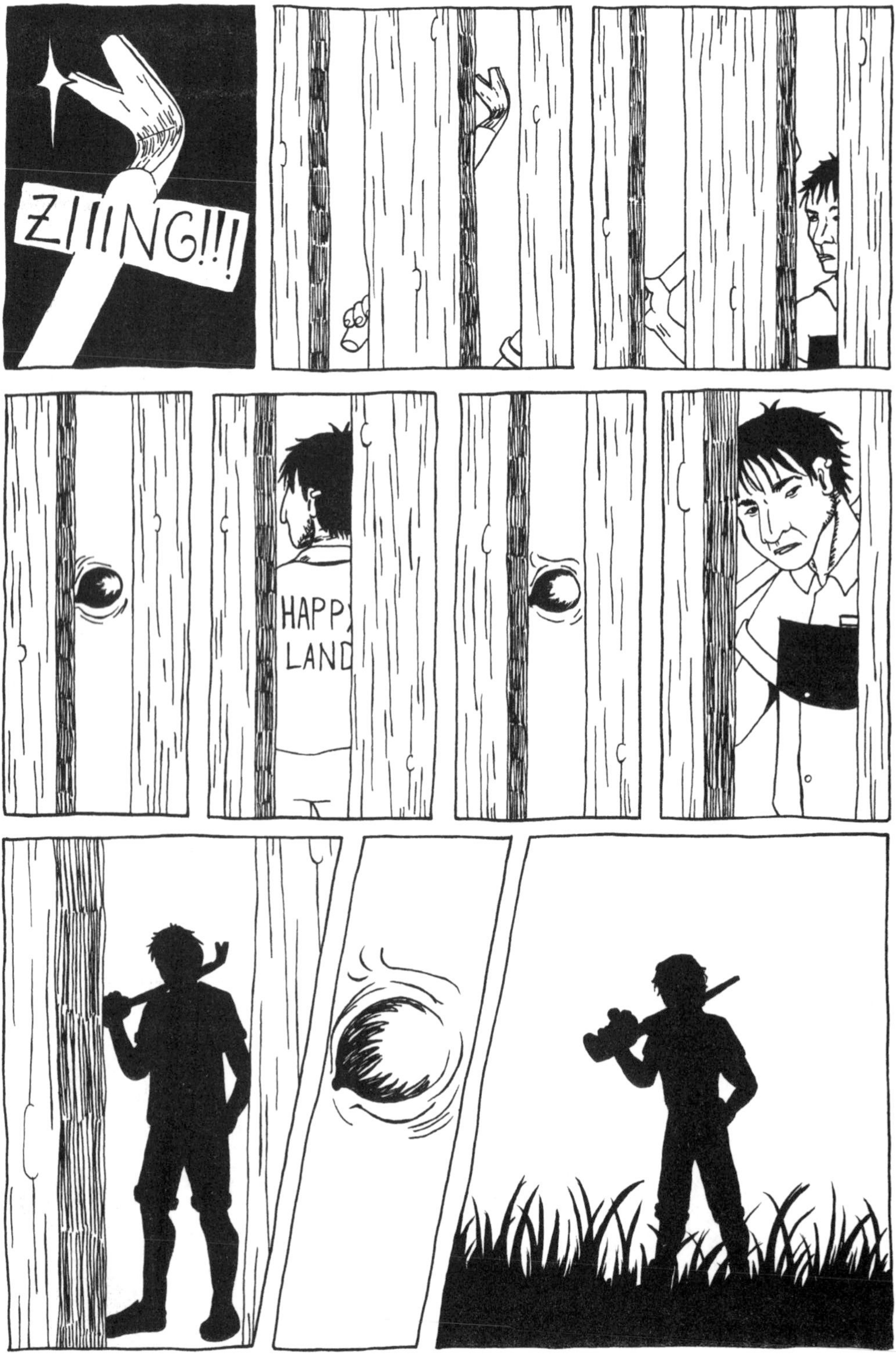
ZIIING!!!
HAPPY
LAND

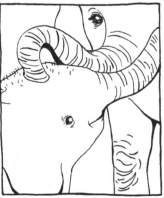

BLAM!

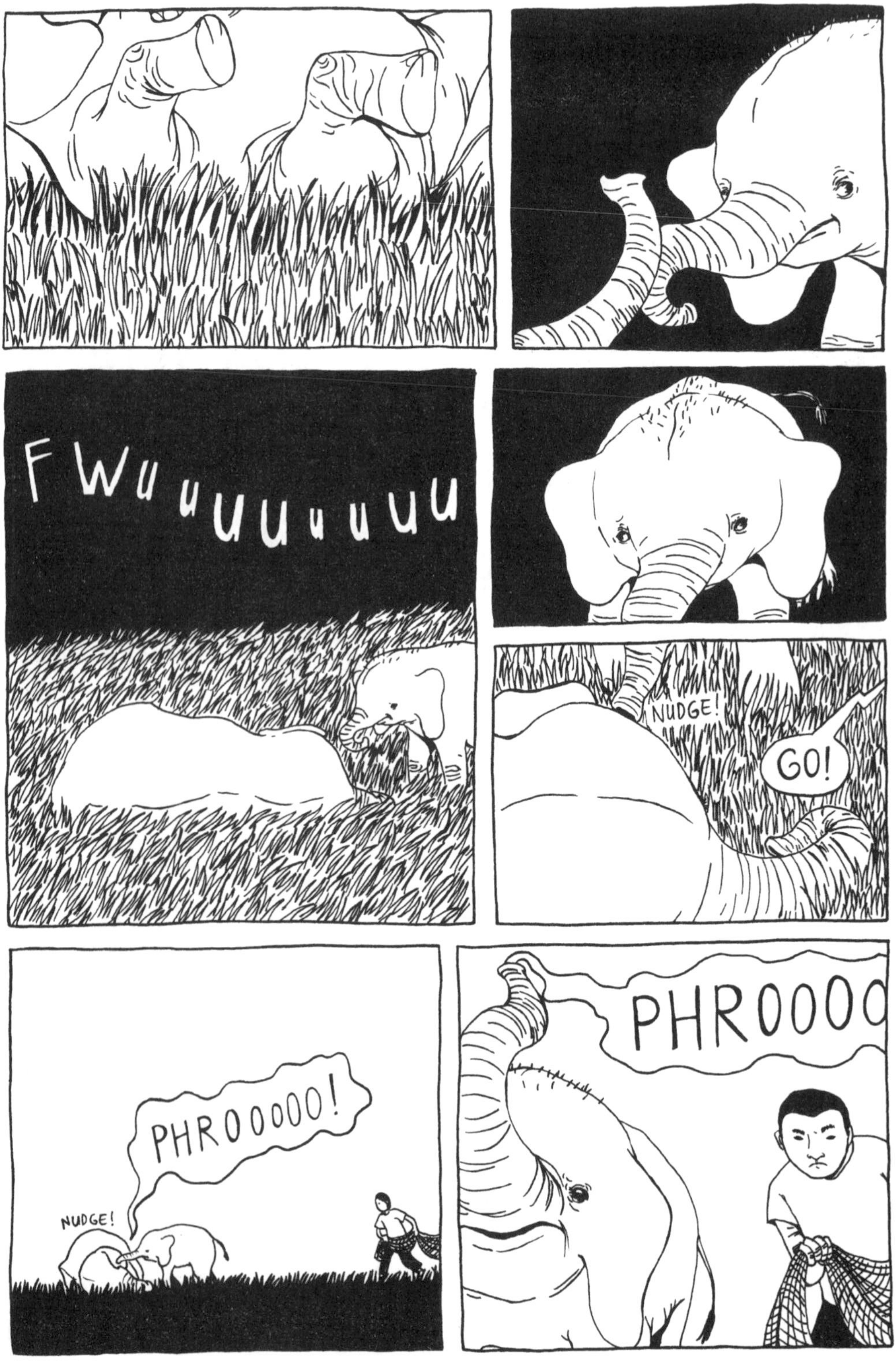
FWuuuuuuuu
NUDGE!
GO!
NUDGE!
PHROOOOO!
PHROOOO

GOT HIM!
PHROOO!
NOWHERE TO RUN!
IS THIS ONE GOOD, CHIEF?
PHROOOOOOOO!
YEAH... THIS ONE WILL FETCH A GOOD PRICE.
SHOO!
YARGH!
MOVE IT!

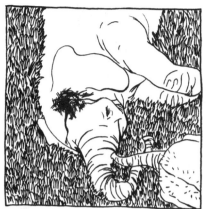

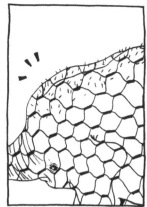

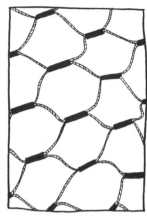

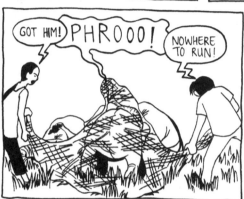

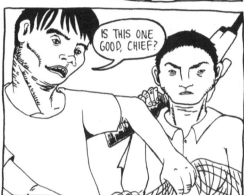

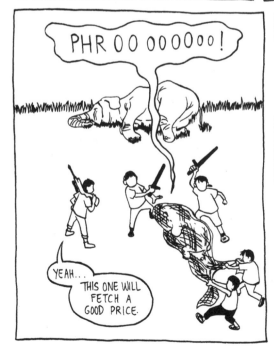

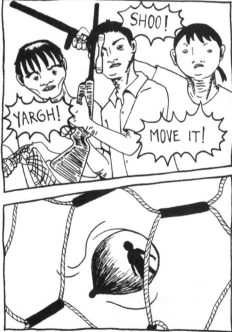

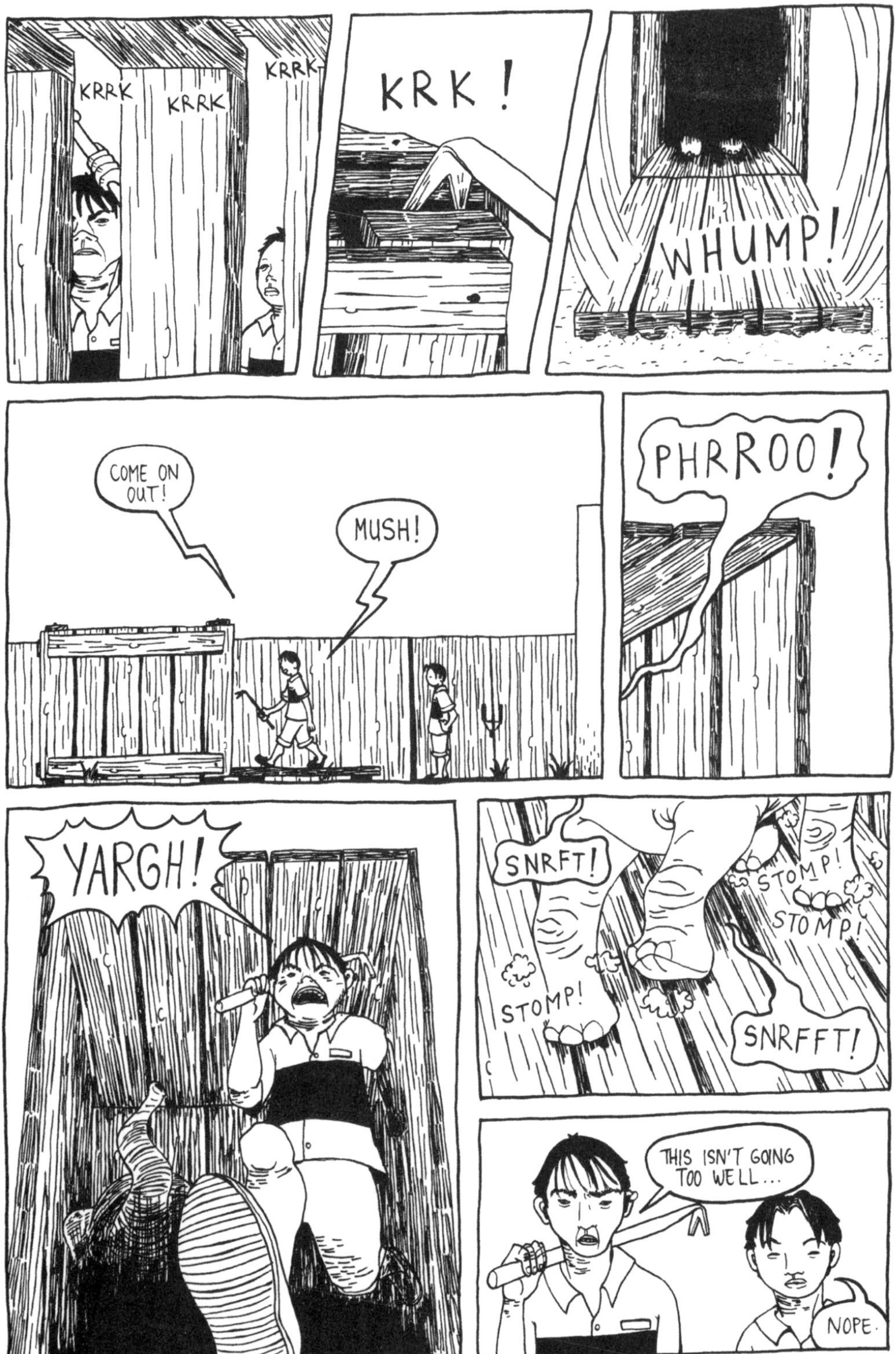
KRRK
KRRK
KRRK
KRK!
WHUMP!
COME ON OUT!
MUSH!
PHRROO!
YARGH!
SNRFT!
STOMP!
STOMP!
STOMP!
SNRFFT!
THIS ISN'T GOING TOO WELL...
NOPE.

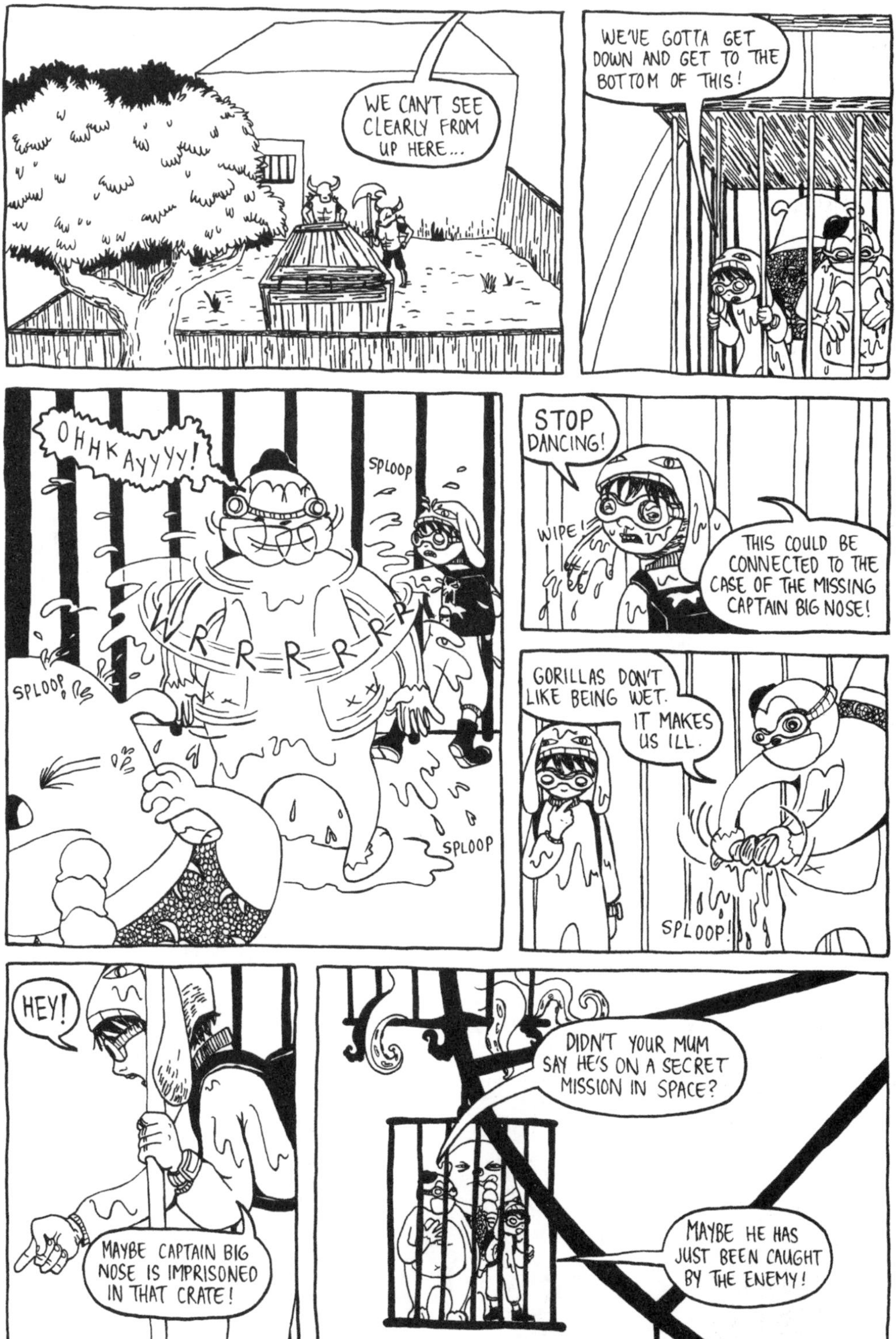
WE CAN'T SEE CLEARLY FROM UP HERE...
WE'VE GOTTA GET DOWN AND GET TO THE BOTTOM OF THIS!
OHHKAYYYY!
SPLOOP
WRRRRRR
SPLOOP
SPLOOP
STOP DANCING!
WIPE!
THIS COULD BE CONNECTED TO THE CASE OF THE MISSING CAPTAIN BIG NOSE!
GORILLAS DON'T LIKE BEING WET.
IT MAKES US ILL.
SPLOOP!
HEY!
MAYBE CAPTAIN BIG NOSE IS IMPRISONED IN THAT CRATE!
DIDN'T YOUR MUM SAY HE'S ON A SECRET MISSION IN SPACE?
MAYBE HE HAS JUST BEEN CAUGHT BY THE ENEMY!

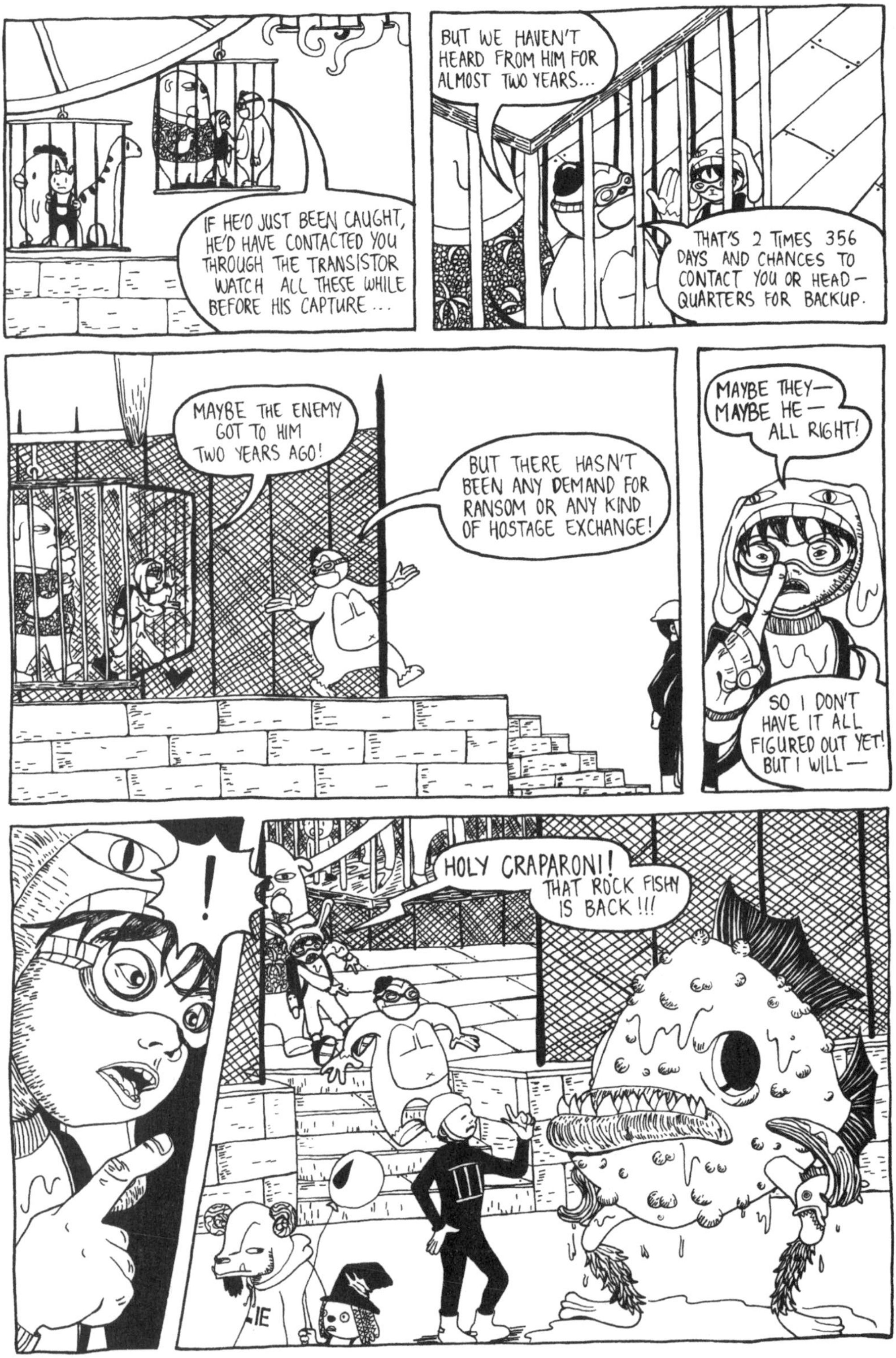
IF HE'D JUST BEEN CAUGHT, HE'D HAVE CONTACTED YOU THROUGH THE TRANSISTOR WATCH ALL THESE WHILE BEFORE HIS CAPTURE...
BUT WE HAVEN'T HEARD FROM HIM FOR ALMOST TWO YEARS...
THAT'S 2 TIMES 356 DAYS AND CHANCES TO CONTACT YOU OR HEAD-QUARTERS FOR BACKUP.
MAYBE THE ENEMY GOT TO HIM TWO YEARS AGO!
BUT THERE HASN'T BEEN ANY DEMAND FOR RANSOM OR ANY KIND OF HOSTAGE EXCHANGE!
MAYBE THEY— MAYBE HE— ALL RIGHT!
SO I DON'T HAVE IT ALL FIGURED OUT YET! BUT I WILL—
!
HOLY CRAPARONI! THAT ROCK FISHY IS BACK!!!
LIE

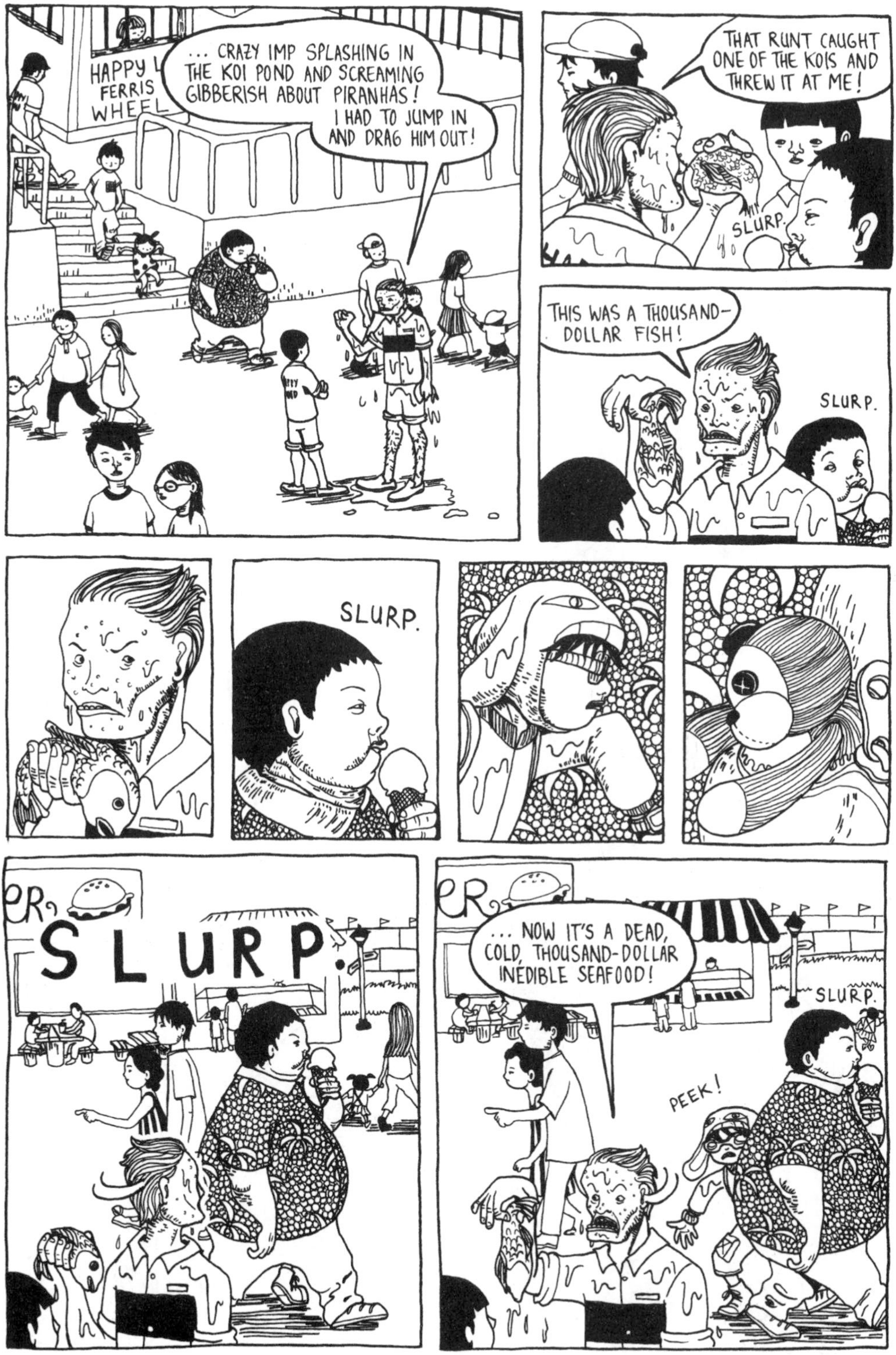
HAPPY
FERRIS WHEEL
... CRAZY IMP SPLASHING IN THE KOI POND AND SCREAMING GIBBERISH ABOUT PIRANHAS!
I HAD TO JUMP IN AND DRAG HIM OUT!
THAT RUNT CAUGHT ONE OF THE KOIS AND THREW IT AT ME!
SLURP.
THIS WAS A THOUSAND-DOLLAR FISH!
SLURP.
SLURP.
SLURP.
... NOW IT'S A DEAD, COLD, THOUSAND-DOLLAR INEDIBLE SEAFOOD!
SLURP.
PEEK!

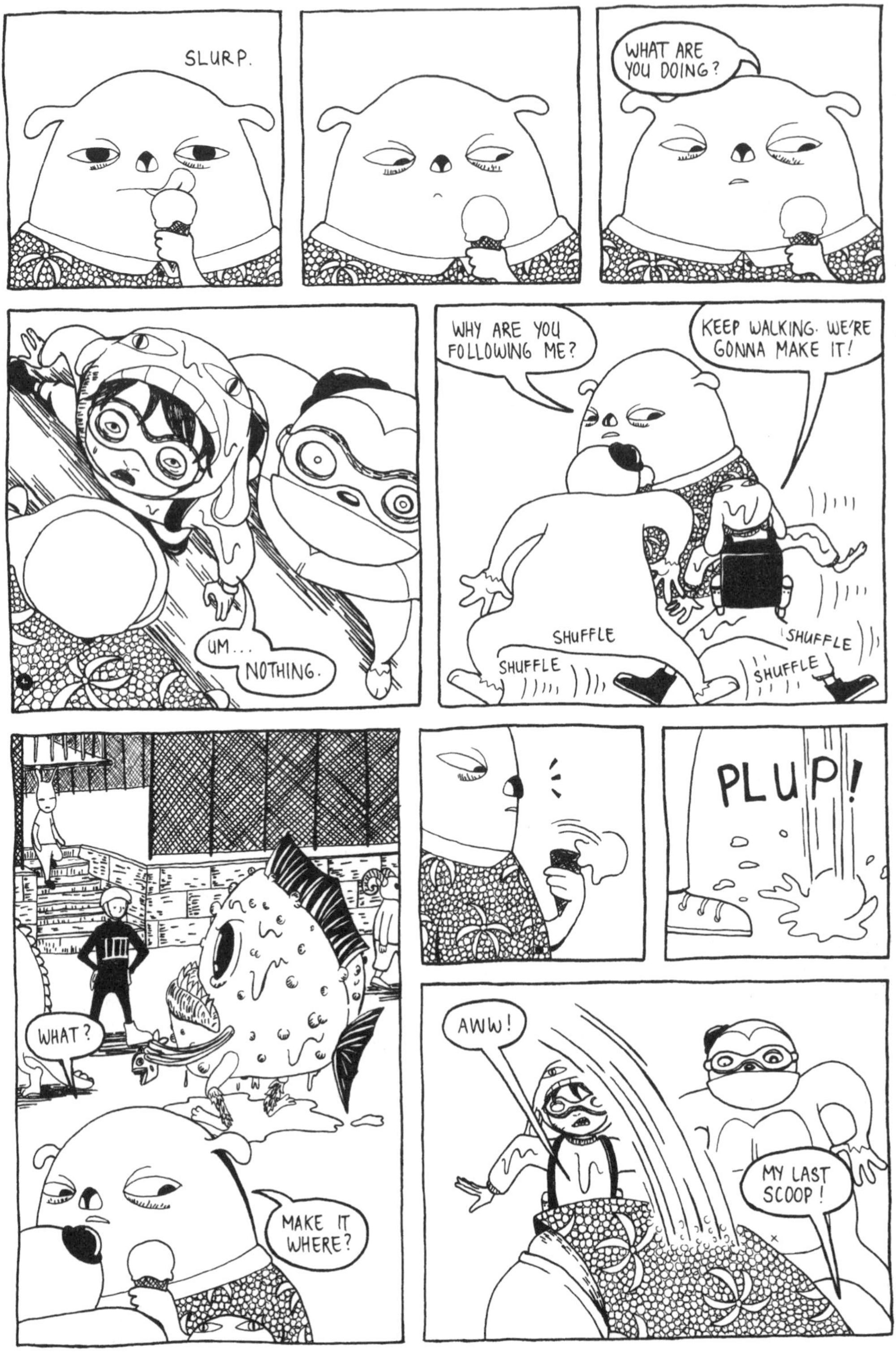
SLURP.
WHAT ARE YOU DOING?
UM... NOTHING.
WHY ARE YOU FOLLOWING ME?
KEEP WALKING. WE'RE GONNA MAKE IT!
SHUFFLE
SHUFFLE
SHUFFLE
SHUFFLE
WHAT?
MAKE IT WHERE?
PLUP!
AWW!
MY LAST SCOOP!

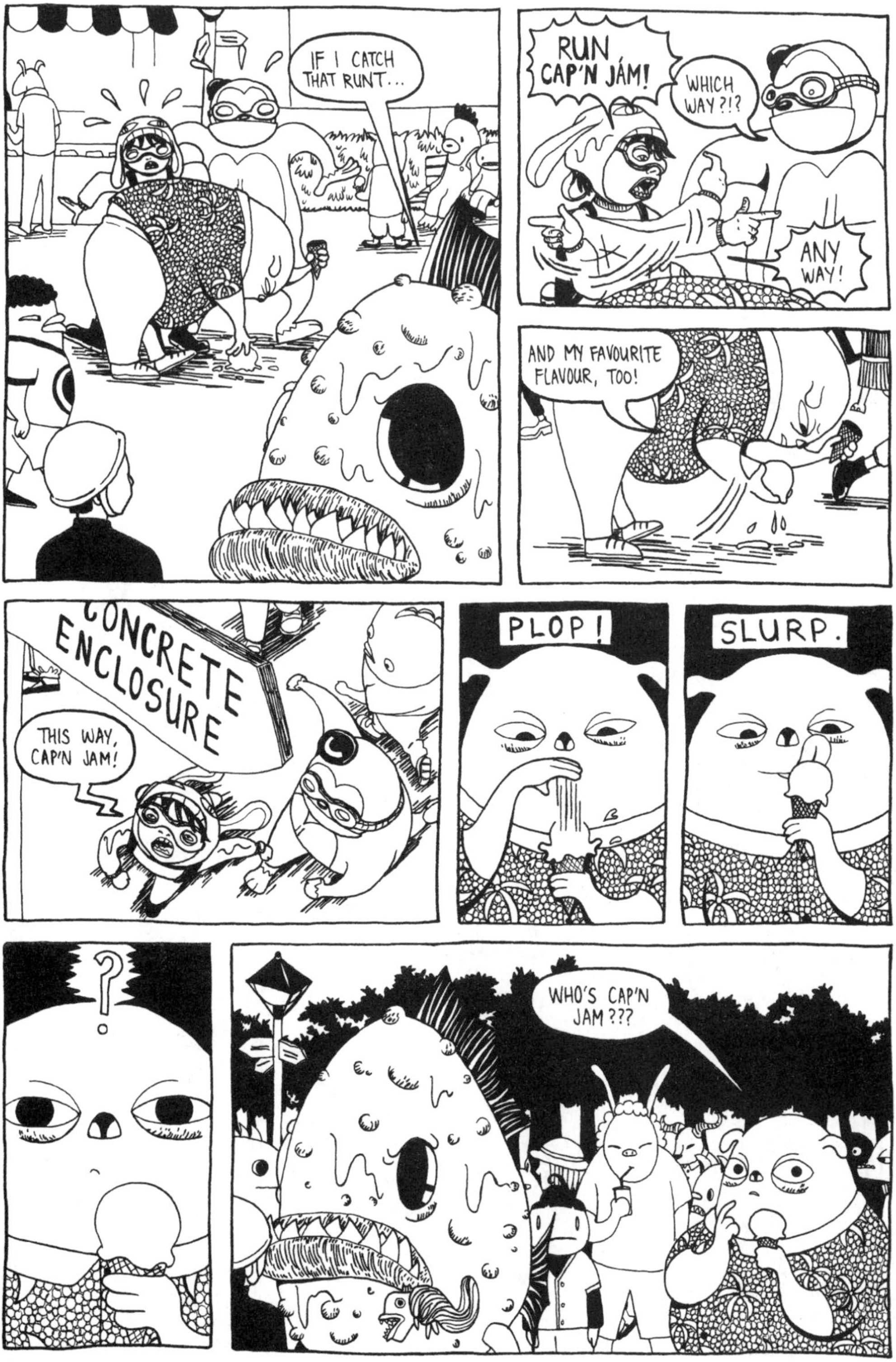
IF I CATCH THAT RUNT...
RUN, CAP'N JÁM!
WHICH WAY?!?
ANY WAY!
AND MY FAVOURITE FLAVOUR, TOO!
CONCRETE ENCLOSURE
THIS WAY, CAP'N JAM!
PLOP!
SLURP.
?
WHO'S CAP'N JAM???

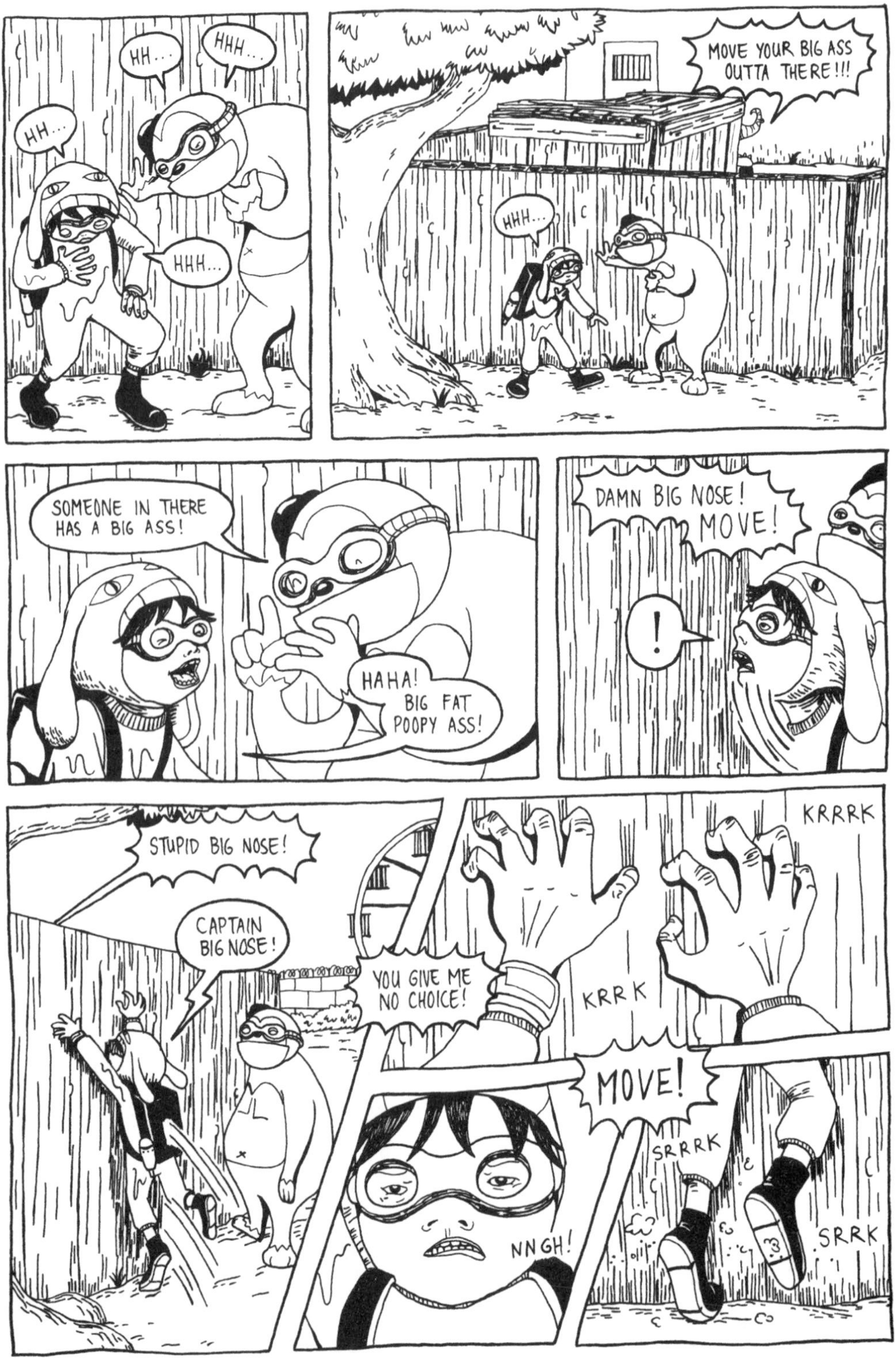
HH...
HH...
HHH...
HHH...
MOVE YOUR BIG ASS OUTTA THERE!!!
HHH...
SOMEONE IN THERE HAS A BIG ASS!
HAHA! BIG FAT POOPY ASS!
DAMN BIG NOSE! MOVE!
!
STUPID BIG NOSE!
CAPTAIN BIG NOSE!
YOU GIVE ME NO CHOICE!
KRRRK
KRRK
MOVE!
NNGH!
SRRRK
SRRK

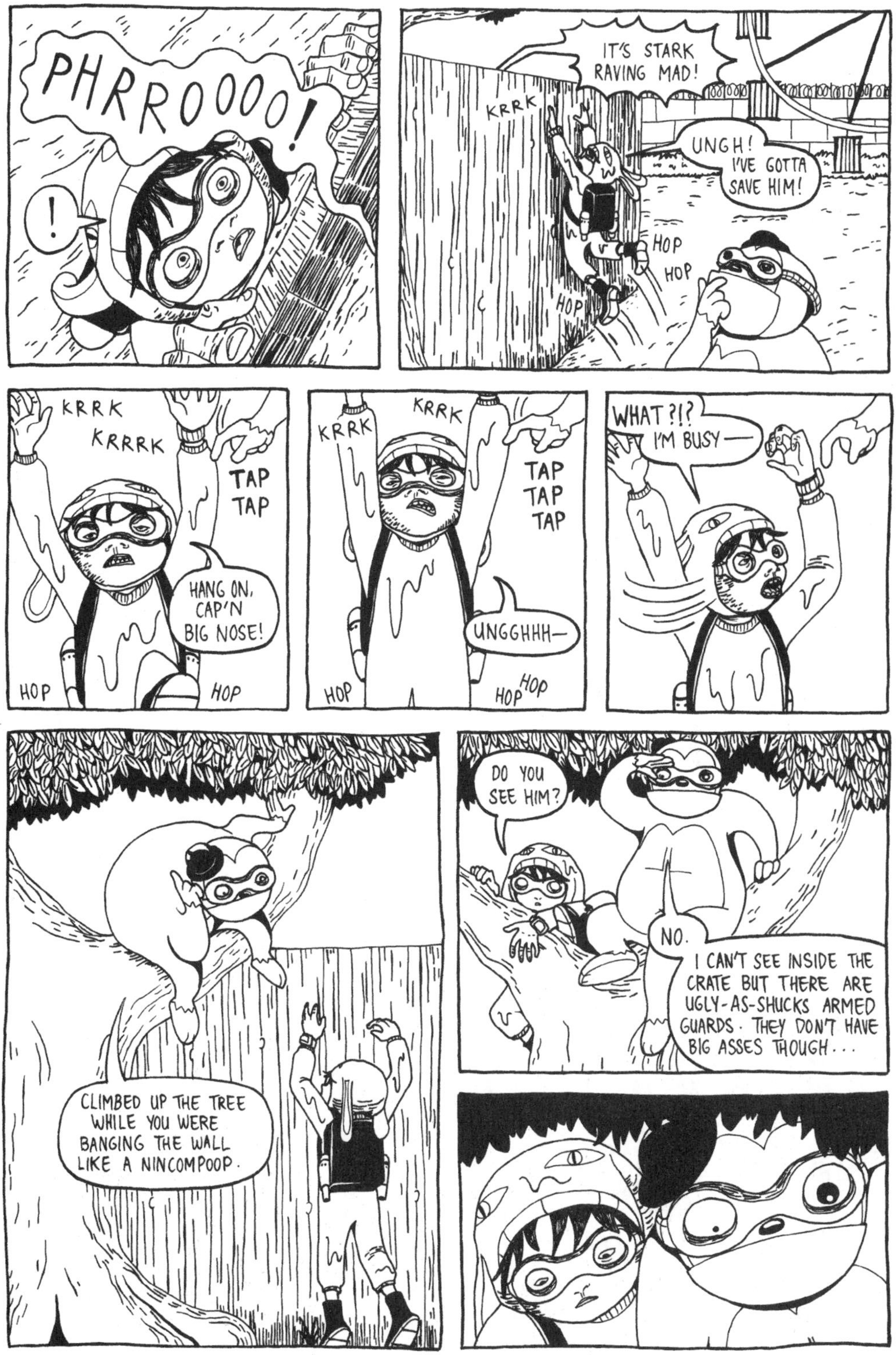
PHRROOOO!
!
IT'S STARK RAVING MAD!
KRRK
UNGH! I'VE GOTTA SAVE HIM!
HOP
HOP
HOP
KRRK
KRRRK
TAP TAP
HANG ON, CAP'N BIG NOSE!
HOP
HOP
KRRK
KRRK
TAP TAP TAP
UNGGHHH—
HOP
HOP HOP
WHAT?!?
I'M BUSY—
CLIMBED UP THE TREE WHILE YOU WERE BANGING THE WALL LIKE A NINCOMPOOP.
DO YOU SEE HIM?
NO.
I CAN'T SEE INSIDE THE CRATE BUT THERE ARE UGLY-AS-SHUCKS ARMED GUARDS. THEY DON'T HAVE BIG ASSES THOUGH...

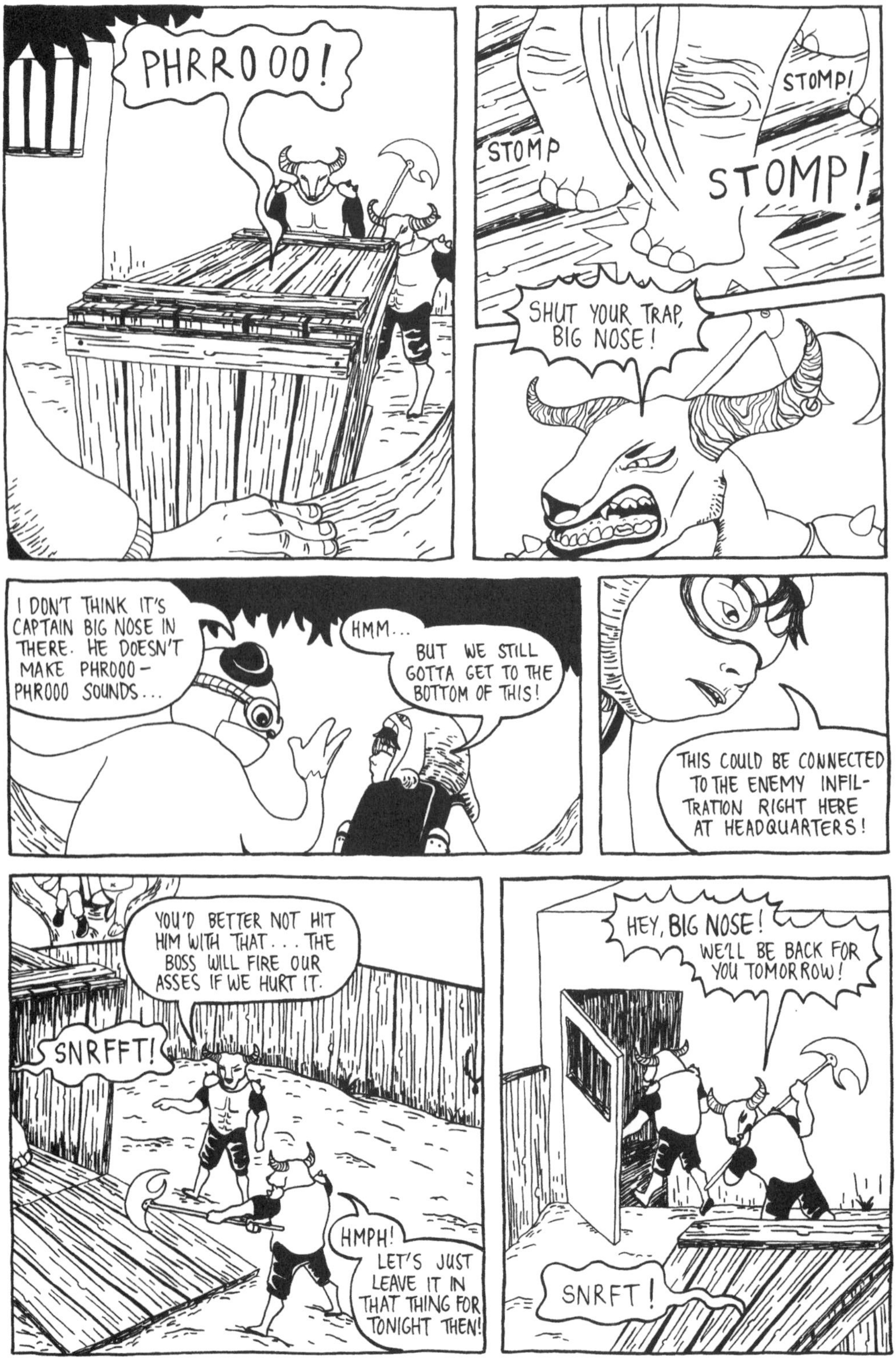
PHRROOO!
STOMP
STOMP!
STOMP!
SHUT YOUR TRAP, BIG NOSE!
I DON'T THINK IT'S CAPTAIN BIG NOSE IN THERE. HE DOESN'T MAKE PHROOO-PHROOO SOUNDS...
HMM...
BUT WE STILL GOTTA GET TO THE BOTTOM OF THIS!
THIS COULD BE CONNECTED TO THE ENEMY INFIL-TRATION RIGHT HERE AT HEADQUARTERS!
YOU'D BETTER NOT HIT HIM WITH THAT... THE BOSS WILL FIRE OUR ASSES IF WE HURT IT.
SNRFFT!
HMPH!
LET'S JUST LEAVE IT IN THAT THING FOR TONIGHT THEN!
HEY, BIG NOSE!
WE'LL BE BACK FOR YOU TOMORROW!
SNRFT!

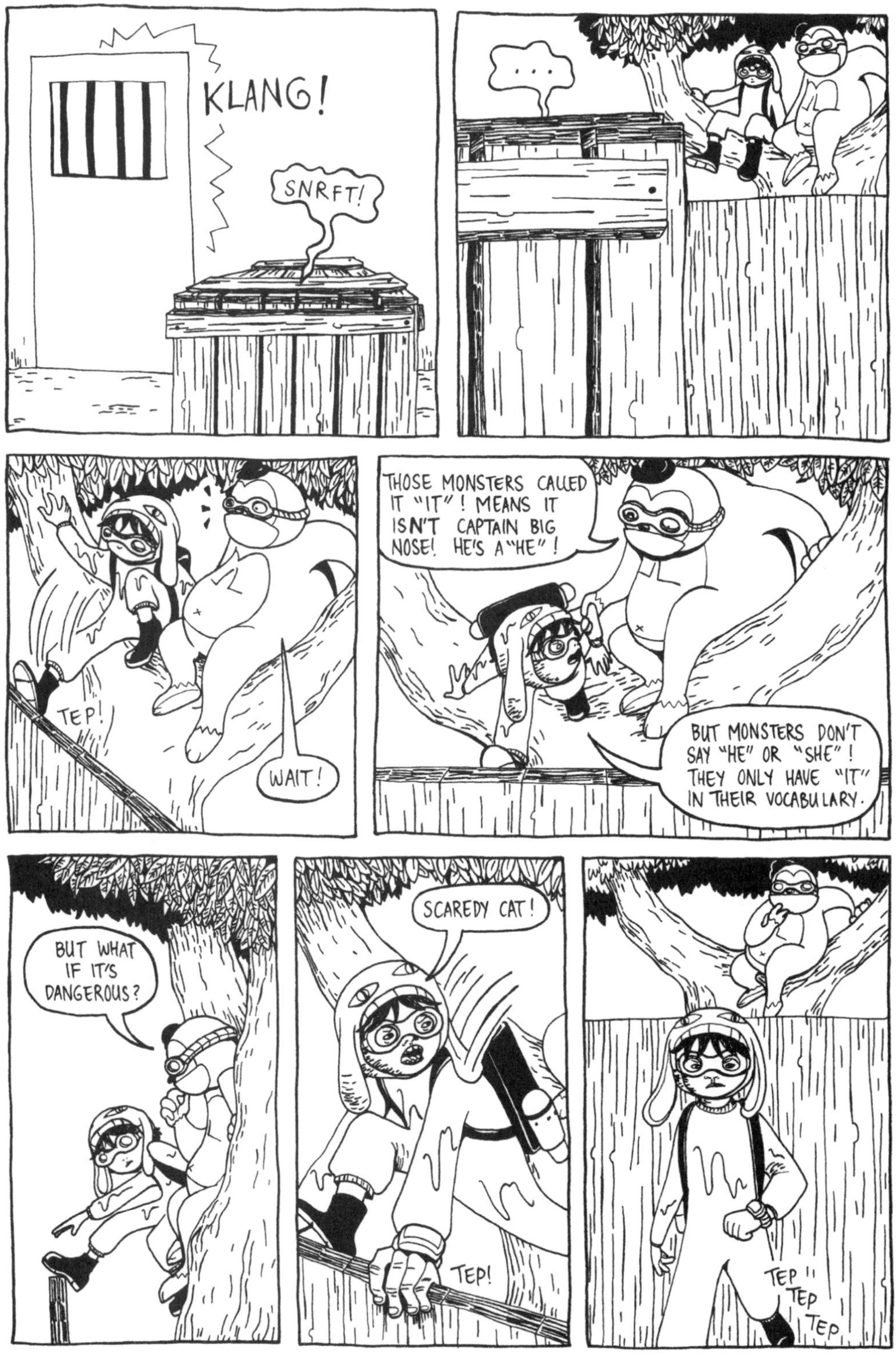
KLANG!
SNRFT!
. . .
TEP!
WAIT!
THOSE MONSTERS CALLED IT "IT"! MEANS IT ISN'T CAPTAIN BIG NOSE! HE'S A "HE"!
BUT MONSTERS DON'T SAY "HE" OR "SHE"! THEY ONLY HAVE "IT" IN THEIR VOCABULARY.
BUT WHAT IF IT'S DANGEROUS?
SCAREDY CAT!
TEP!
TEP TEP TEP

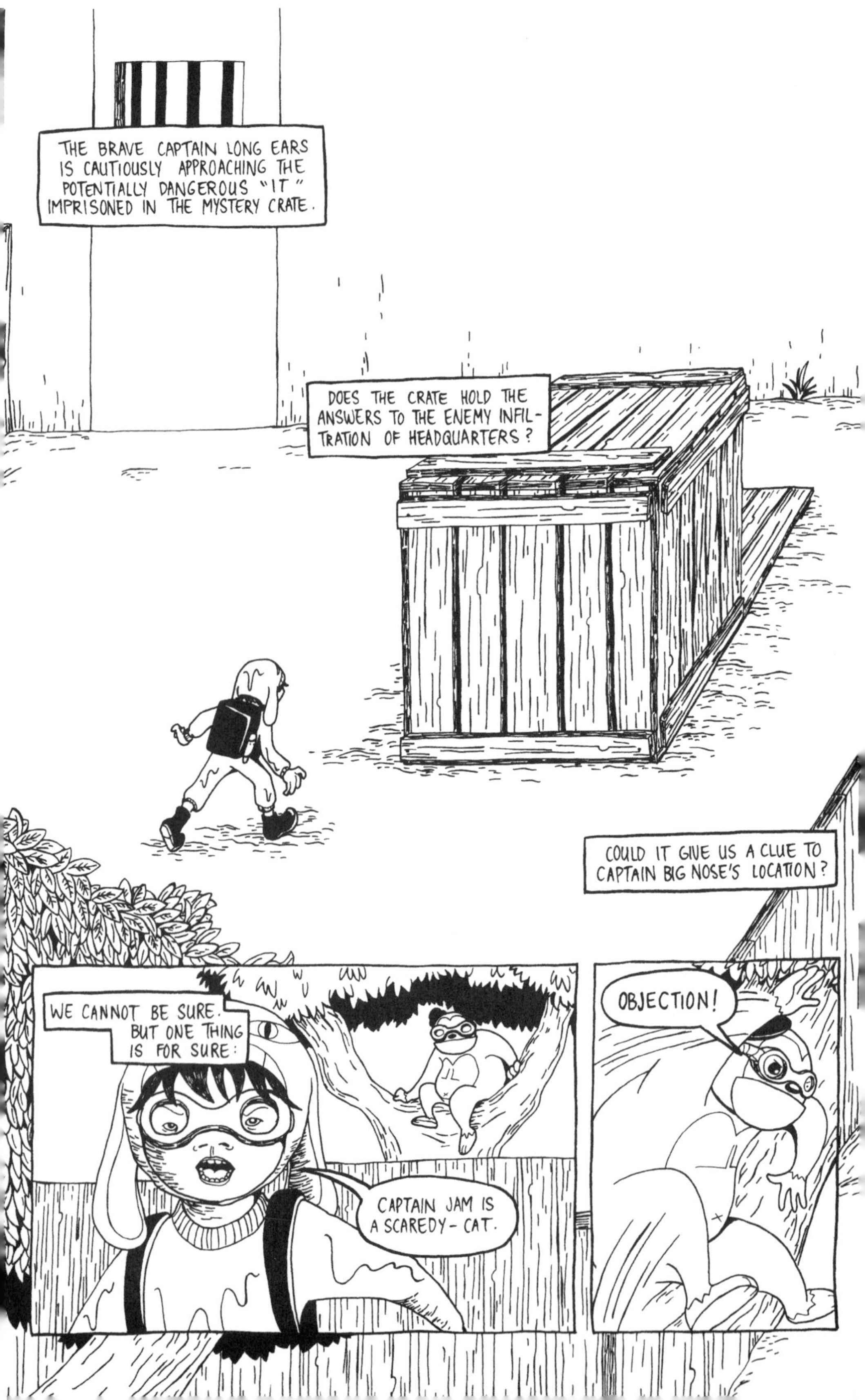
THE BRAVE CAPTAIN LONG EARS IS CAUTIOUSLY APPROACHING THE POTENTIALLY DANGEROUS "IT" IMPRISONED IN THE MYSTERY CRATE.
DOES THE CRATE HOLD THE ANSWERS TO THE ENEMY INFILTRATION OF HEADQUARTERS?
COULD IT GIVE US A CLUE TO CAPTAIN BIG NOSE'S LOCATION?
WE CANNOT BE SURE. BUT ONE THING IS FOR SURE:
CAPTAIN JAM IS A SCAREDY-CAT.
OBJECTION!

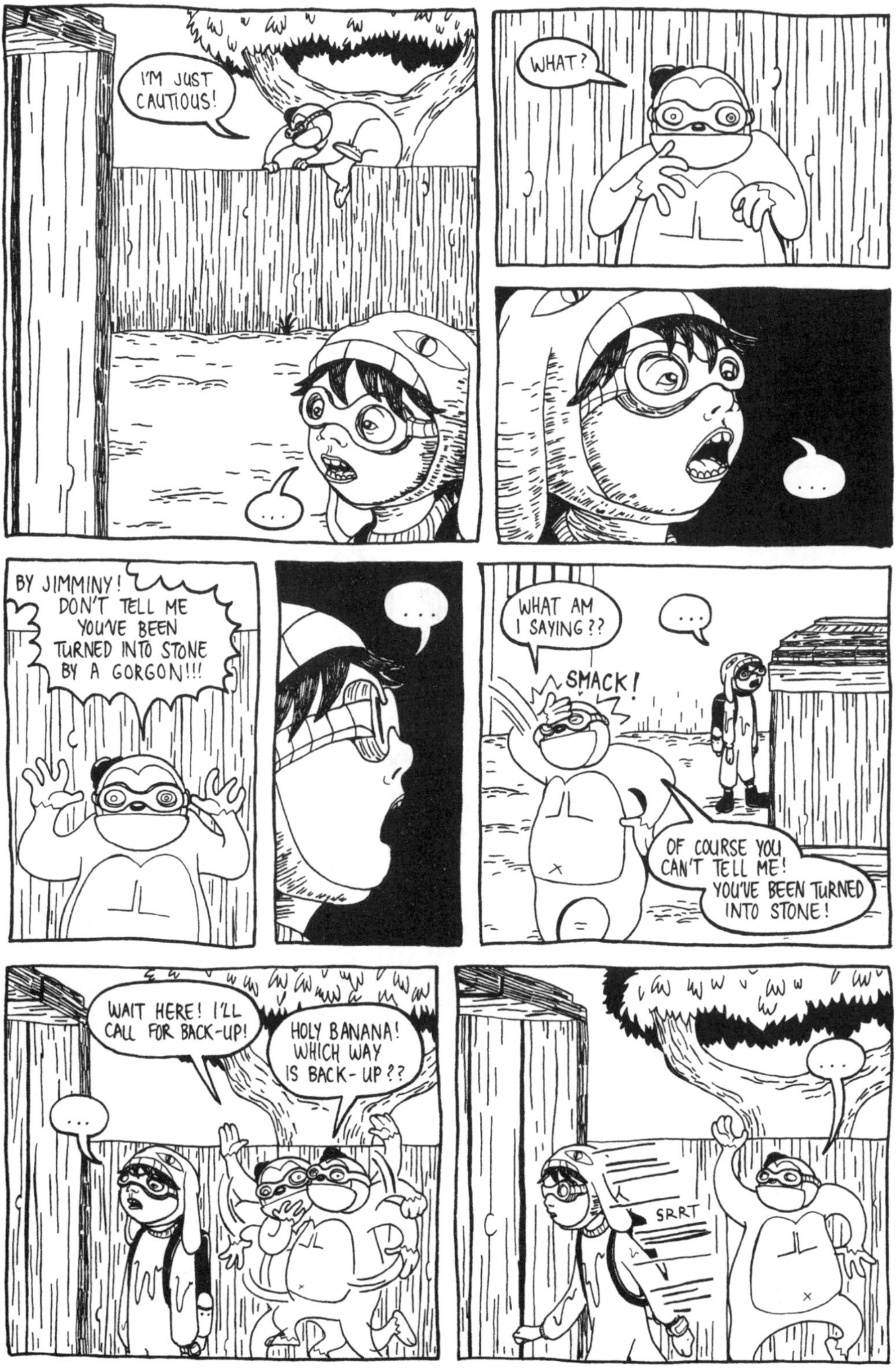

I'M JUST CAUTIOUS!
...
WHAT?
...
BY JIMMINY! DON'T TELL ME YOU'VE BEEN TURNED INTO STONE BY A GORGON!!!
...
WHAT AM I SAYING??
...
SMACK!
OF COURSE YOU CAN'T TELL ME! YOU'VE BEEN TURNED INTO STONE!
...
WAIT HERE! I'LL CALL FOR BACK-UP!
HOLY BANANA! WHICH WAY IS BACK-UP??
...
SRRT

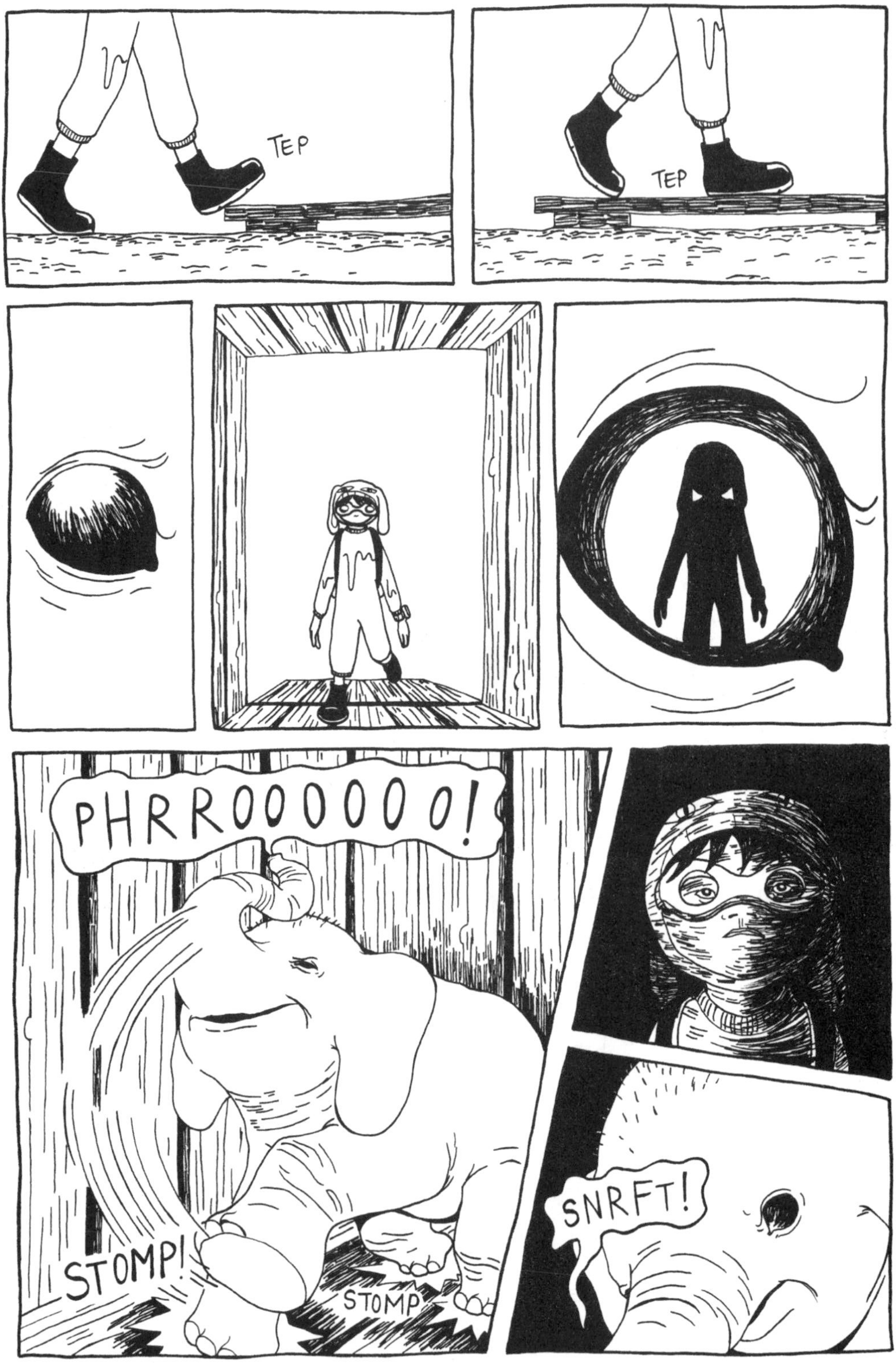
TEP
TEP
PHRROOOOOO!
STOMP!
STOMP
SNRFT!

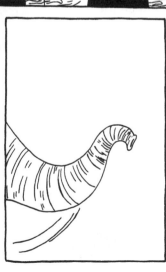

PUK.

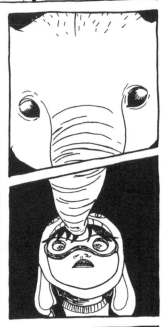

PUK.

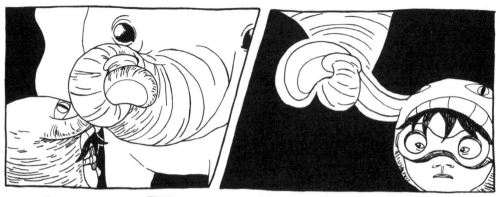

SHUCKS SHUCKS SHUCKS SHUCKS! THE GORGON HAS HYPNOTISED CAP'N LONG EARS INTO ITS LAIR!

CALM DOWN, CAP'N JAM... KEEP YOUR SHIRT ON, KEEP YOUR HAIR ON AND YOU'LL KEEP YOUR HEAD.

TEP.

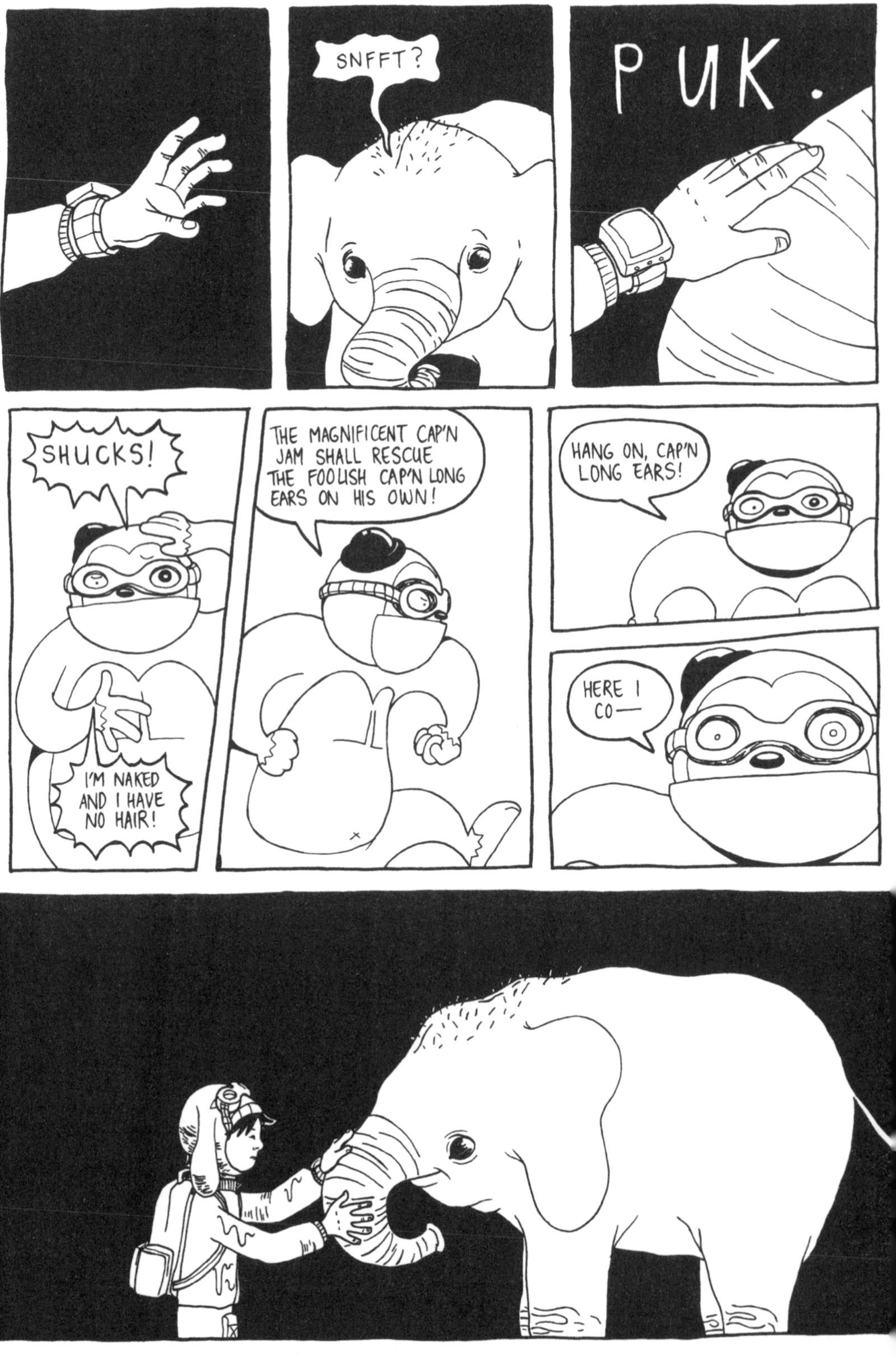
SNFFT?
PUK.
SHUCKS!
I'M NAKED AND I HAVE NO HAIR!
THE MAGNIFICENT CAP'N JAM SHALL RESCUE THE FOOLISH CAP'N LONG EARS ON HIS OWN!
HANG ON, CAP'N LONG EARS!
HERE I CO—

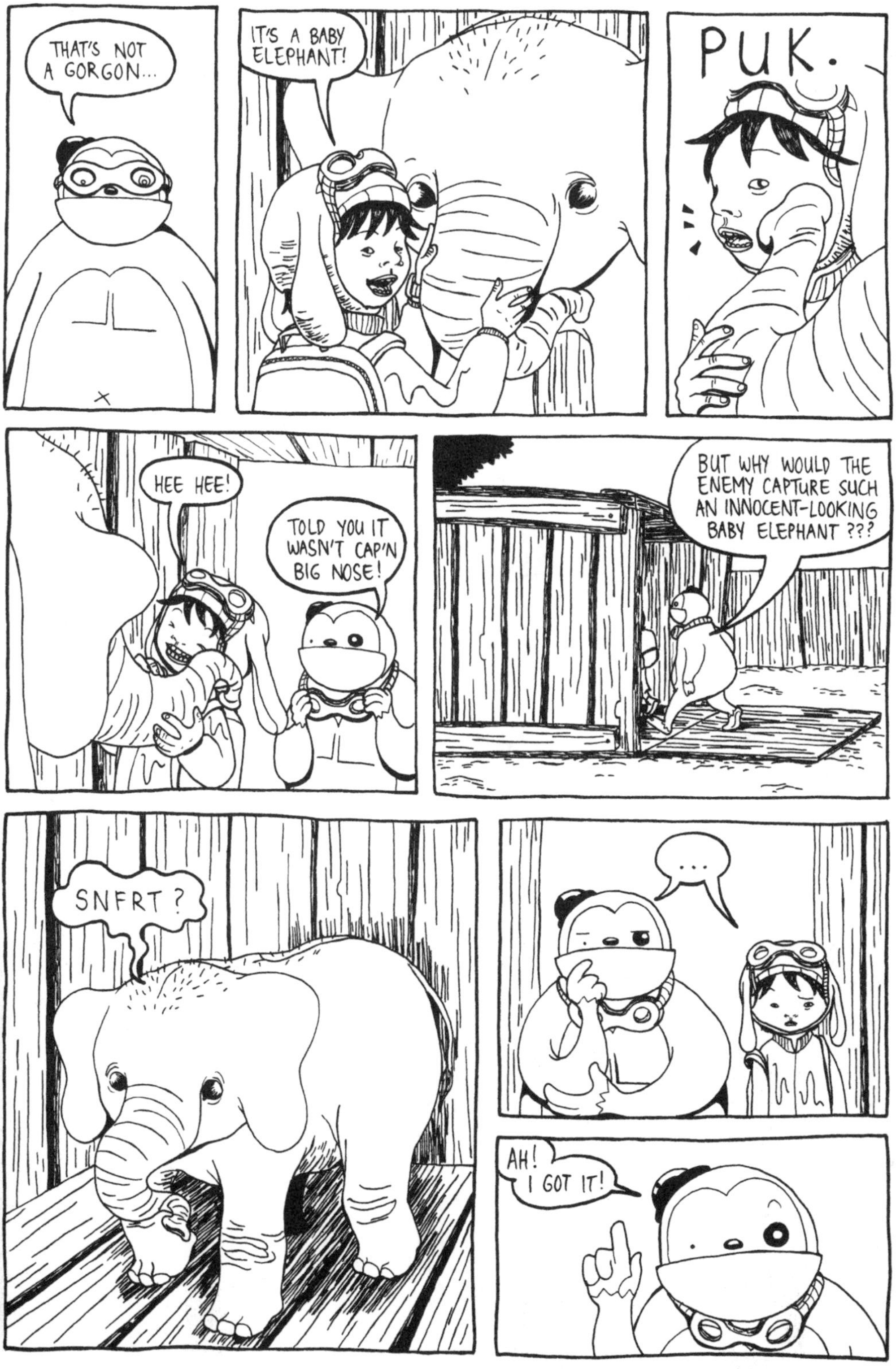
THAT'S NOT A GORGON...
IT'S A BABY ELEPHANT!
PUK.
HEE HEE!
TOLD YOU IT WASN'T CAP'N BIG NOSE!
BUT WHY WOULD THE ENEMY CAPTURE SUCH AN INNOCENT-LOOKING BABY ELEPHANT???
SNFRT?
...
AH! I GOT IT!

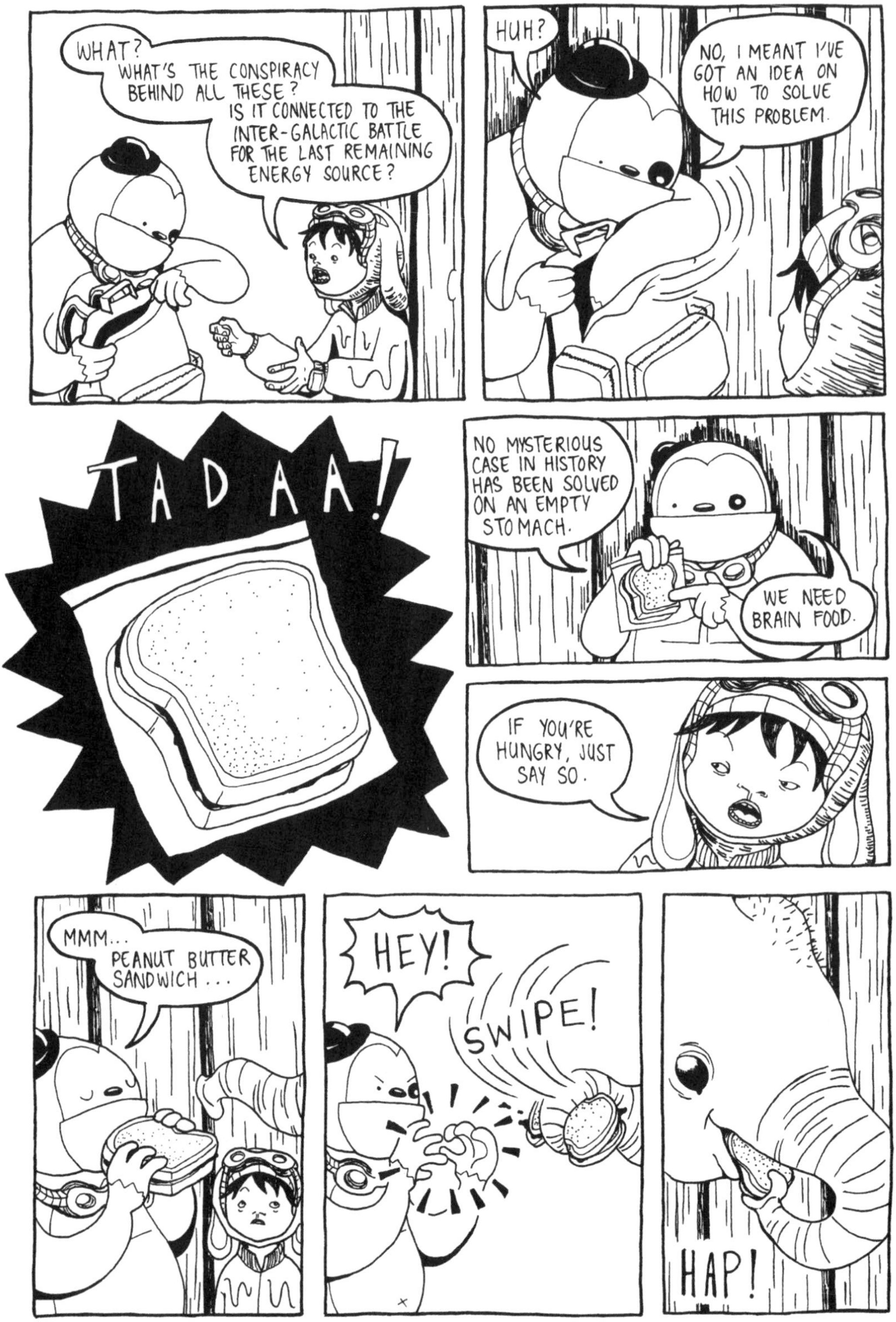
WHAT?
WHAT'S THE CONSPIRACY BEHIND ALL THESE?
IS IT CONNECTED TO THE INTER-GALACTIC BATTLE FOR THE LAST REMAINING ENERGY SOURCE?
HUH?
NO, I MEANT I'VE GOT AN IDEA ON HOW TO SOLVE THIS PROBLEM.
TADAA!
NO MYSTERIOUS CASE IN HISTORY HAS BEEN SOLVED ON AN EMPTY STOMACH.
WE NEED BRAIN FOOD.
IF YOU'RE HUNGRY, JUST SAY SO.
MMM... PEANUT BUTTER SANDWICH...
HEY!
SWIPE!
HAP!

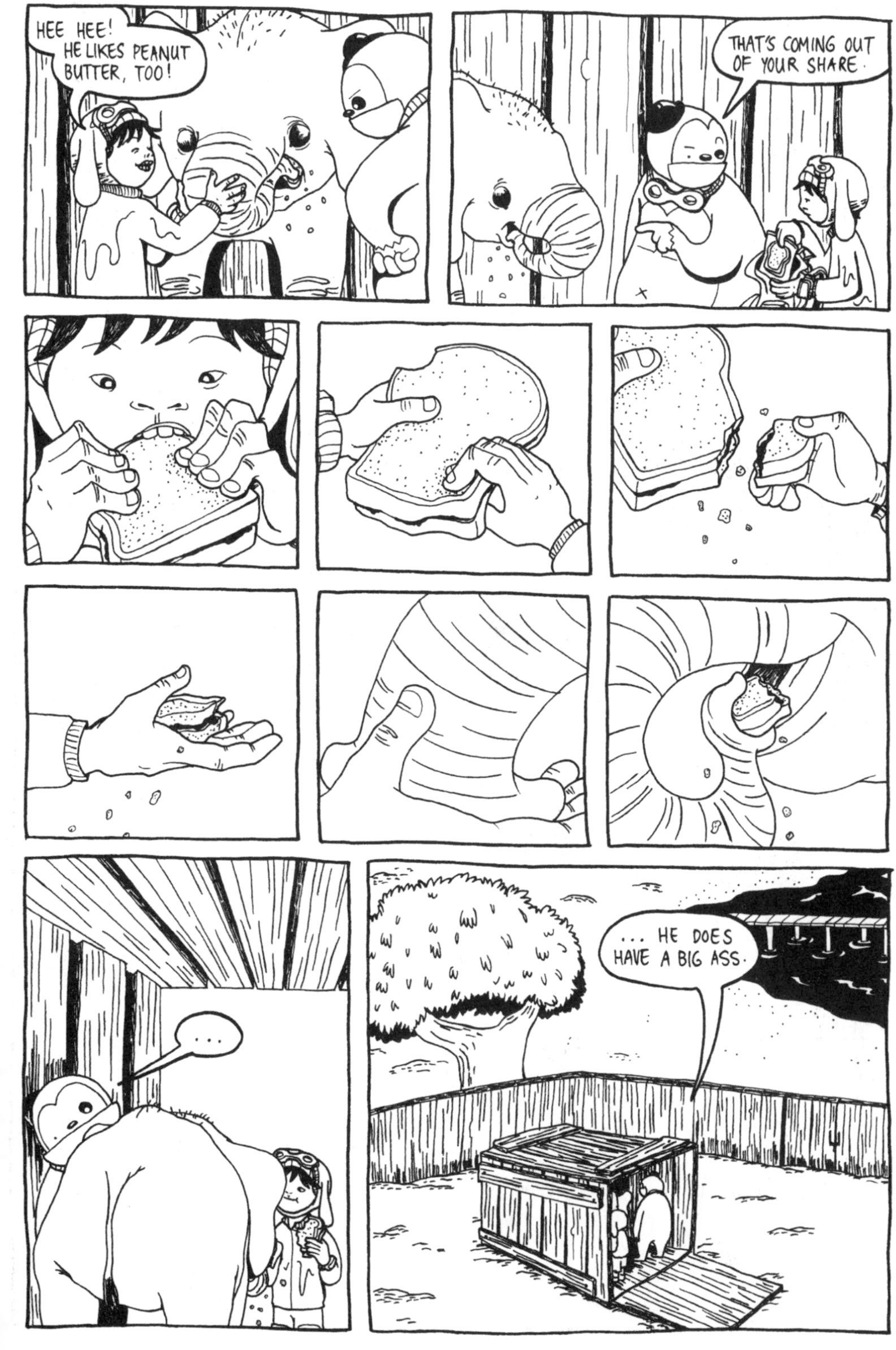
HEE HEE!
HE LIKES PEANUT BUTTER, TOO!
THAT'S COMING OUT OF YOUR SHARE.
...
... HE DOES HAVE A BIG ASS.

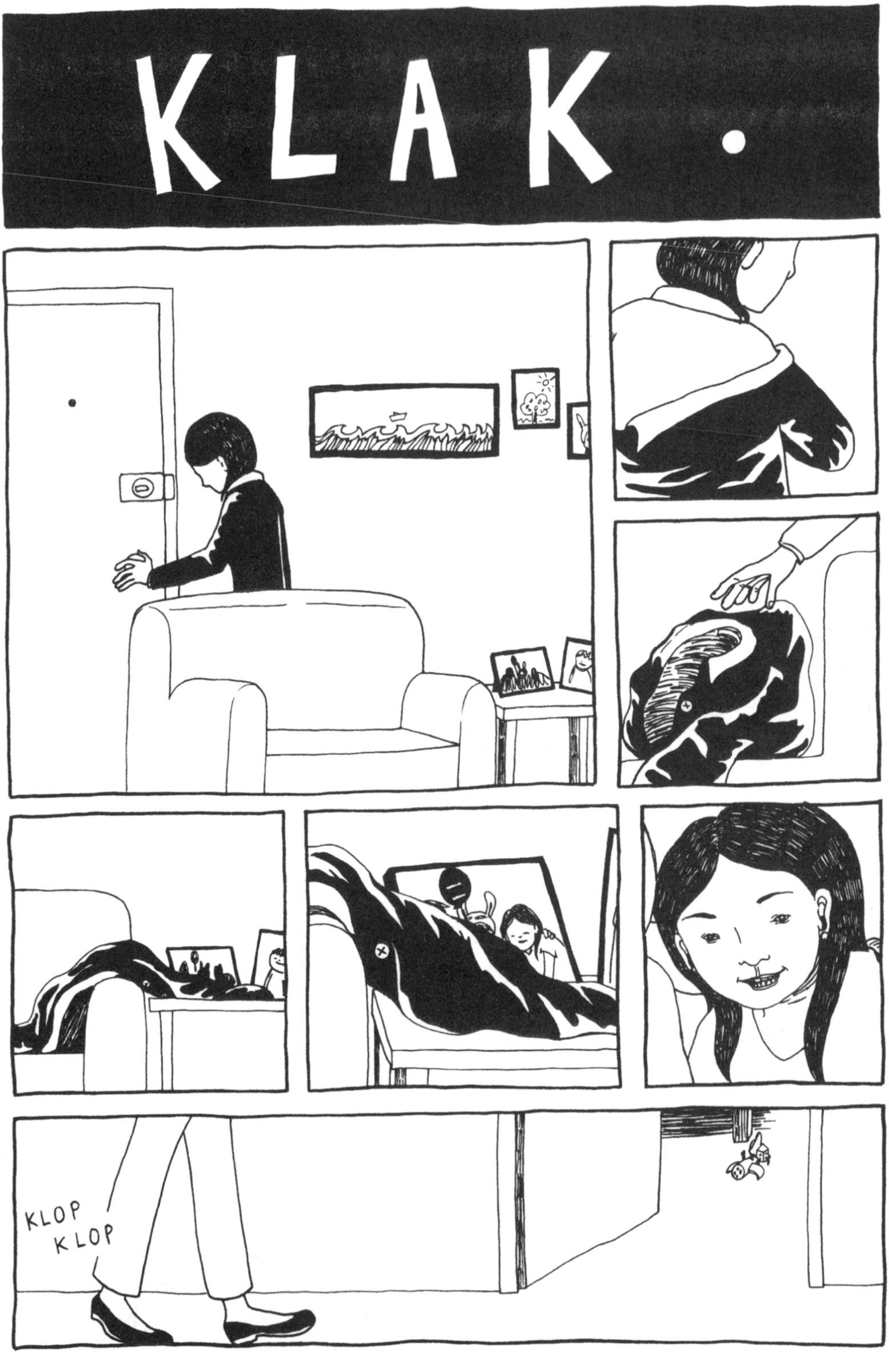
KLAK.
KLOP
KLOP

KLOP
KLOP

inja★
ules!

KLOP

KLOP

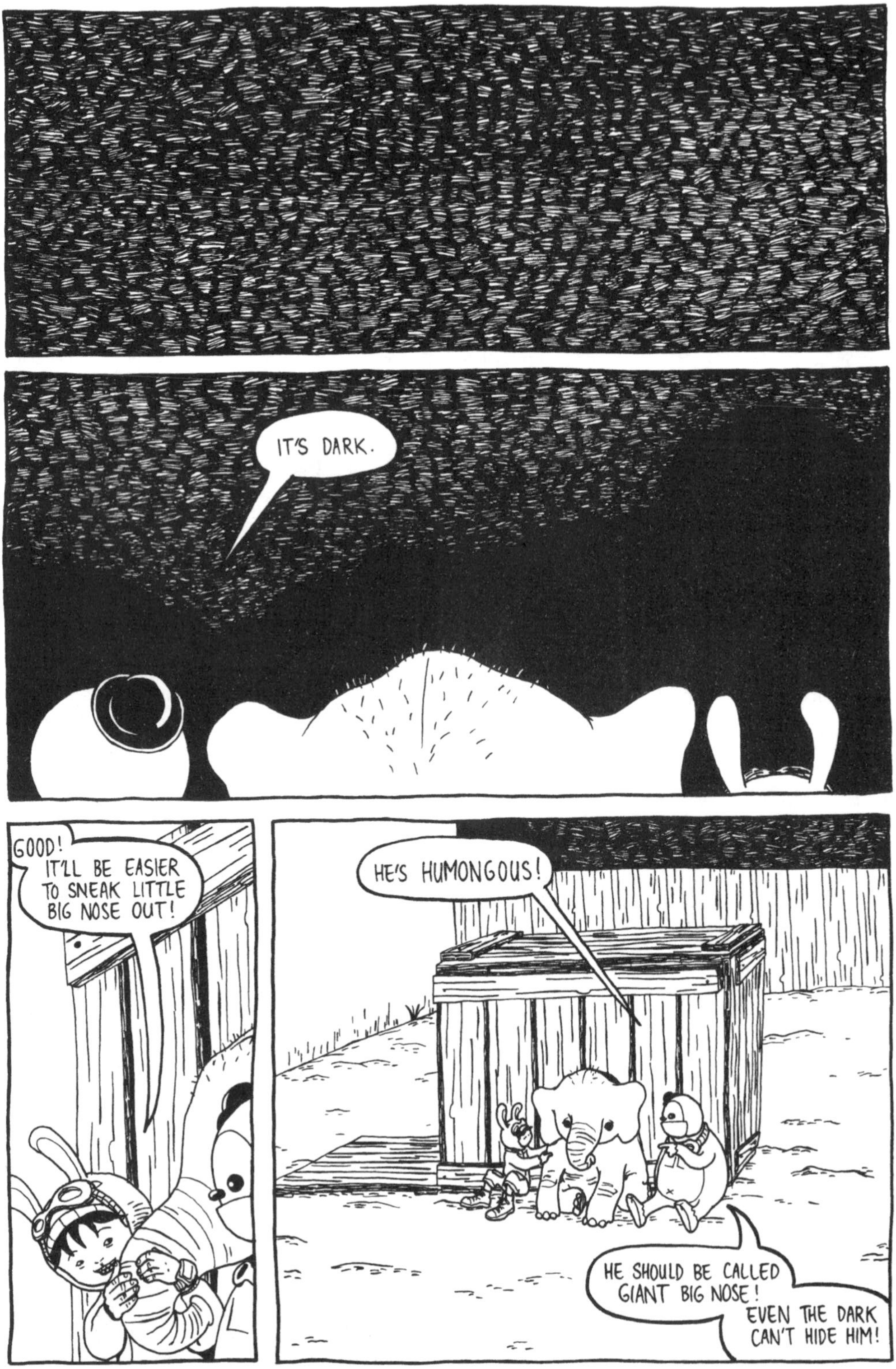
IT'S DARK.
GOOD! IT'LL BE EASIER TO SNEAK LITTLE BIG NOSE OUT!
HE'S HUMONGOUS!
HE SHOULD BE CALLED GIANT BIG NOSE! EVEN THE DARK CAN'T HIDE HIM!

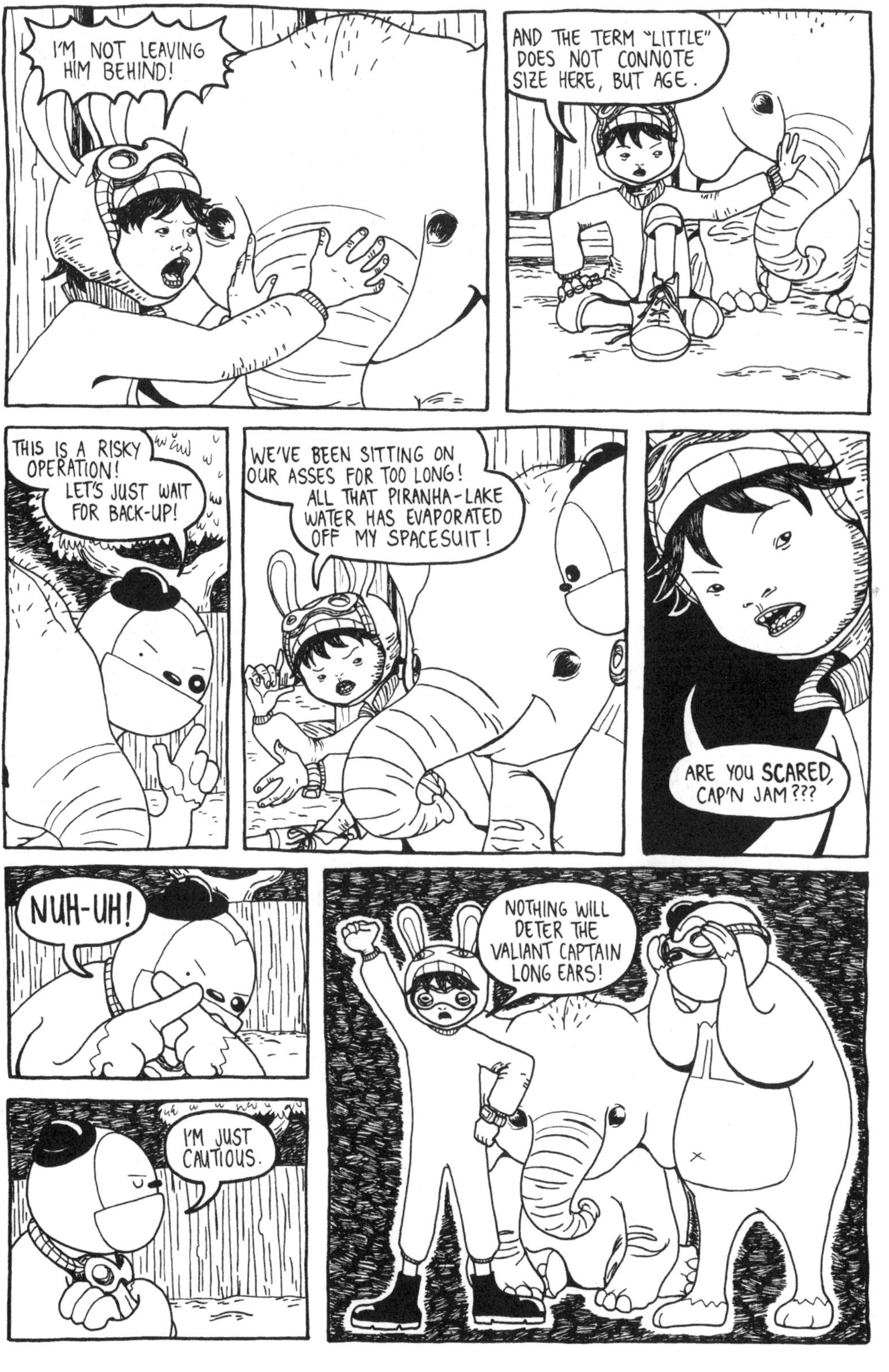
I'M NOT LEAVING HIM BEHIND!
AND THE TERM "LITTLE" DOES NOT CONNOTE SIZE HERE, BUT AGE.
THIS IS A RISKY OPERATION! LET'S JUST WAIT FOR BACK-UP!
WE'VE BEEN SITTING ON OUR ASSES FOR TOO LONG! ALL THAT PIRANHA-LAKE WATER HAS EVAPORATED OFF MY SPACESUIT!
ARE YOU SCARED, CAP'N JAM???
NUH-UH!
I'M JUST CAUTIOUS.
NOTHING WILL DETER THE VALIANT CAPTAIN LONG EARS!

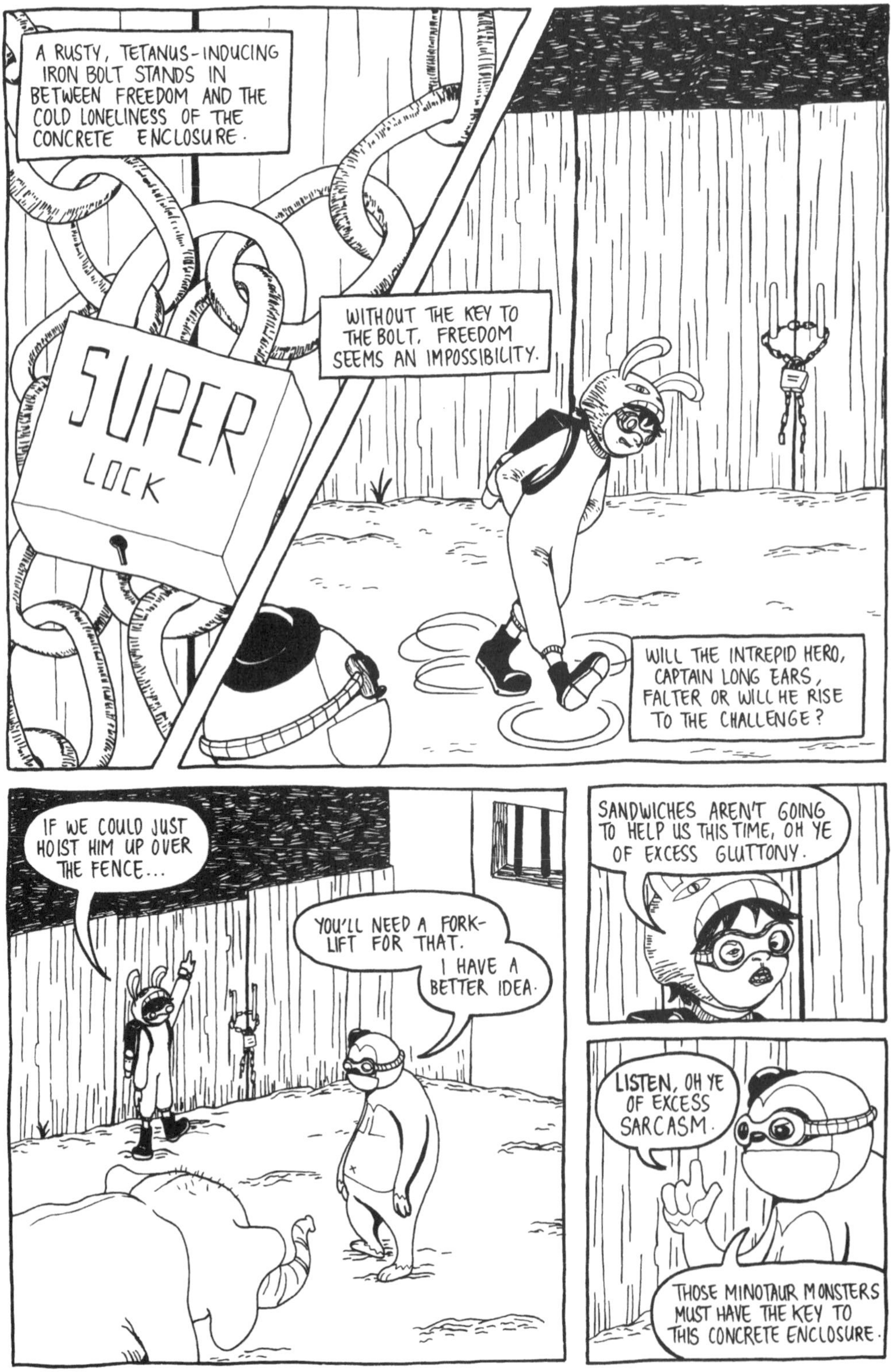
A RUSTY, TETANUS-INDUCING IRON BOLT STANDS IN BETWEEN FREEDOM AND THE COLD LONELINESS OF THE CONCRETE ENCLOSURE.
SUPER LOCK
WITHOUT THE KEY TO THE BOLT, FREEDOM SEEMS AN IMPOSSIBILITY.
WILL THE INTREPID HERO, CAPTAIN LONG EARS, FALTER OR WILL HE RISE TO THE CHALLENGE?
IF WE COULD JUST HOIST HIM UP OVER THE FENCE...
YOU'LL NEED A FORK-LIFT FOR THAT.
I HAVE A BETTER IDEA.
SANDWICHES AREN'T GOING TO HELP US THIS TIME, OH YE OF EXCESS GLUTTONY.
LISTEN, OH YE OF EXCESS SARCASM.
THOSE MINOTAUR MONSTERS MUST HAVE THE KEY TO THIS CONCRETE ENCLOSURE.

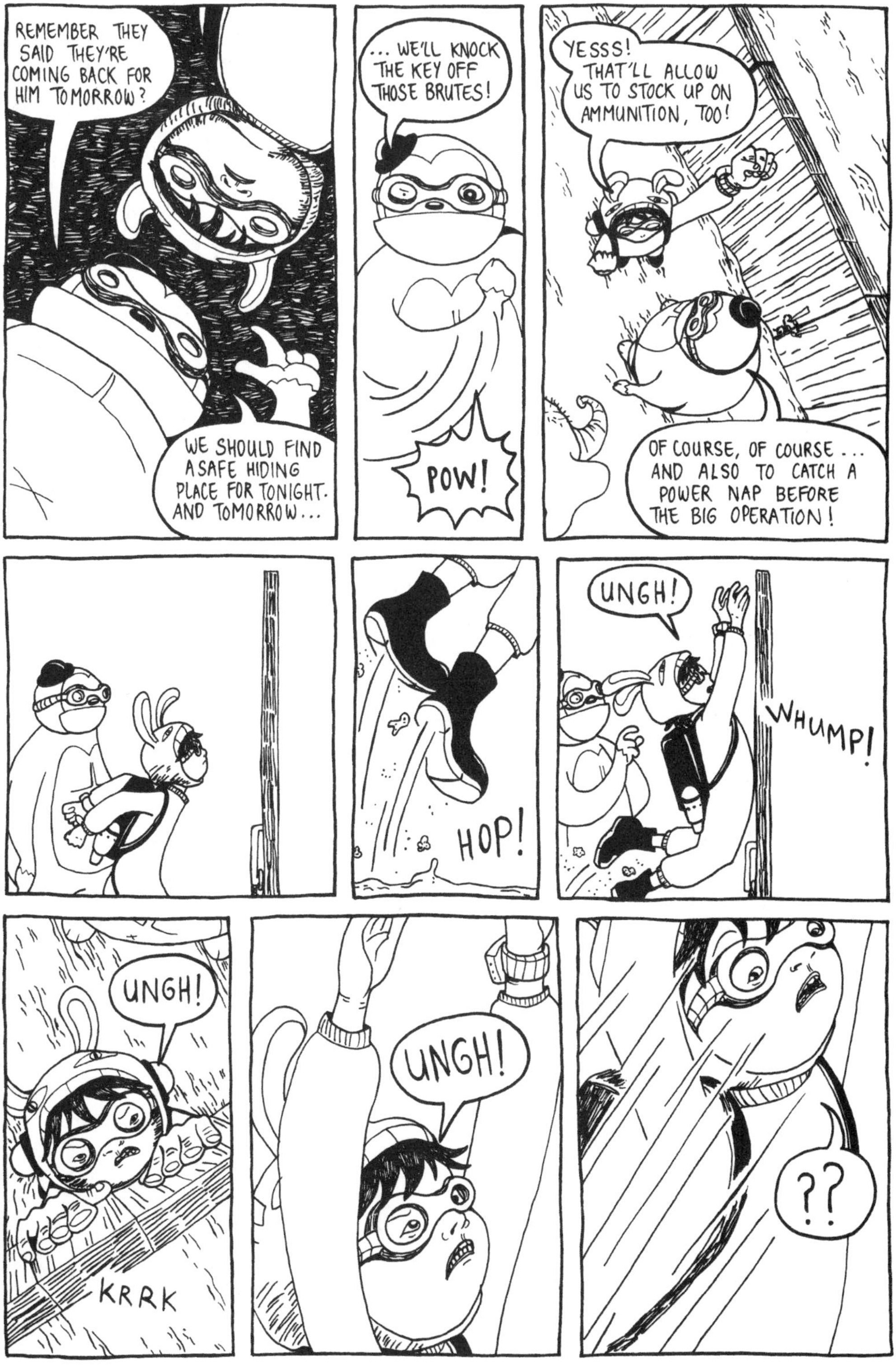
REMEMBER THEY SAID THEY'RE COMING BACK FOR HIM TOMORROW?
WE SHOULD FIND A SAFE HIDING PLACE FOR TONIGHT. AND TOMORROW...
... WE'LL KNOCK THE KEY OFF THOSE BRUTES!
POW!
YESSS! THAT'LL ALLOW US TO STOCK UP ON AMMUNITION, TOO!
OF COURSE, OF COURSE... AND ALSO TO CATCH A POWER NAP BEFORE THE BIG OPERATION!
HOP!
UNGH!
WHUMP!
UNGH!
KRRK
UNGH!
??

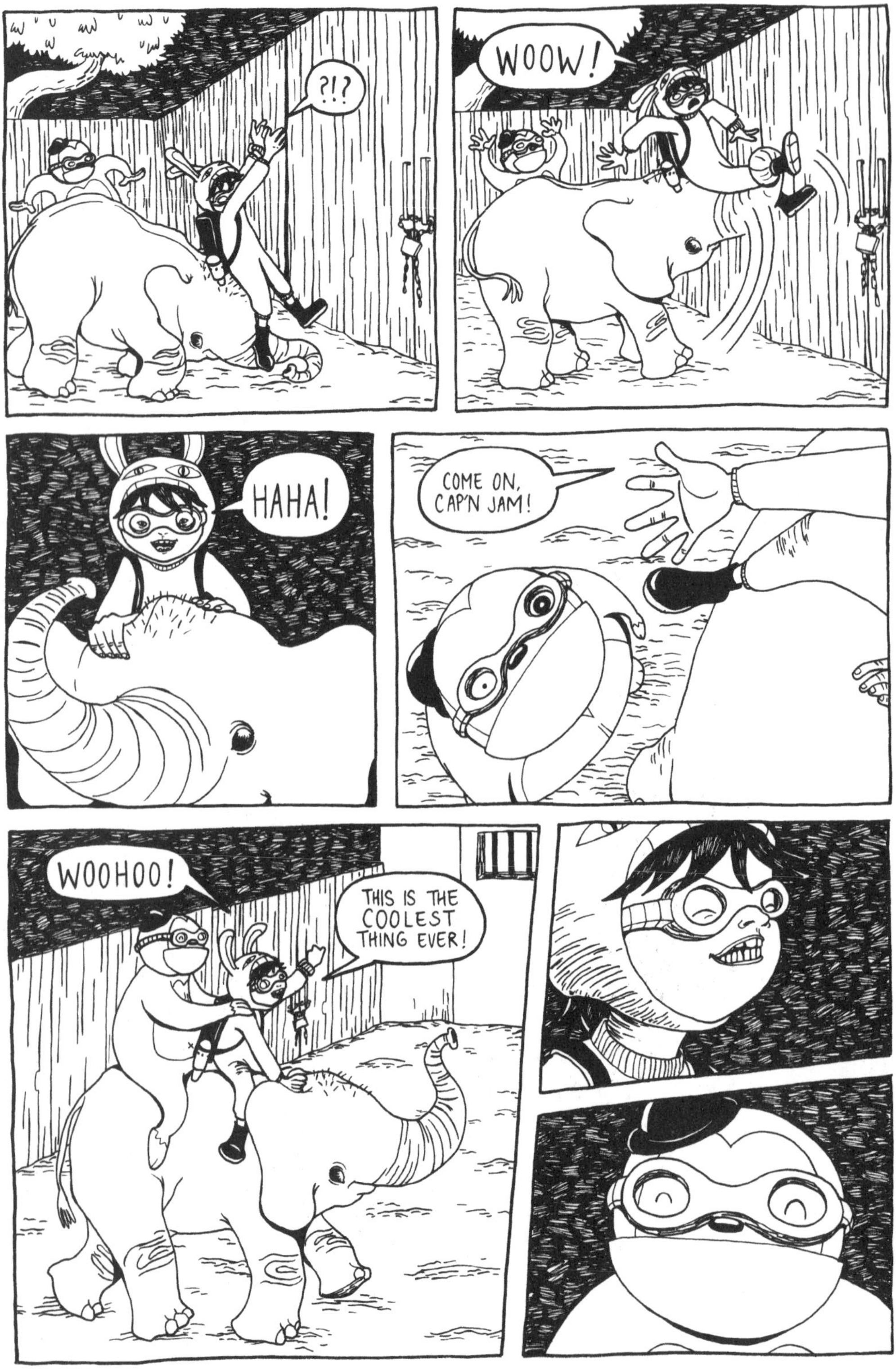
?!?
WOOW!
HAHA!
COME ON, CAP'N JAM!
WOOHOO!
THIS IS THE COOLEST THING EVER!

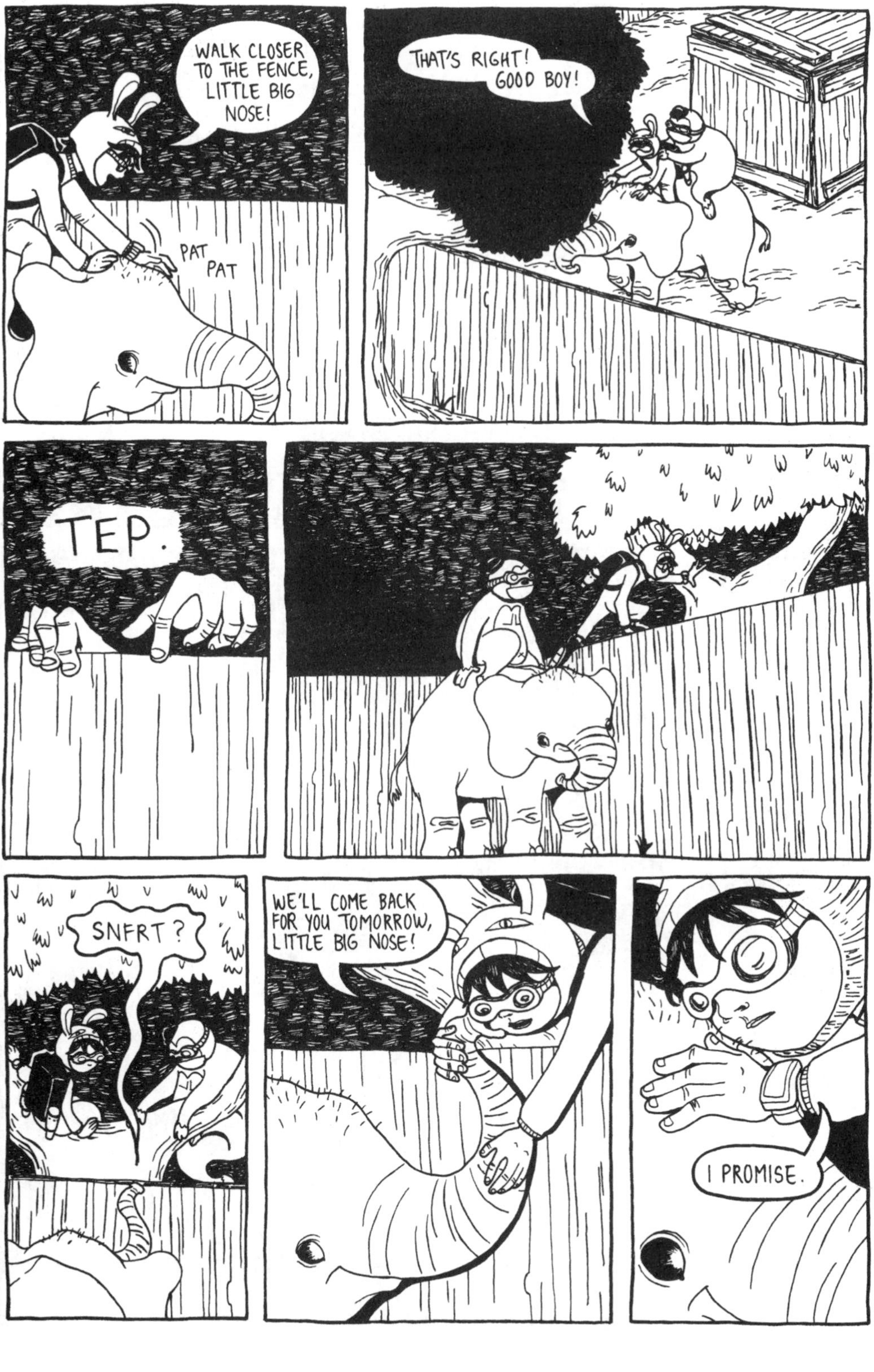
WALK CLOSER TO THE FENCE, LITTLE BIG NOSE!
PAT PAT
THAT'S RIGHT! GOOD BOY!
TEP.
SNFRT?
WE'LL COME BACK FOR YOU TOMORROW, LITTLE BIG NOSE!
I PROMISE.

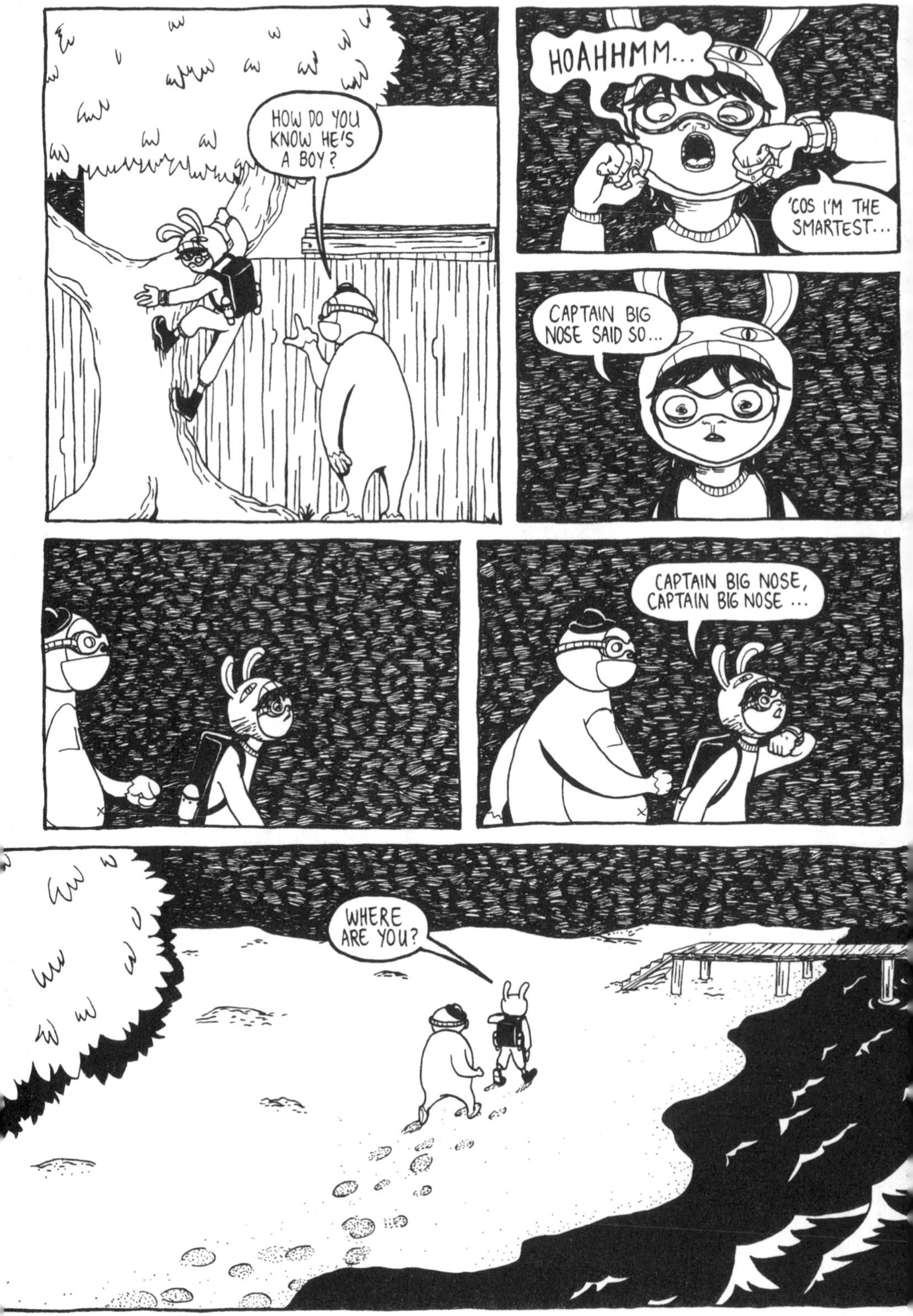
HOW DO YOU KNOW HE'S A BOY?
HOAHHMM...
'COS I'M THE SMARTEST...
CAPTAIN BIG NOSE SAID SO...
CAPTAIN BIG NOSE, CAPTAIN BIG NOSE ...
WHERE ARE YOU?

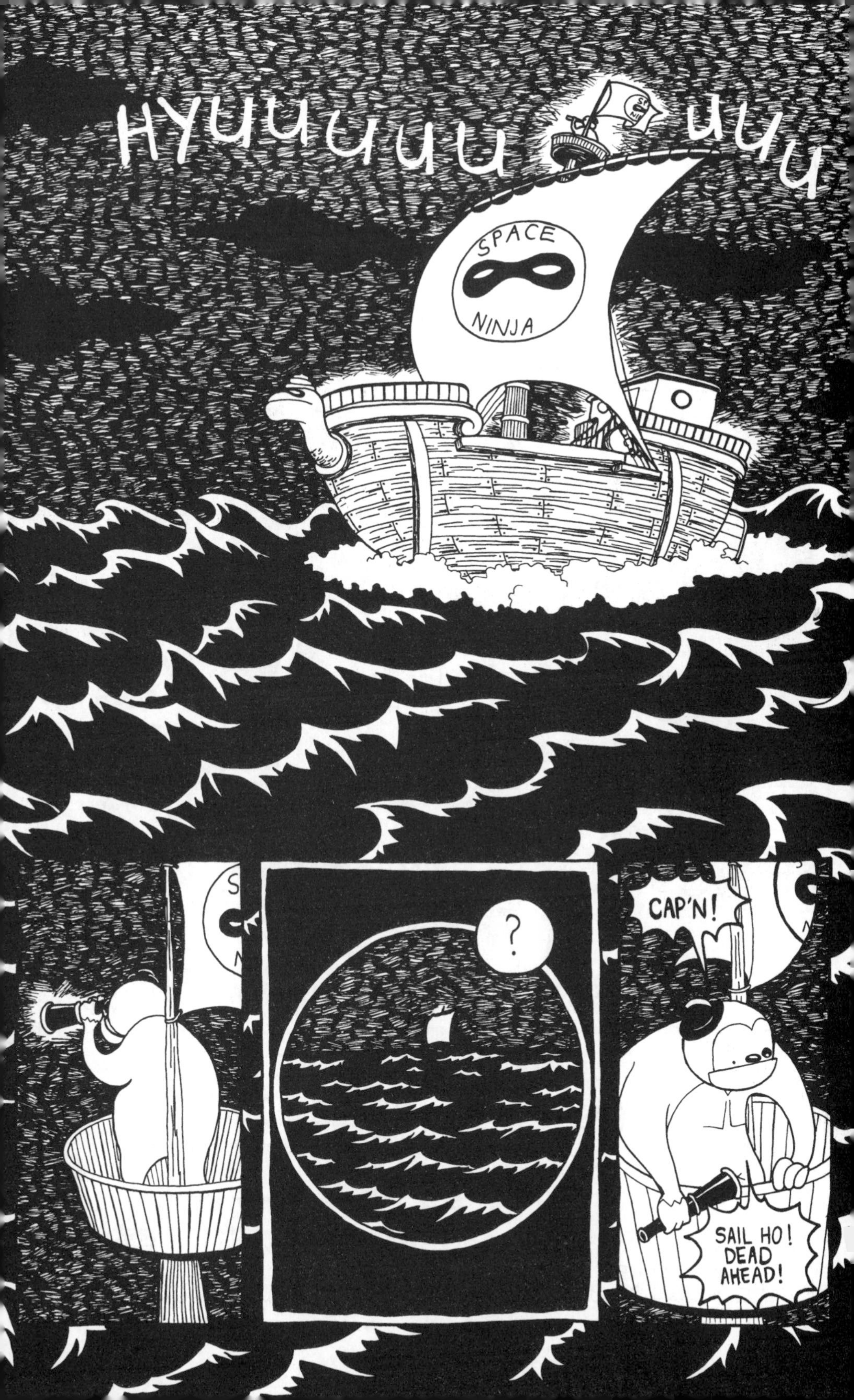
HYUUUUUUU UUU
SPACE NINJA
?
CAP'N!
SAIL HO! DEAD AHEAD!

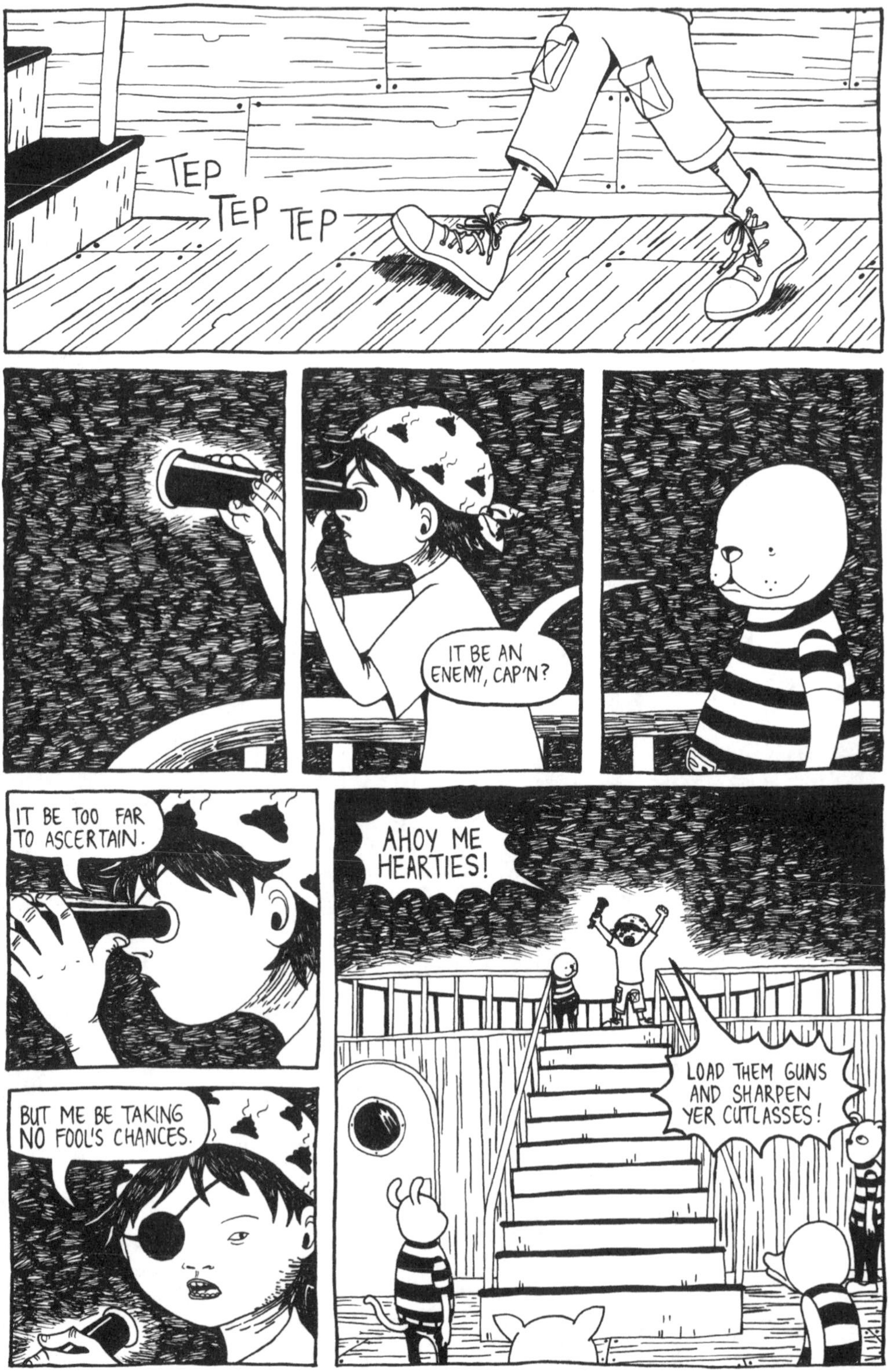
TEP
TEP TEP
IT BE AN ENEMY, CAP'N?
IT BE TOO FAR TO ASCERTAIN.
BUT ME BE TAKING NO FOOL'S CHANCES.
AHOY ME HEARTIES!
LOAD THEM GUNS AND SHARPEN YER CUTLASSES!

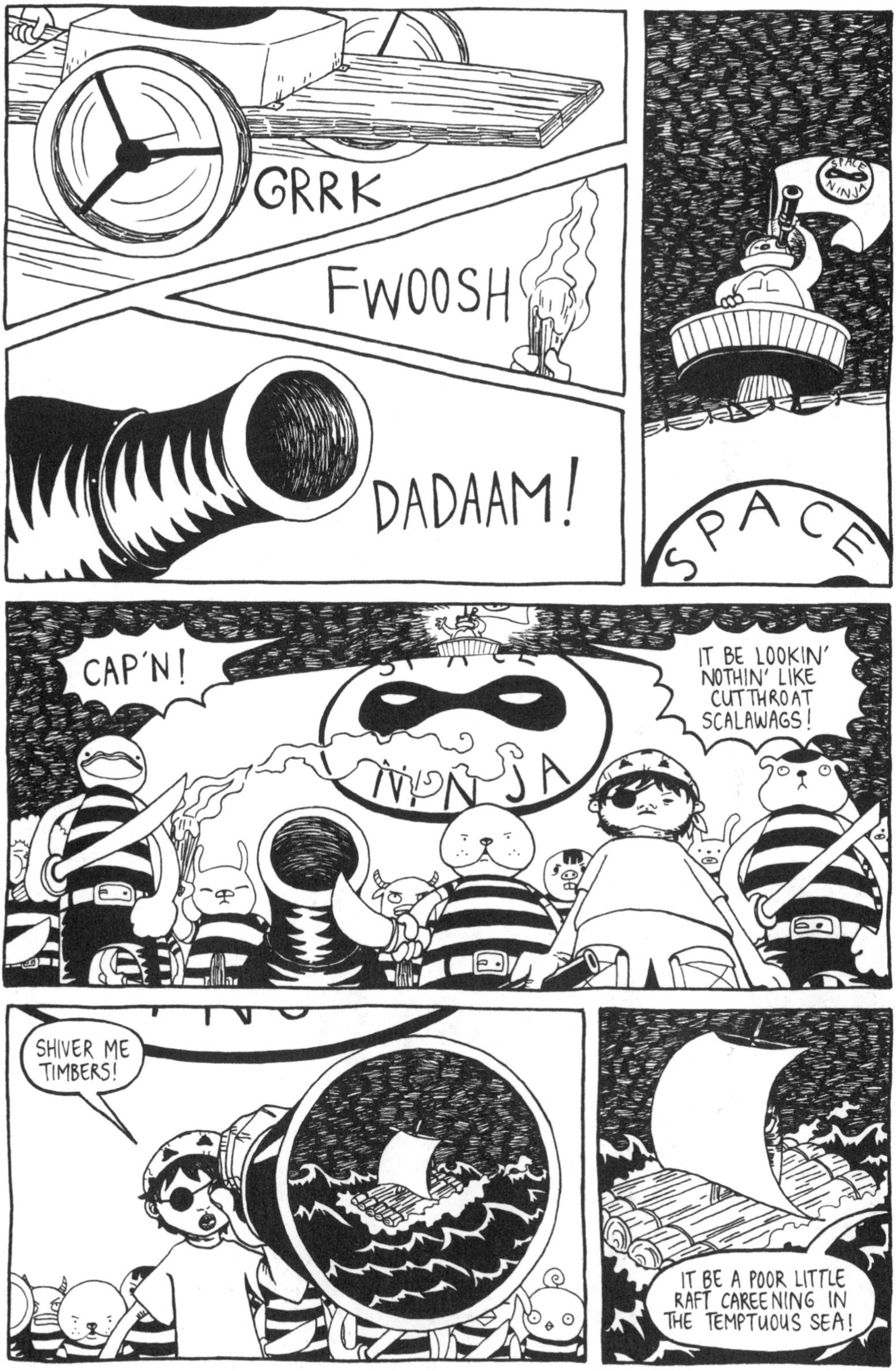
GRRK
FWOOSH
DADAAM!
SPACE NINJA
SPACE
CAP'N!
IT BE LOOKIN' NOTHIN' LIKE CUTTHROAT SCALAWAGS!
NINJA
SHIVER ME TIMBERS!
IT BE A POOR LITTLE RAFT CAREENING IN THE TEMPTUOUS SEA!

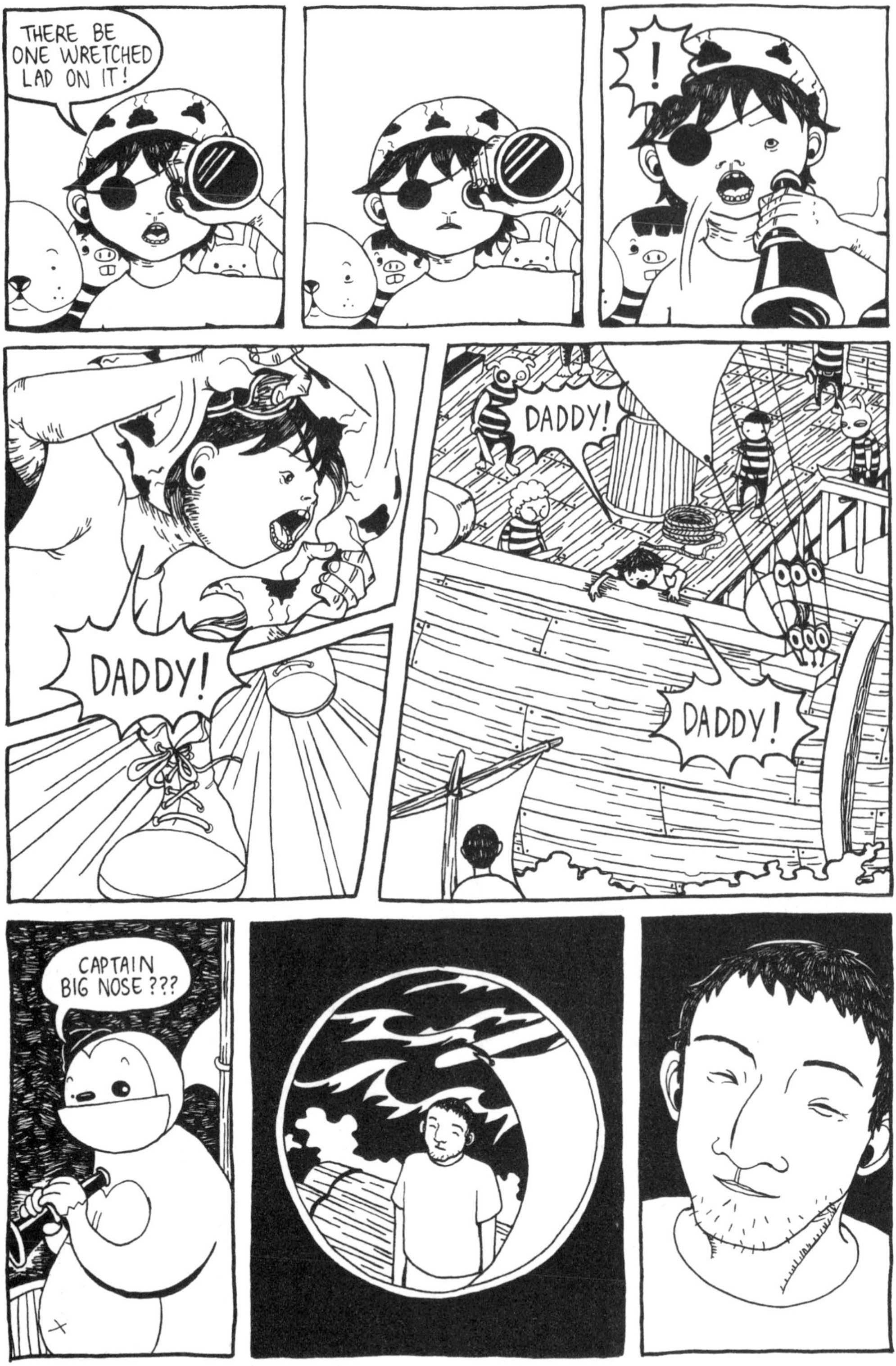
THERE BE ONE WRETCHED LAD ON IT!
!
DADDY!
DADDY!
DADDY!
CAPTAIN BIG NOSE???

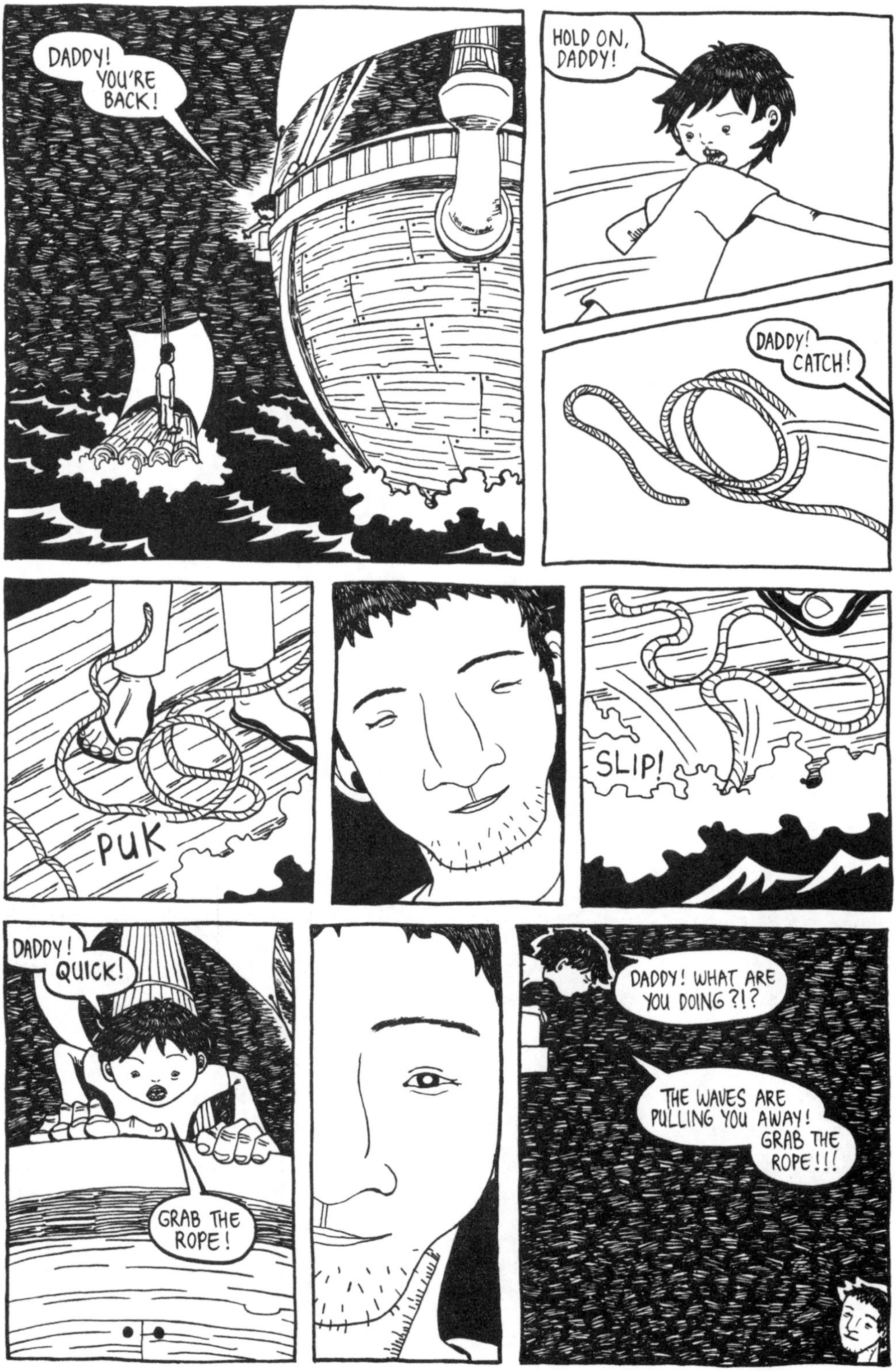
DADDY! YOU'RE BACK!
HOLD ON, DADDY!
DADDY! CATCH!
PUK
SLIP!
DADDY! QUICK!
GRAB THE ROPE!
DADDY! WHAT ARE YOU DOING?!?
THE WAVES ARE PULLING YOU AWAY! GRAB THE ROPE!!!

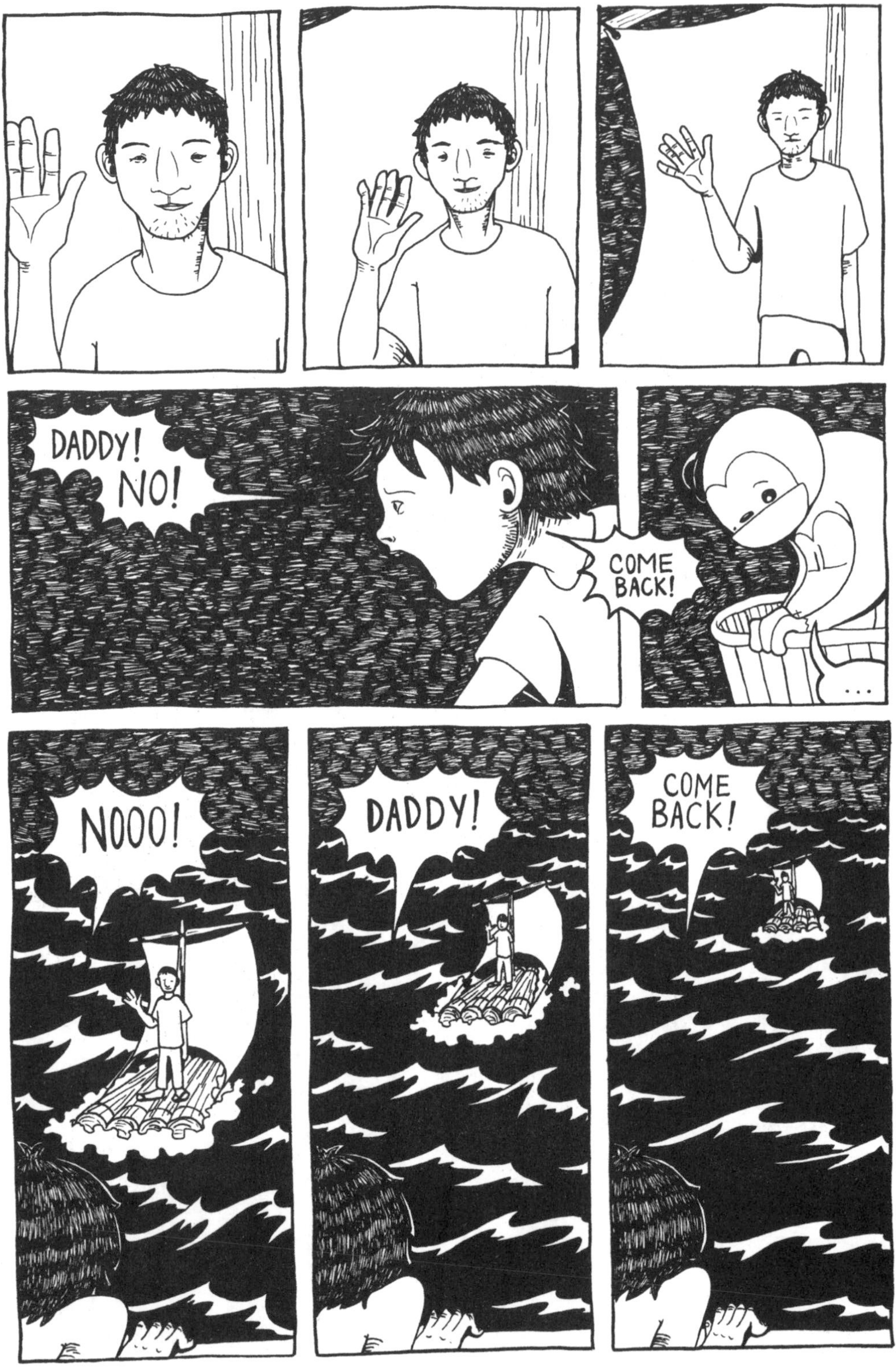
DADDY! NO!
COME BACK!
...
NOOO!
DADDY!
COME BACK!

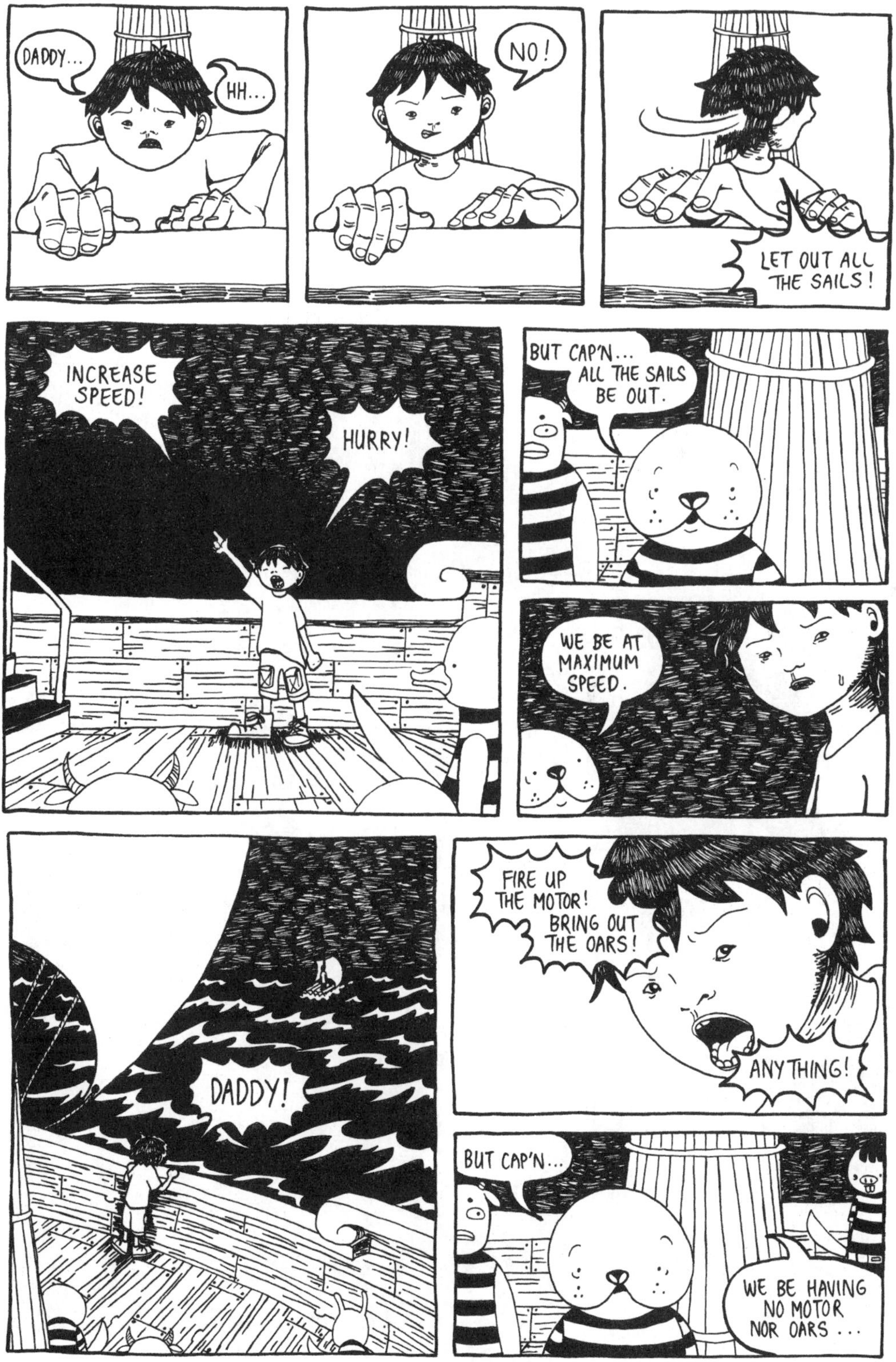
DADDY...
HH...
NO!
LET OUT ALL THE SAILS!
INCREASE SPEED!
HURRY!
BUT CAP'N... ALL THE SAILS BE OUT.
WE BE AT MAXIMUM SPEED.
DADDY!
FIRE UP THE MOTOR! BRING OUT THE OARS!
ANYTHING!
BUT CAP'N...
WE BE HAVING NO MOTOR NOR OARS...

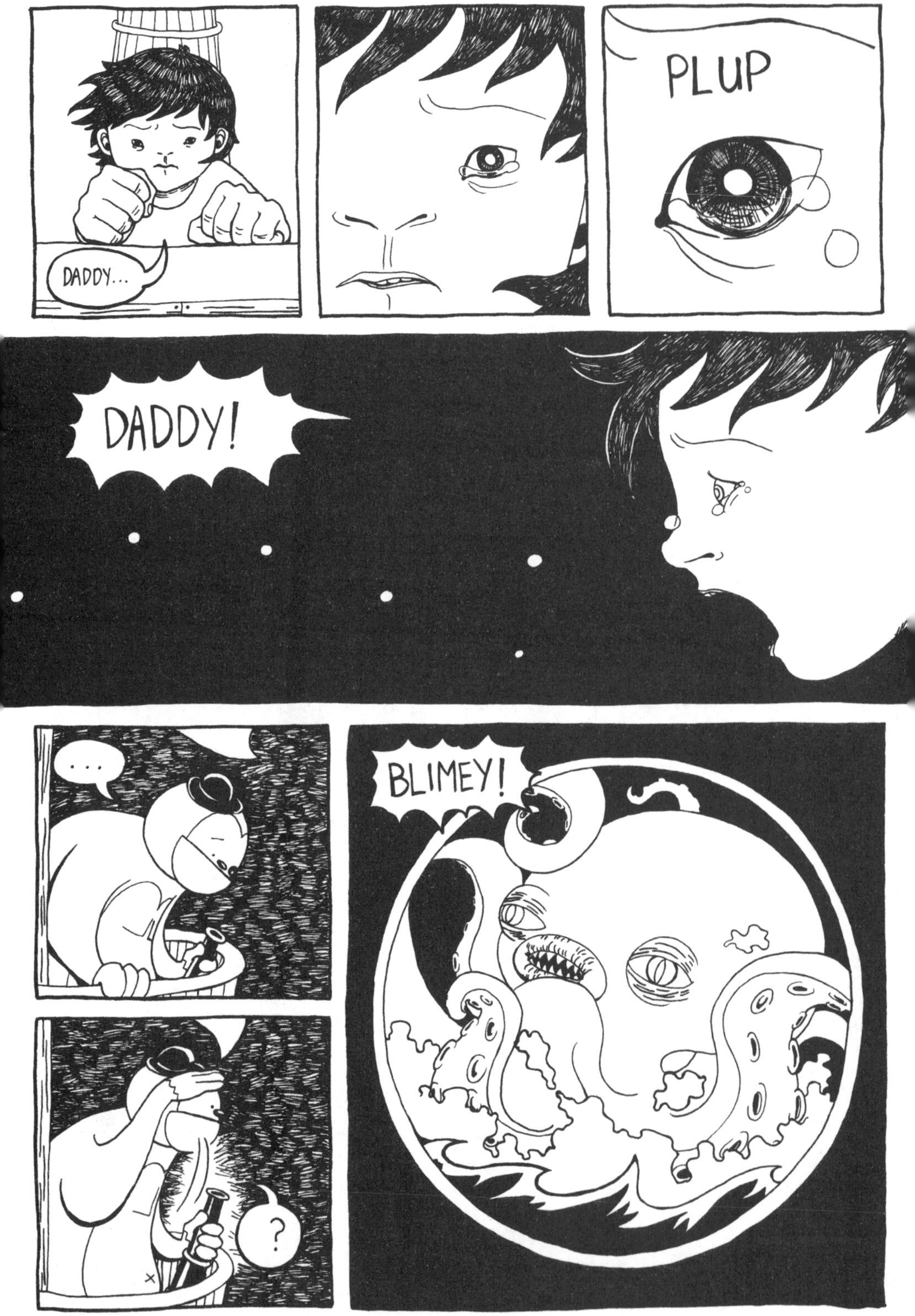
DADDY...
PLUP
DADDY!
...
BLIMEY!
?

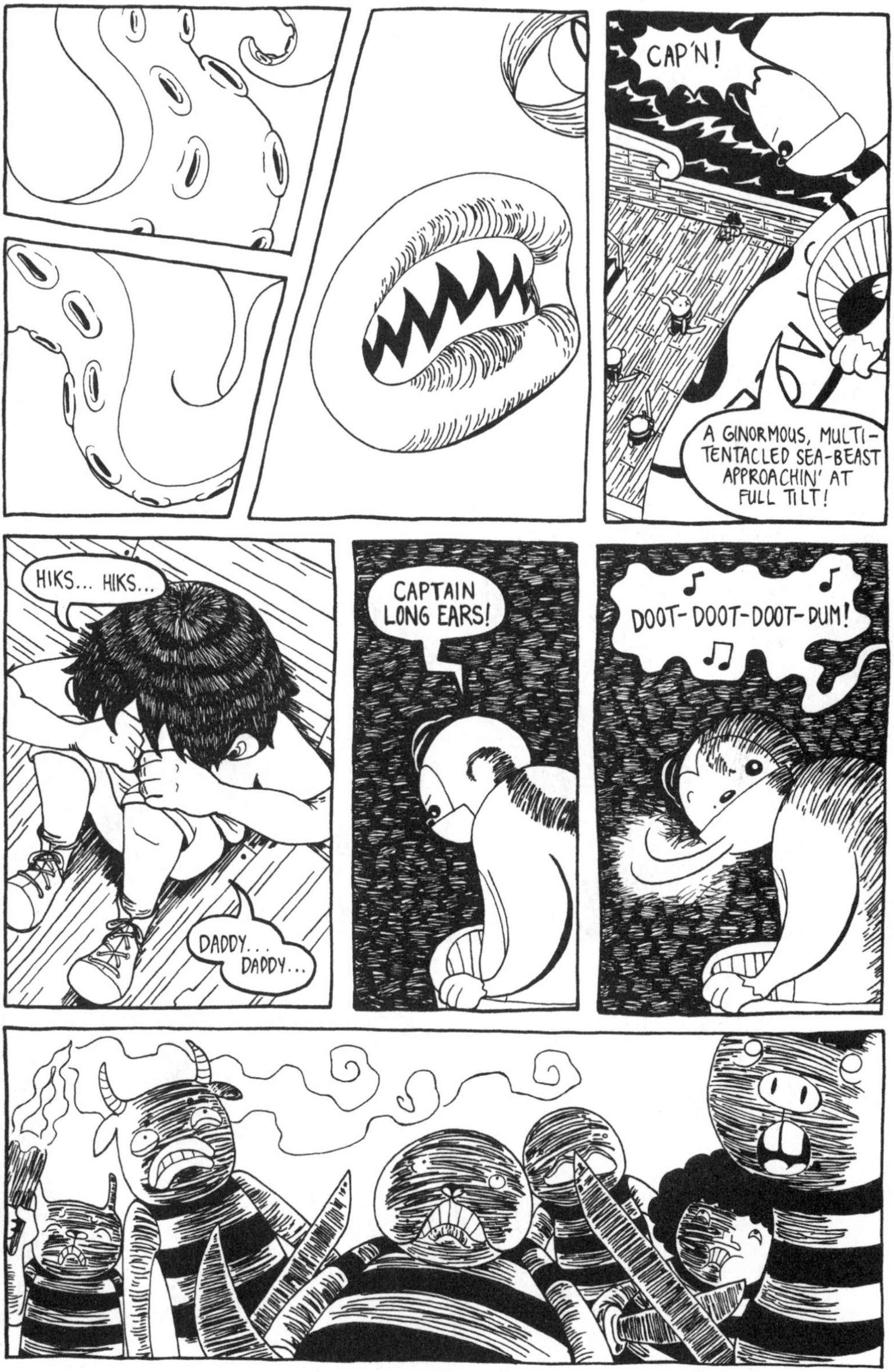
CAP'N!
A GINORMOUS, MULTI-TENTACLED SEA-BEAST APPROACHIN' AT FULL TILT!
HIKS... HIKS...
DADDY.... DADDY...
CAPTAIN LONG EARS!
DOOT-DOOT-DOOT-DUM!

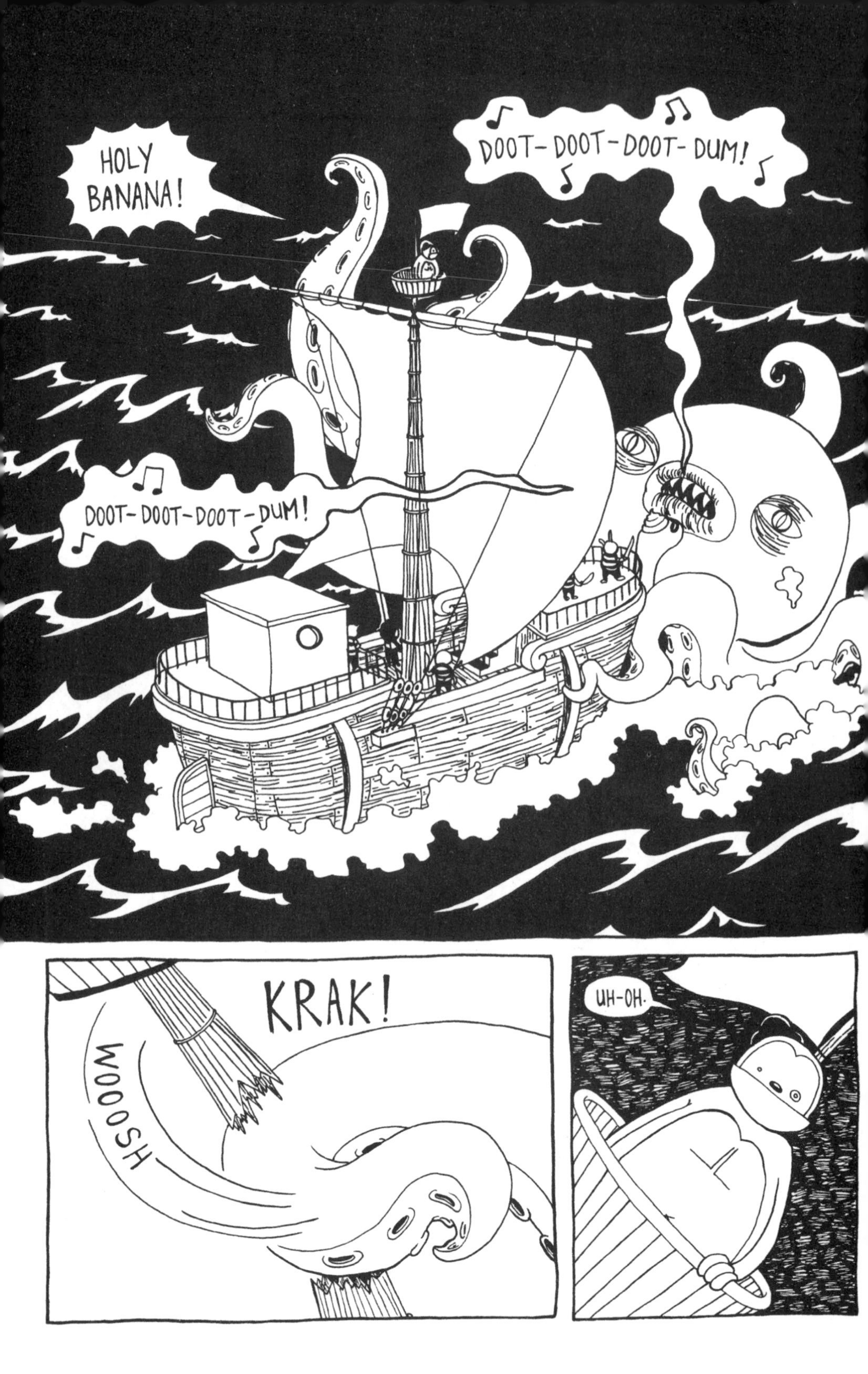
HOLY BANANA!
DOOT-DOOT-DOOT-DUM!
DOOT-DOOT-DOOT-DUM!
KRAK!
WOOOSH
UH-OH.

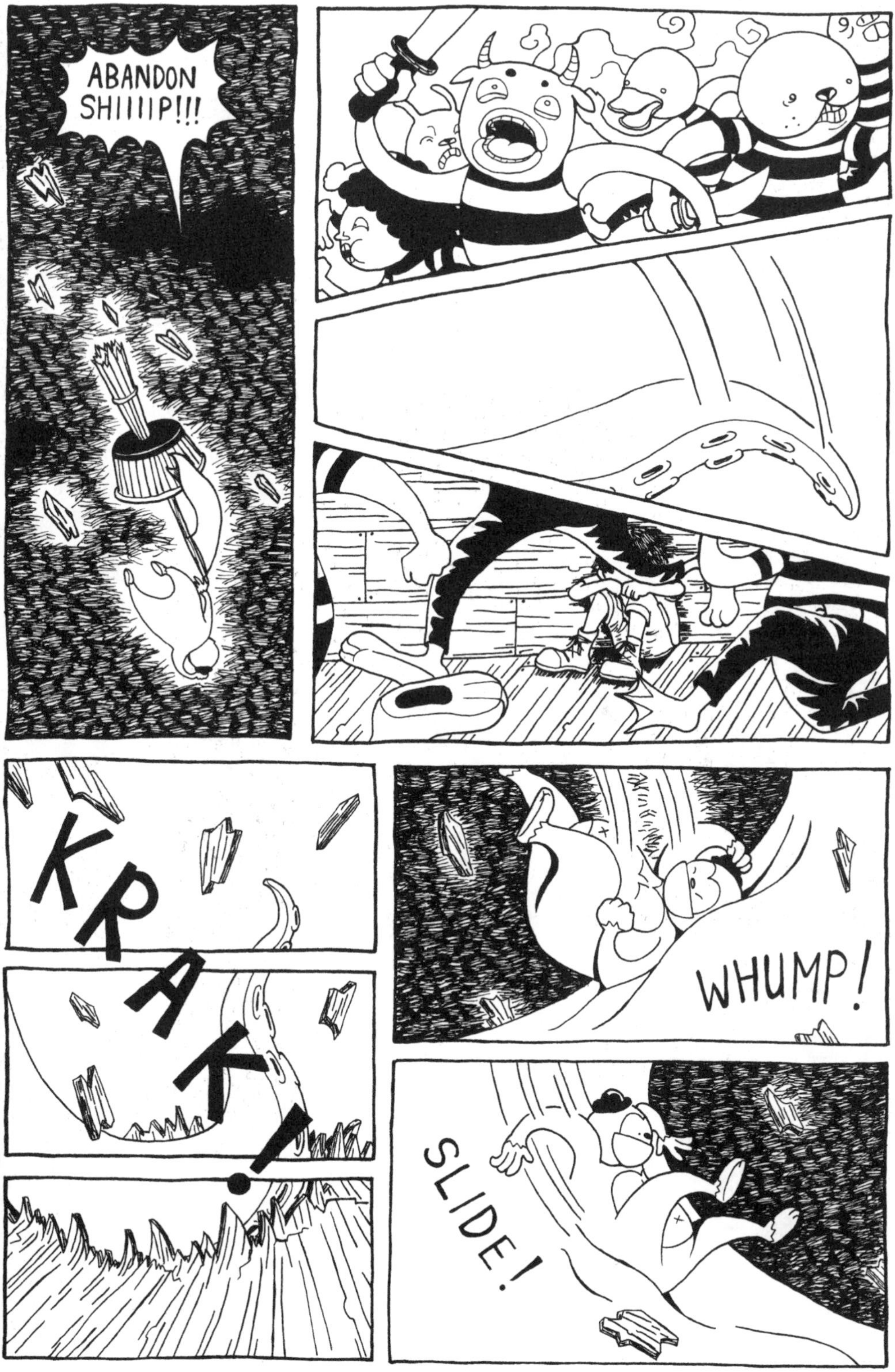
ABANDON SHIIIIP!!!
KRAAK!!
WHUMP!
SLIDE!

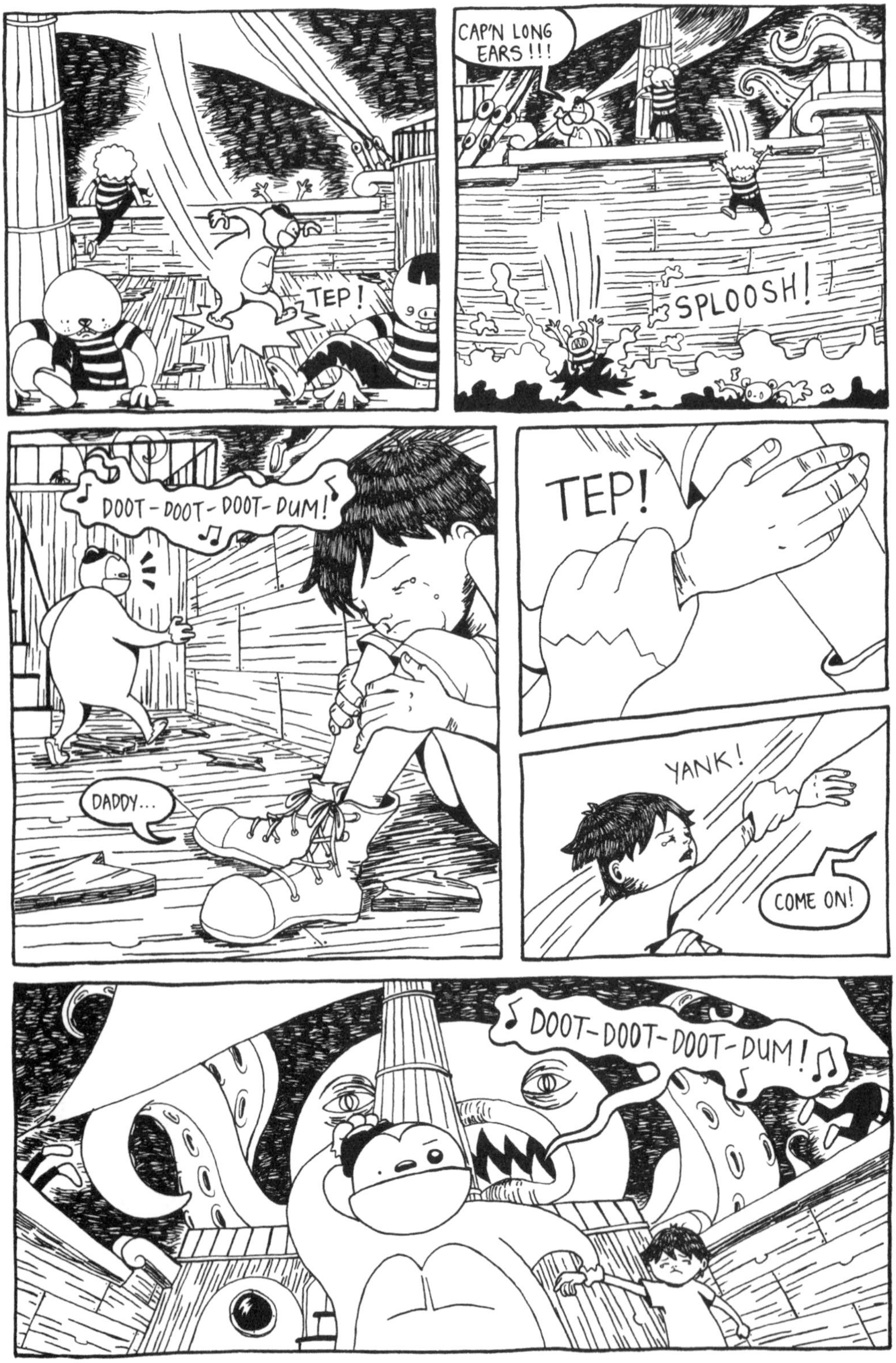
TEP!
CAP'N LONG EARS!!!
SPLOOSH!
DOOT-DOOT-DOOT-DUM!
DADDY...
TEP!
YANK!
COME ON!
DOOT-DOOT-DOOT-DUM!

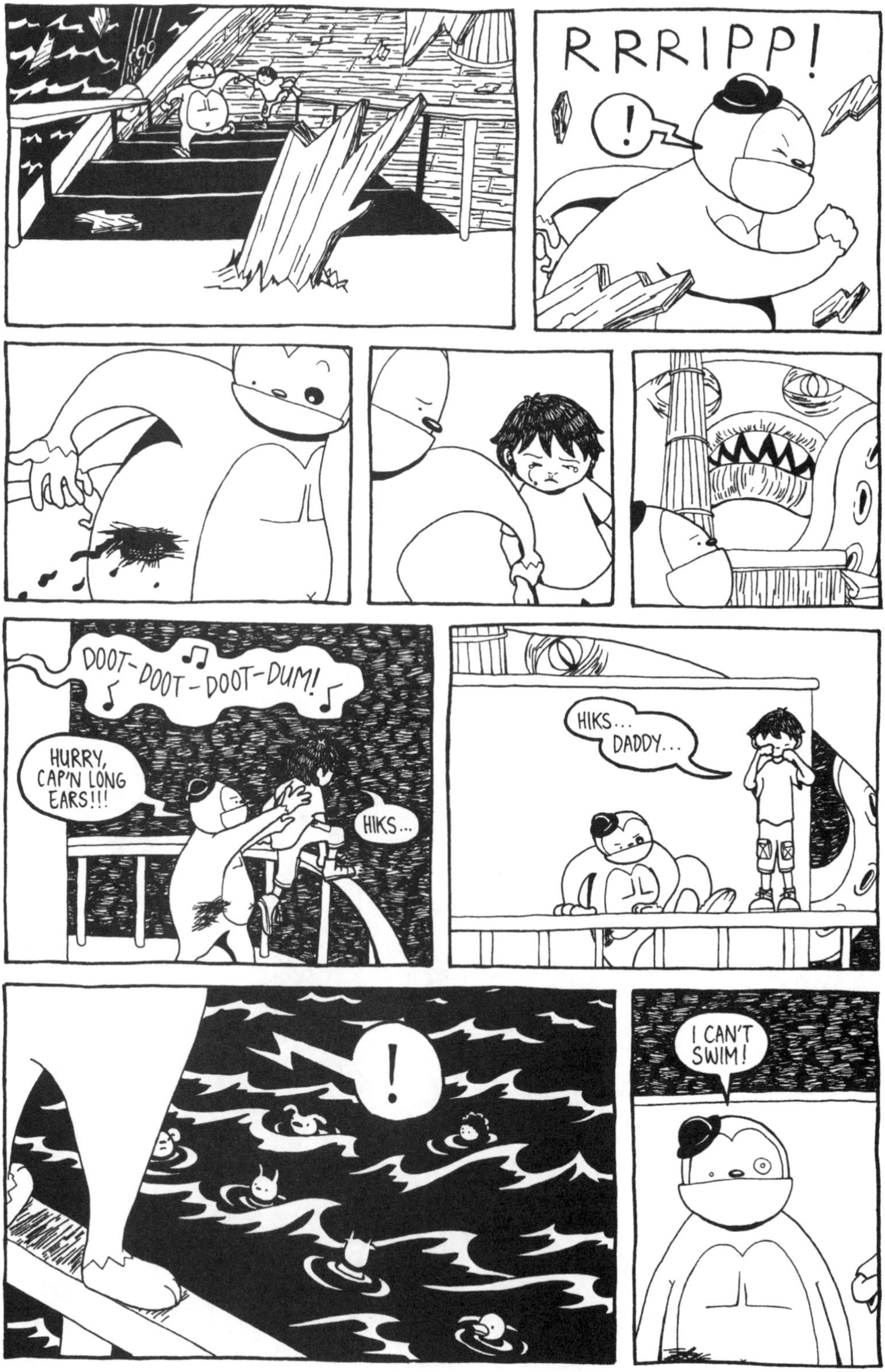
RRRIPP!
!
DOOT-DOOT-DOOT-DUM!
HURRY, CAP'N LONG EARS!!!
HIKS...
HIKS... DADDY...
!
I CAN'T SWIM!

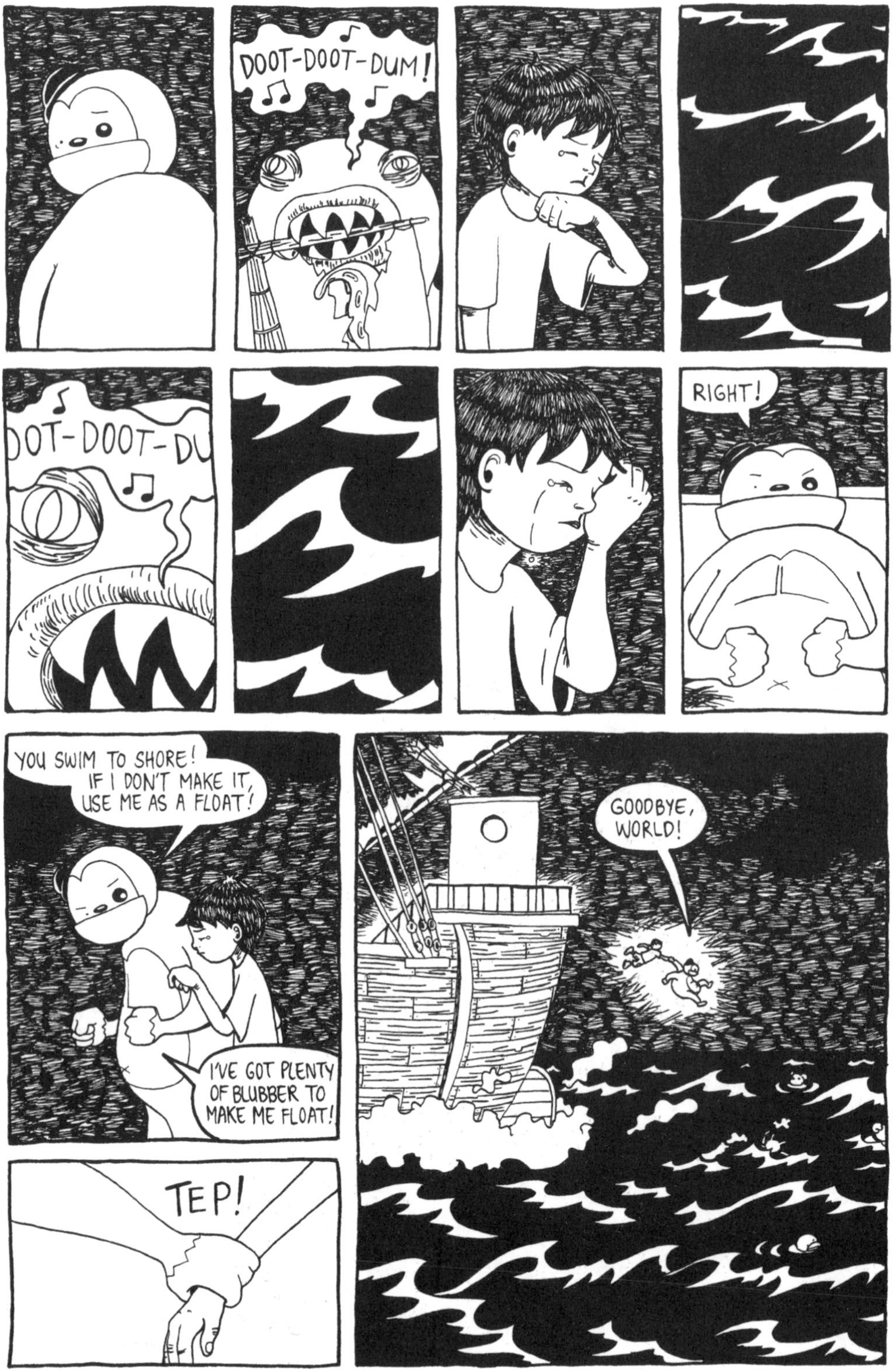

DOOT-DOOT-DUM!
OOT-DOOT-DU
RIGHT!
YOU SWIM TO SHORE! IF I DON'T MAKE IT, USE ME AS A FLOAT!
I'VE GOT PLENTY OF BLUBBER TO MAKE ME FLOAT!
TEP!
GOODBYE, WORLD!

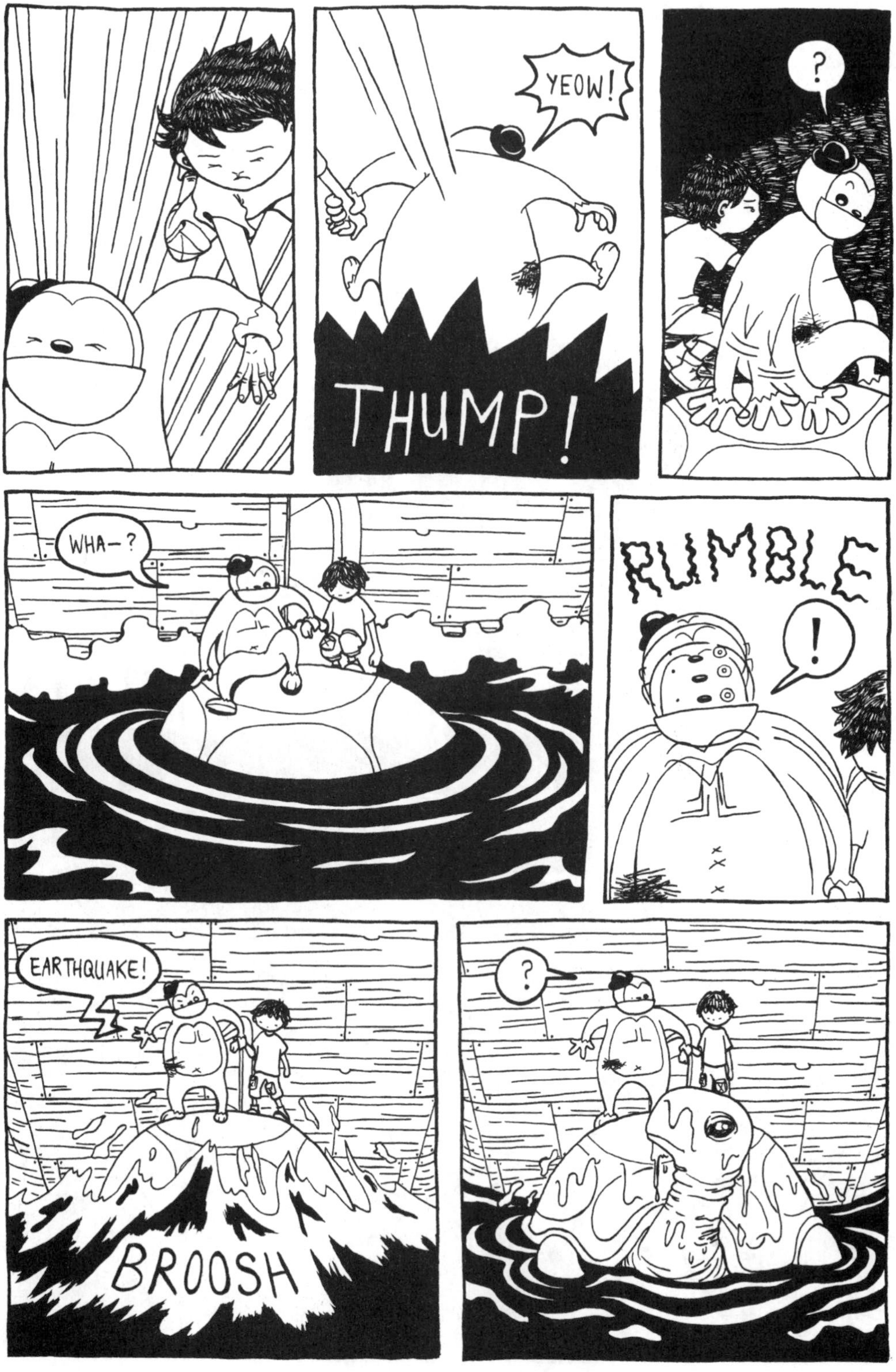
YEOW!
THUMP!
?
WHA-?
RUMBLE
!
EARTHQUAKE!
BROOSH
?

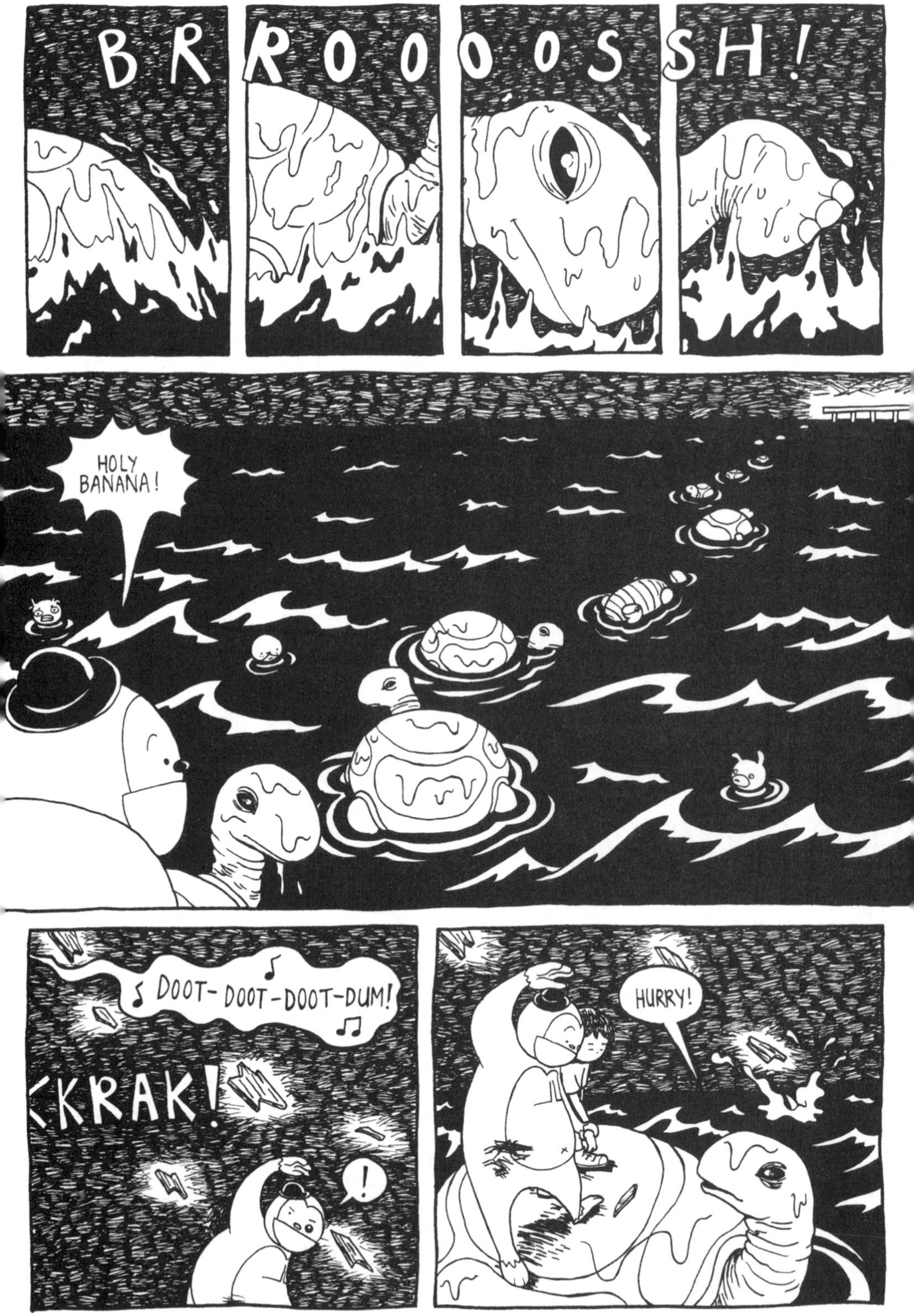
BRROOOOSSH!
HOLY BANANA!
DOOT-DOOT-DOOT-DUM!
KRAK!
!
HURRY!

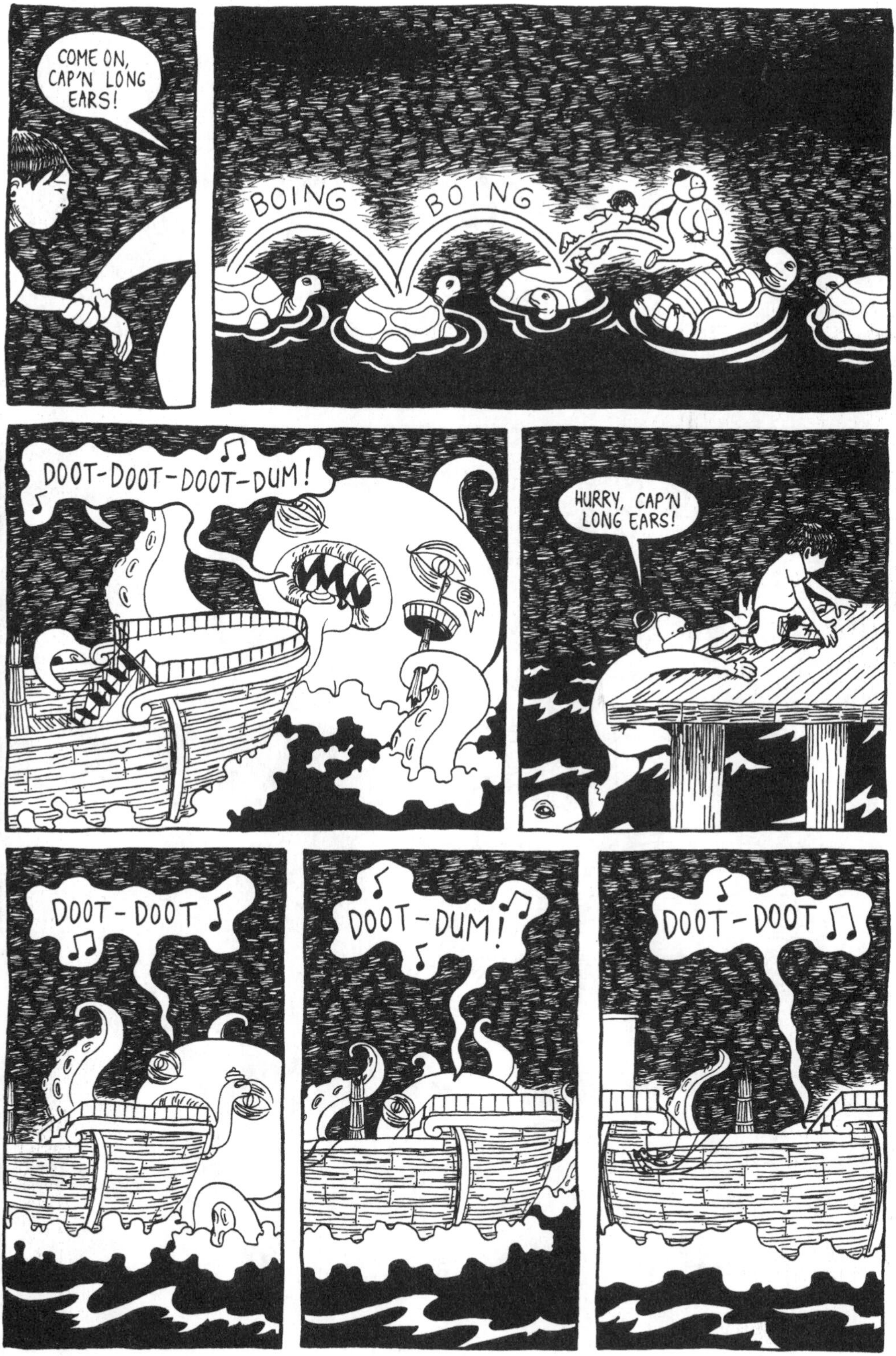
COME ON, CAP'N LONG EARS!
BOING
BOING
DOOT-DOOT-DOOT-DUM!
HURRY, CAP'N LONG EARS!
DOOT-DOOT
DOOT-DUM!
DOOT-DOOT

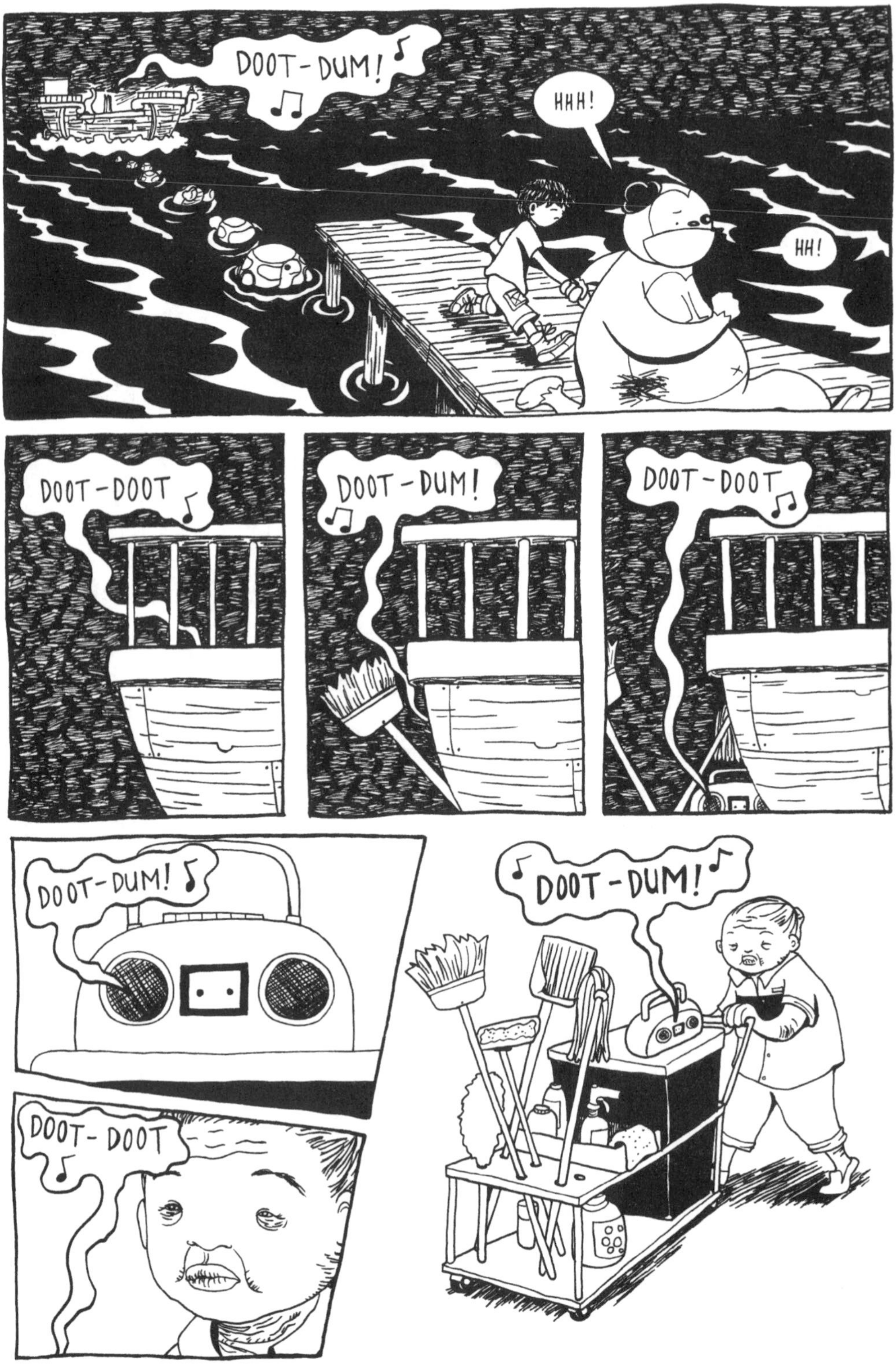
DOOT-DUM!
HHH!
HH!
DOOT-DOOT
DOOT-DUM!
DOOT-DOOT
DOOT-DUM!
DOOT-DOOT
DOOT-DUM!

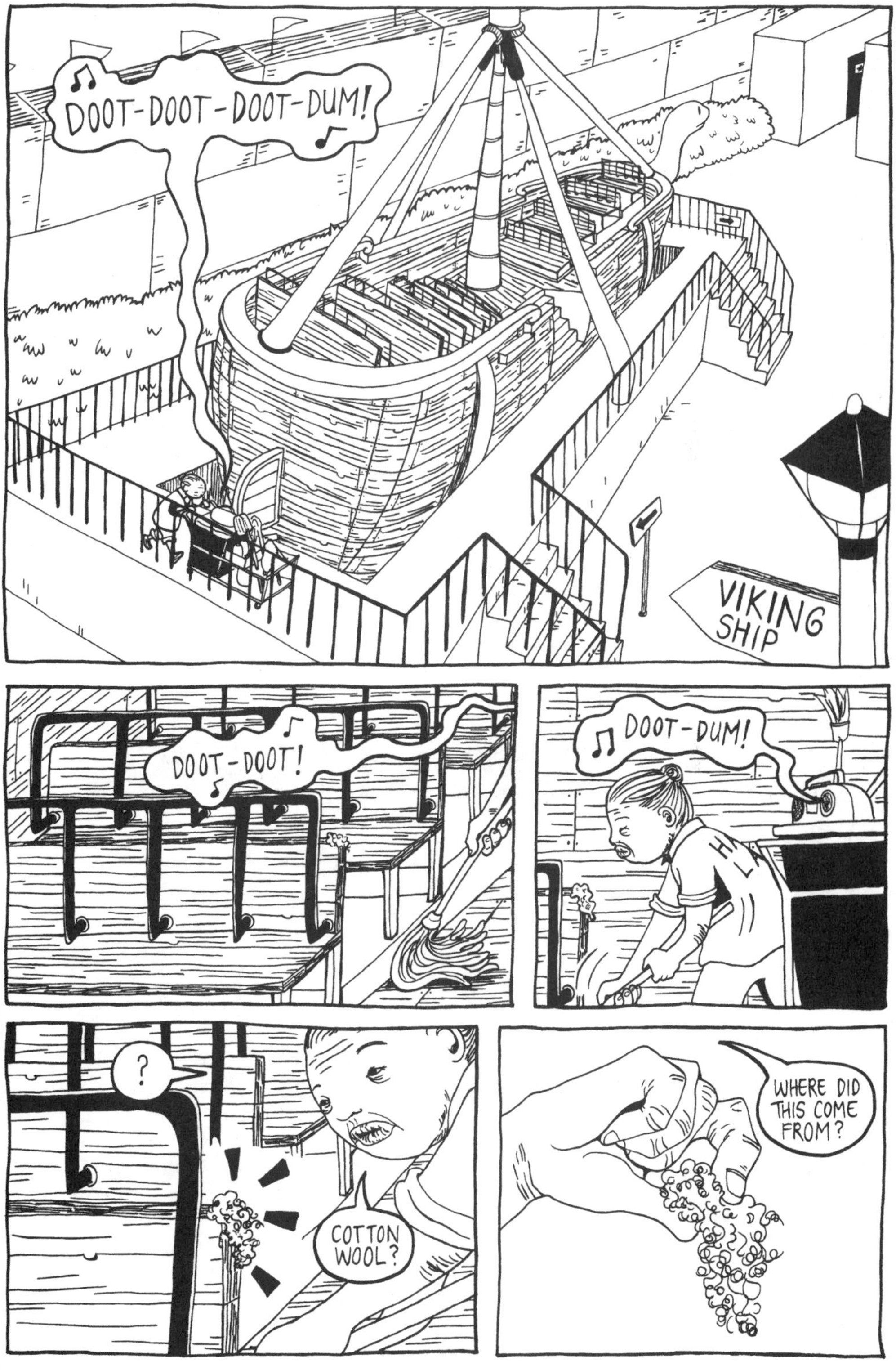
DOOT-DOOT-DOOT-DUM!
VIKING SHIP
DOOT-DOOT!
DOOT-DUM!
?
COTTON WOOL?
WHERE DID THIS COME FROM?

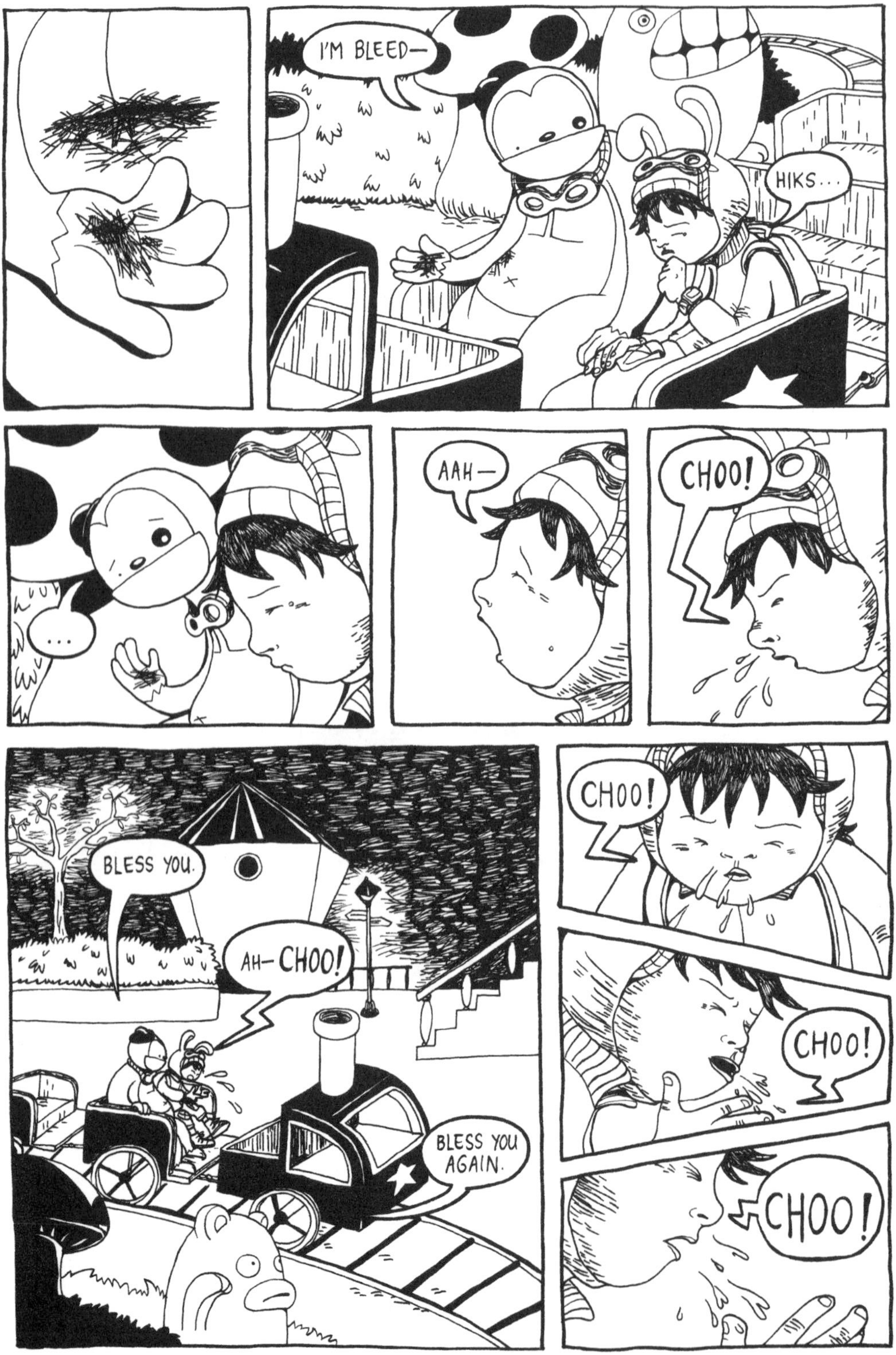
I'M BLEED—
HIKS...
...
AAH—
CHOO!
BLESS YOU.
AH—CHOO!
BLESS YOU AGAIN.
CHOO!
CHOO!
CHOO!

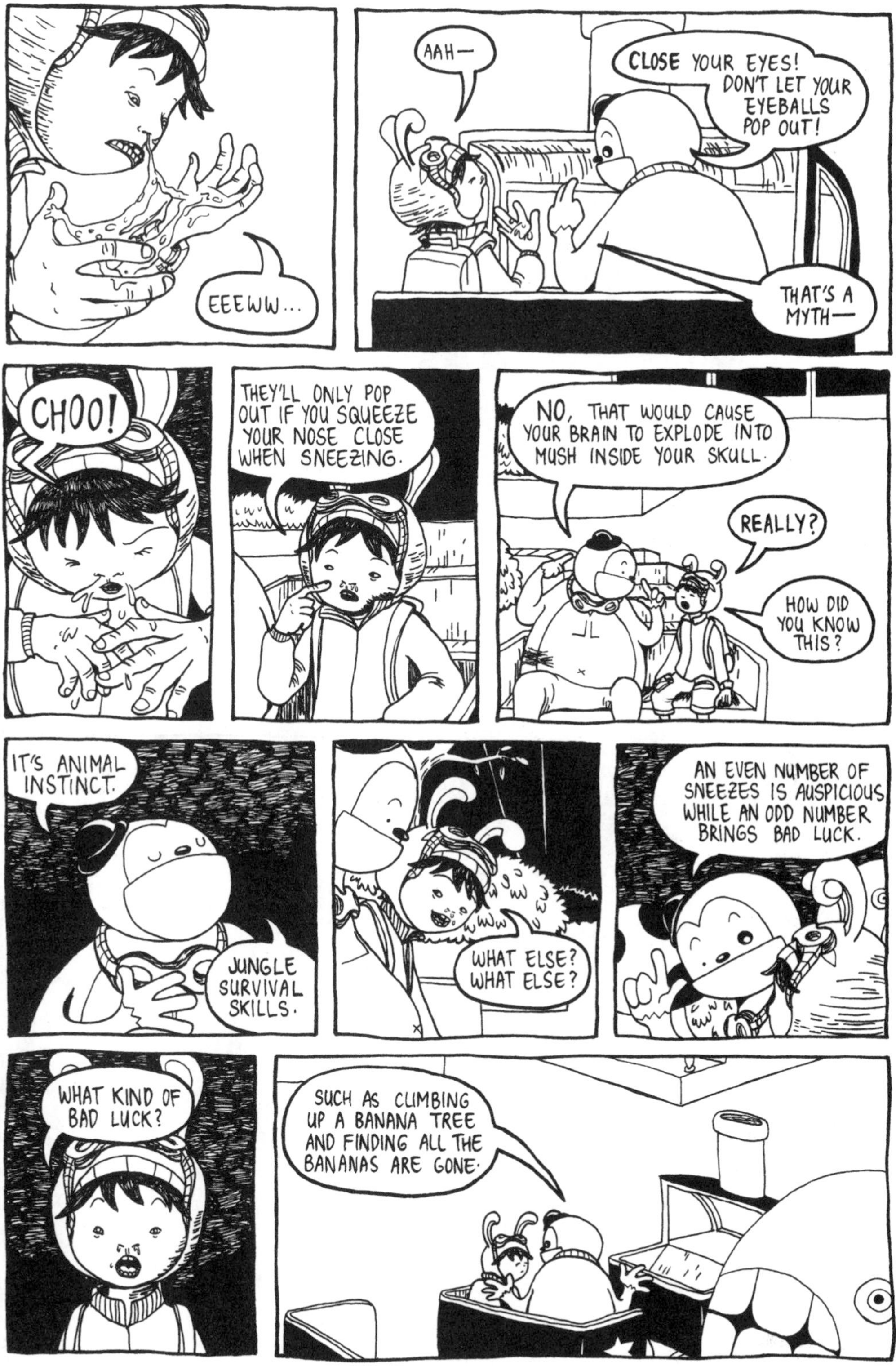
EEEWW...
AAH—
CLOSE YOUR EYES! DON'T LET YOUR EYEBALLS POP OUT!
THAT'S A MYTH—
CHOO!
THEY'LL ONLY POP OUT IF YOU SQUEEZE YOUR NOSE CLOSE WHEN SNEEZING.
NO, THAT WOULD CAUSE YOUR BRAIN TO EXPLODE INTO MUSH INSIDE YOUR SKULL.
REALLY?
HOW DID YOU KNOW THIS?
IT'S ANIMAL INSTINCT.
JUNGLE SURVIVAL SKILLS.
WHAT ELSE? WHAT ELSE?
AN EVEN NUMBER OF SNEEZES IS AUSPICIOUS WHILE AN ODD NUMBER BRINGS BAD LUCK.
WHAT KIND OF BAD LUCK?
SUCH AS CLIMBING UP A BANANA TREE AND FINDING ALL THE BANANAS ARE GONE.

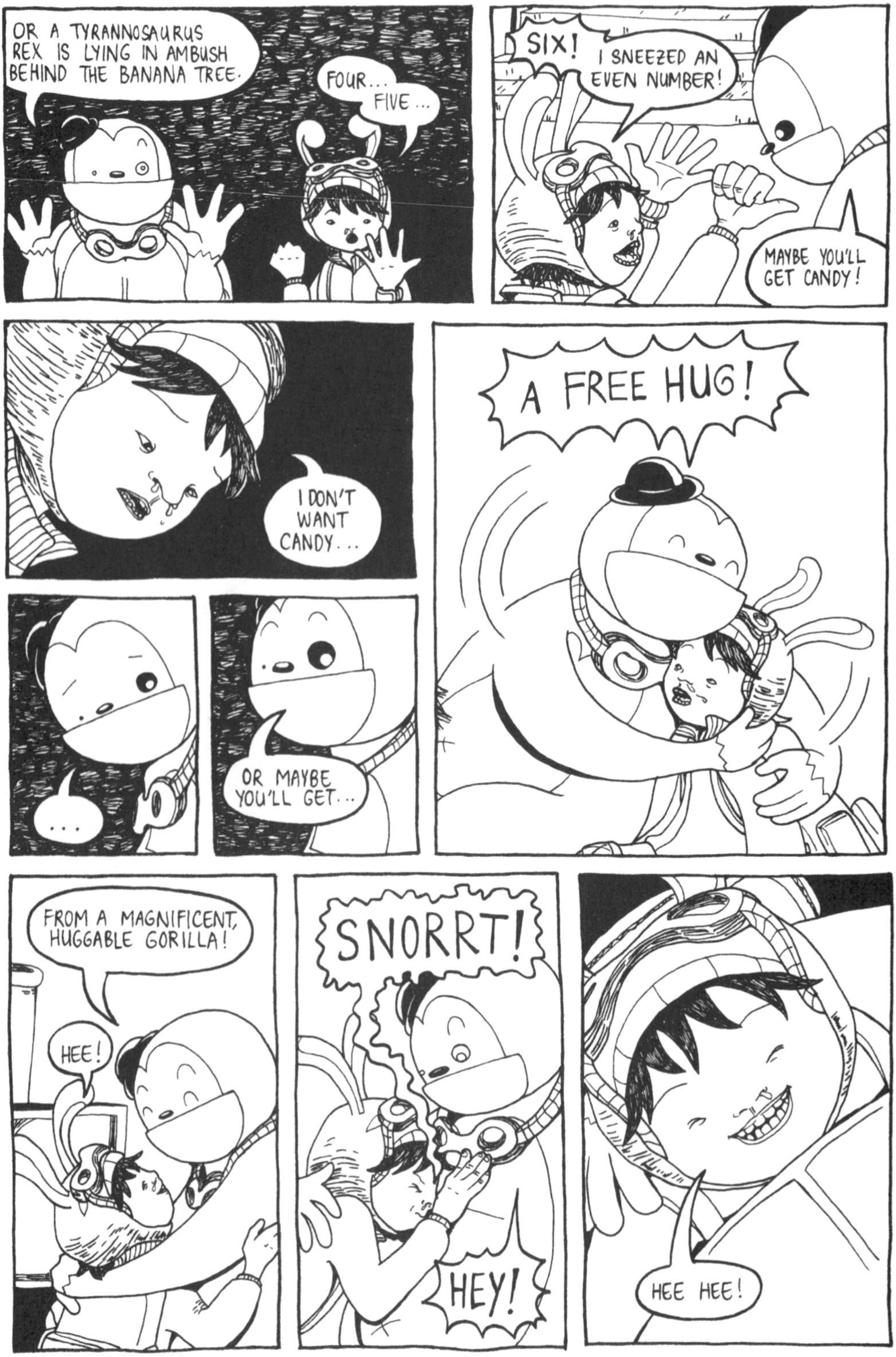
OR A TYRANNOSAURUS REX IS LYING IN AMBUSH BEHIND THE BANANA TREE.
FOUR... FIVE...
SIX!
I SNEEZED AN EVEN NUMBER!
MAYBE YOU'LL GET CANDY!
I DON'T WANT CANDY...
...
OR MAYBE YOU'LL GET...
A FREE HUG!
FROM A MAGNIFICENT, HUGGABLE GORILLA!
HEE!
SNORRT!
HEY!
HEE HEE!

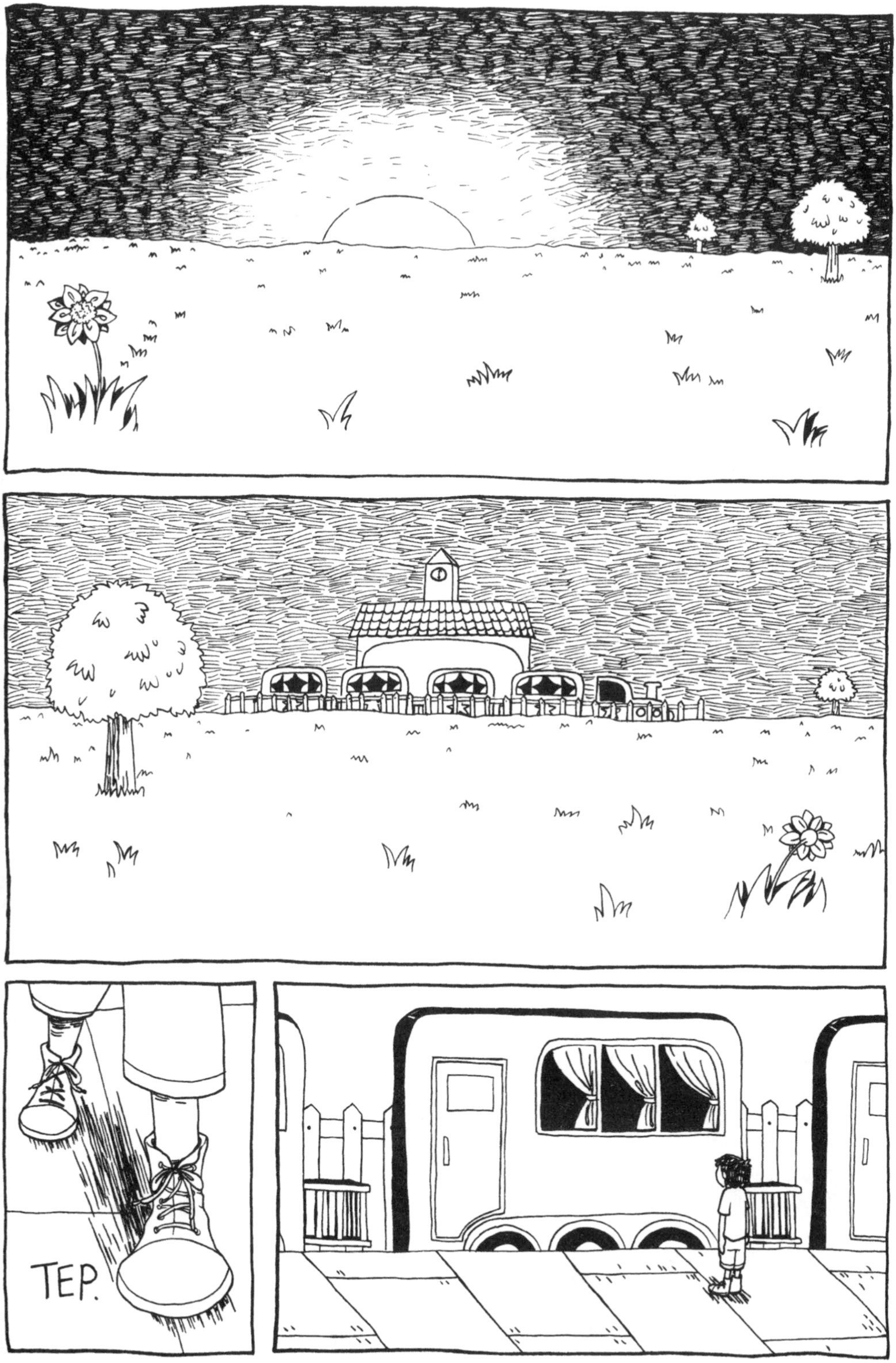
TEP.

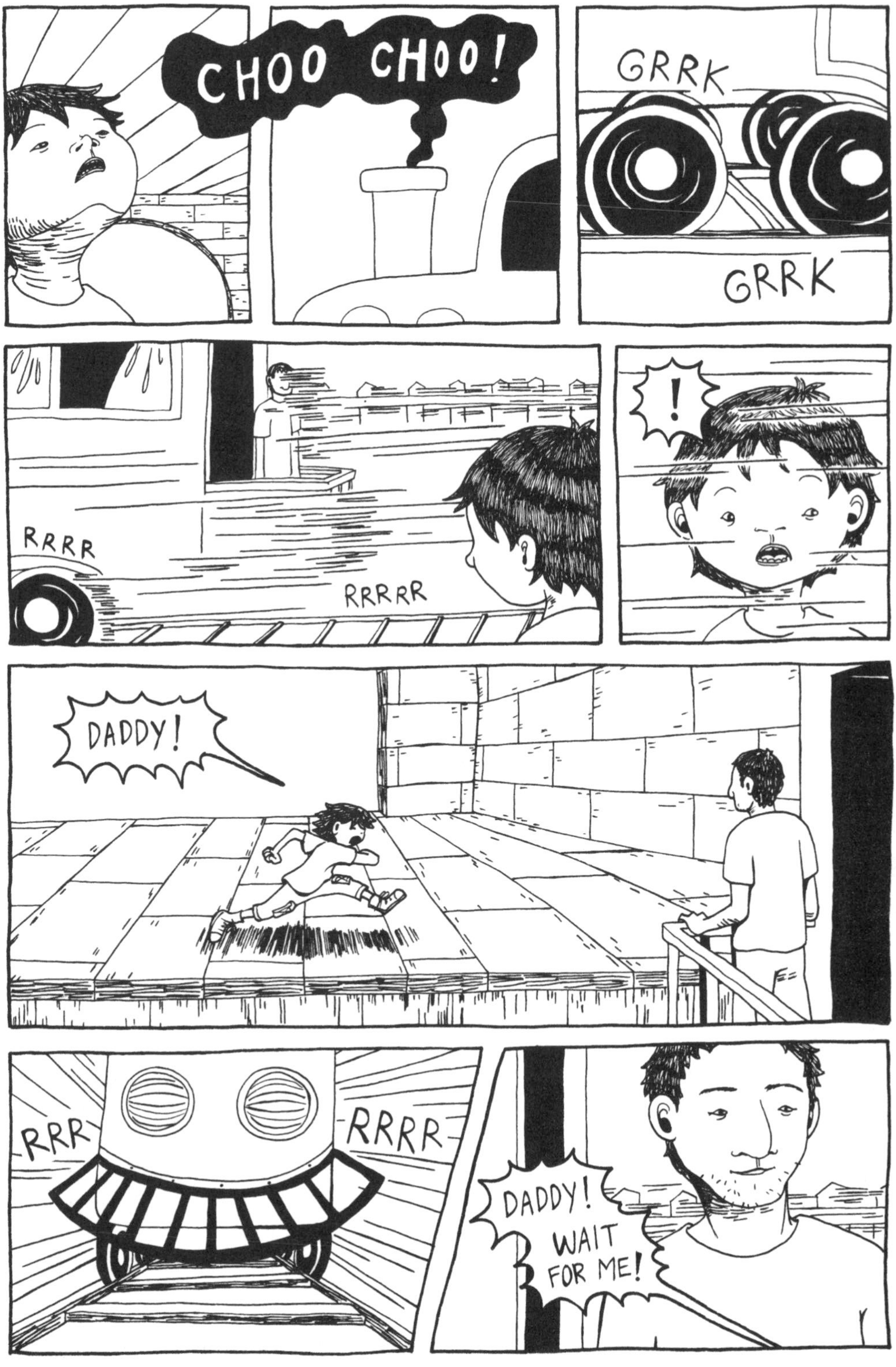
CHOO CHOO!
GRRK
GRRK
RRRR
RRRRR
!
DADDY!
RRR
RRRR
DADDY! WAIT FOR ME!

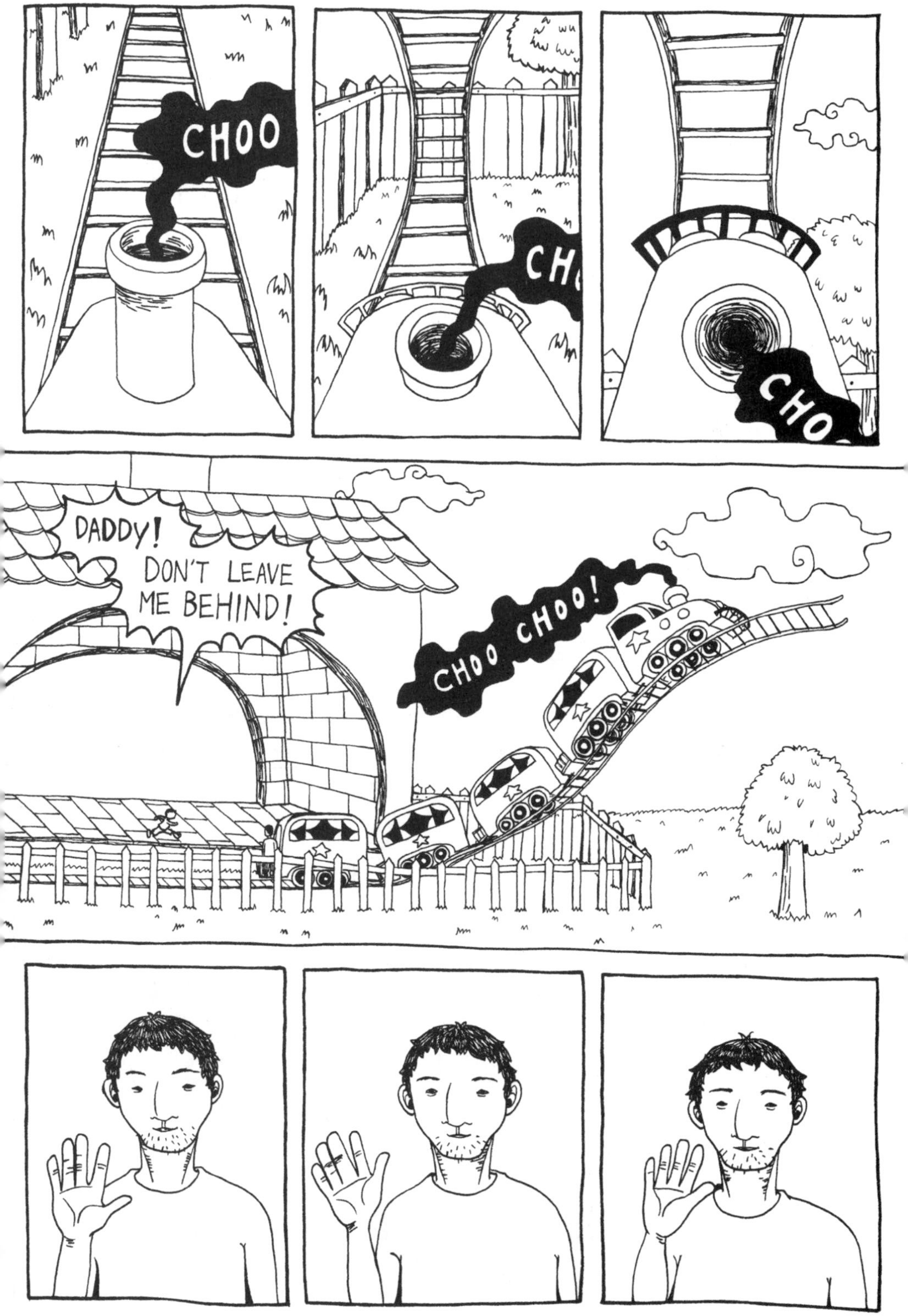
CHOO
CH
CHO
DADDY!
DON'T LEAVE ME BEHIND!
CHOO CHOO!

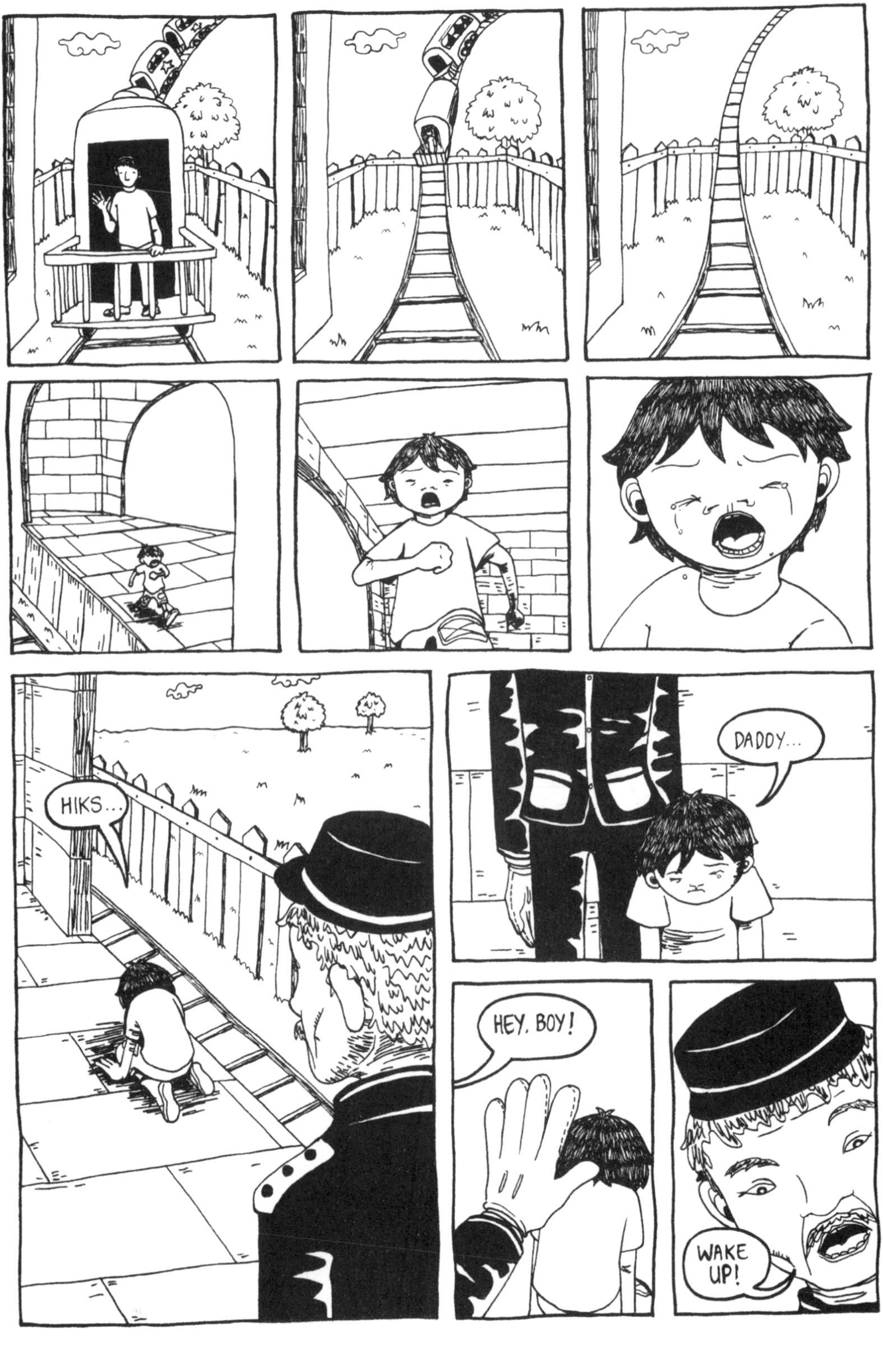
HIKS...
DADDY...
HEY, BOY!
WAKE UP!

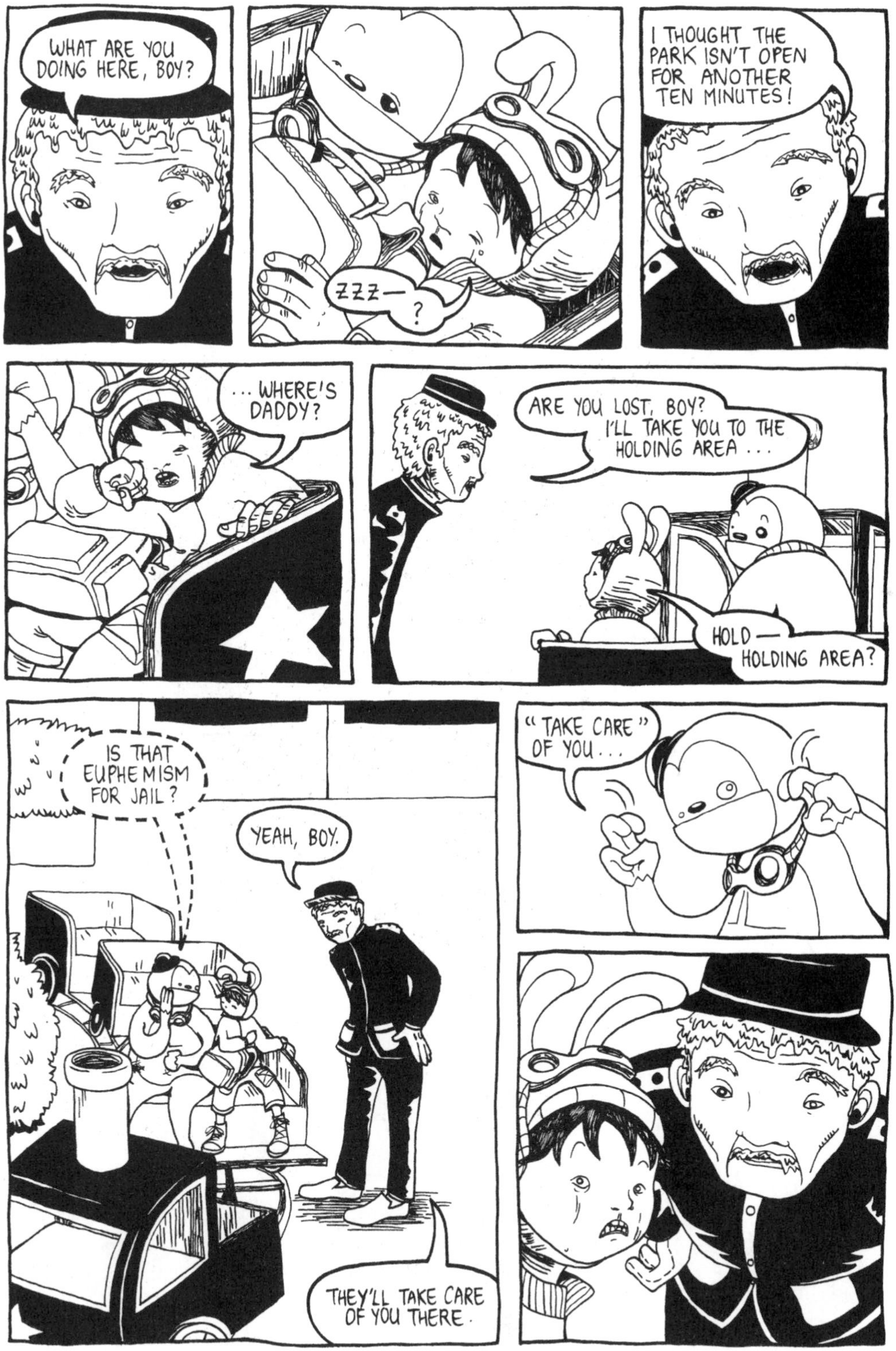
WHAT ARE YOU DOING HERE, BOY?
ZZZ— ?
I THOUGHT THE PARK ISN'T OPEN FOR ANOTHER TEN MINUTES!
... WHERE'S DADDY?
ARE YOU LOST, BOY? I'LL TAKE YOU TO THE HOLDING AREA ...
HOLD— HOLDING AREA?
IS THAT EUPHEMISM FOR JAIL?
YEAH, BOY.
THEY'LL TAKE CARE OF YOU THERE.
"TAKE CARE" OF YOU...

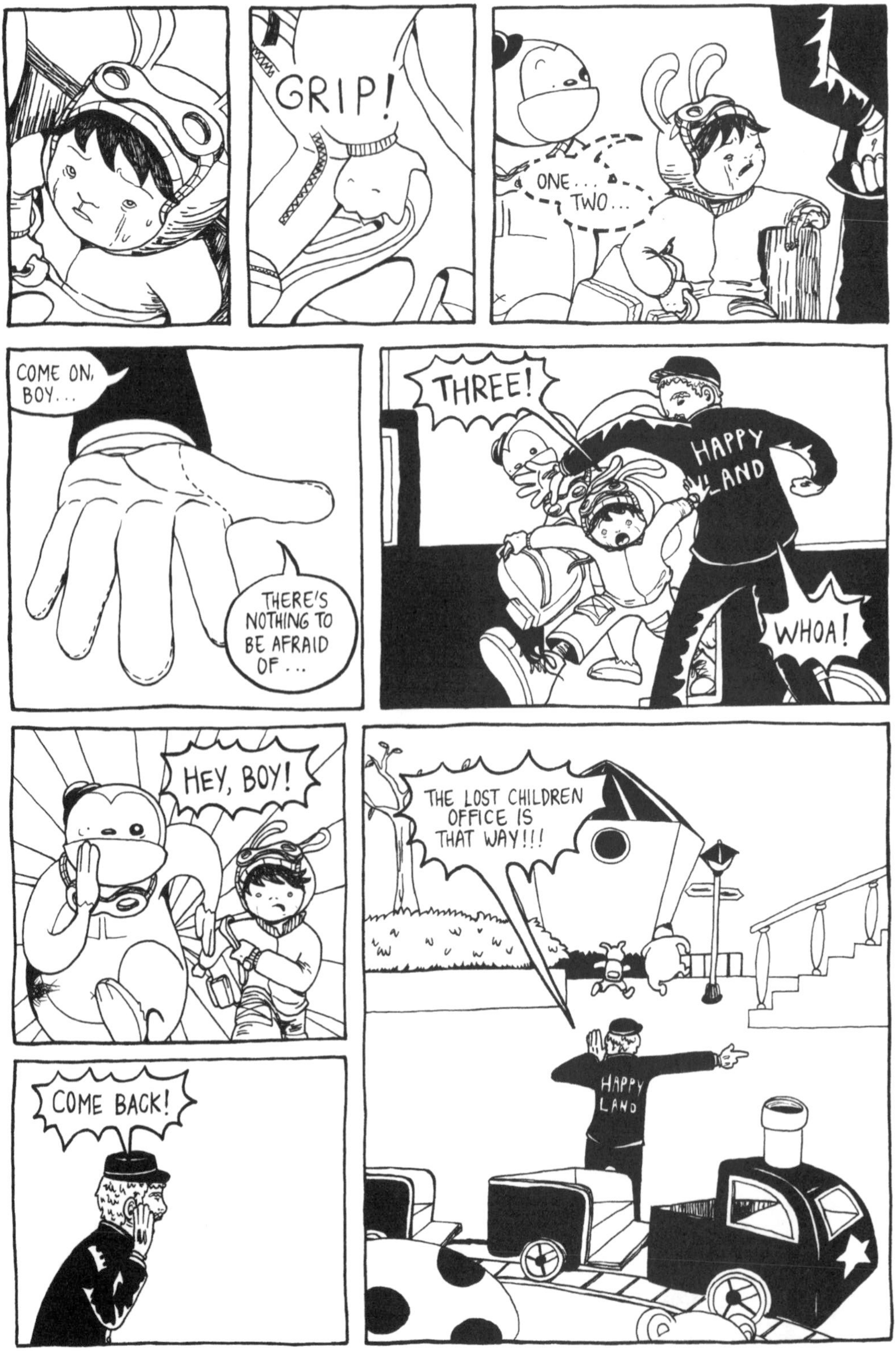
GRIP!
ONE... TWO...
COME ON, BOY...
THERE'S NOTHING TO BE AFRAID OF...
THREE!
HAPPY LAND
WHOA!
HEY, BOY!
THE LOST CHILDREN OFFICE IS THAT WAY!!!
HAPPY LAND
COME BACK!

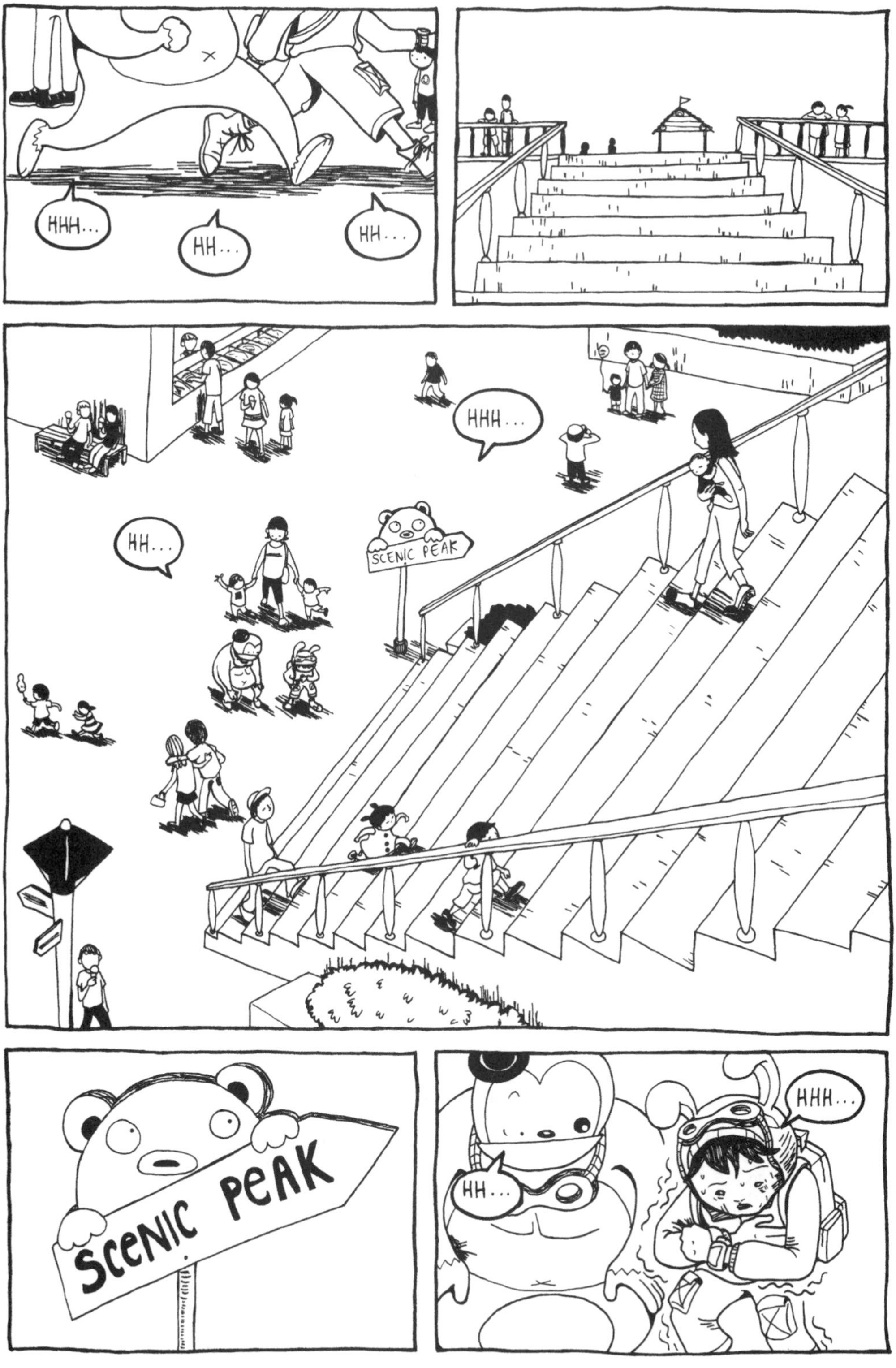
HHH...
HH...
HH...
HHH...
HH...
SCENIC PEAK
SCENIC PEAK
HH...
HHH...

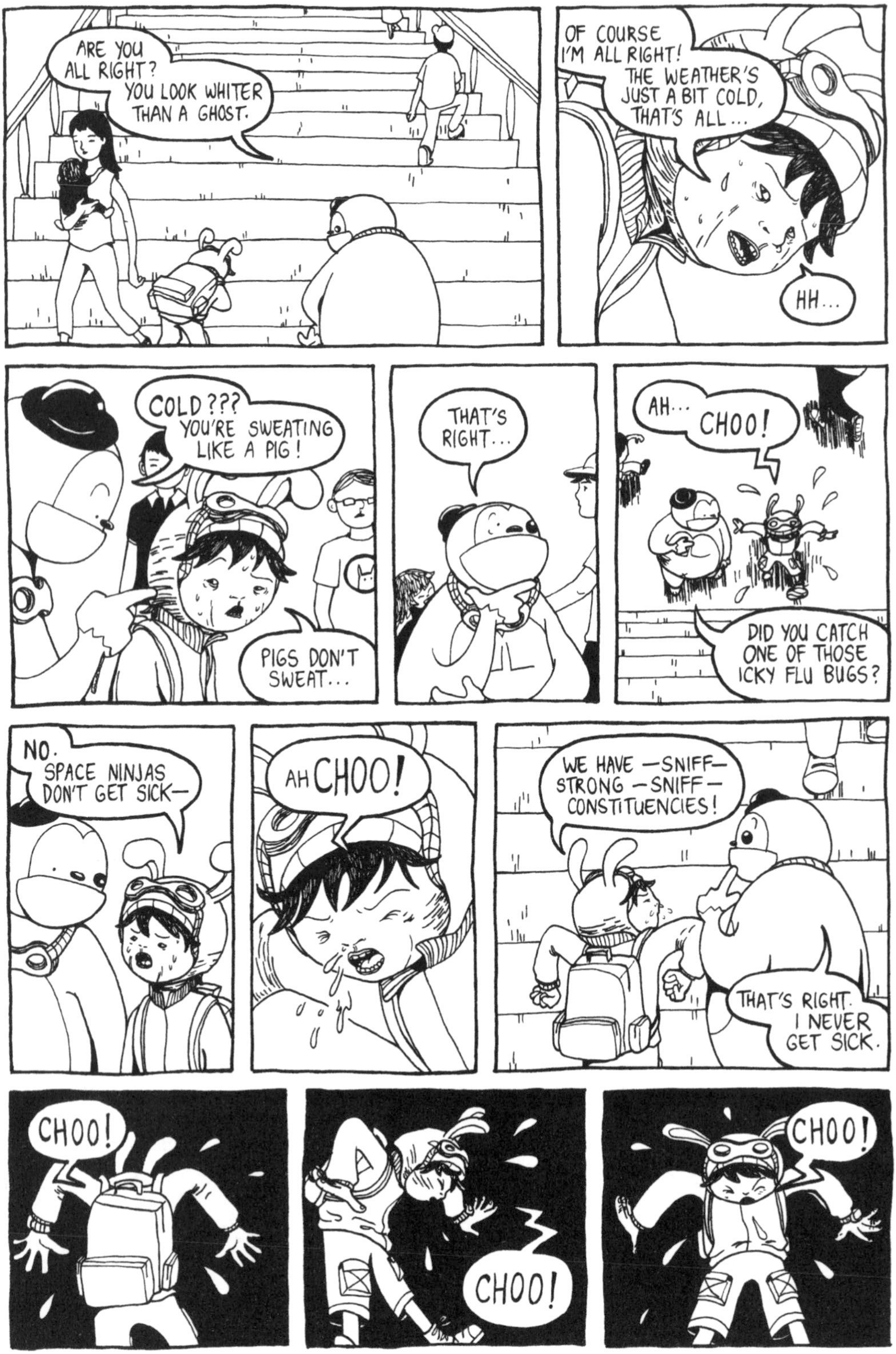
ARE YOU ALL RIGHT? YOU LOOK WHITER THAN A GHOST.
OF COURSE I'M ALL RIGHT!
THE WEATHER'S JUST A BIT COLD, THAT'S ALL...
HH...
COLD??? YOU'RE SWEATING LIKE A PIG!
PIGS DON'T SWEAT...
THAT'S RIGHT...
AH... CHOO!
DID YOU CATCH ONE OF THOSE ICKY FLU BUGS?
NO. SPACE NINJAS DON'T GET SICK—
AH CHOO!
WE HAVE —SNIFF— STRONG —SNIFF— CONSTITUENCIES!
THAT'S RIGHT. I NEVER GET SICK.
CHOO!
CHOO!
CHOO!

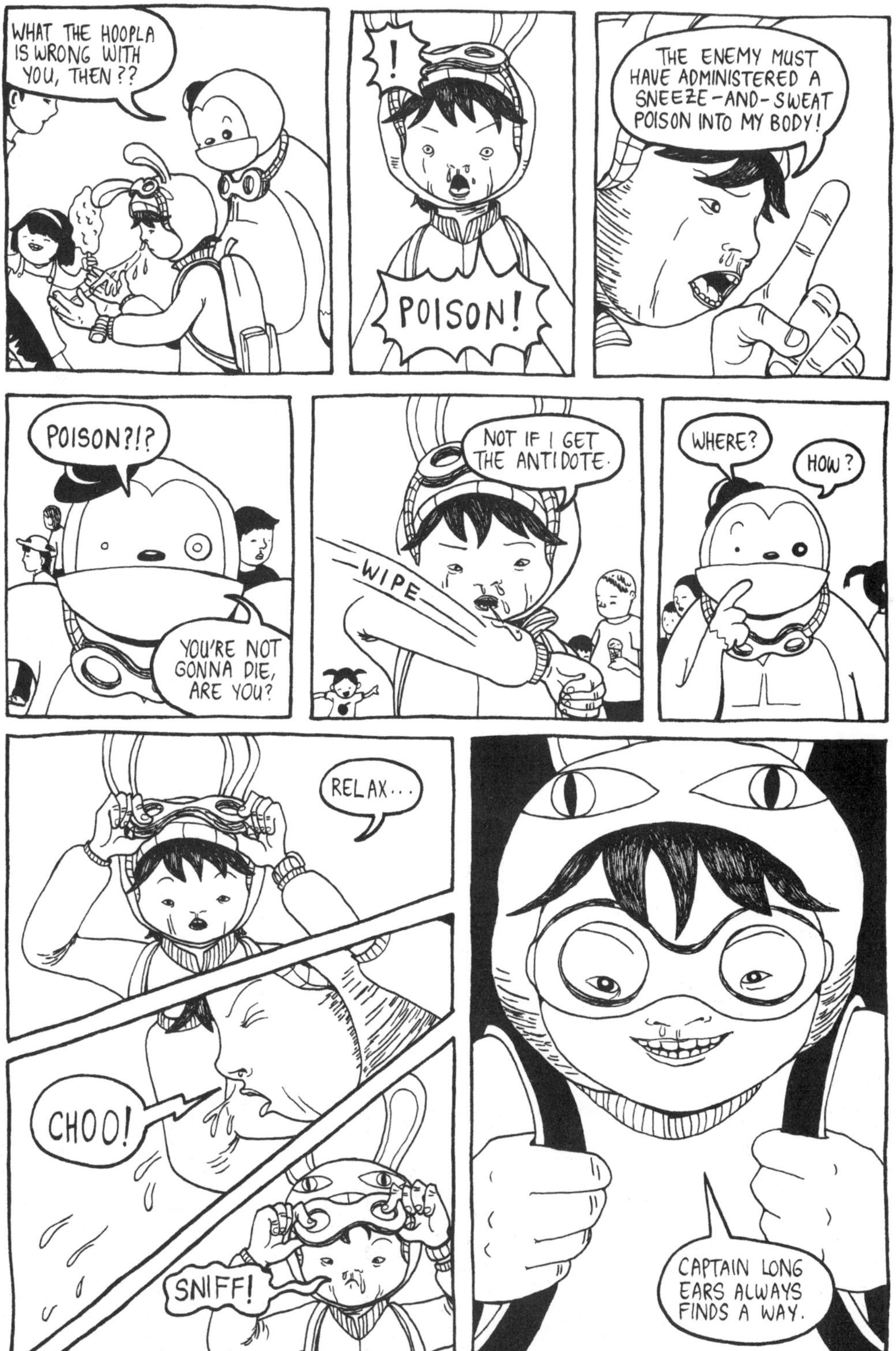
WHAT THE HOOPLA IS WRONG WITH YOU, THEN??
!
POISON!
THE ENEMY MUST HAVE ADMINISTERED A SNEEZE-AND-SWEAT POISON INTO MY BODY!
POISON?!?
YOU'RE NOT GONNA DIE, ARE YOU?
NOT IF I GET THE ANTIDOTE.
WIPE
WHERE?
HOW?
RELAX...
CHOO!
SNIFF!
CAPTAIN LONG EARS ALWAYS FINDS A WAY.

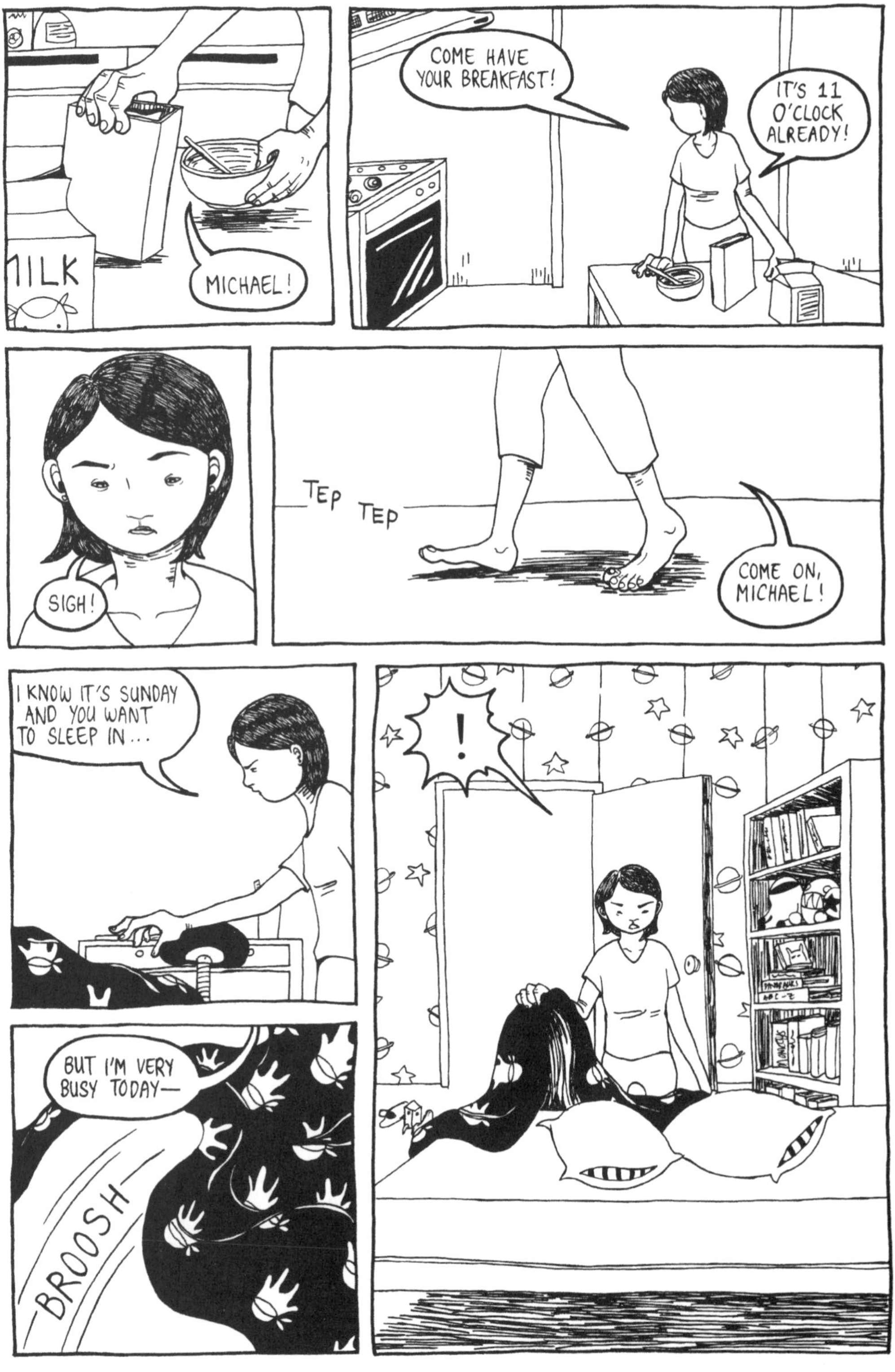
MICHAEL!
COME HAVE YOUR BREAKFAST!
IT'S 11 O'CLOCK ALREADY!
SIGH!
TEP TEP
COME ON, MICHAEL!
I KNOW IT'S SUNDAY AND YOU WANT TO SLEEP IN...
BUT I'M VERY BUSY TODAY—
BROOSH
!

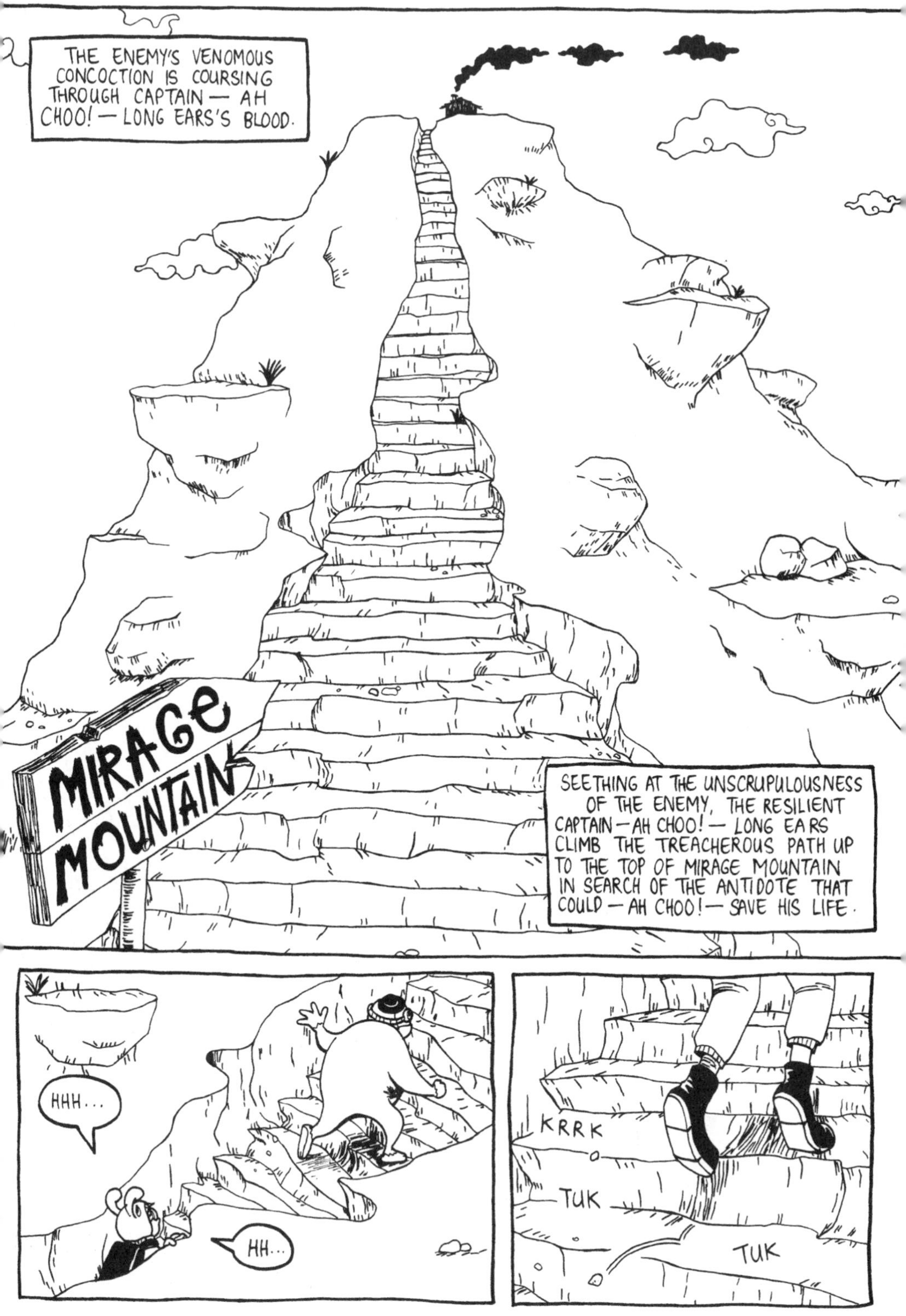
THE ENEMY'S VENOMOUS CONCOCTION IS COURSING THROUGH CAPTAIN — AH CHOO! — LONG EARS'S BLOOD.
MIRAGE MOUNTAIN
SEETHING AT THE UNSCRUPULOUSNESS OF THE ENEMY, THE RESILIENT CAPTAIN — AH CHOO! — LONG EARS CLIMB THE TREACHEROUS PATH UP TO THE TOP OF MIRAGE MOUNTAIN IN SEARCH OF THE ANTIDOTE THAT COULD — AH CHOO! — SAVE HIS LIFE.
HHH...
HH...
KRRK
TUK
TUK

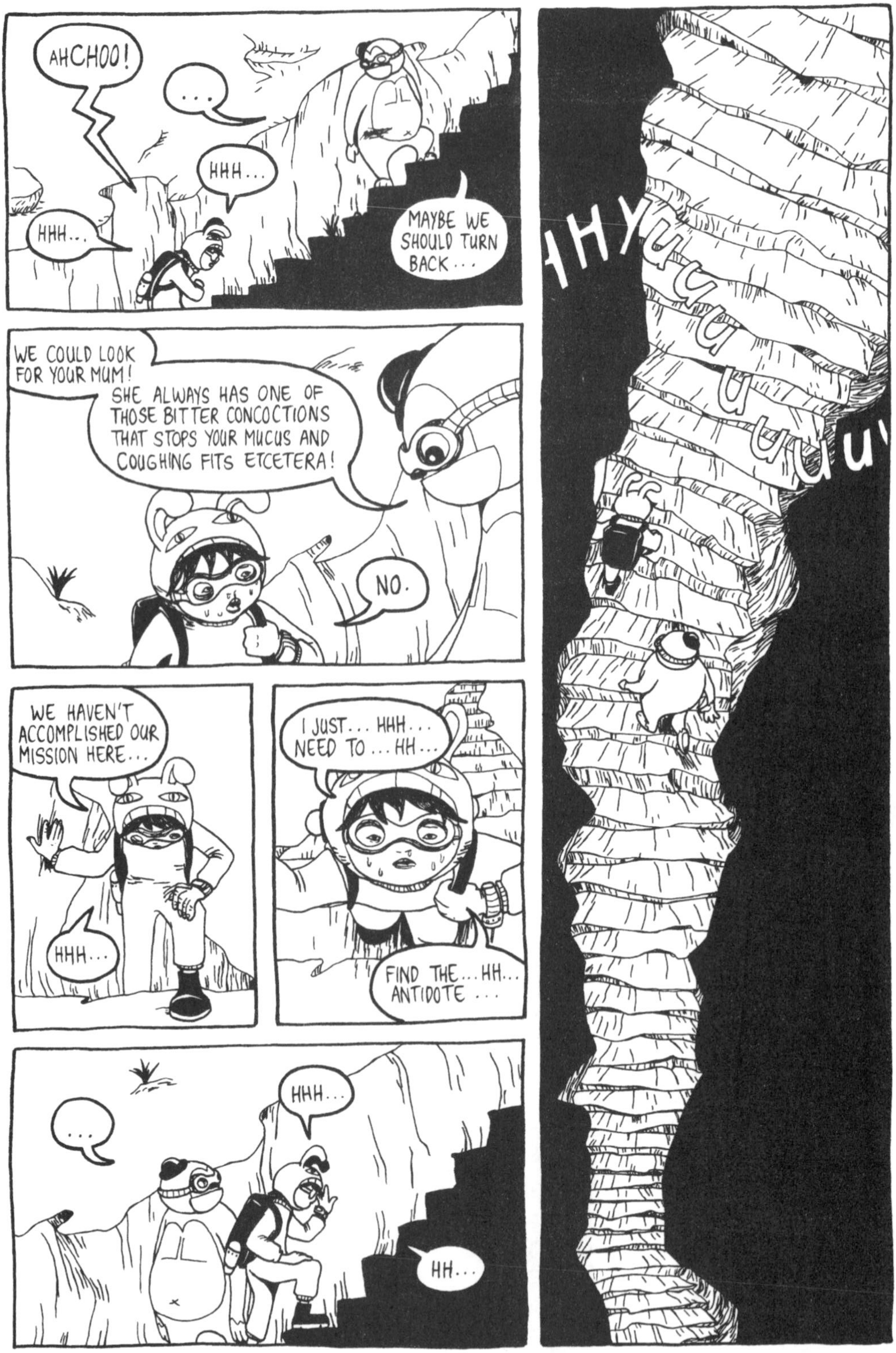
AHCHOO!
...
HHH...
HHH...
MAYBE WE SHOULD TURN BACK...
WE COULD LOOK FOR YOUR MUM!
SHE ALWAYS HAS ONE OF THOSE BITTER CONCOCTIONS THAT STOPS YOUR MUCUS AND COUGHING FITS ETCETERA!
NO.
WE HAVEN'T ACCOMPLISHED OUR MISSION HERE...
HHH...
I JUST... HHH... NEED TO... HH...
FIND THE... HH... ANTIDOTE...
...
HHH...
HH...

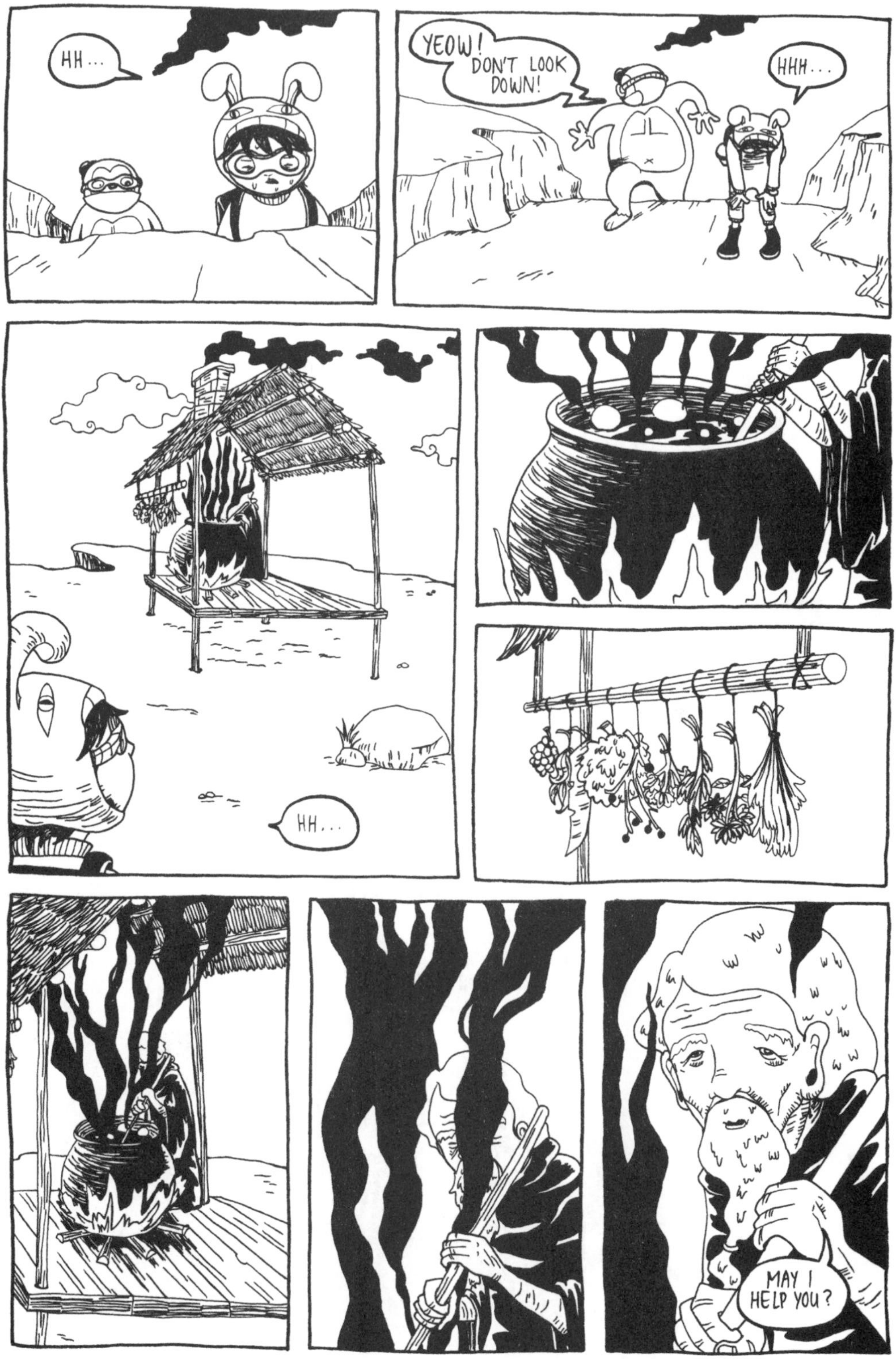
HH...
YEOW! DON'T LOOK DOWN!
HHH...
HH...
MAY I HELP YOU?

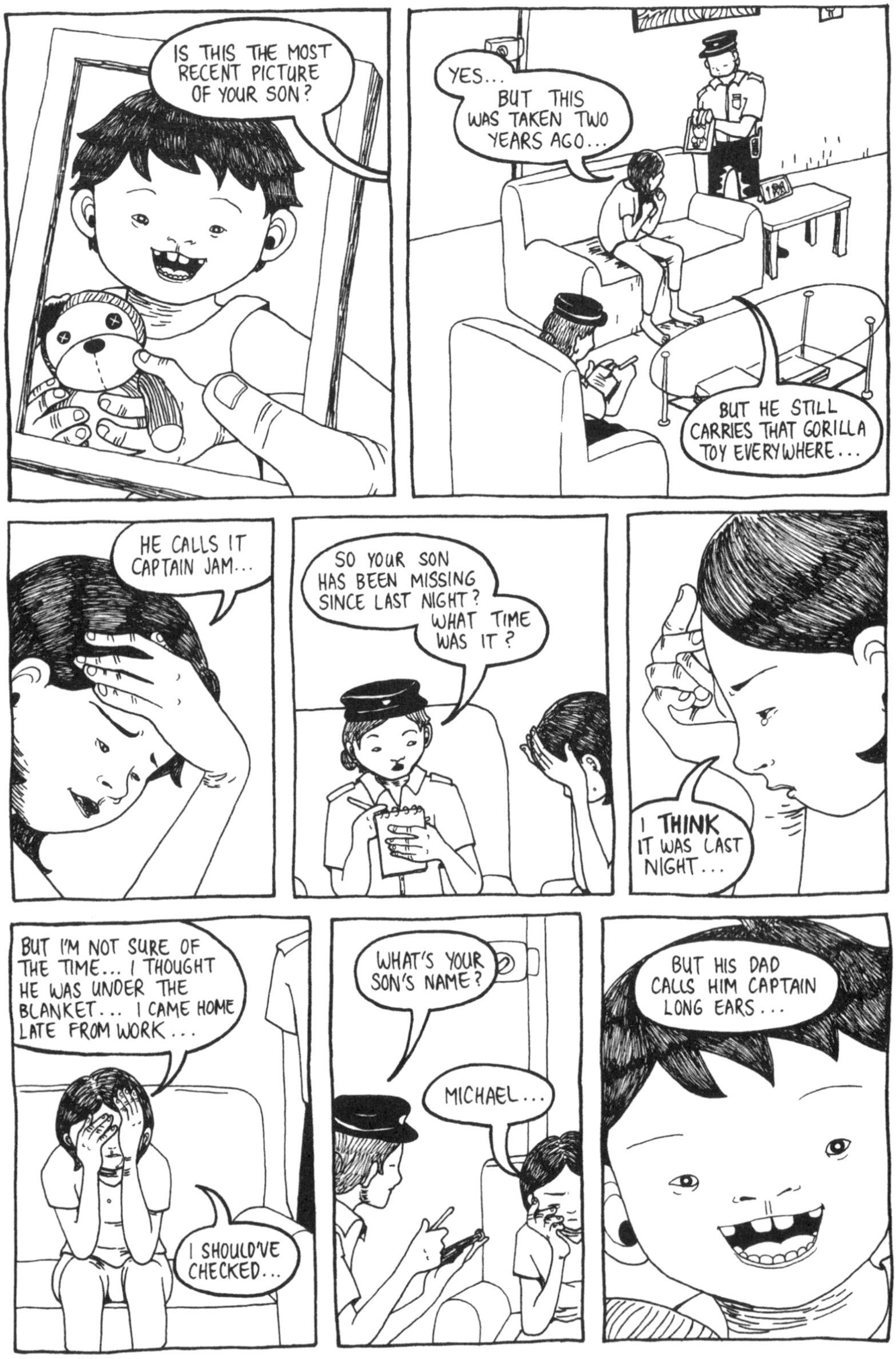
IS THIS THE MOST RECENT PICTURE OF YOUR SON?
YES... BUT THIS WAS TAKEN TWO YEARS AGO...
BUT HE STILL CARRIES THAT GORILLA TOY EVERYWHERE...
HE CALLS IT CAPTAIN JAM...
SO YOUR SON HAS BEEN MISSING SINCE LAST NIGHT? WHAT TIME WAS IT?
I **THINK** IT WAS LAST NIGHT...
BUT I'M NOT SURE OF THE TIME... I THOUGHT HE WAS UNDER THE BLANKET... I CAME HOME LATE FROM WORK...
I SHOULD'VE CHECKED...
WHAT'S YOUR SON'S NAME?
MICHAEL...
BUT HIS DAD CALLS HIM CAPTAIN LONG EARS...

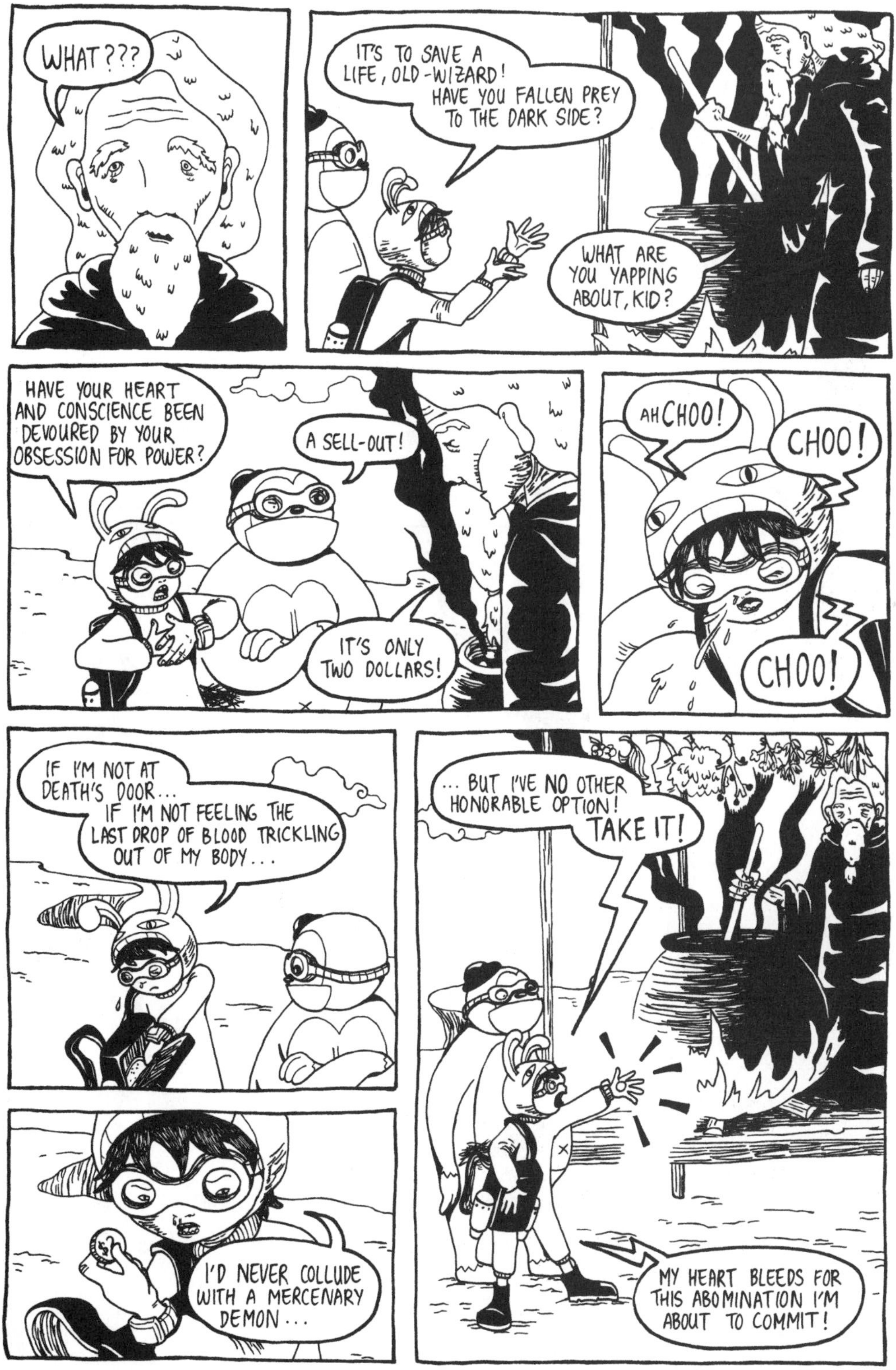
WHAT???
IT'S TO SAVE A LIFE, OLD-WIZARD! HAVE YOU FALLEN PREY TO THE DARK SIDE?
WHAT ARE YOU YAPPING ABOUT, KID?
HAVE YOUR HEART AND CONSCIENCE BEEN DEVOURED BY YOUR OBSESSION FOR POWER?
A SELL-OUT!
IT'S ONLY TWO DOLLARS!
AH CHOO!
CHOO!
CHOO!
IF I'M NOT AT DEATH'S DOOR... IF I'M NOT FEELING THE LAST DROP OF BLOOD TRICKLING OUT OF MY BODY...
I'D NEVER COLLUDE WITH A MERCENARY DEMON...
... BUT I'VE NO OTHER HONORABLE OPTION!
TAKE IT!
MY HEART BLEEDS FOR THIS ABOMINATION I'M ABOUT TO COMMIT!

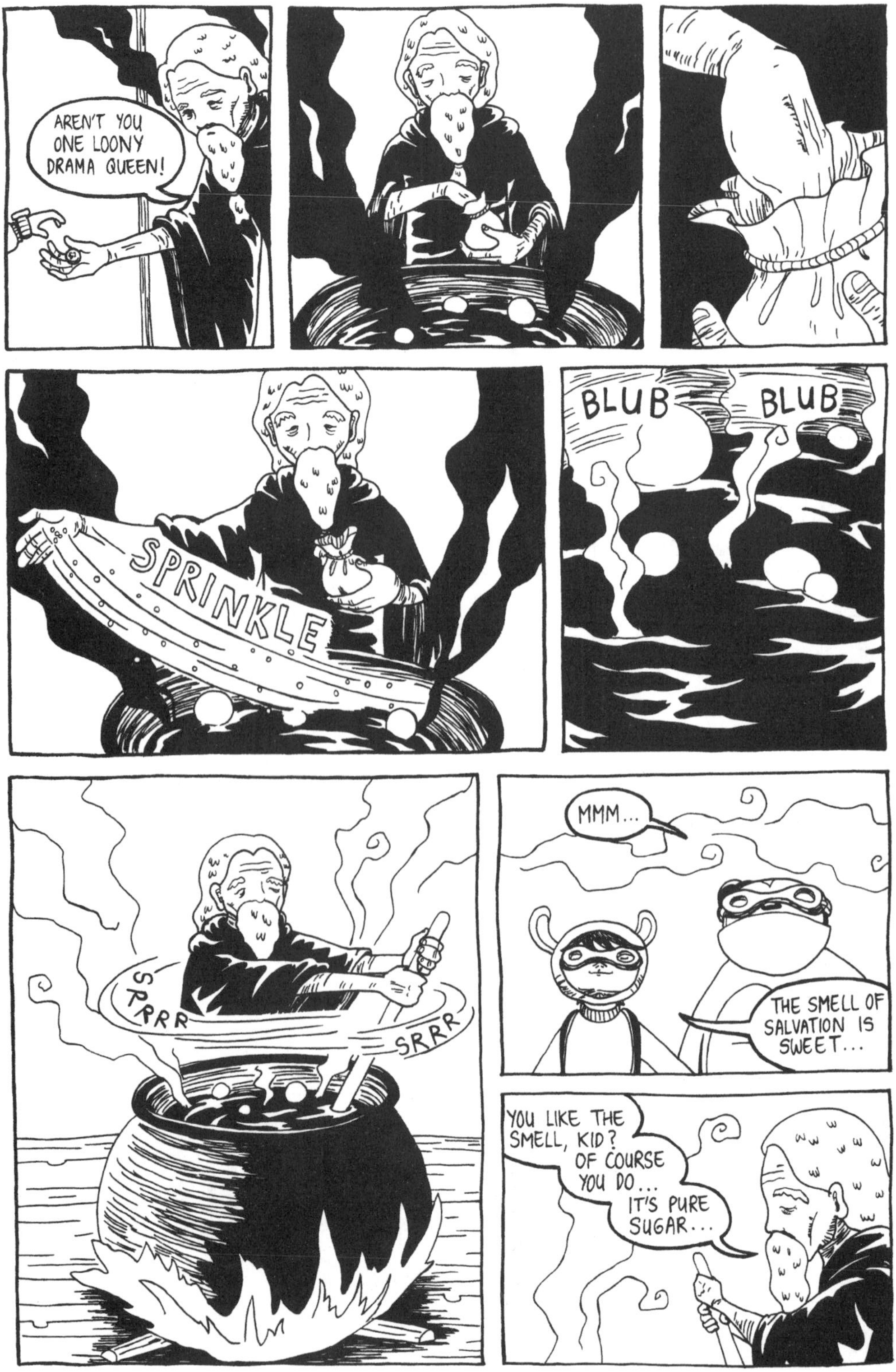
AREN'T YOU ONE LOONY DRAMA QUEEN!
SPRINKLE
BLUB
BLUB
SRRRR
SRRR
MMM...
THE SMELL OF SALVATION IS SWEET...
YOU LIKE THE SMELL, KID?
OF COURSE YOU DO...
IT'S PURE SUGAR...

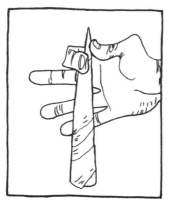

PLUP

DRIP   DRIP

HERE, KID.

GIMME GIMME!

HAP!

FASTER!

HAP!

HAP!

HURRY! BEFORE THE POISON TOTALLY INCAPACITATES YOU!

WHOA, KID! SLOW DOWN!

HAP!

HAP!

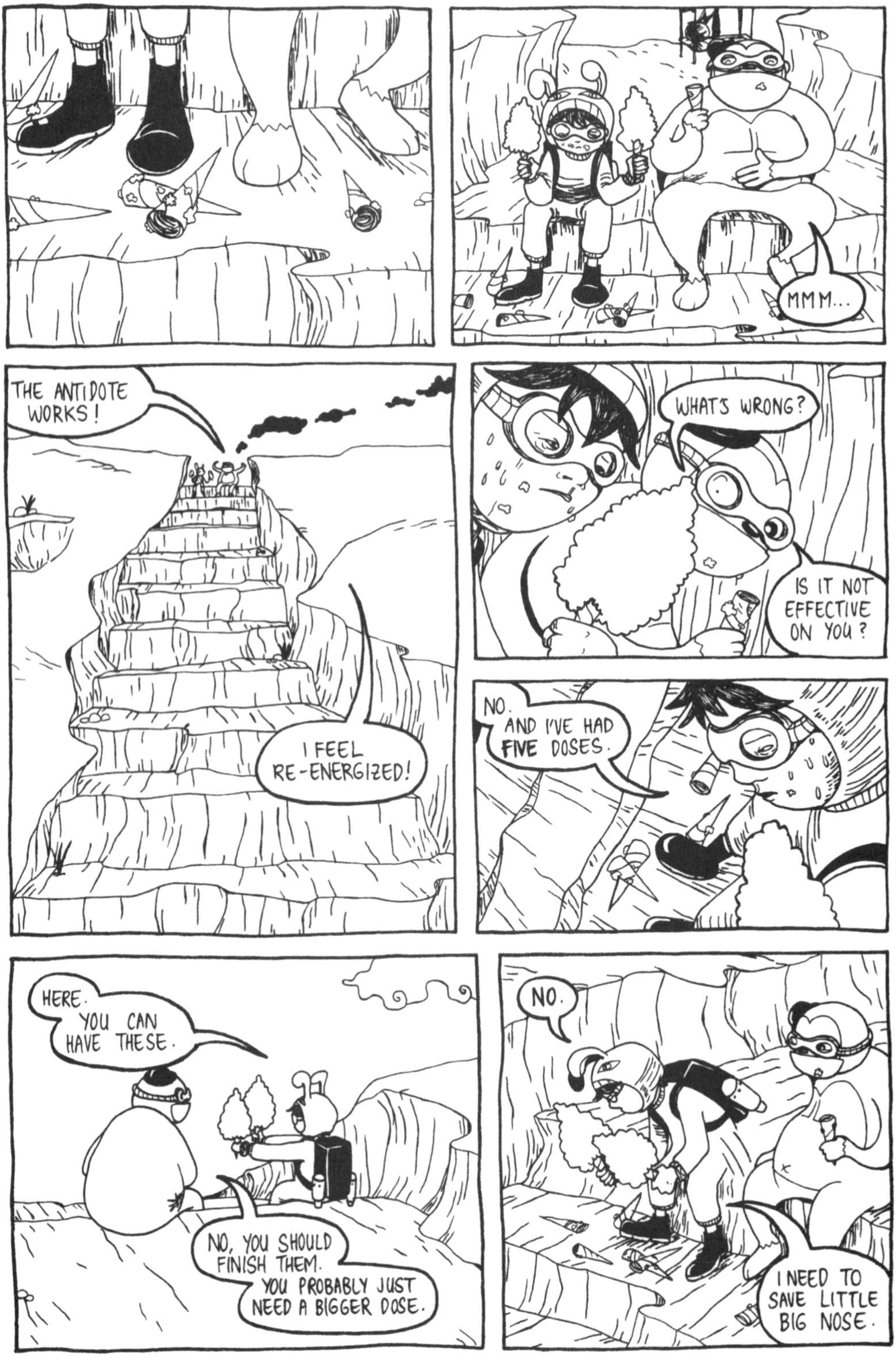
MMM...
THE ANTIDOTE WORKS!
I FEEL RE-ENERGIZED!
WHAT'S WRONG?
IS IT NOT EFFECTIVE ON YOU?
NO. AND I'VE HAD **FIVE** DOSES.
HERE. YOU CAN HAVE THESE.
NO, YOU SHOULD FINISH THEM. YOU PROBABLY JUST NEED A BIGGER DOSE.
NO.
I NEED TO SAVE LITTLE BIG NOSE.

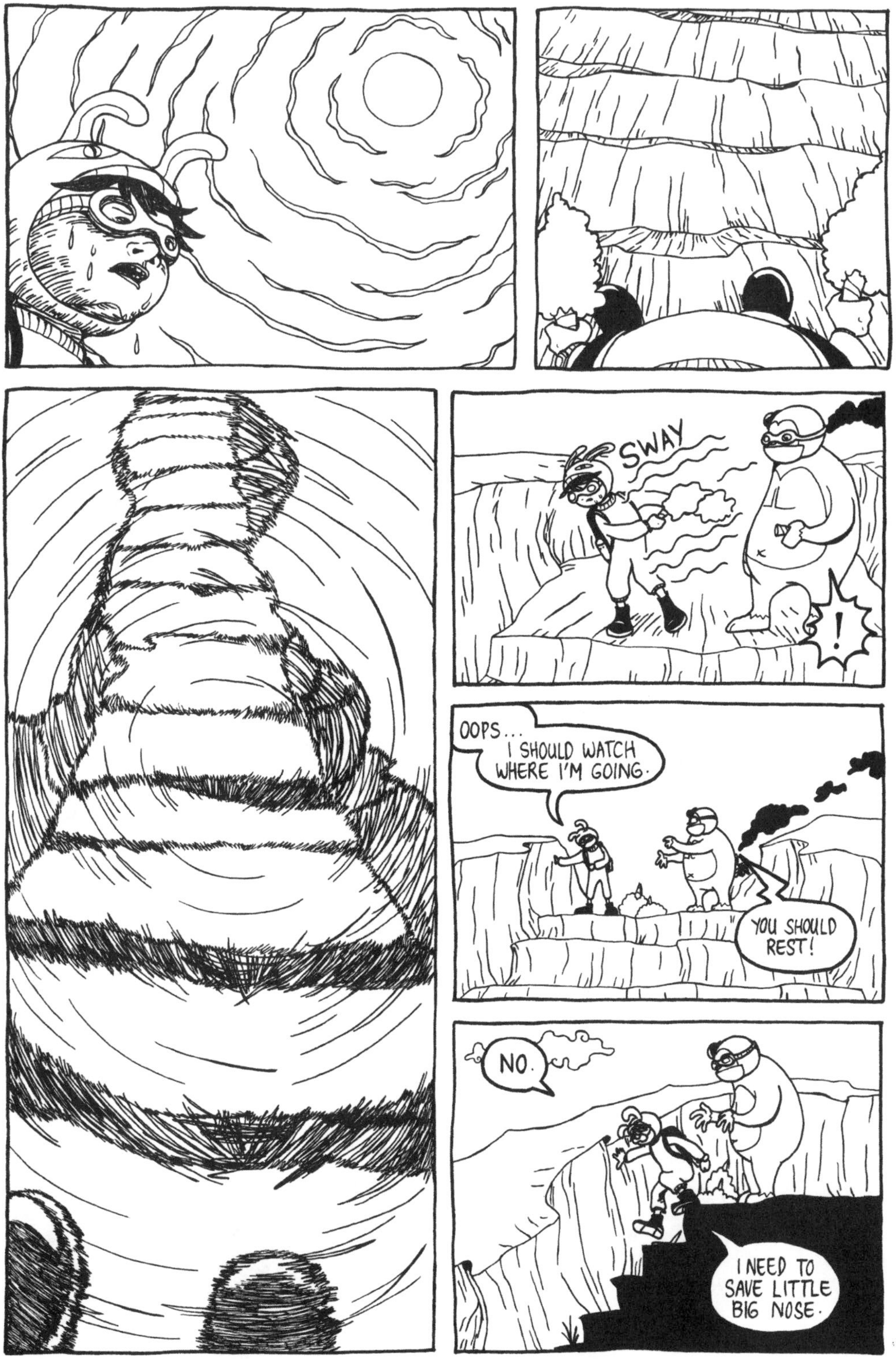
SWAY
!
OOPS... I SHOULD WATCH WHERE I'M GOING.
YOU SHOULD REST!
NO.
I NEED TO SAVE LITTLE BIG NOSE.

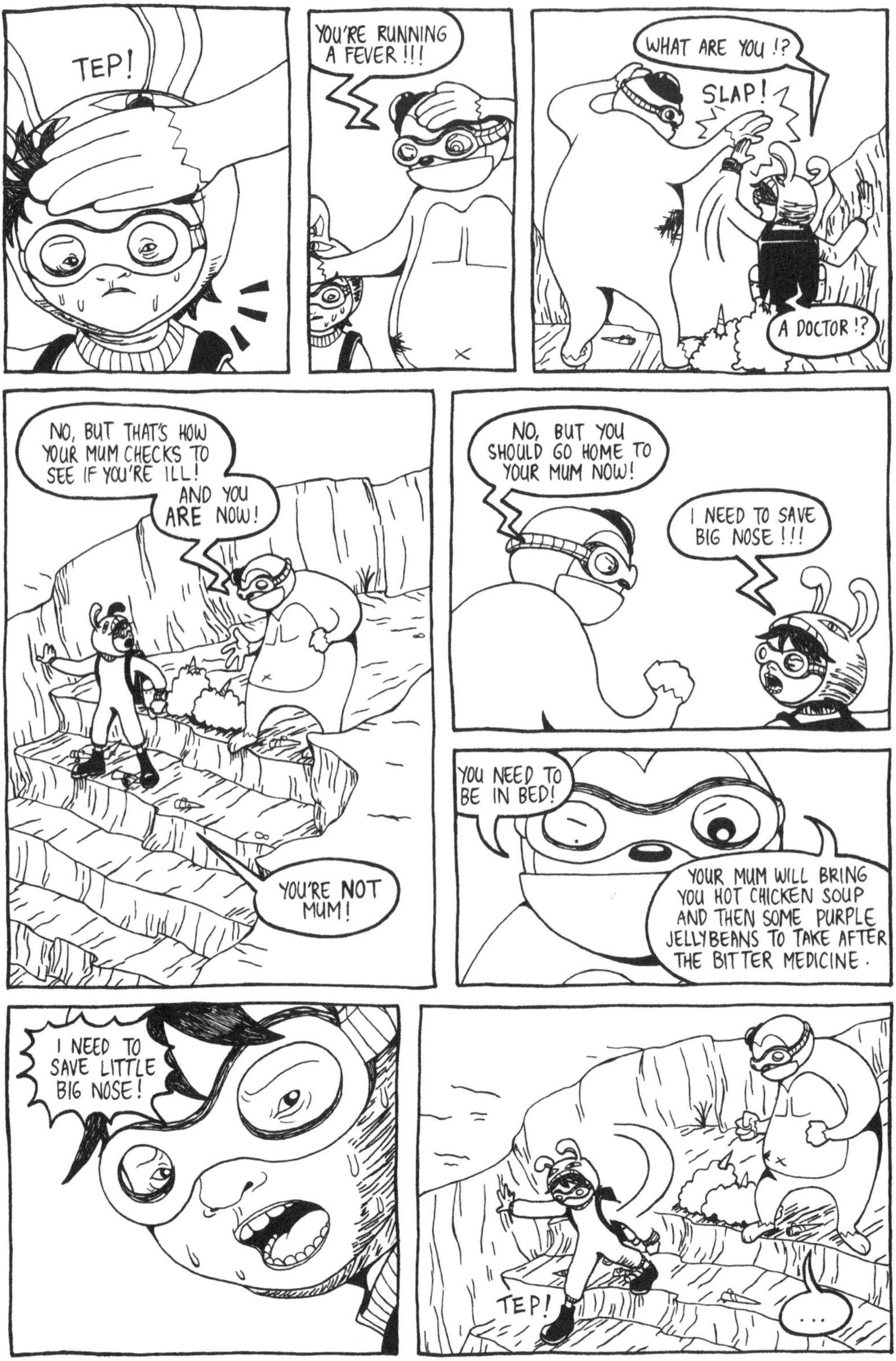
TEP!
YOU'RE RUNNING A FEVER!!!
WHAT ARE YOU!?
SLAP!
A DOCTOR!?
NO, BUT THAT'S HOW YOUR MUM CHECKS TO SEE IF YOU'RE ILL!
AND YOU ARE NOW!
YOU'RE NOT MUM!
NO, BUT YOU SHOULD GO HOME TO YOUR MUM NOW!
I NEED TO SAVE BIG NOSE!!!
YOU NEED TO BE IN BED!
YOUR MUM WILL BRING YOU HOT CHICKEN SOUP AND THEN SOME PURPLE JELLYBEANS TO TAKE AFTER THE BITTER MEDICINE.
I NEED TO SAVE LITTLE BIG NOSE!
TEP!
...

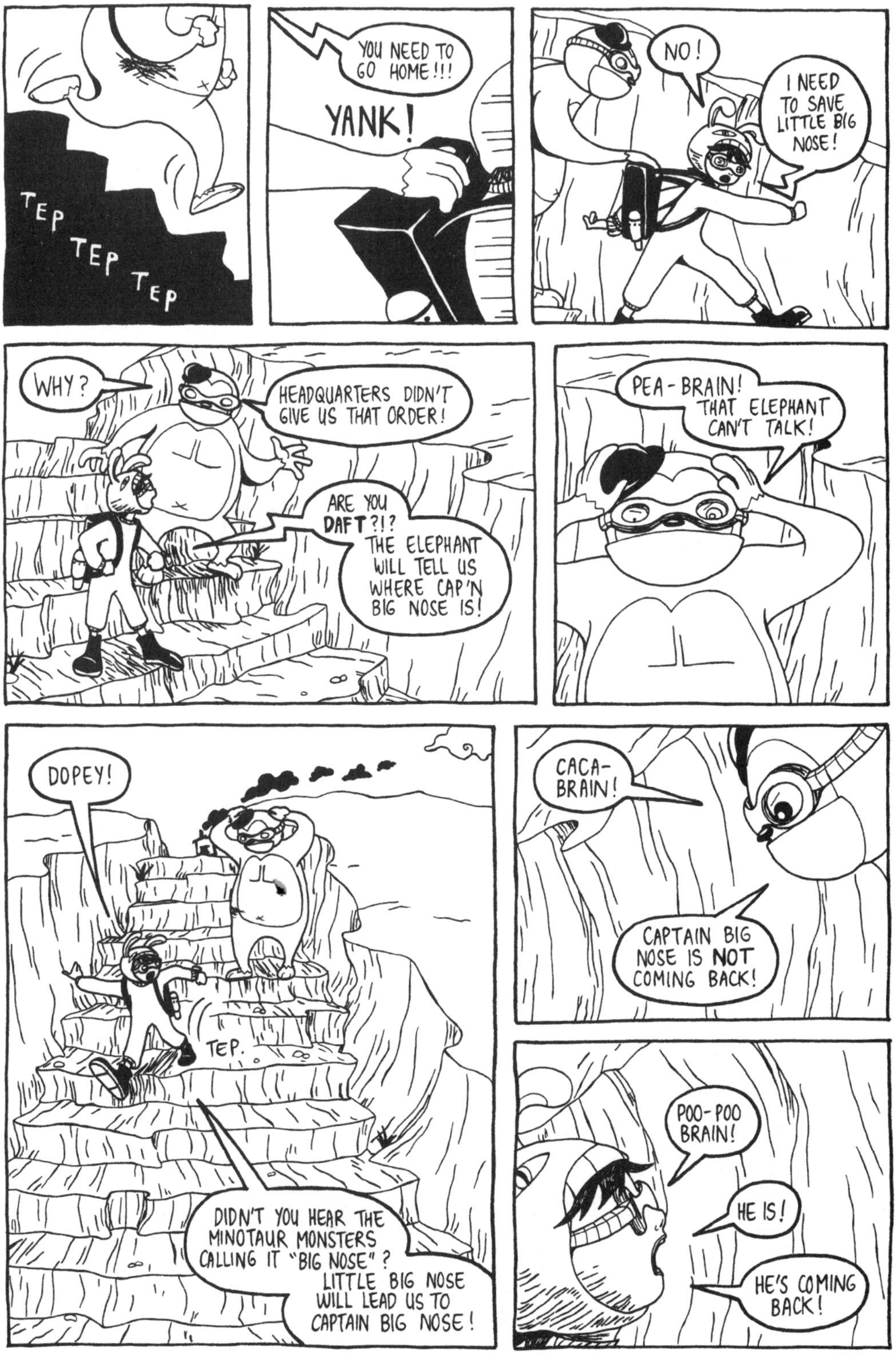
TEP TEP TEP
YOU NEED TO GO HOME!!!
YANK!
NO!
I NEED TO SAVE LITTLE BIG NOSE!
WHY?
HEADQUARTERS DIDN'T GIVE US THAT ORDER!
ARE YOU DAFT?!? THE ELEPHANT WILL TELL US WHERE CAP'N BIG NOSE IS!
PEA-BRAIN! THAT ELEPHANT CAN'T TALK!
DOPEY!
TEP.
DIDN'T YOU HEAR THE MINOTAUR MONSTERS CALLING IT "BIG NOSE"? LITTLE BIG NOSE WILL LEAD US TO CAPTAIN BIG NOSE!
CACA-BRAIN!
CAPTAIN BIG NOSE IS NOT COMING BACK!
POO-POO BRAIN!
HE IS!
HE'S COMING BACK!

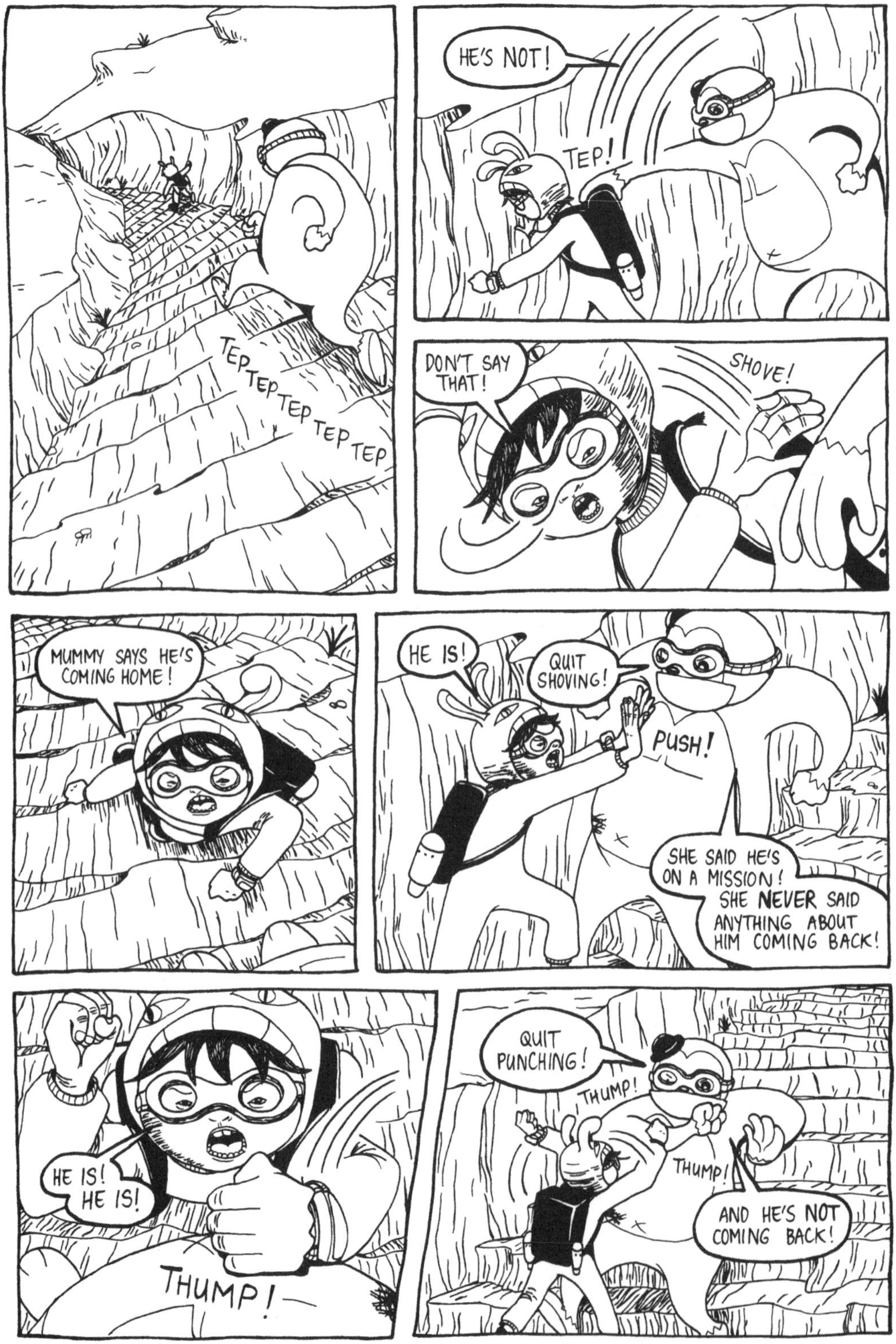
TEP TEP TEP TEP TEP
HE'S NOT!
TEP!
DON'T SAY THAT!
SHOVE!
MUMMY SAYS HE'S COMING HOME!
HE IS!
QUIT SHOVING!
PUSH!
SHE SAID HE'S ON A MISSION! SHE NEVER SAID ANYTHING ABOUT HIM COMING BACK!
HE IS! HE IS!
THUMP!
QUIT PUNCHING!
THUMP!
THUMP!
AND HE'S NOT COMING BACK!

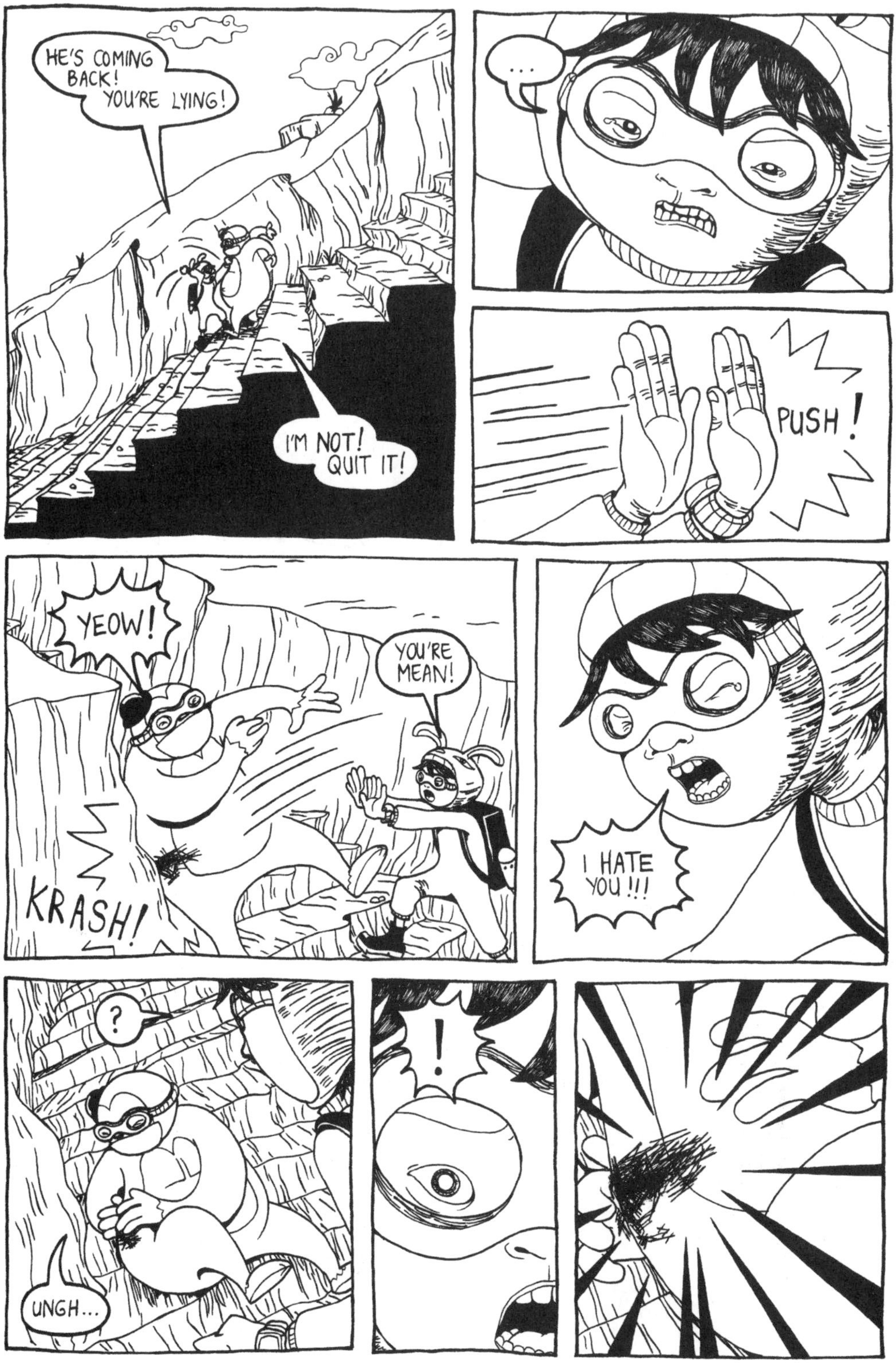
HE'S COMING BACK! YOU'RE LYING!
I'M NOT! QUIT IT!
...
PUSH!
YEOW!
YOU'RE MEAN!
KRASH!
I HATE YOU!!!
?
UNGH...
!

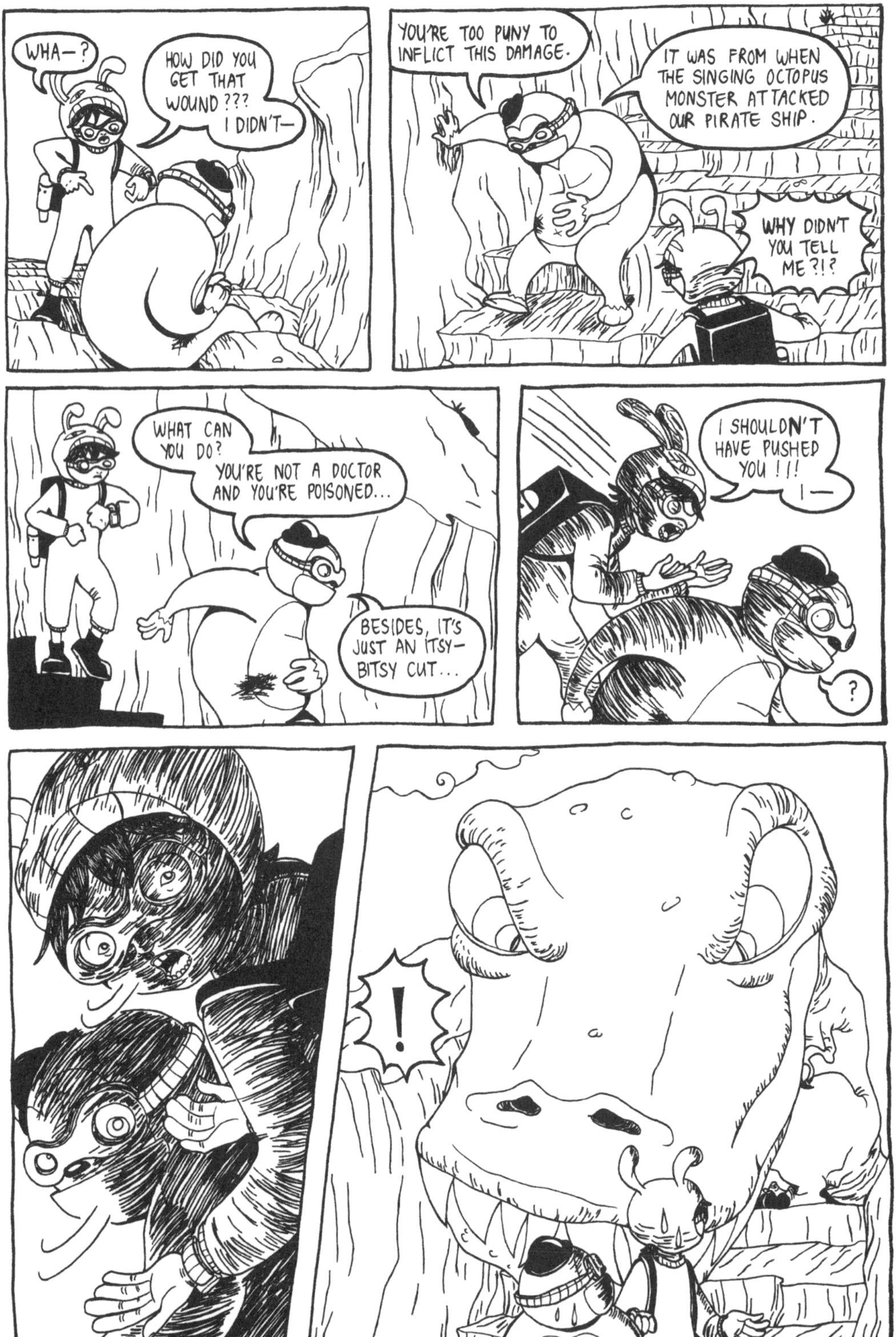
WHA—?
HOW DID YOU GET THAT WOUND??? I DIDN'T—
YOU'RE TOO PUNY TO INFLICT THIS DAMAGE.
IT WAS FROM WHEN THE SINGING OCTOPUS MONSTER ATTACKED OUR PIRATE SHIP.
WHY DIDN'T YOU TELL ME?!?
WHAT CAN YOU DO? YOU'RE NOT A DOCTOR AND YOU'RE POISONED...
BESIDES, IT'S JUST AN ITSY-BITSY CUT...
I SHOULDN'T HAVE PUSHED YOU!!! I—
?
!

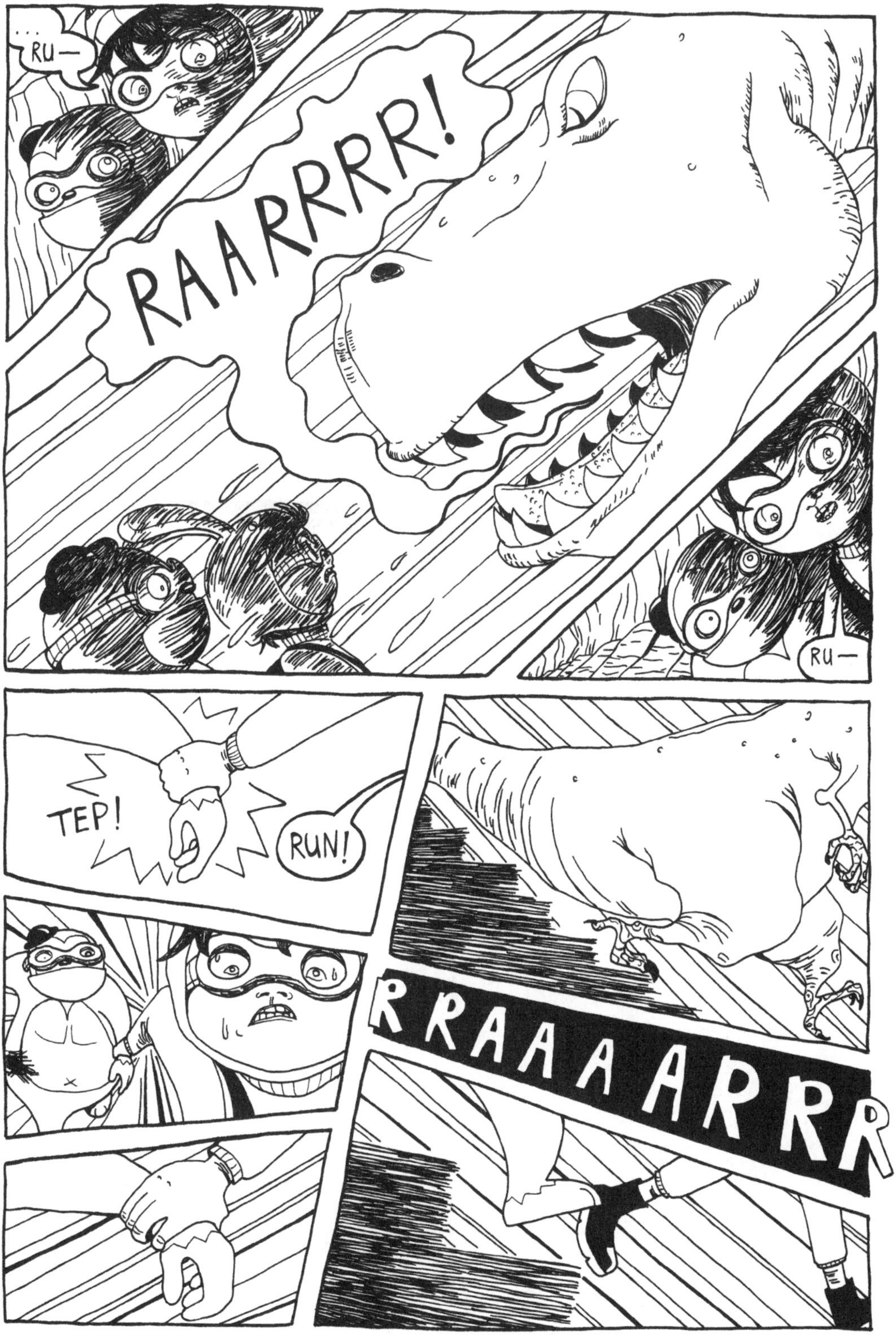
...
RU—
RAARRRRR!
RU—
TEP!
RUN!
RRAAAARRR

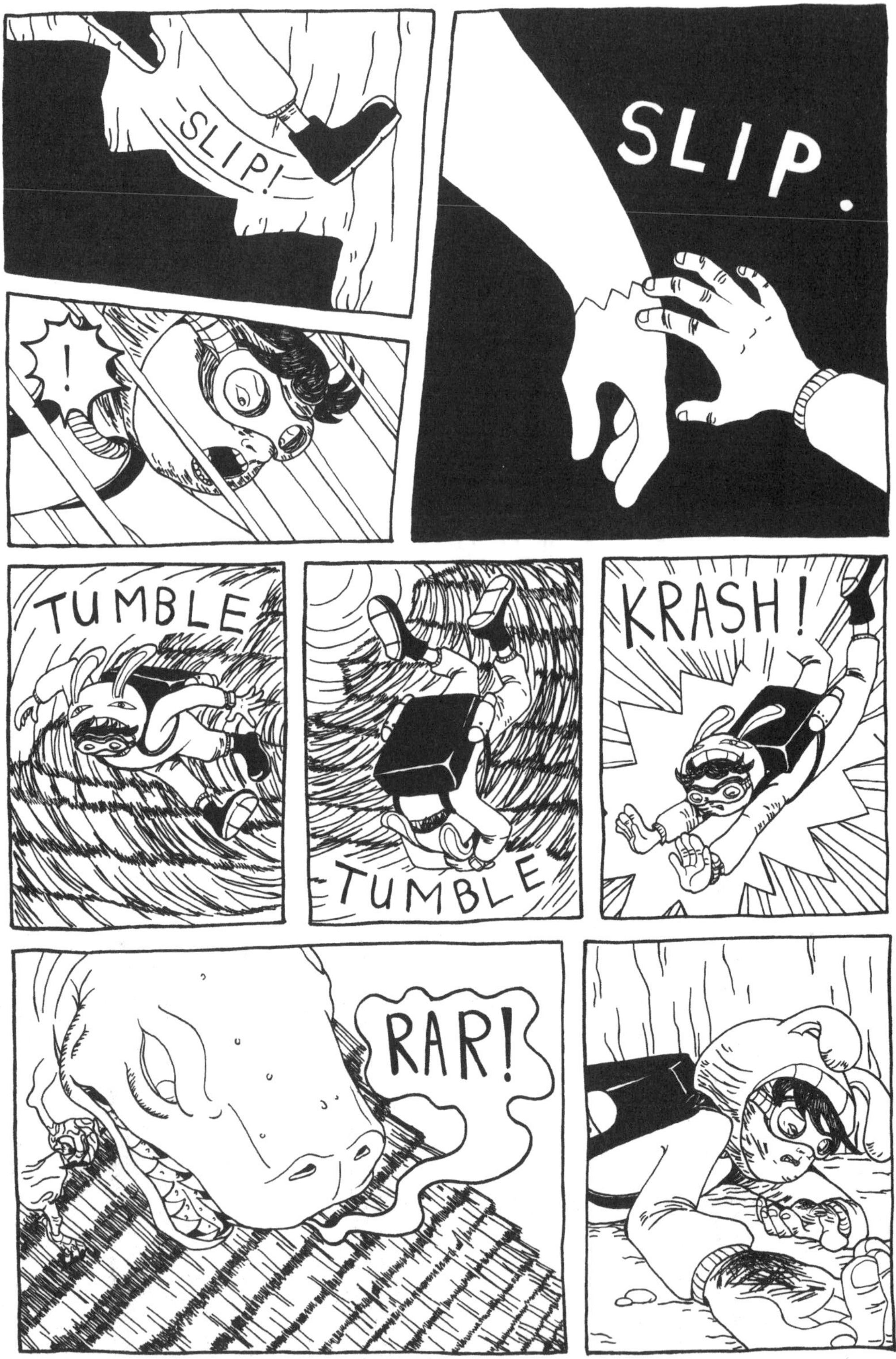
SLIP!
SLIP.
!
TUMBLE
TUMBLE
KRASH!
RAR!

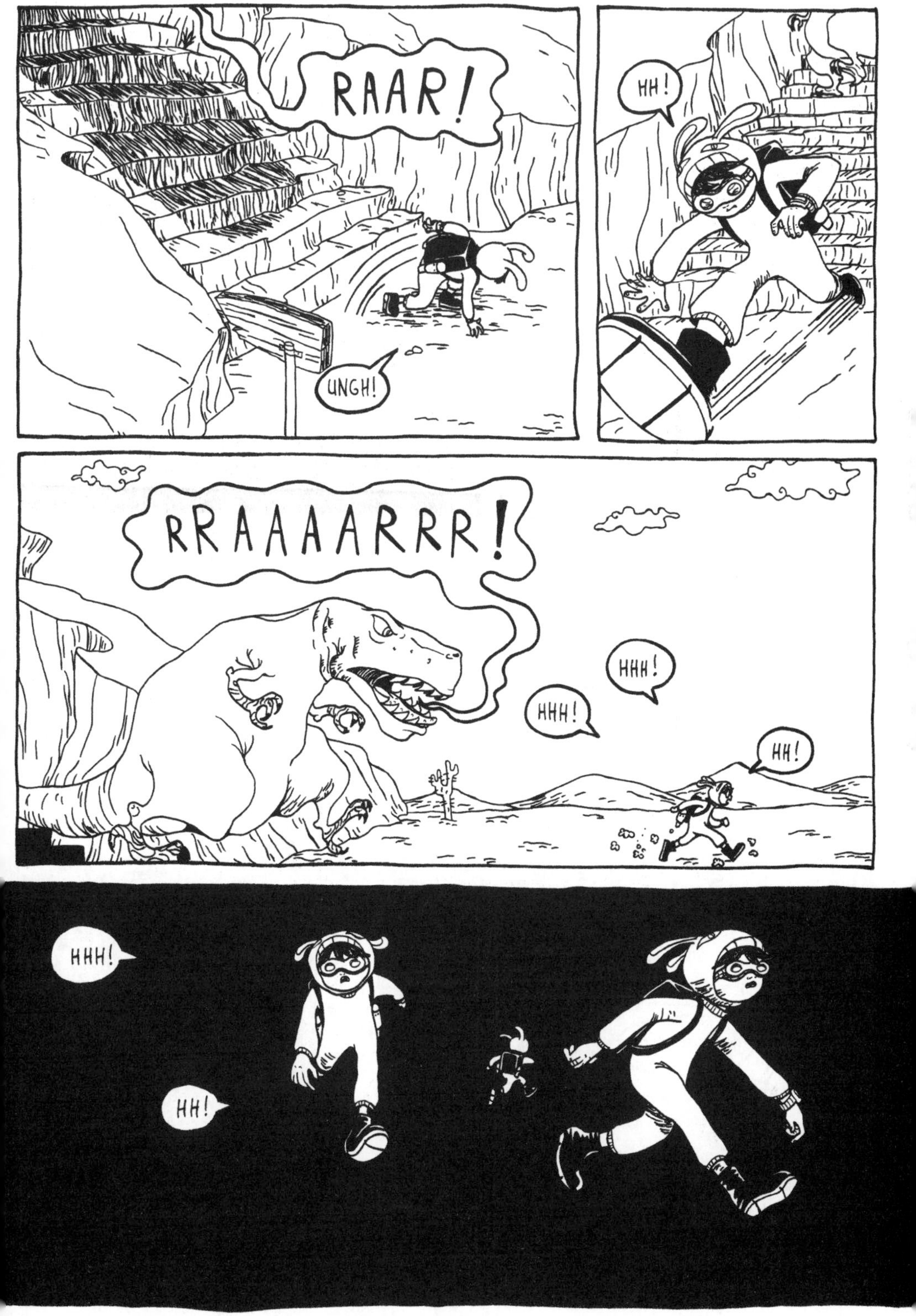
RAAR!
UNGH!
HH!
RRAAAARRR!
HHH!
HHH!
HH!
HHH!
HH!

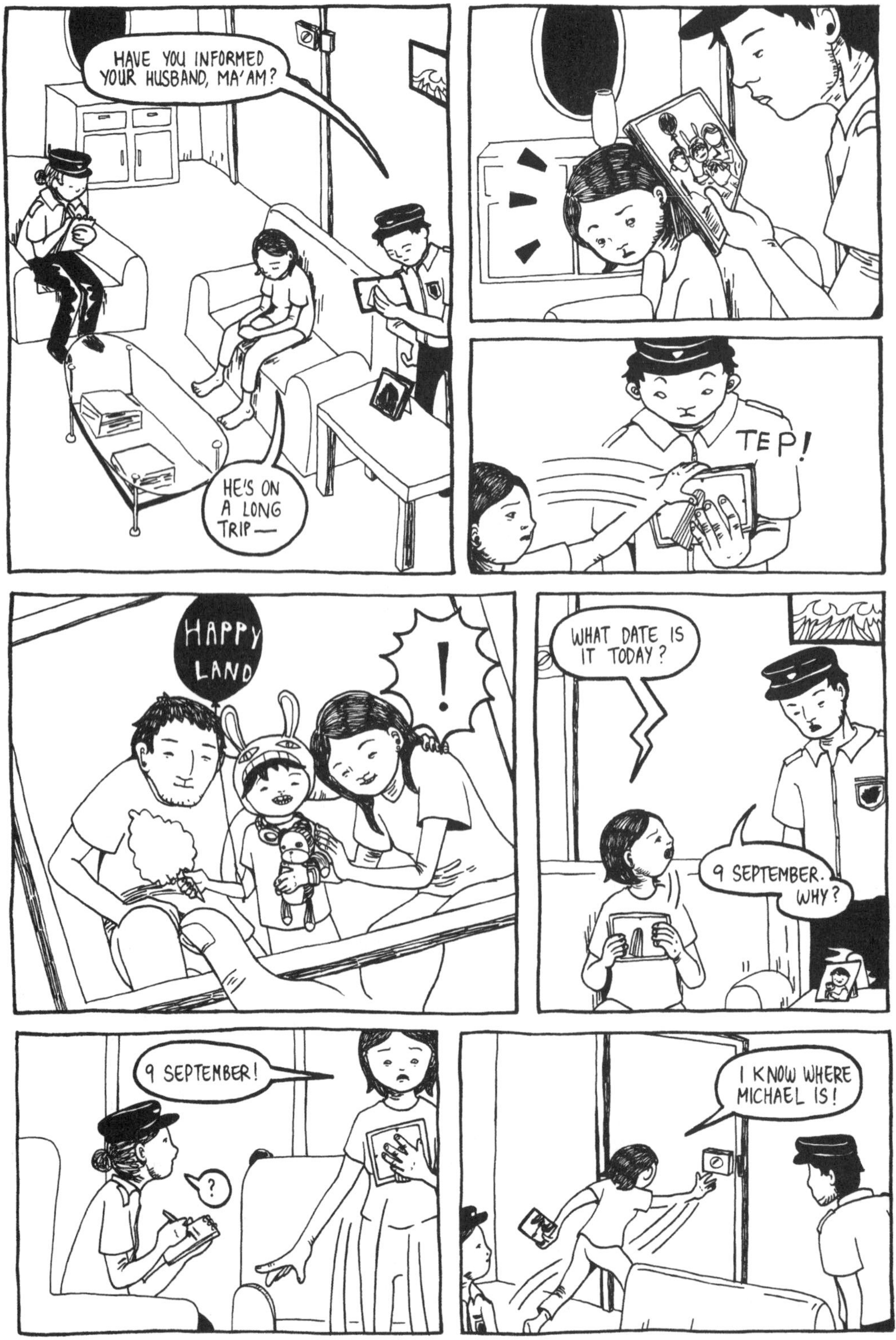
HAVE YOU INFORMED YOUR HUSBAND, MA'AM?
HE'S ON A LONG TRIP—
TEP!
HAPPY LAND
!
WHAT DATE IS IT TODAY?
9 SEPTEMBER. WHY?
9 SEPTEMBER!
?
I KNOW WHERE MICHAEL IS!

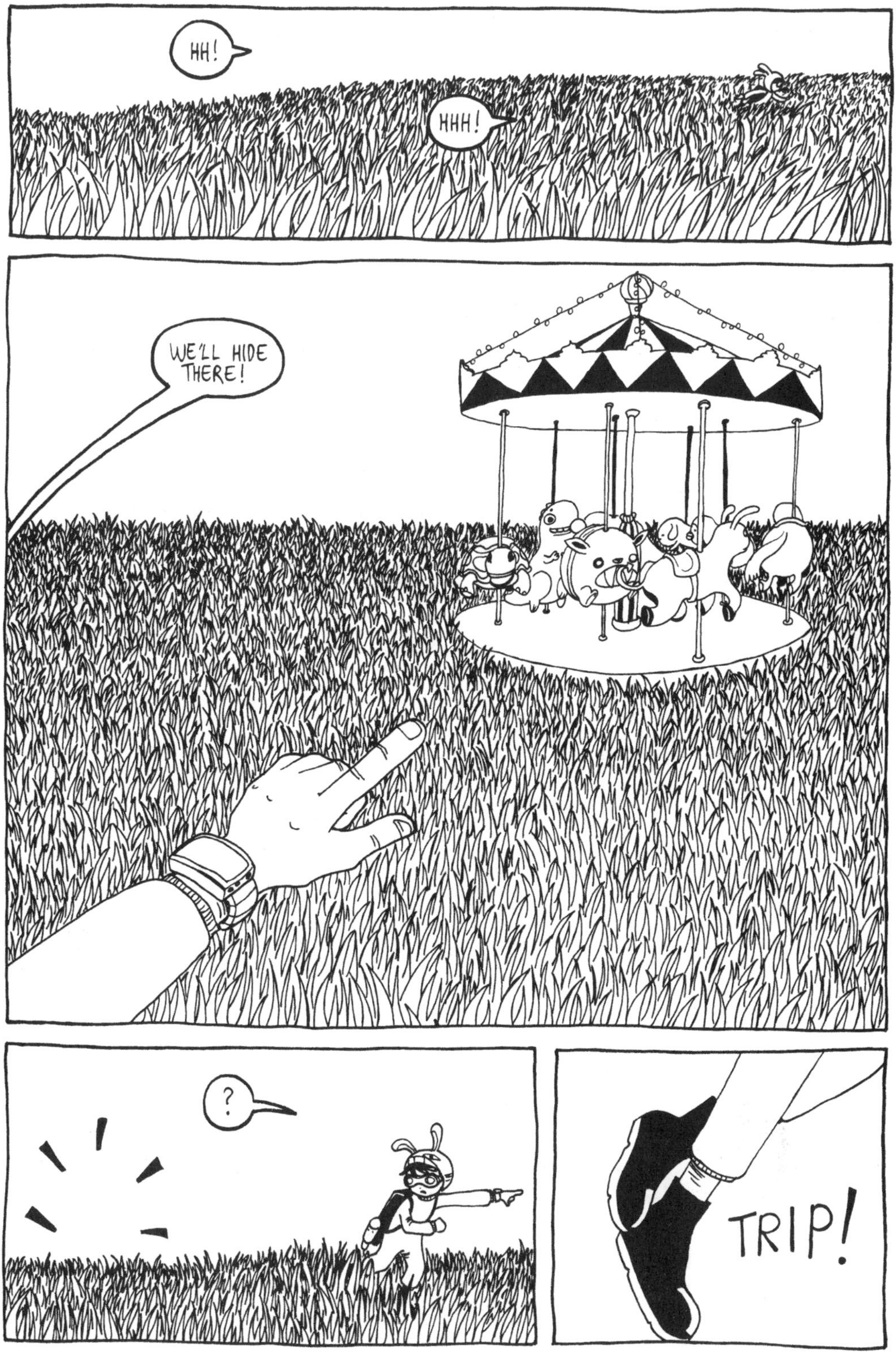
HH!
HHH!
WE'LL HIDE THERE!
?
TRIP!

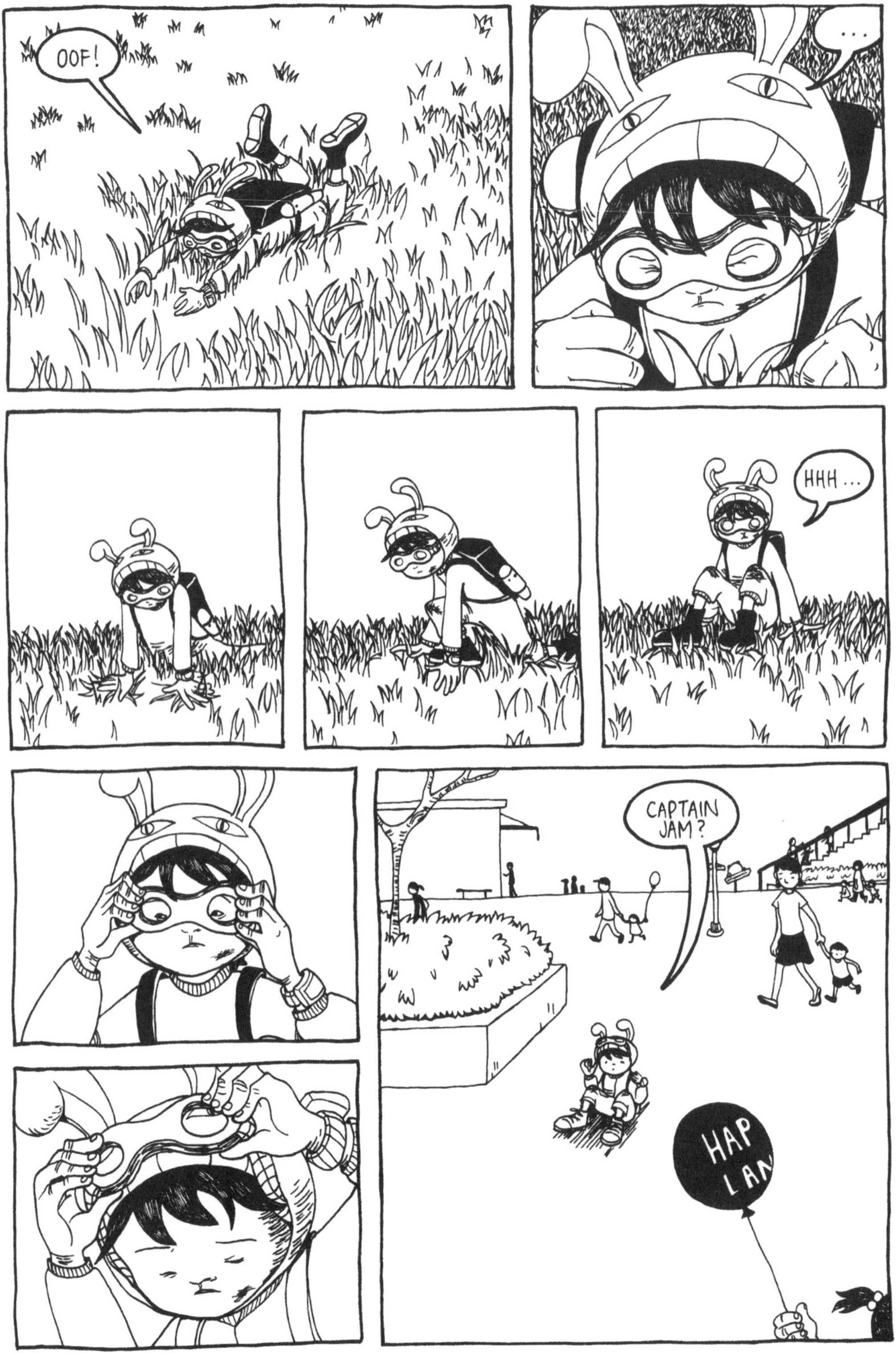
OOF!
...
HHH...
CAPTAIN JAM?
HAP
LAN

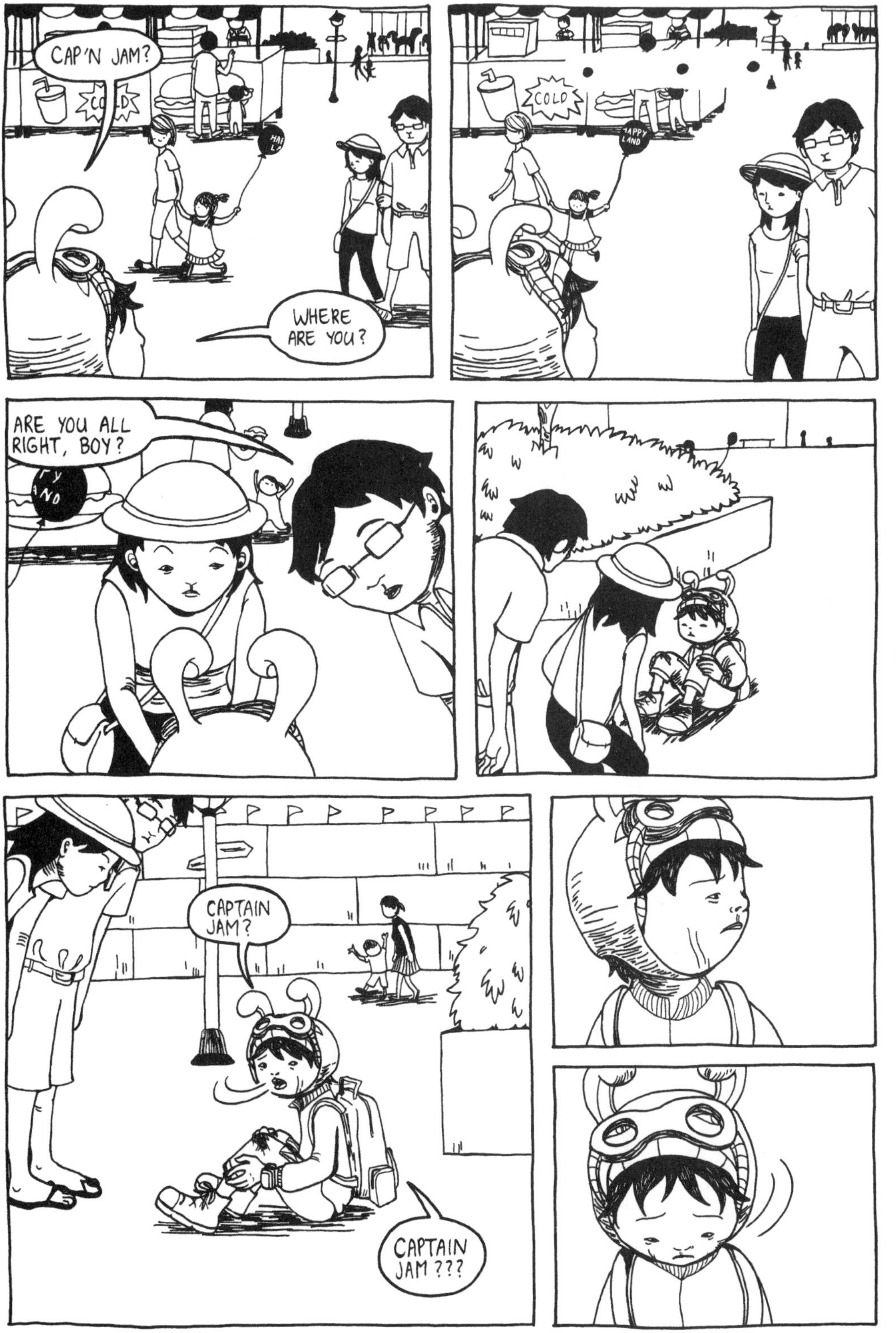
CAP'N JAM?
COLD
WHERE ARE YOU?
COLD
HAPPY LAND
ARE YOU ALL RIGHT, BOY?
CAPTAIN JAM?
CAPTAIN JAM???

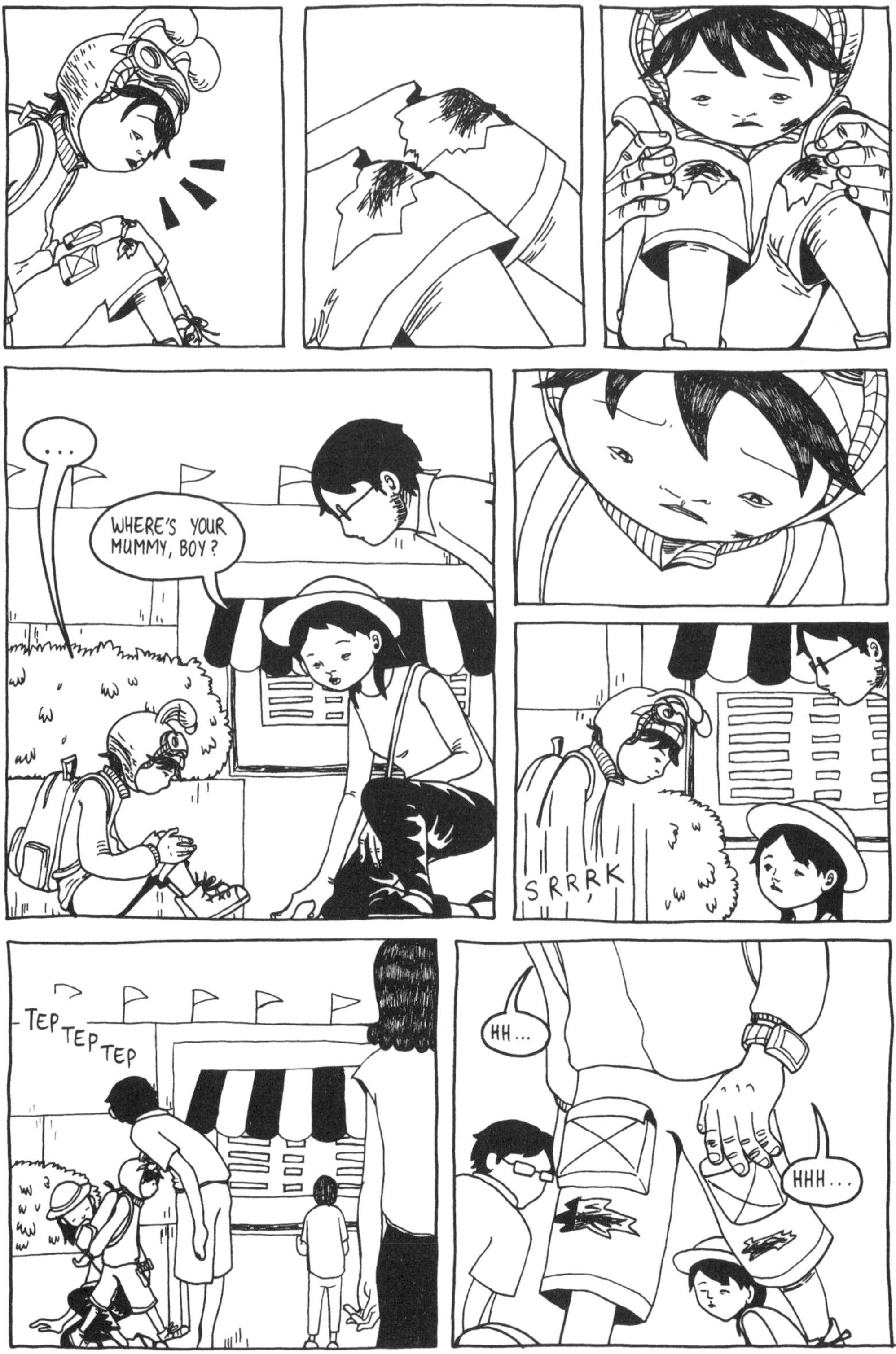
...
WHERE'S YOUR MUMMY, BOY?
SRRRK
TEP TEP TEP
HH...
HHH...

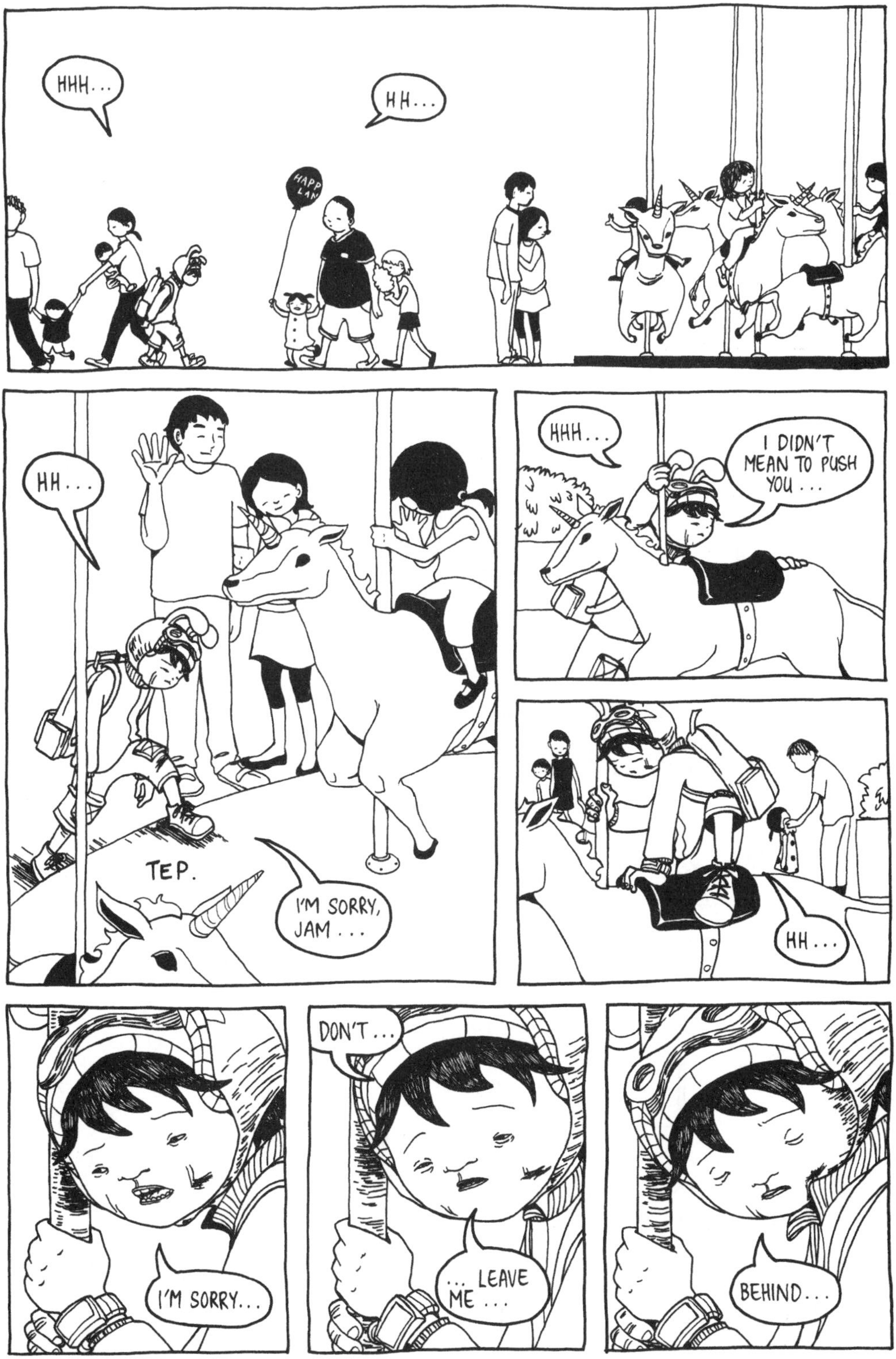
HHH...
HH...
HAPPY LAN
HH...
HHH...
I DIDN'T MEAN TO PUSH YOU...
TEP.
I'M SORRY, JAM...
HH...
I'M SORRY...
DON'T...
... LEAVE ME...
BEHIND...

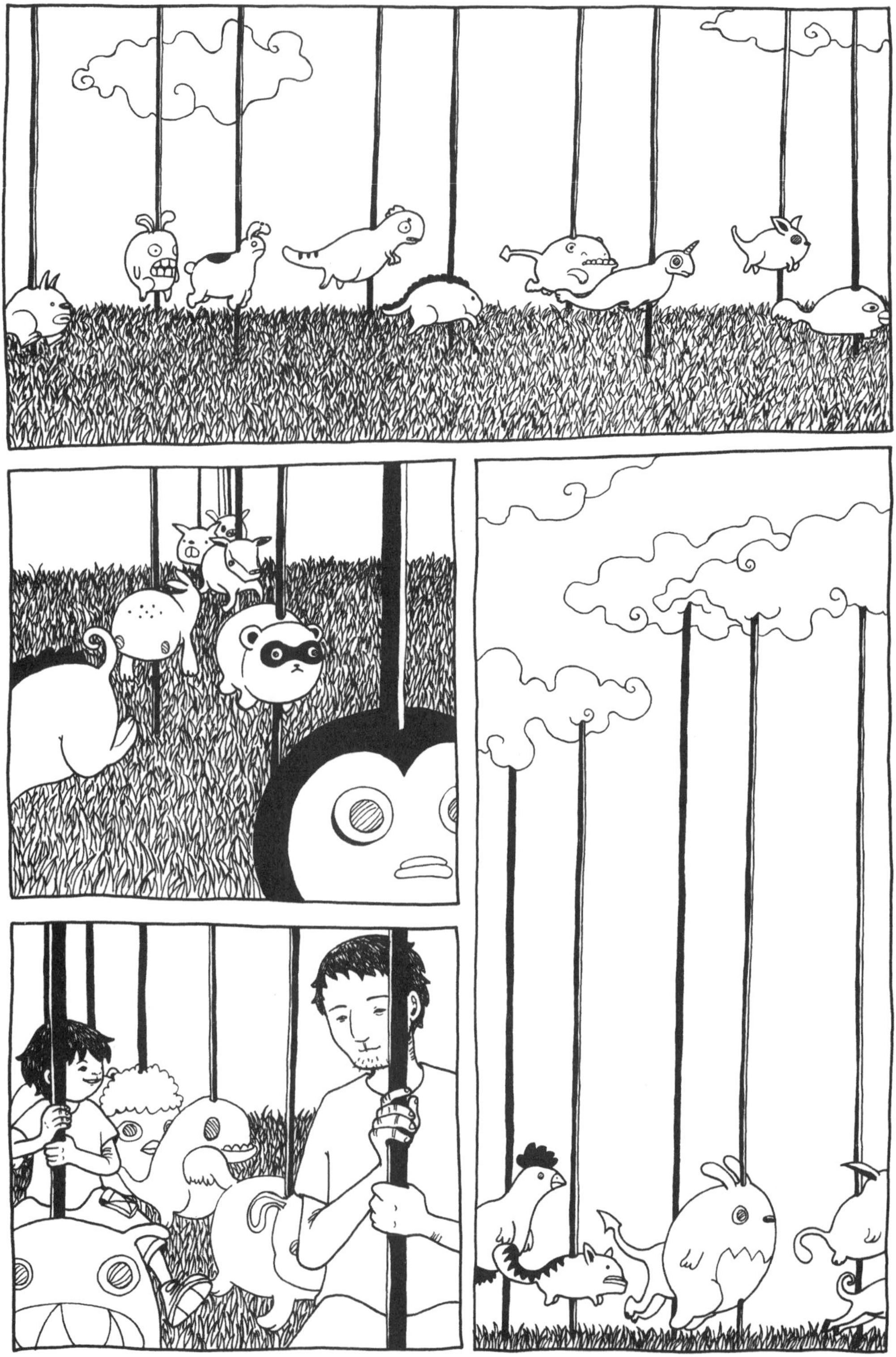

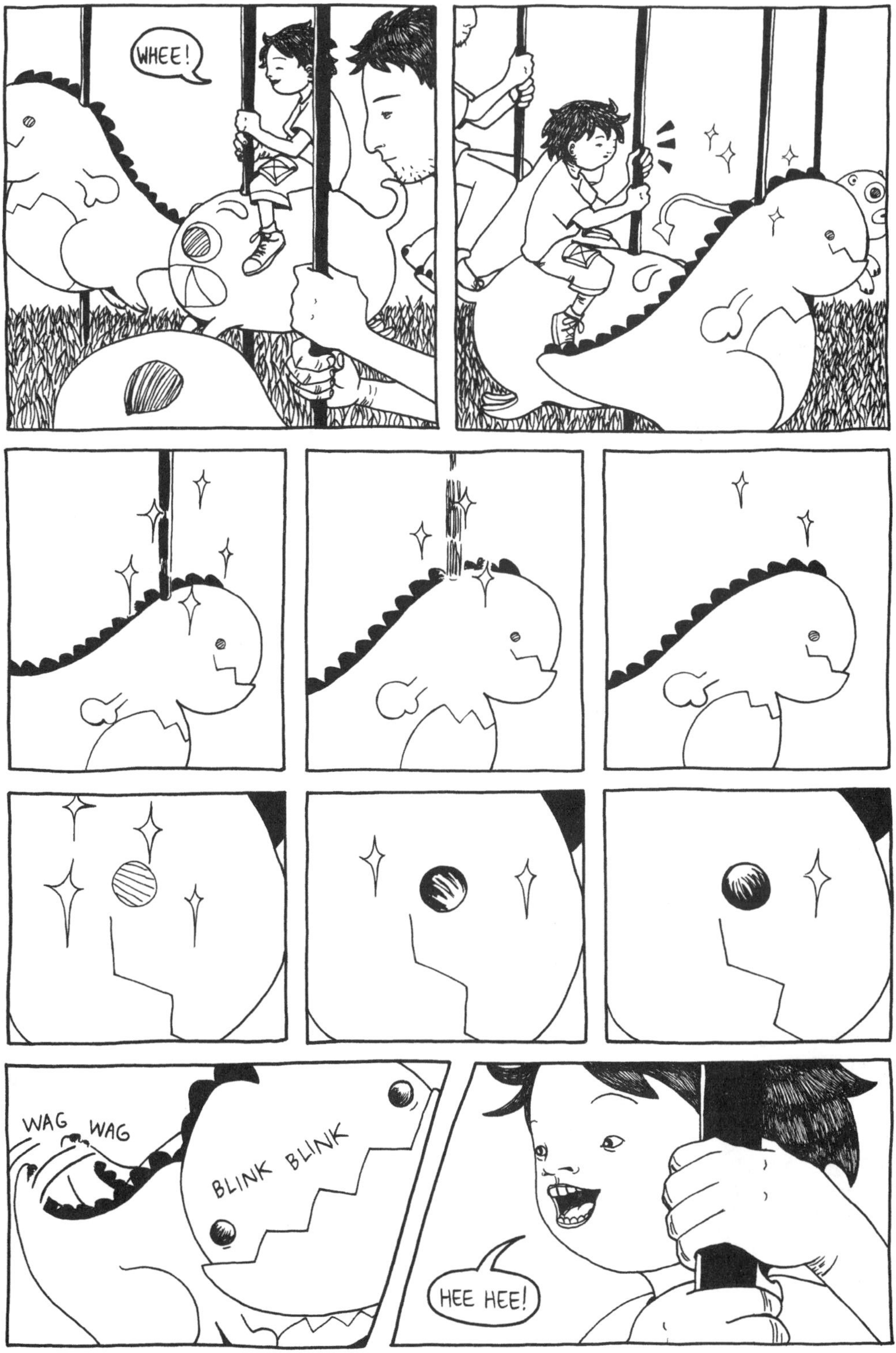
WHEE!
WAG WAG
BLINK BLINK
HEE HEE!

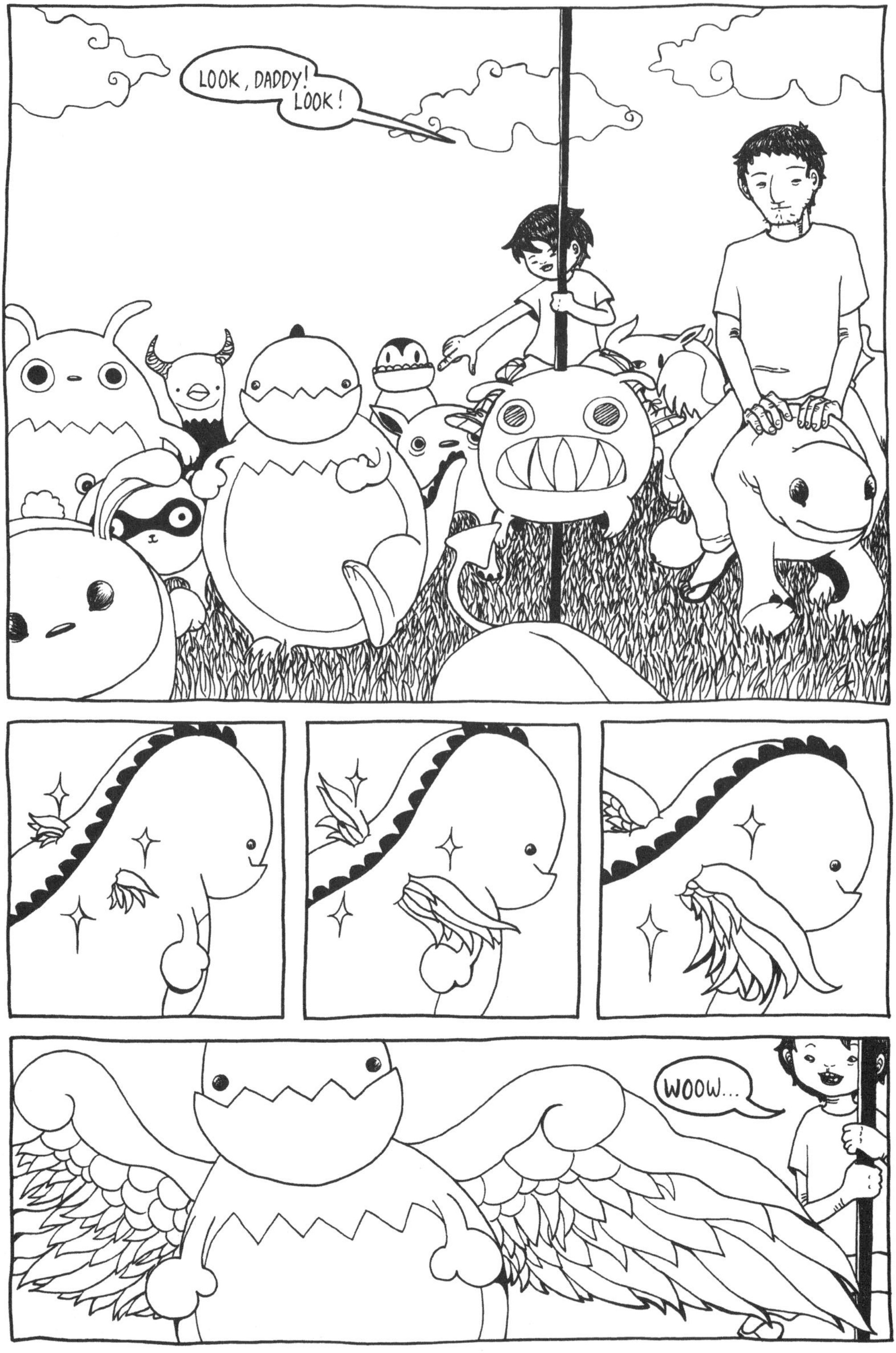

LOOK, DADDY! LOOK!
WOOW...

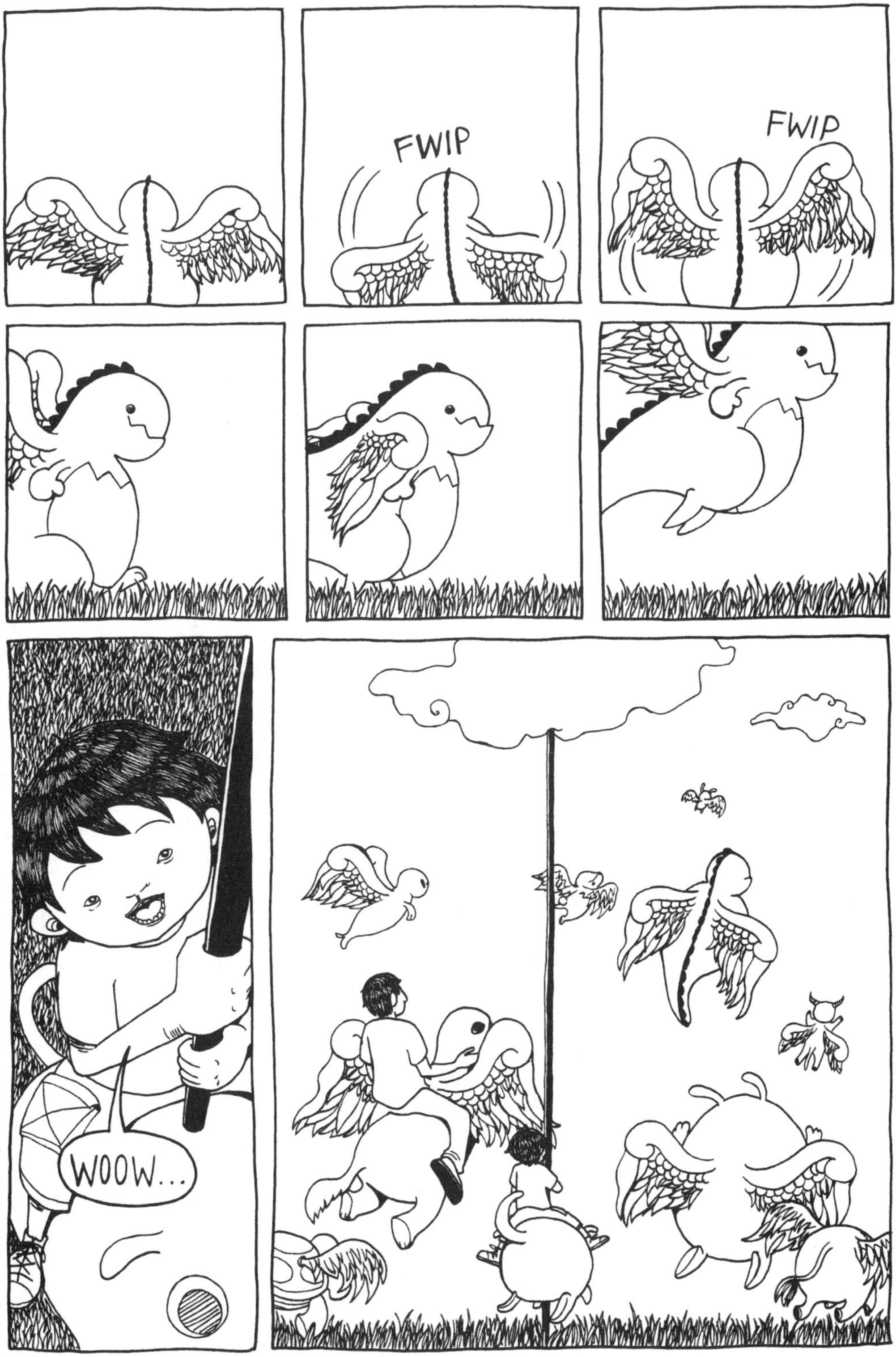
FWIP
FWIP
WOOW...

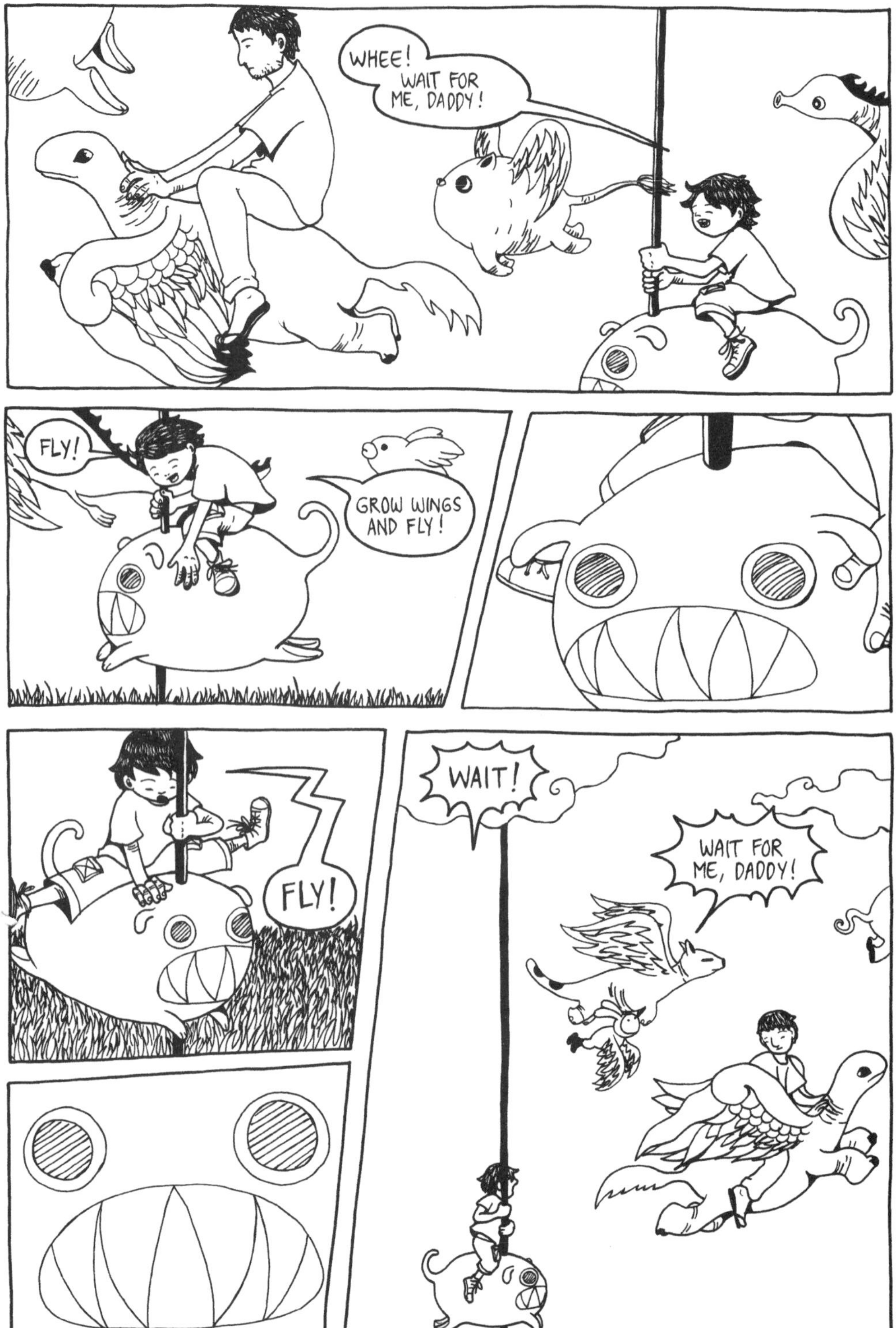
WHEE! WAIT FOR ME, DADDY!
FLY!
GROW WINGS AND FLY!
FLY!
WAIT!
WAIT FOR ME, DADDY!

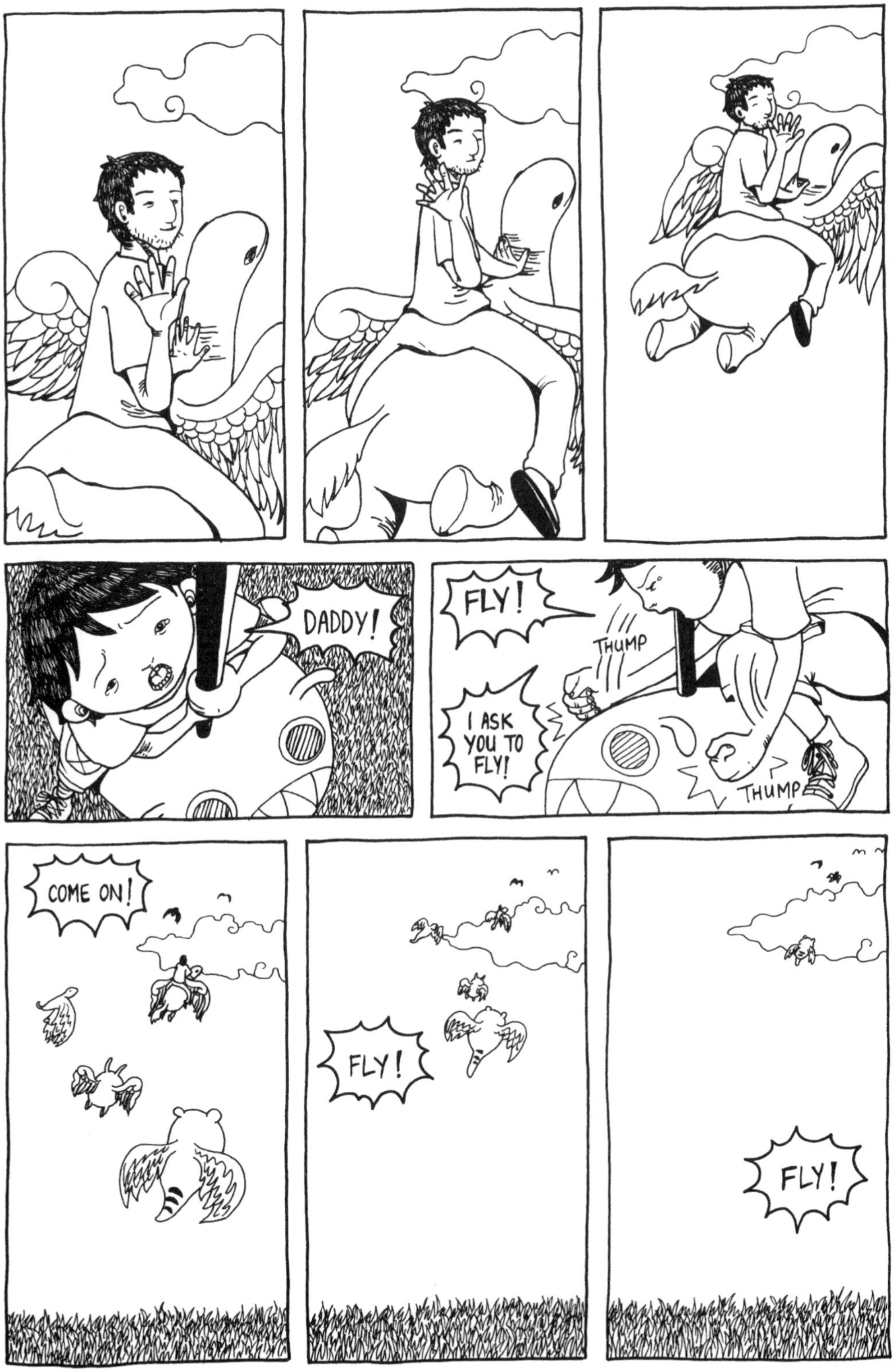
DADDY!
FLY!
THUMP
I ASK YOU TO FLY!
THUMP
COME ON!
FLY!
FLY!

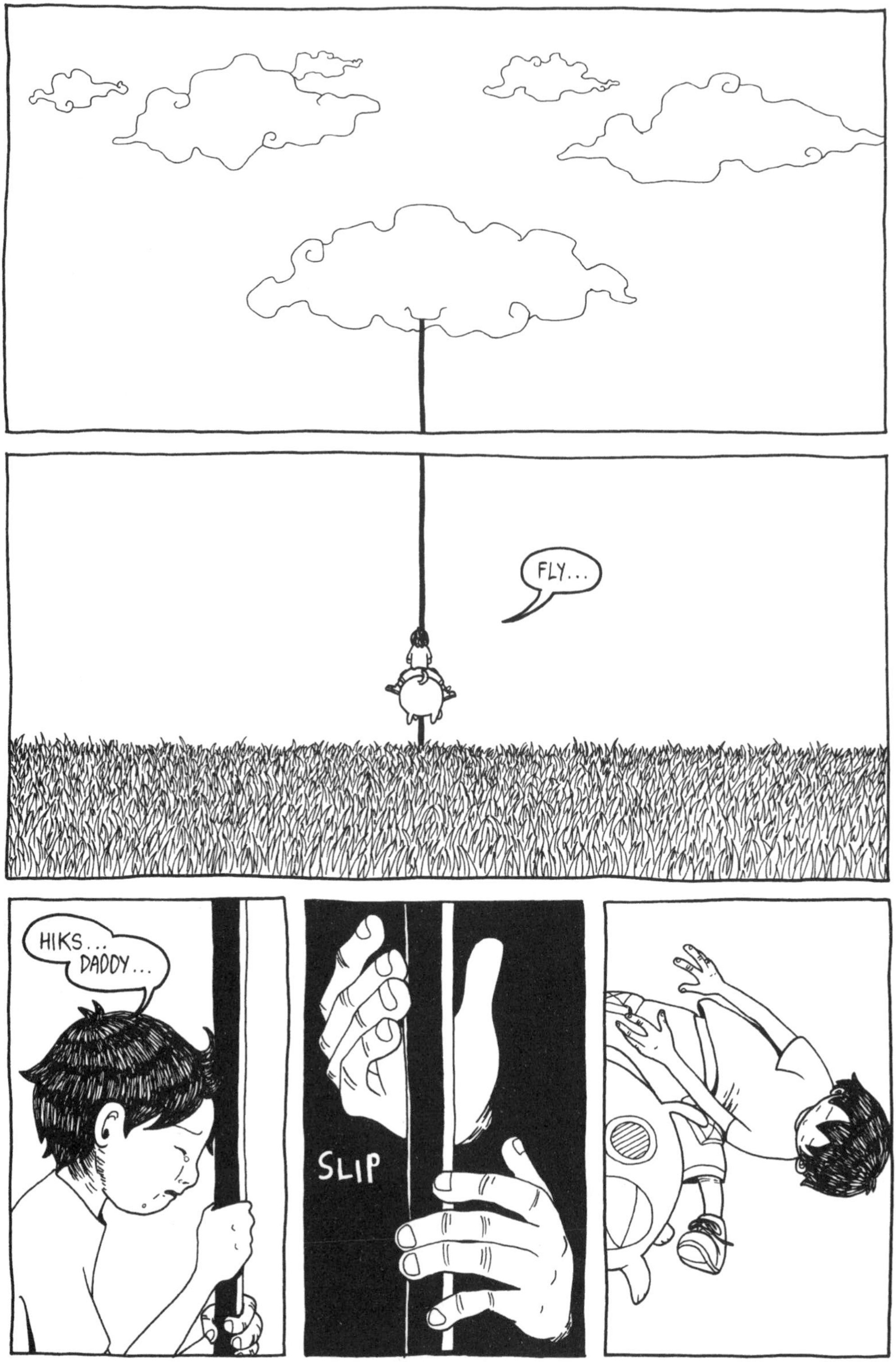
FLY...
HIKS... DADDY...
SLIP

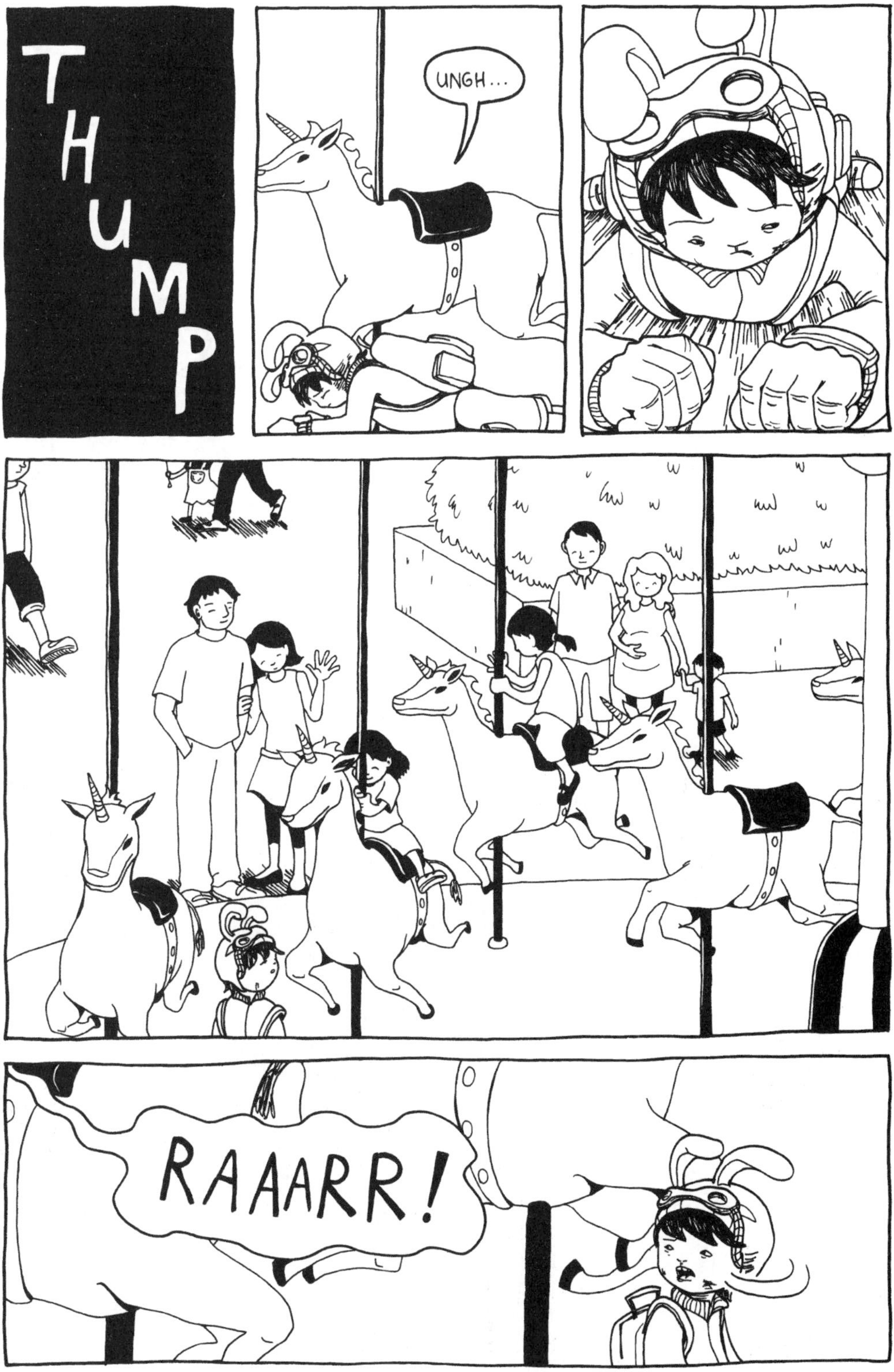
THUMP
UNGH...
RAAARR!

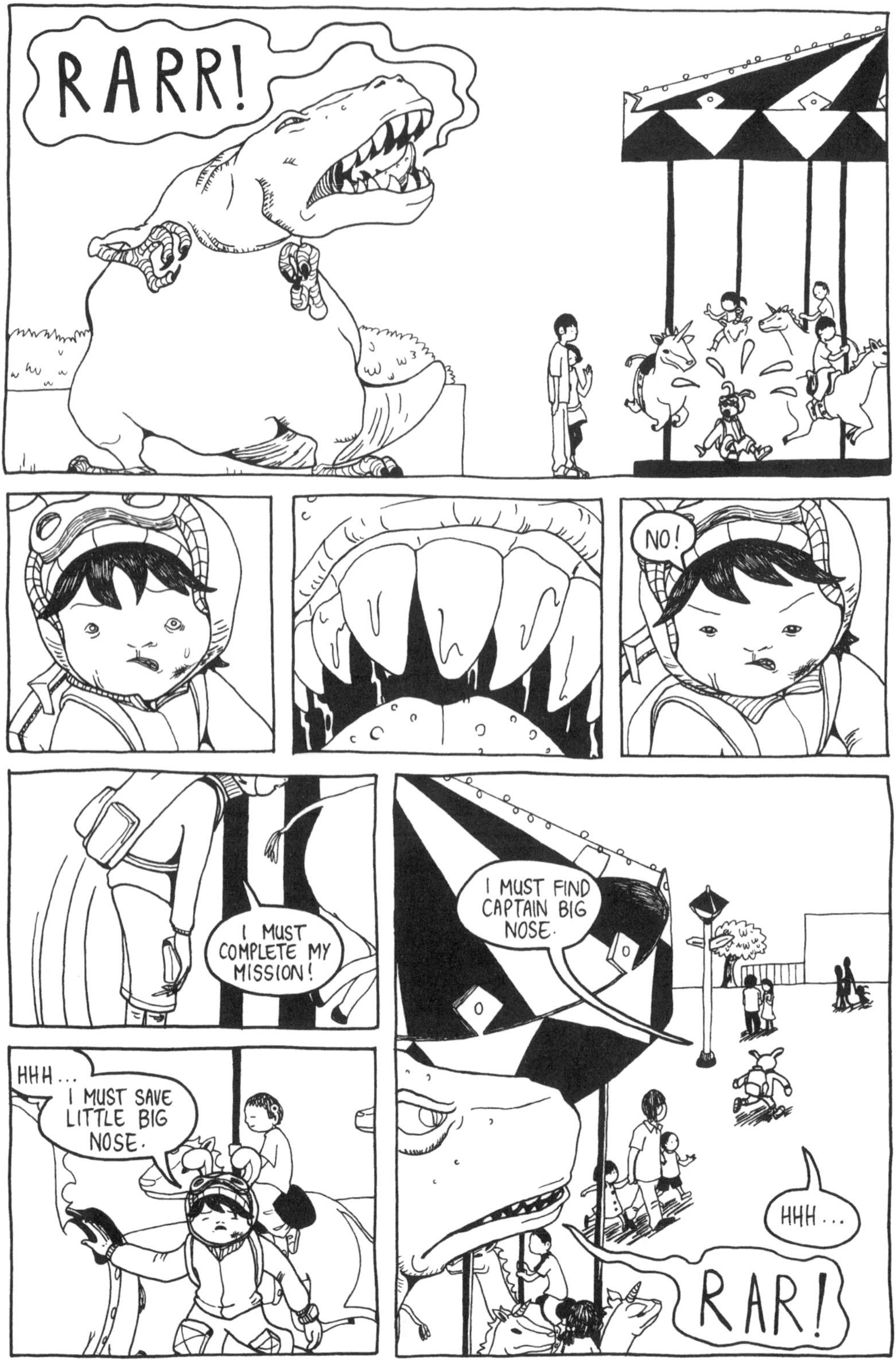
RARR!
NO!
I MUST COMPLETE MY MISSION!
I MUST FIND CAPTAIN BIG NOSE.
HHH...
I MUST SAVE LITTLE BIG NOSE.
HHH...
RAR!

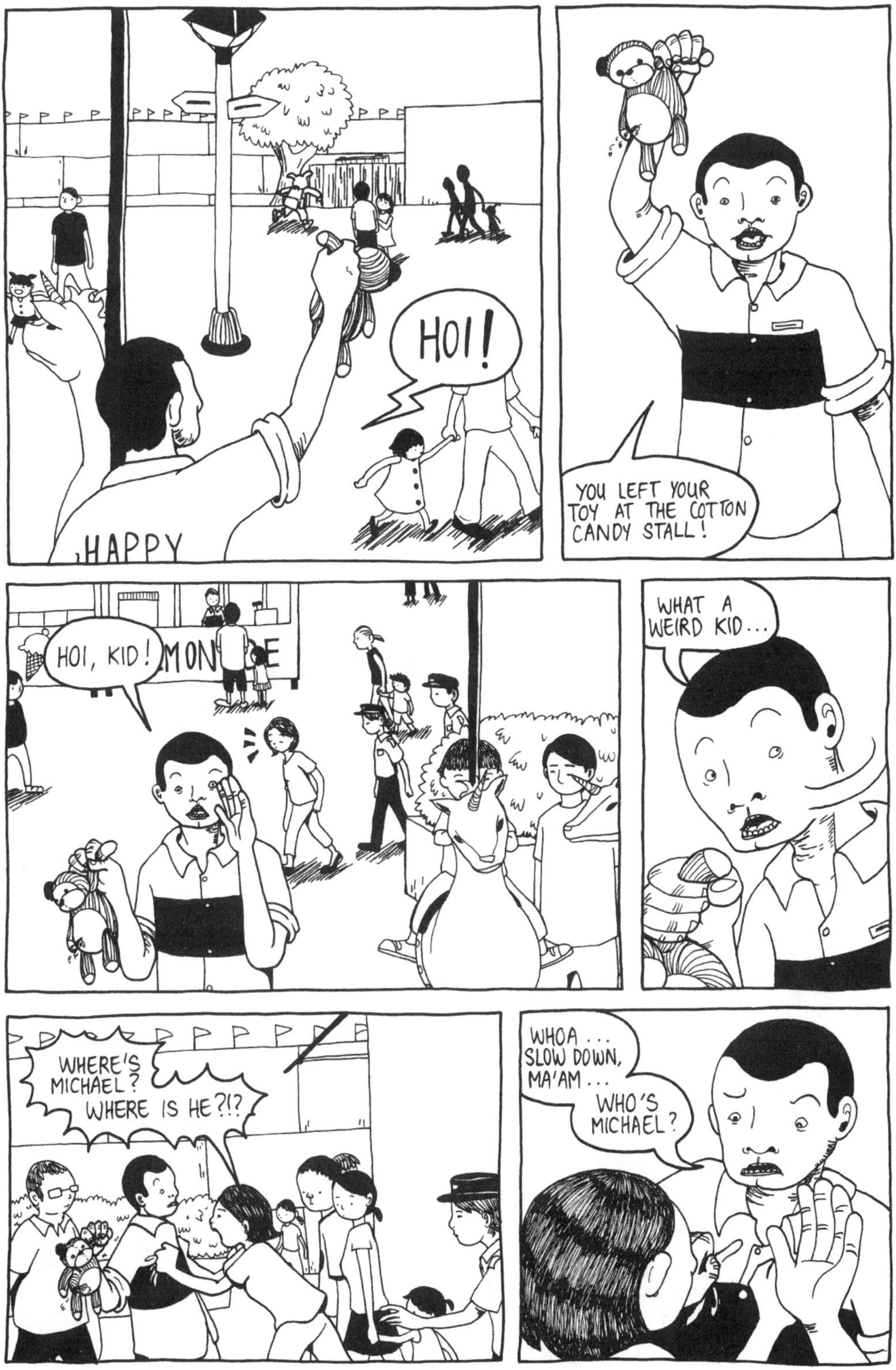
HAPPY
HOI!
YOU LEFT YOUR TOY AT THE COTTON CANDY STALL!
HOI, KID!
MON E
WHAT A WEIRD KID...
WHERE'S MICHAEL? WHERE IS HE?!?
WHOA... SLOW DOWN, MA'AM...
WHO'S MICHAEL?

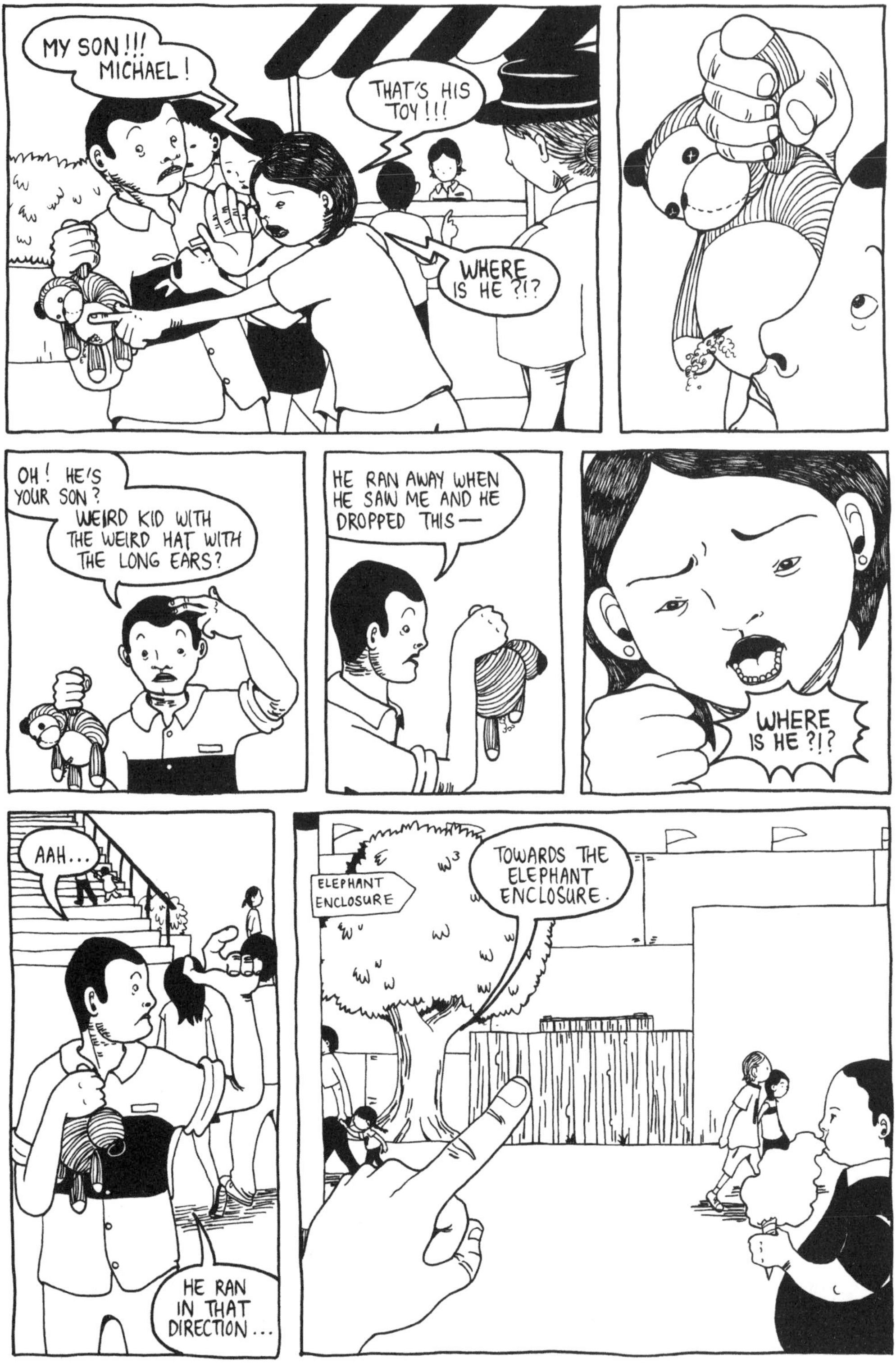
MY SON!!! MICHAEL!
THAT'S HIS TOY!!!
WHERE IS HE ?!?
OH! HE'S YOUR SON? WEIRD KID WITH THE WEIRD HAT WITH THE LONG EARS?
HE RAN AWAY WHEN HE SAW ME AND HE DROPPED THIS—
WHERE IS HE ?!?
AAH...
HE RAN IN THAT DIRECTION...
ELEPHANT ENCLOSURE
TOWARDS THE ELEPHANT ENCLOSURE.

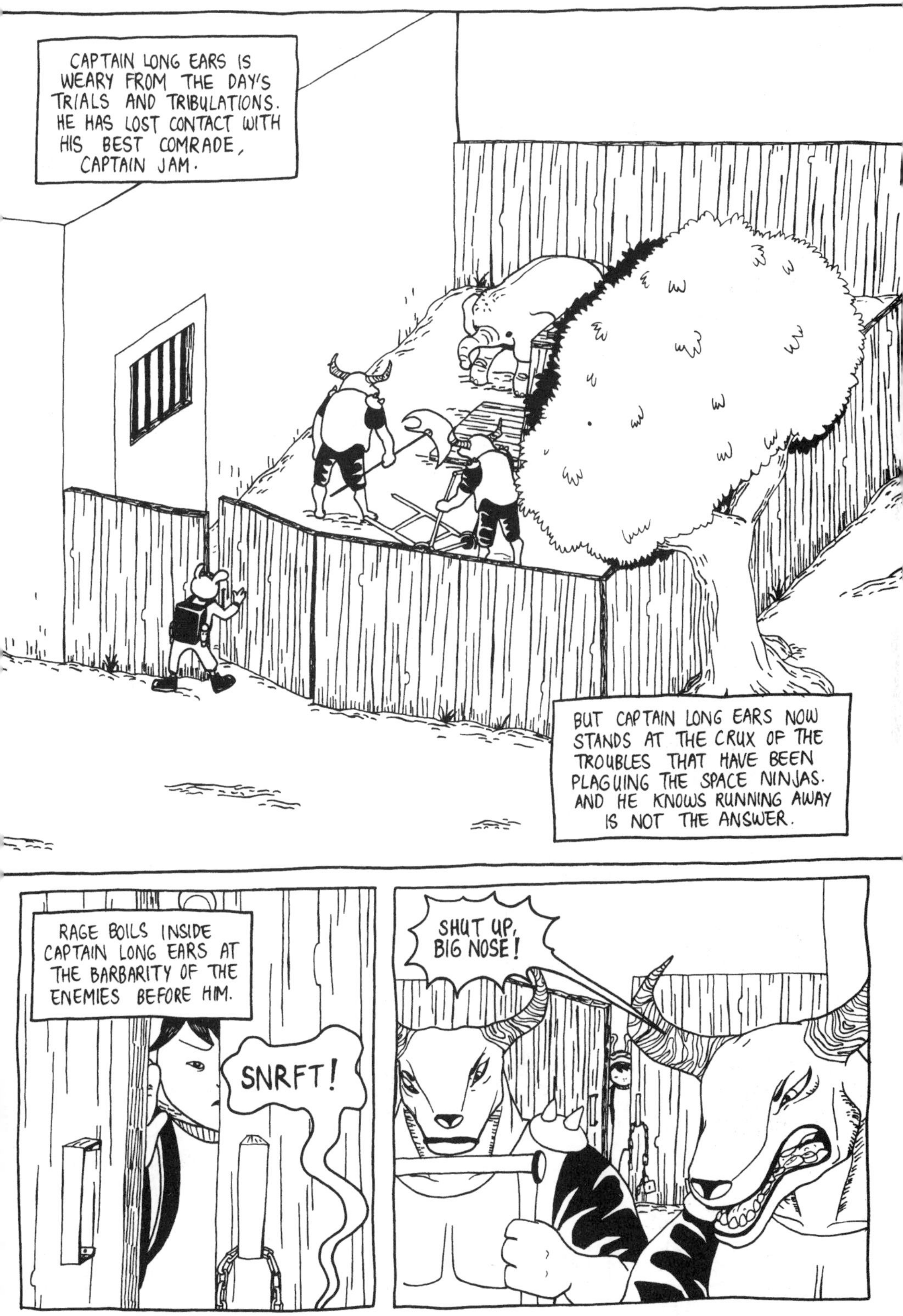
CAPTAIN LONG EARS IS WEARY FROM THE DAY'S TRIALS AND TRIBULATIONS. HE HAS LOST CONTACT WITH HIS BEST COMRADE, CAPTAIN JAM.
BUT CAPTAIN LONG EARS NOW STANDS AT THE CRUX OF THE TROUBLES THAT HAVE BEEN PLAGUING THE SPACE NINJAS. AND HE KNOWS RUNNING AWAY IS NOT THE ANSWER.
RAGE BOILS INSIDE CAPTAIN LONG EARS AT THE BARBARITY OF THE ENEMIES BEFORE HIM.
SNRFT!
SHUT UP, BIG NOSE!

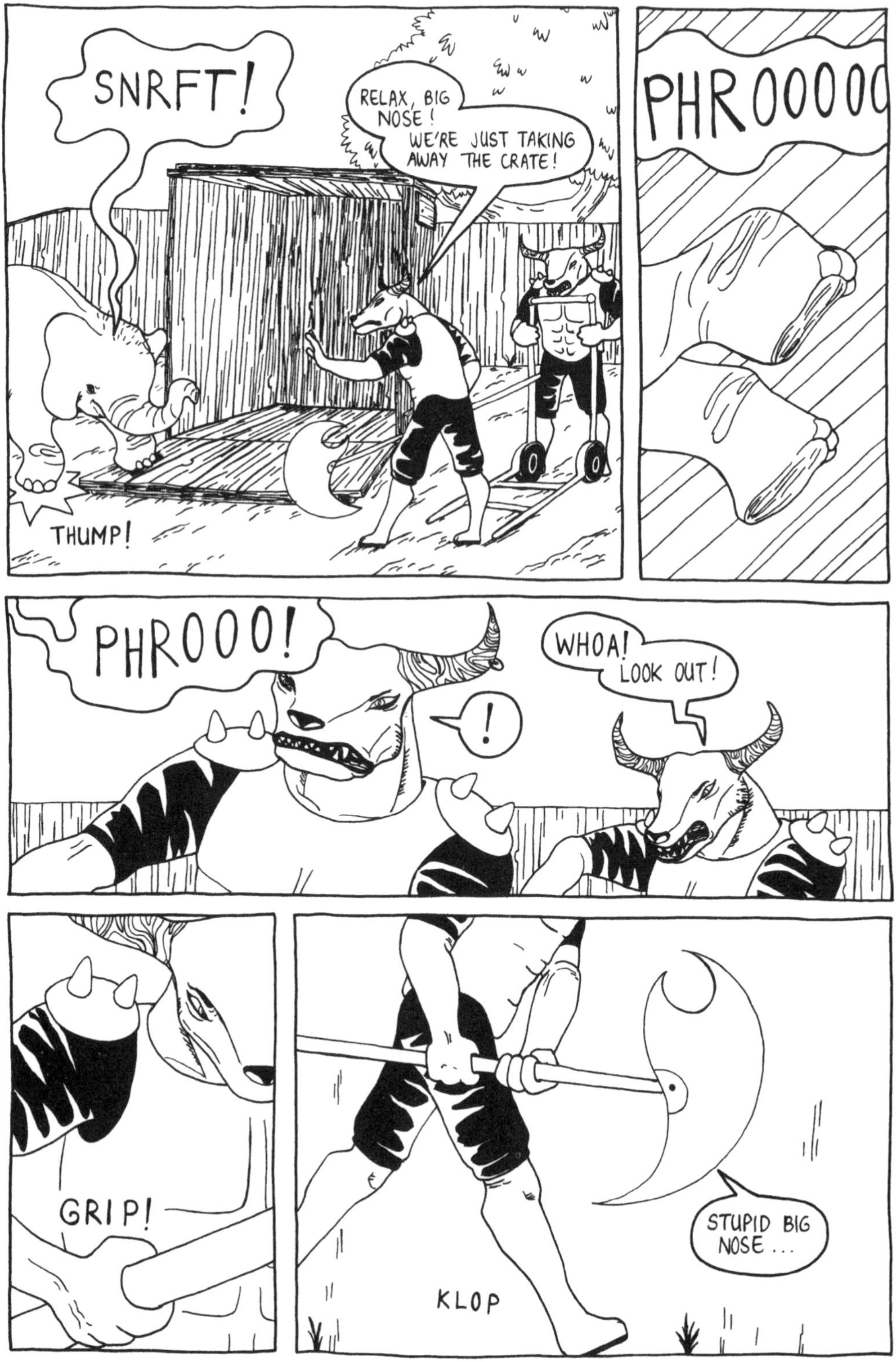
SNRFT!
RELAX, BIG NOSE!
WE'RE JUST TAKING AWAY THE CRATE!
THUMP!
PHROOOOO
PHROOO!
!
WHOA!
LOOK OUT!
GRIP!
STUPID BIG NOSE...
KLOP

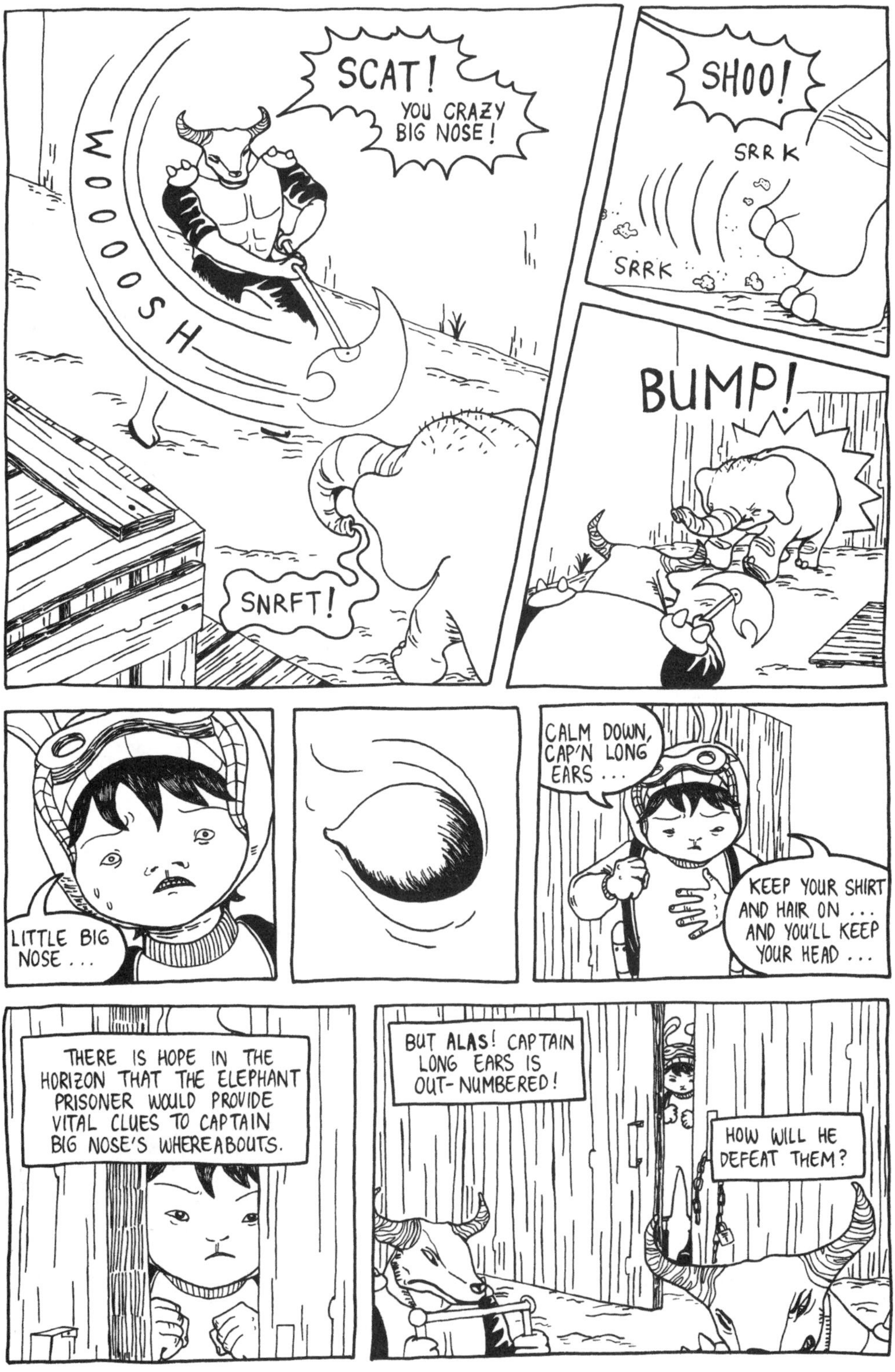
SCAT!
YOU CRAZY BIG NOSE!
WOOOOOSH
SNRFT!
SHOO!
SRRK
SRRK
BUMP!
LITTLE BIG NOSE . . .
CALM DOWN, CAP'N LONG EARS . . .
KEEP YOUR SHIRT AND HAIR ON . . . AND YOU'LL KEEP YOUR HEAD . . .
THERE IS HOPE IN THE HORIZON THAT THE ELEPHANT PRISONER WOULD PROVIDE VITAL CLUES TO CAPTAIN BIG NOSE'S WHEREABOUTS.
BUT ALAS! CAPTAIN LONG EARS IS OUT-NUMBERED!
HOW WILL HE DEFEAT THEM?

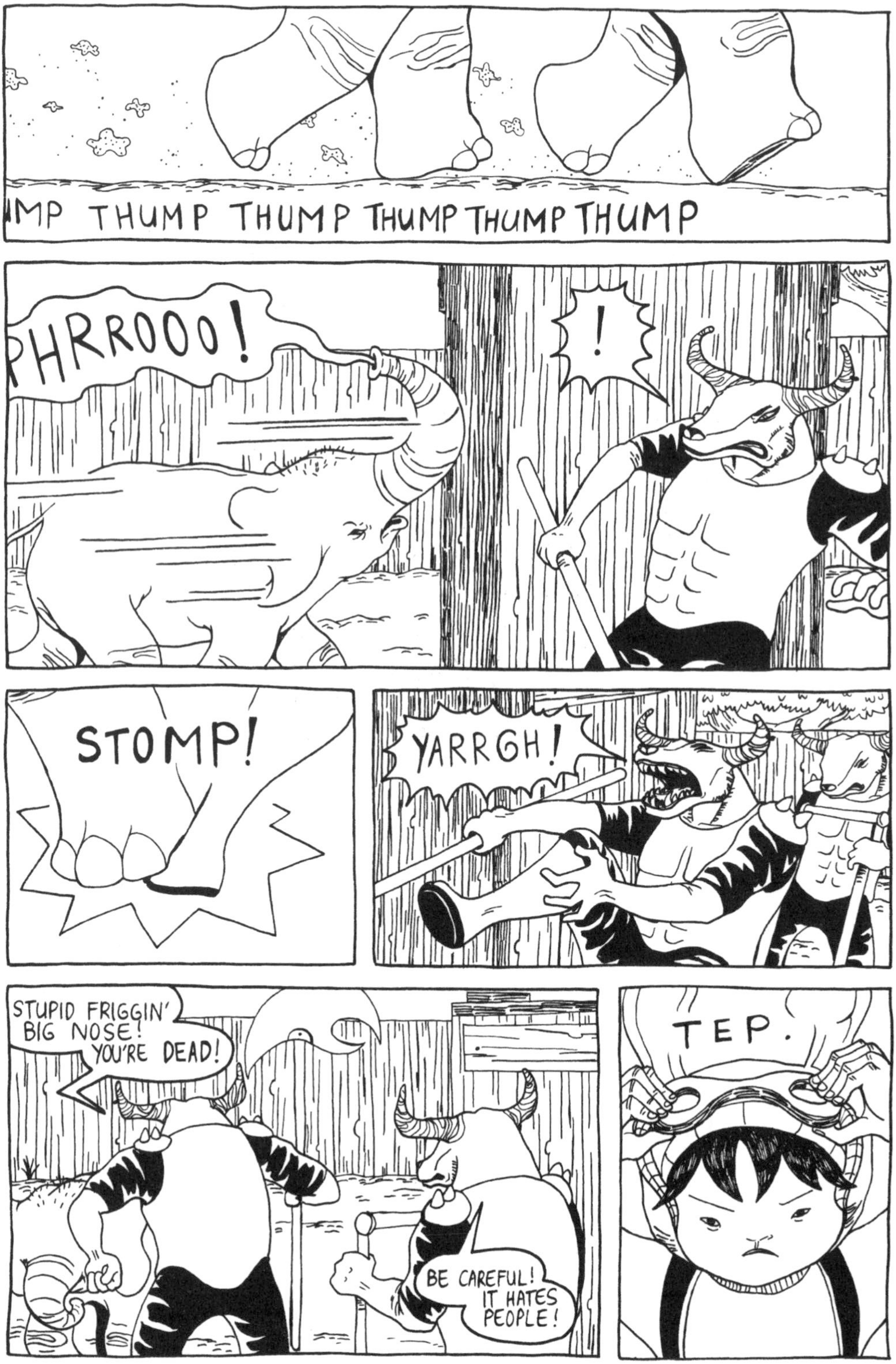
MP THUMP THUMP THUMP THUMP THUMP
PHRROOO!
!
STOMP!
YARRGH!
STUPID FRIGGIN' BIG NOSE! YOU'RE DEAD!
BE CAREFUL! IT HATES PEOPLE!
TEP.

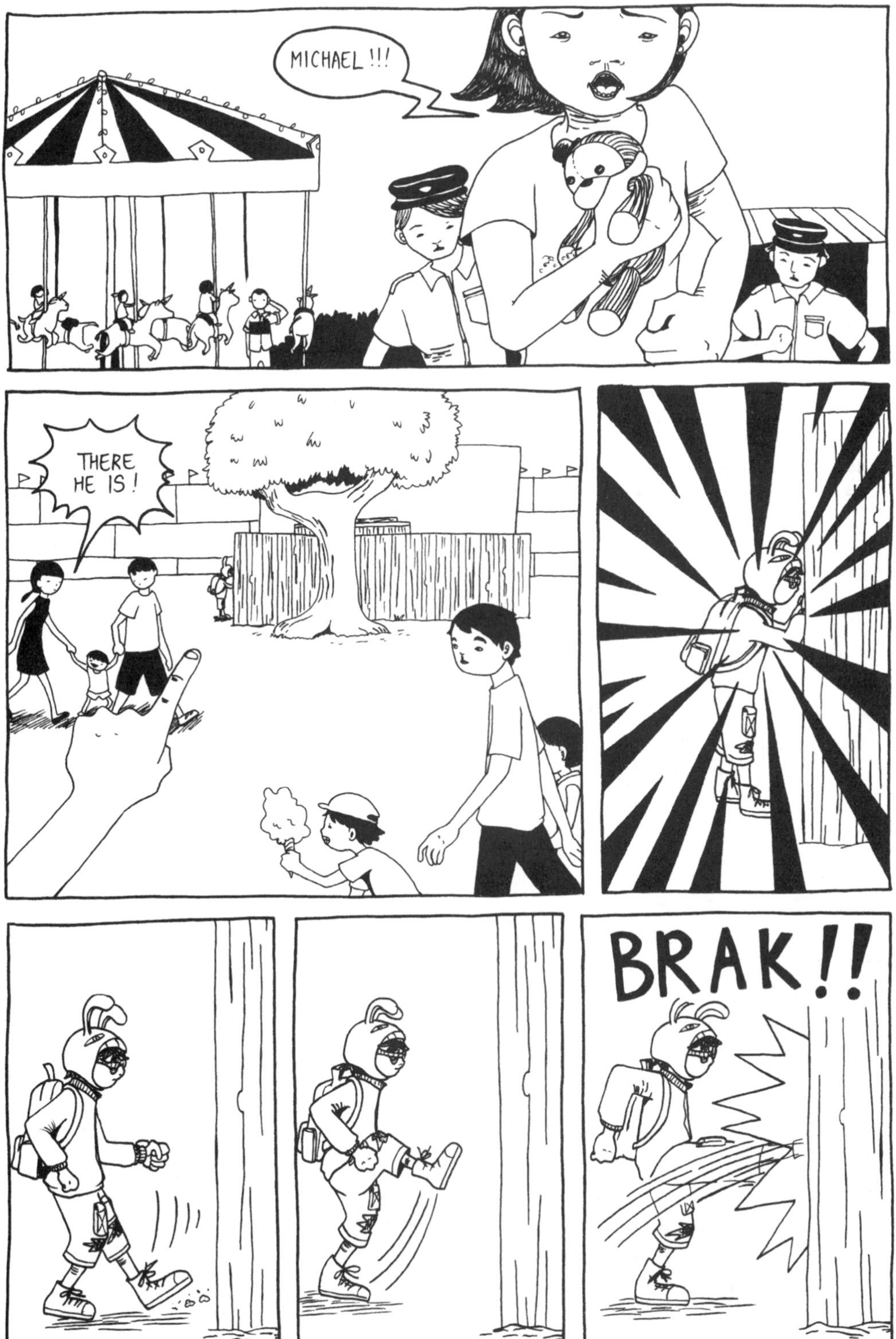
MICHAEL!!!
THERE HE IS!
BRAK!!

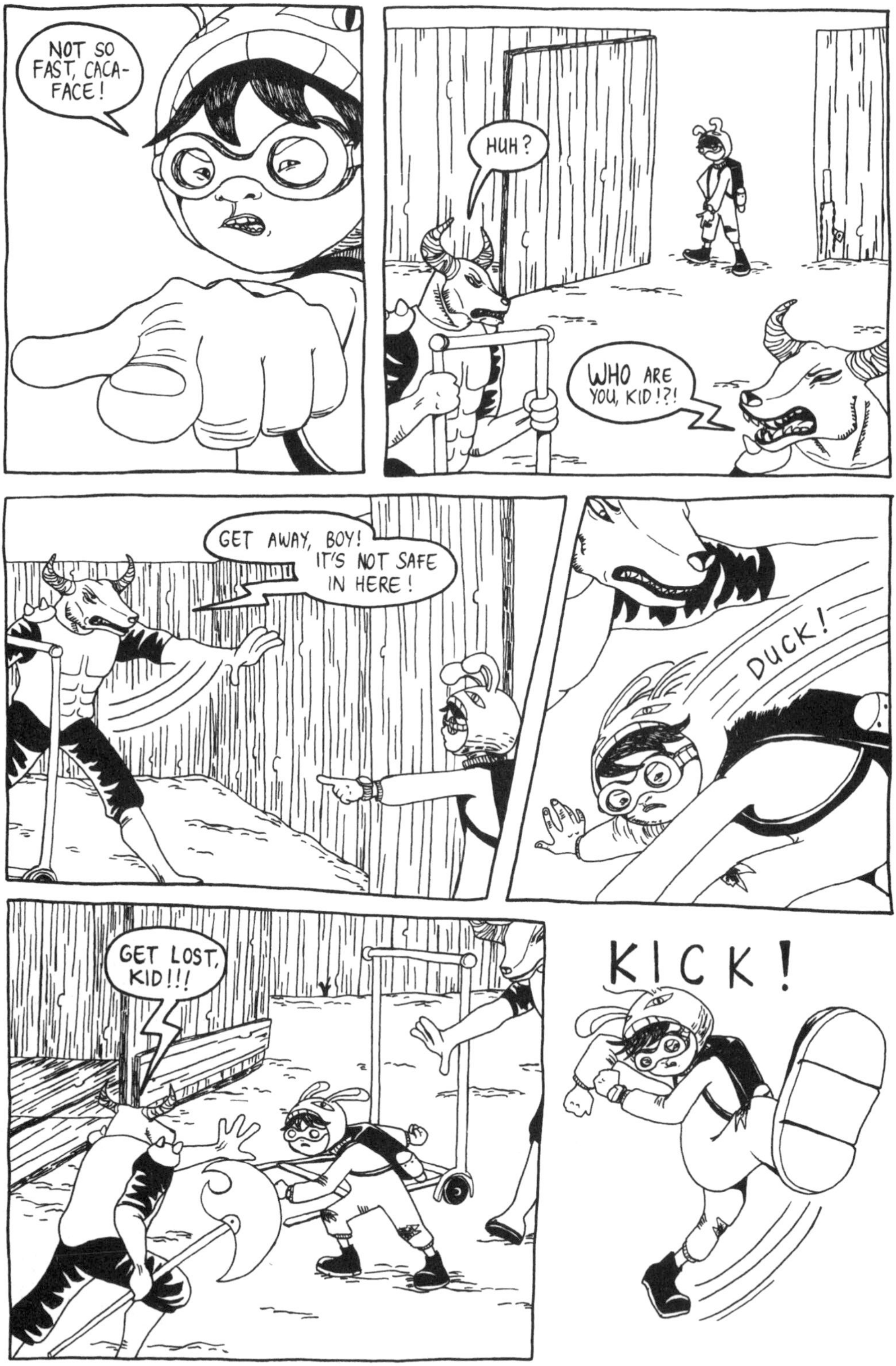
NOT SO FAST, CACA-FACE!
HUH?
WHO ARE YOU, KID!?!
GET AWAY, BOY! IT'S NOT SAFE IN HERE!
DUCK!
GET LOST, KID!!!
KICK!

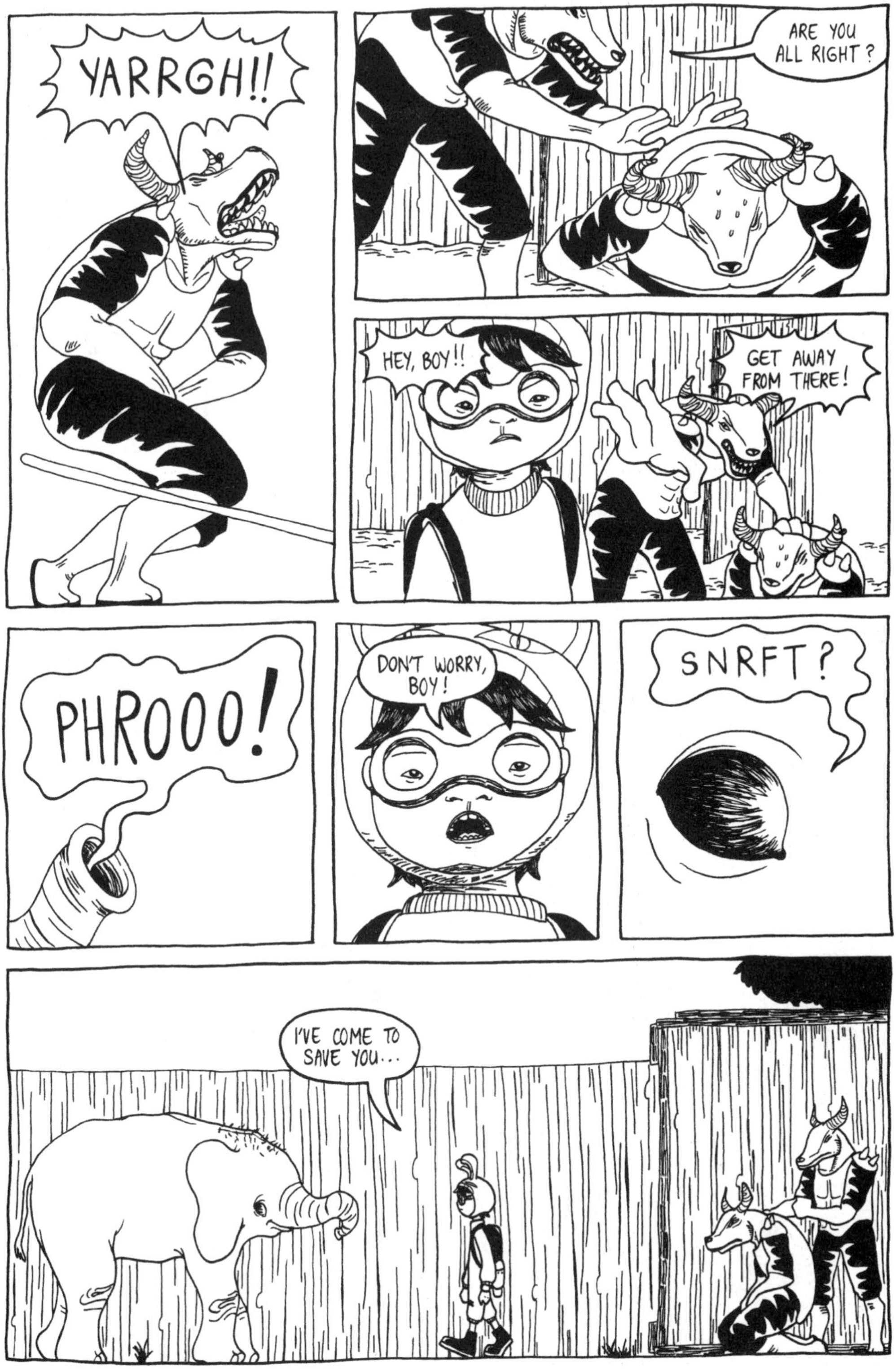
YARRGH!!
ARE YOU ALL RIGHT?
HEY, BOY!!
GET AWAY FROM THERE!
PHROOO!
DON'T WORRY, BOY!
SNRFT?
I'VE COME TO SAVE YOU...

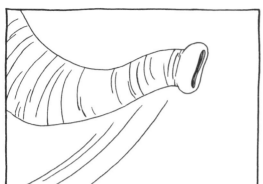

TEP.

EVERYTHING'S GONNA BE ALL RIGHT, BOY...

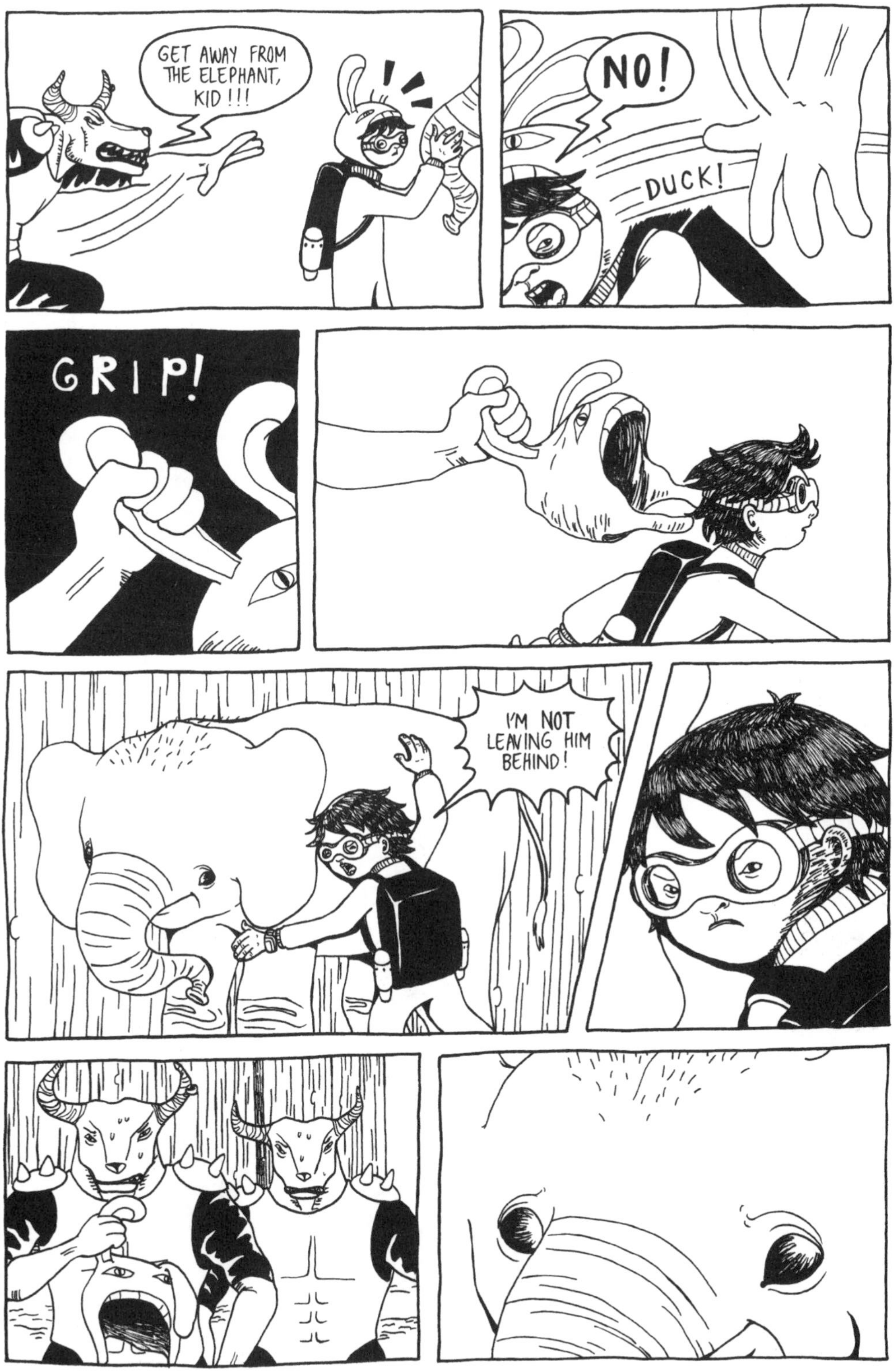
GET AWAY FROM THE ELEPHANT, KID!!!
NO!
DUCK!
GRIP!
I'M NOT LEAVING HIM BEHIND!

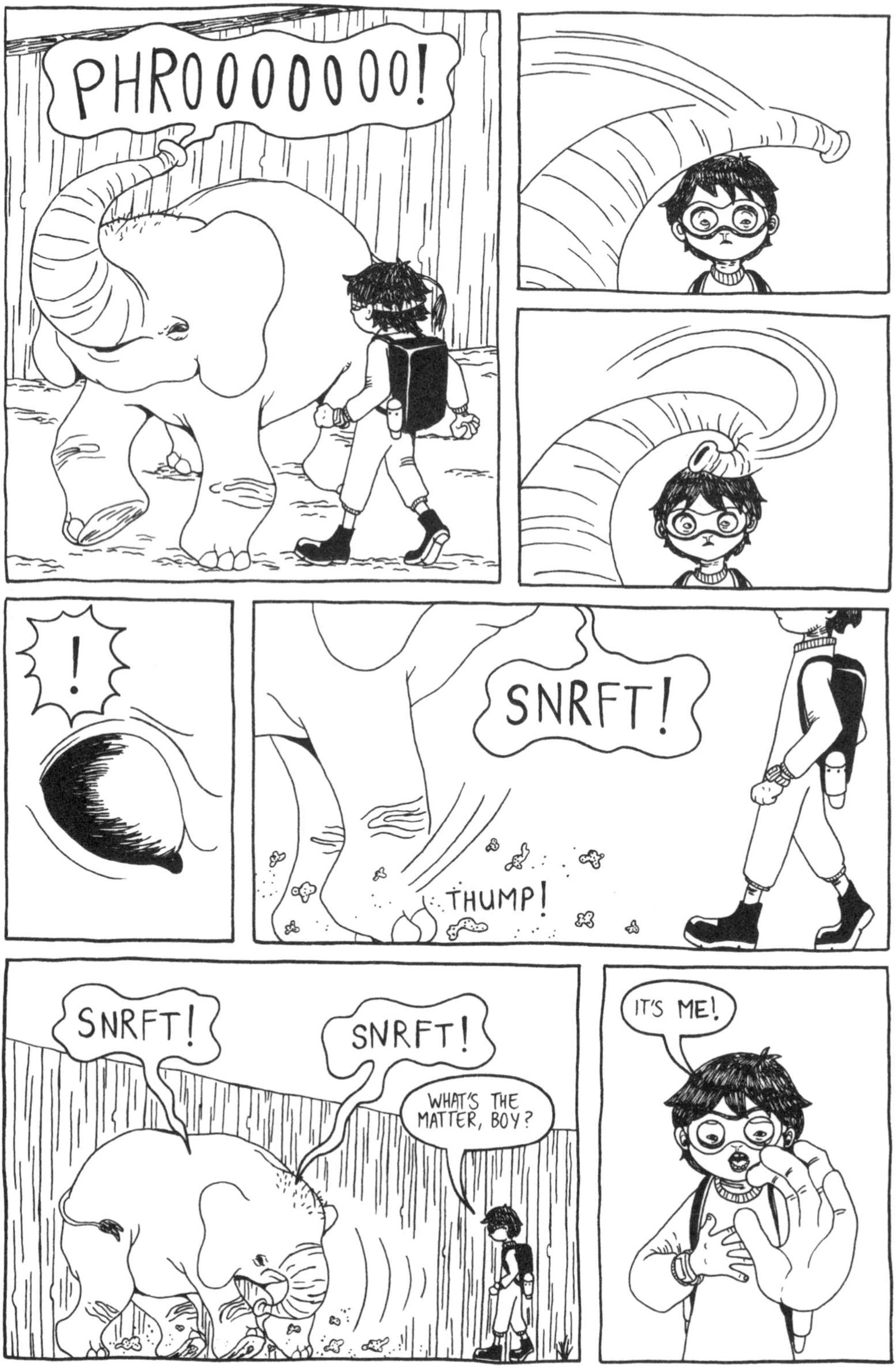
PHROOOOOOO!
!
SNRFT!
THUMP!
SNRFT!
SNRFT!
WHAT'S THE MATTER, BOY?
IT'S ME!

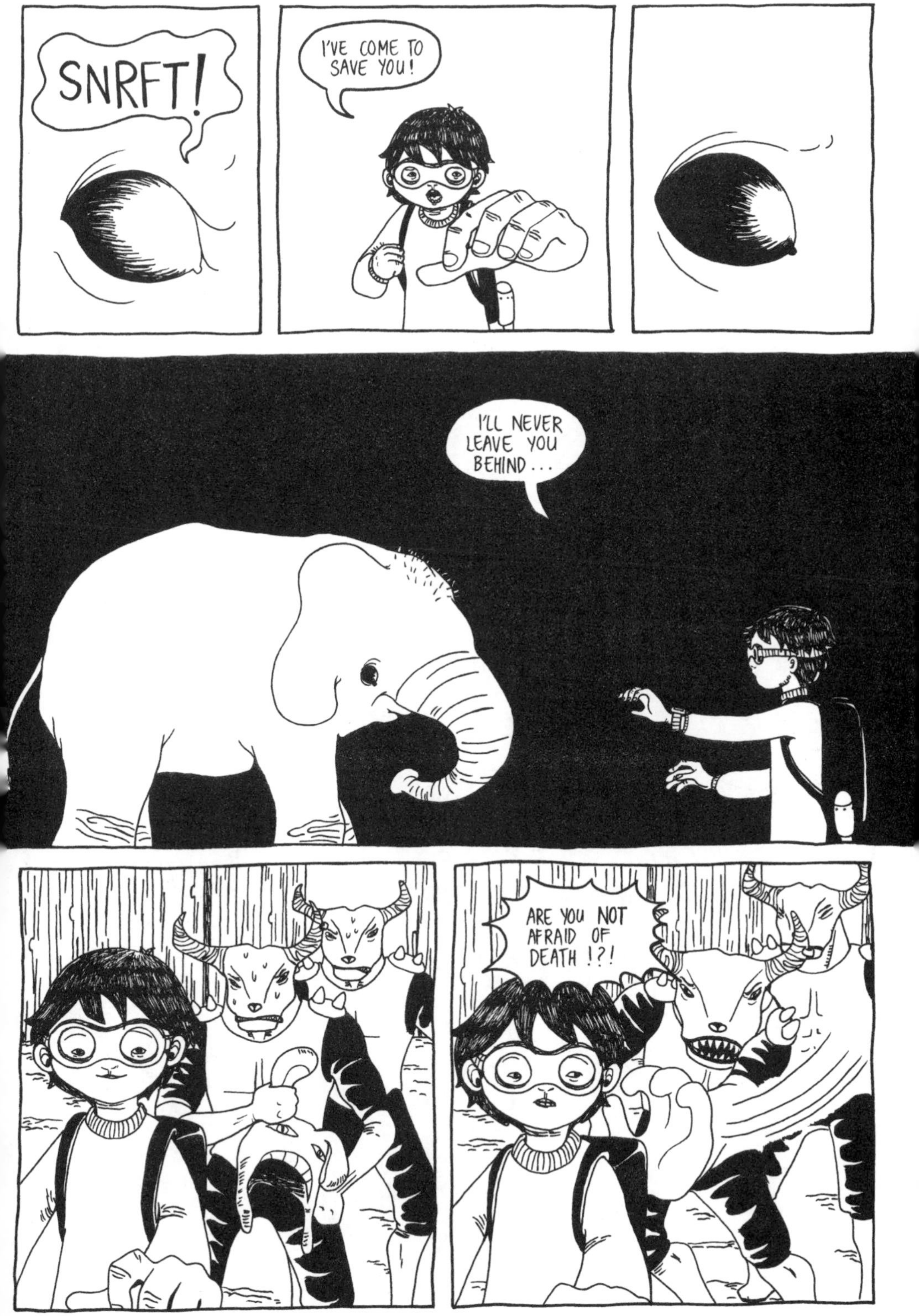
SNRFT!
I'VE COME TO SAVE YOU!
I'LL NEVER LEAVE YOU BEHIND...
ARE YOU NOT AFRAID OF DEATH!?!

!
PHRRROOOOOOO
!?!
THUMP THUMP THUMP
WHUMP!
LOOK OUT!!!

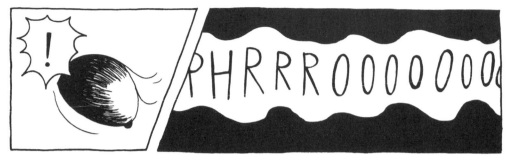

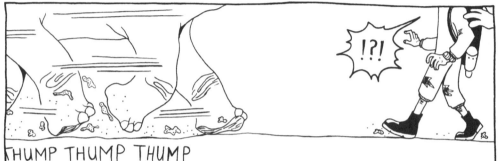

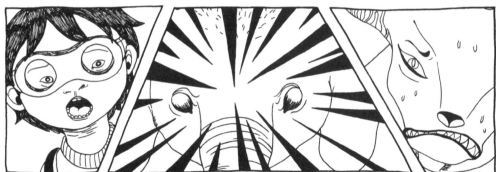

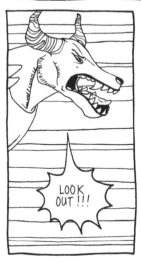

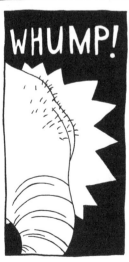

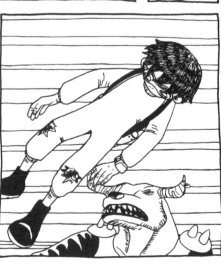

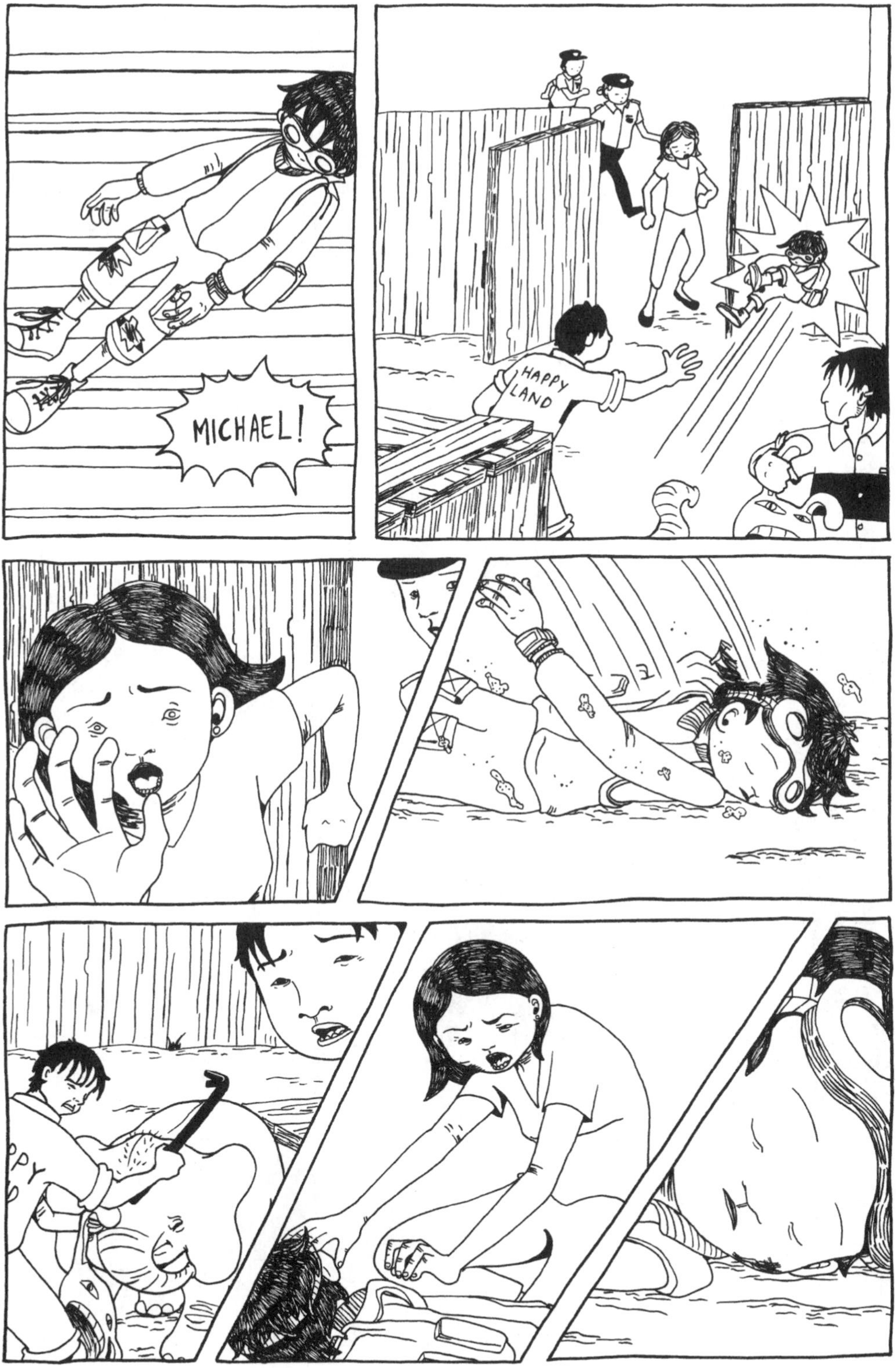
MICHAEL!
HAPPY LAND

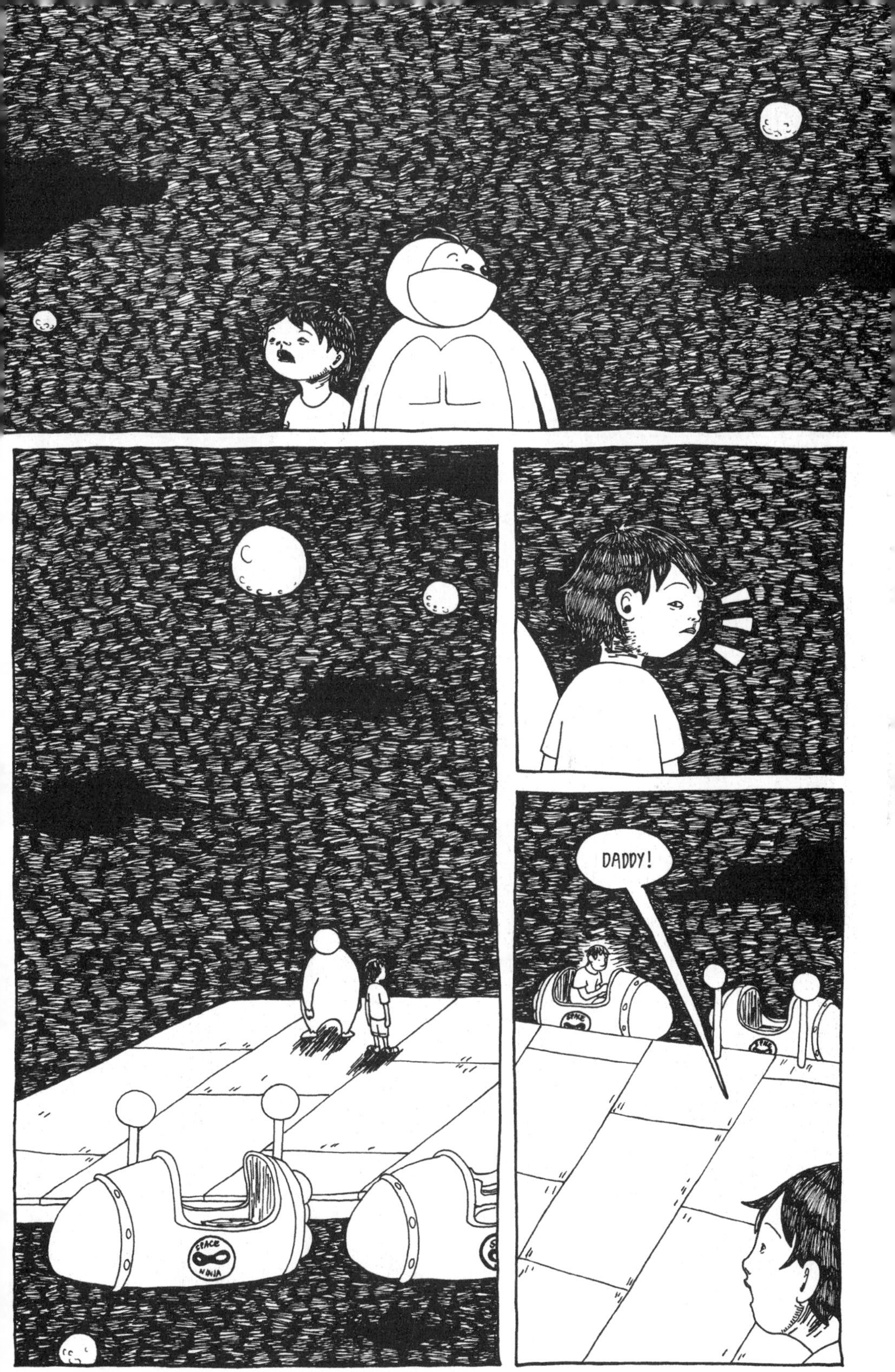
DADDY!

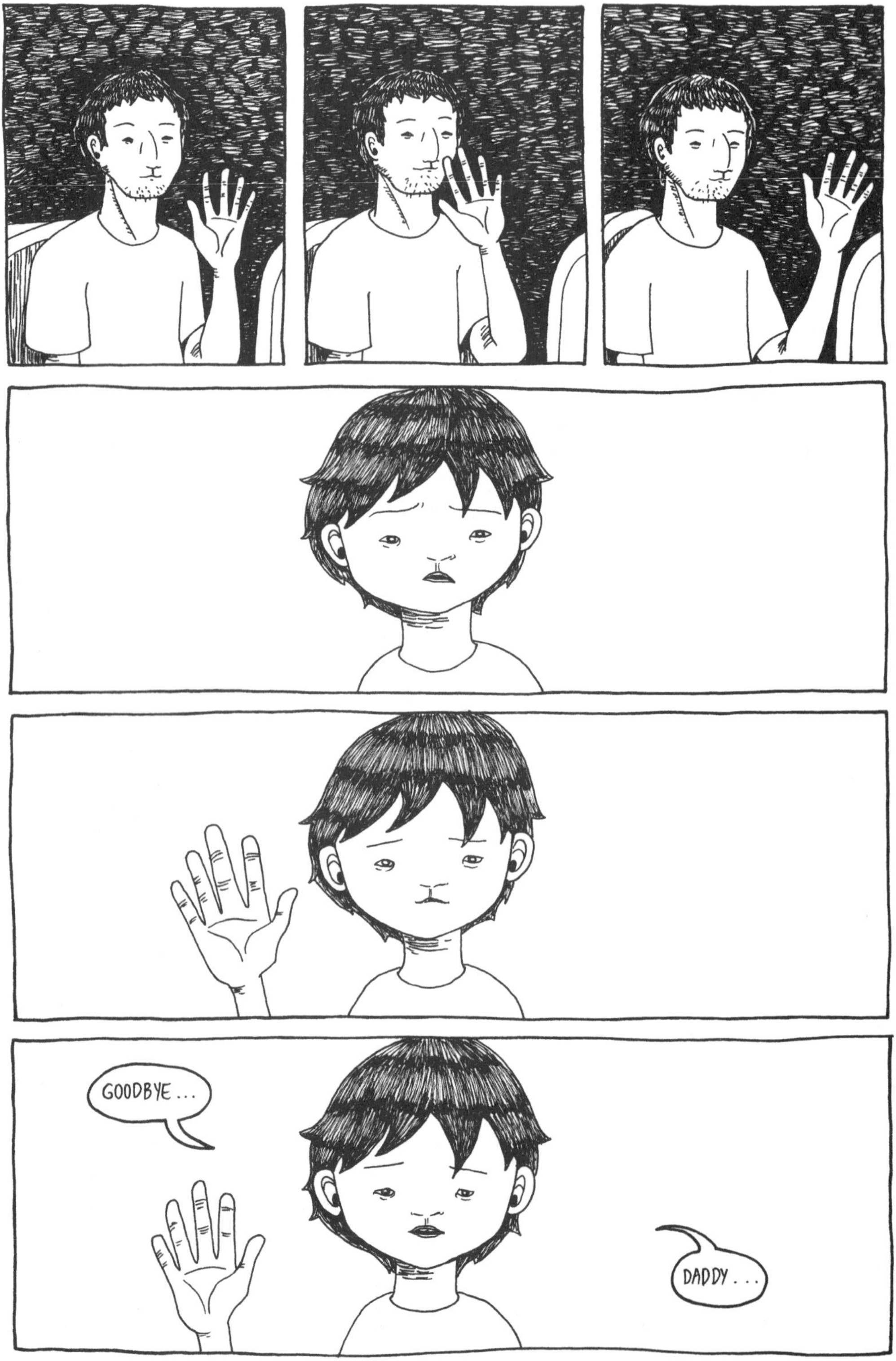
GOODBYE...
DADDY...

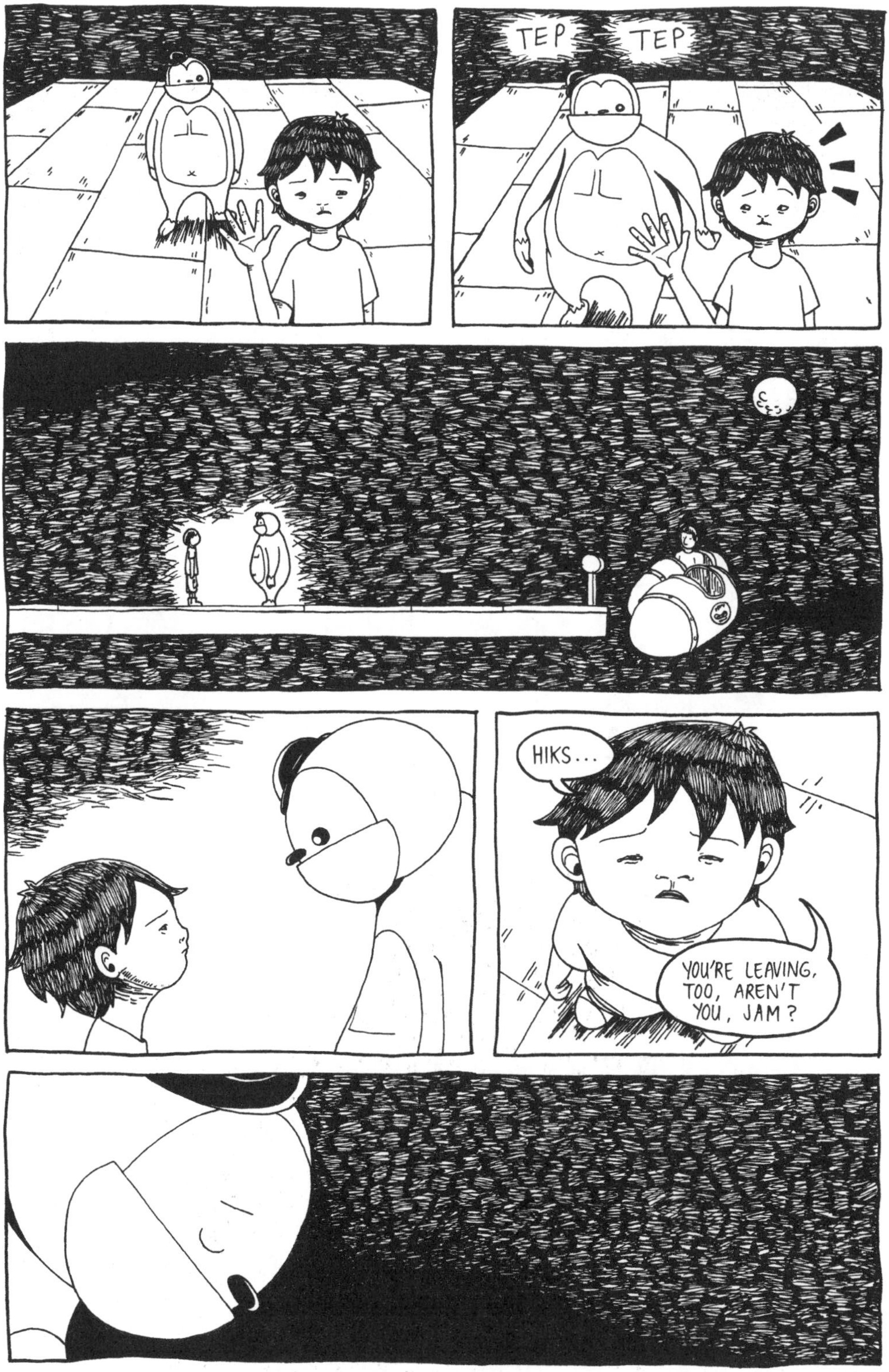
TEP
TEP
HIKS...
YOU'RE LEAVING, TOO, AREN'T YOU, JAM?

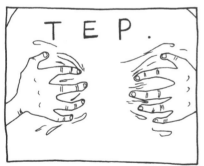

T E P .

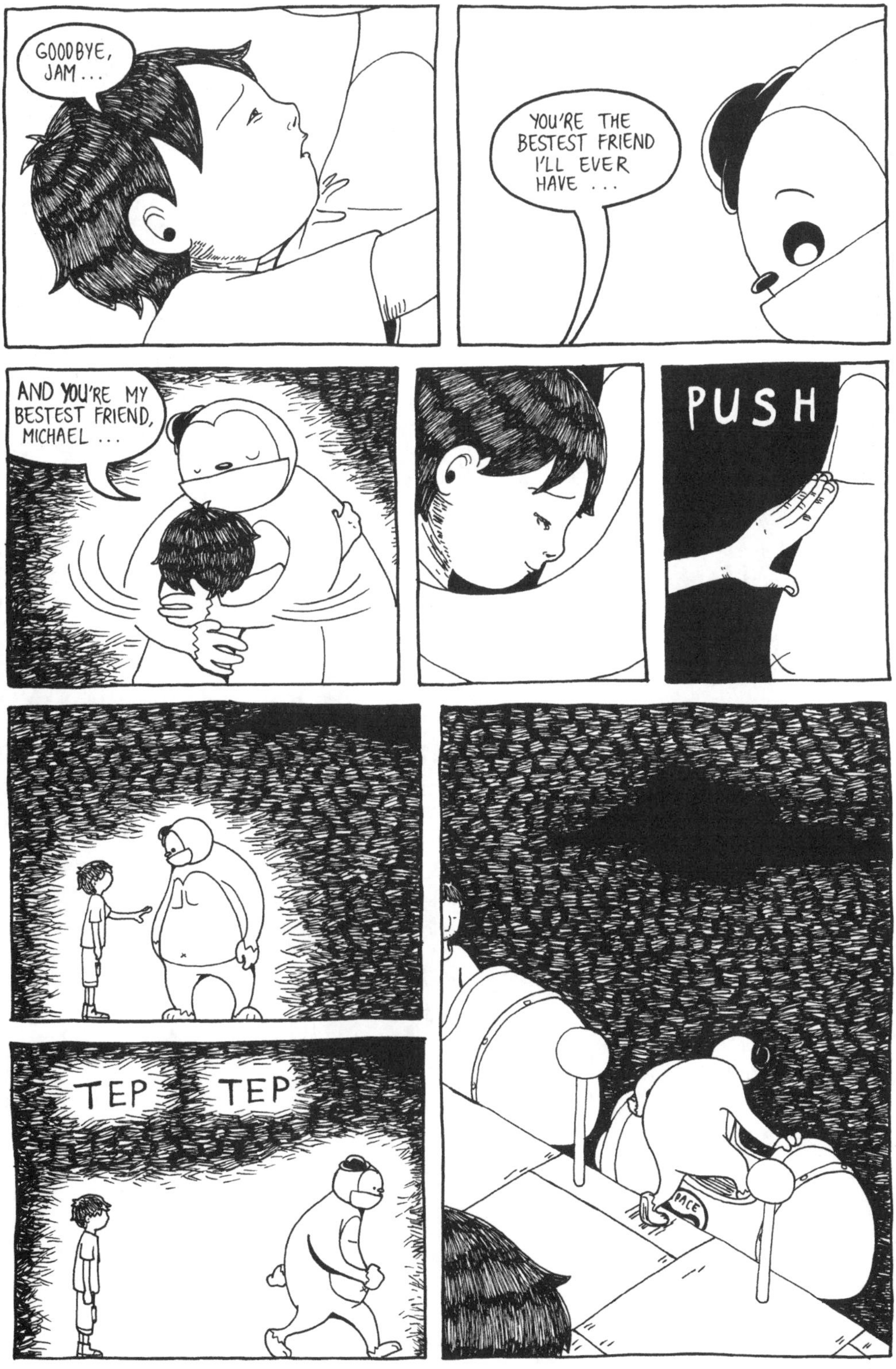
GOODBYE, JAM...
YOU'RE THE BESTEST FRIEND I'LL EVER HAVE . . .
AND YOU'RE MY BESTEST FRIEND, MICHAEL . . .
PUSH
TEP TEP
PACE

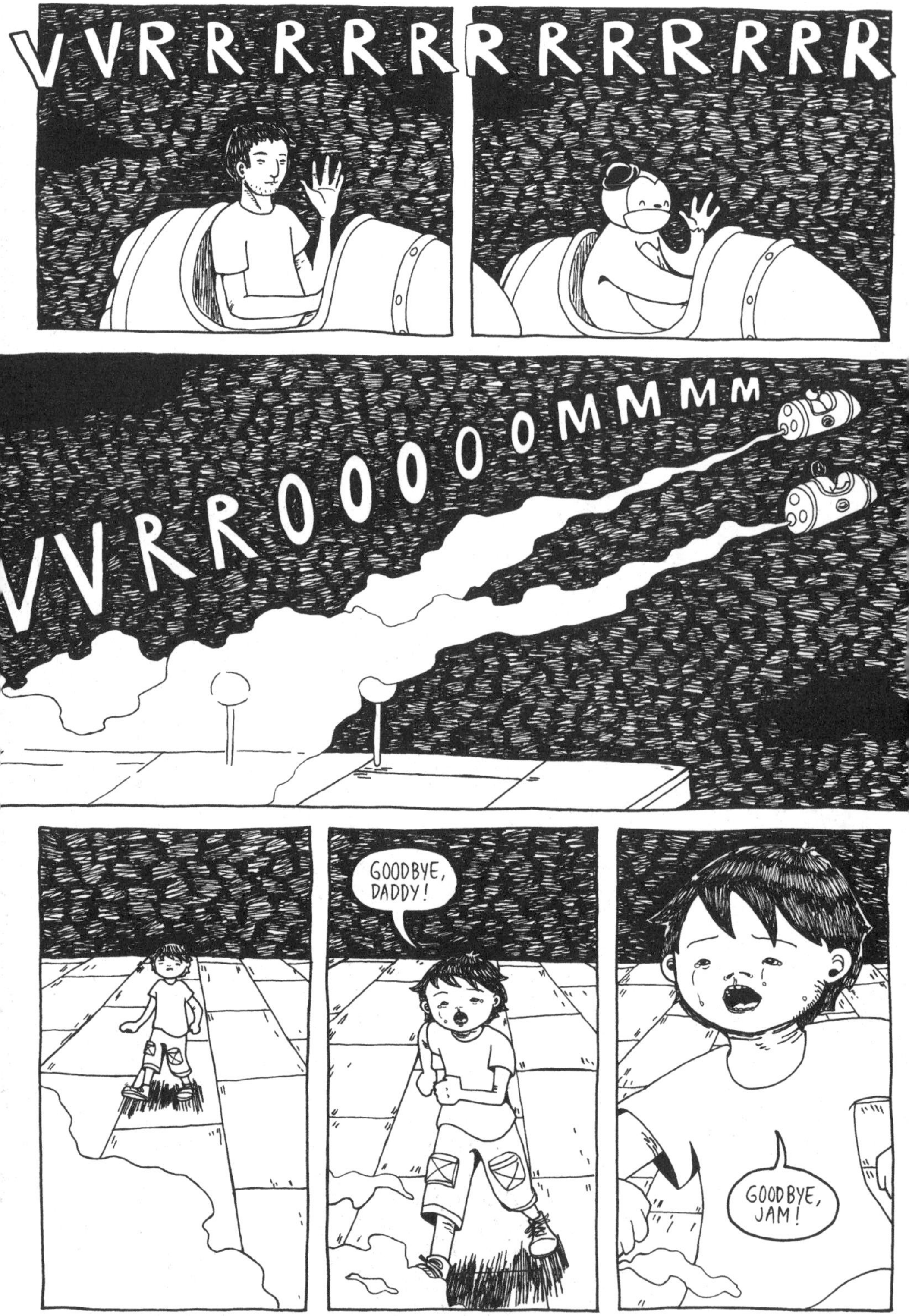
VVRRRRRRRRRRRR
VVRROOOOOOMMMMM
GOODBYE, DADDY!
GOODBYE, JAM!

GOODBYE!

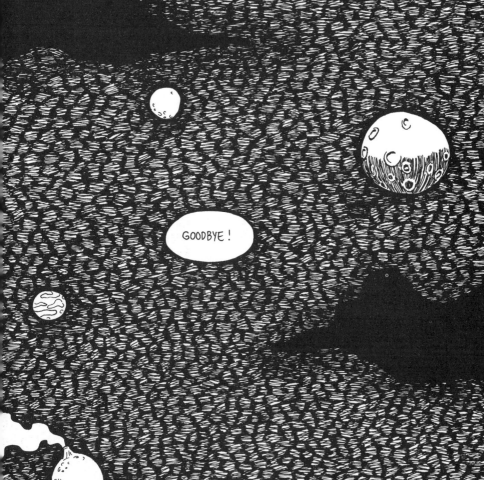

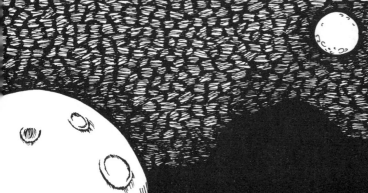

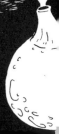

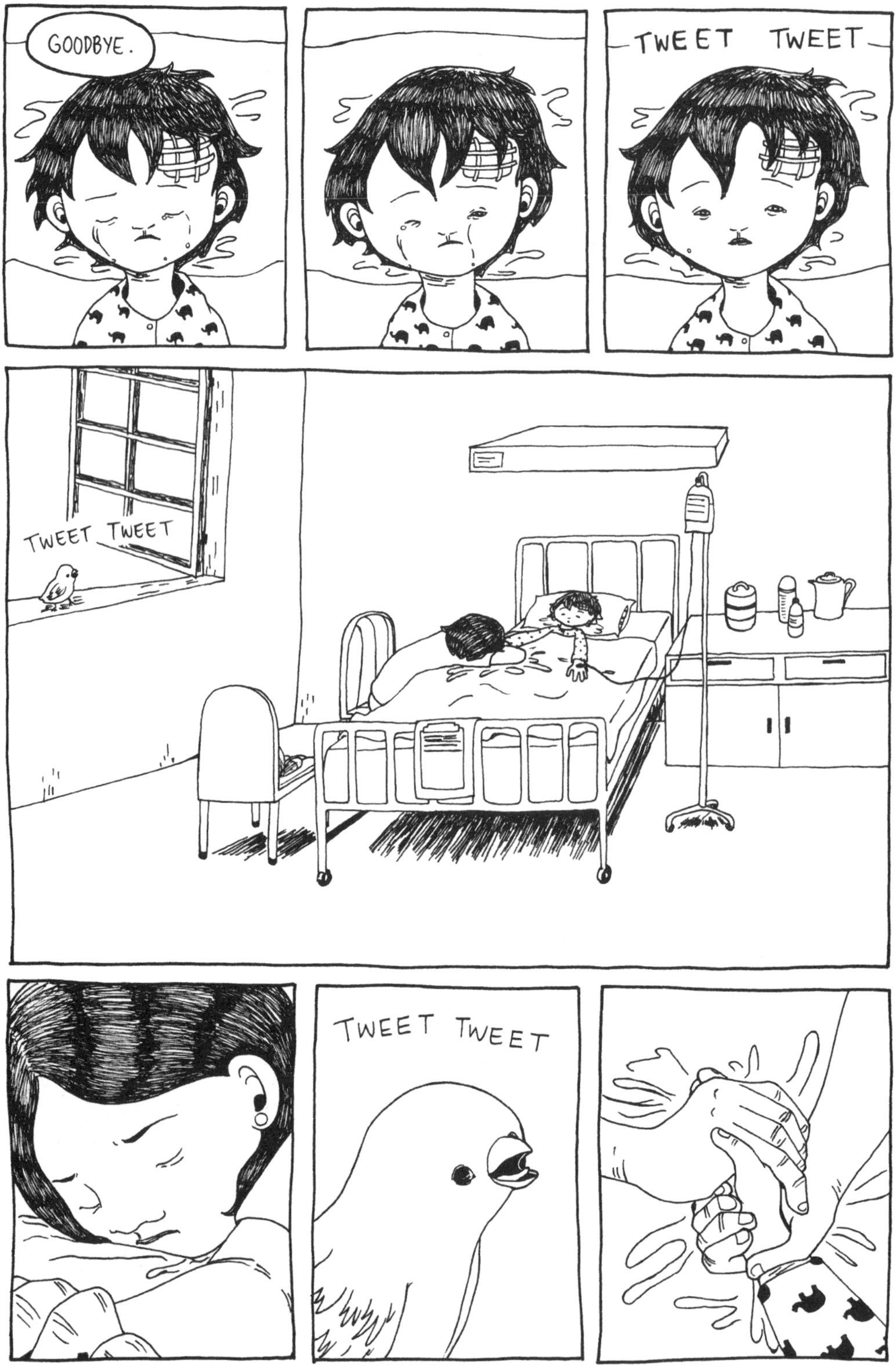
GOODBYE.
TWEET TWEET
TWEET TWEET
TWEET TWEET

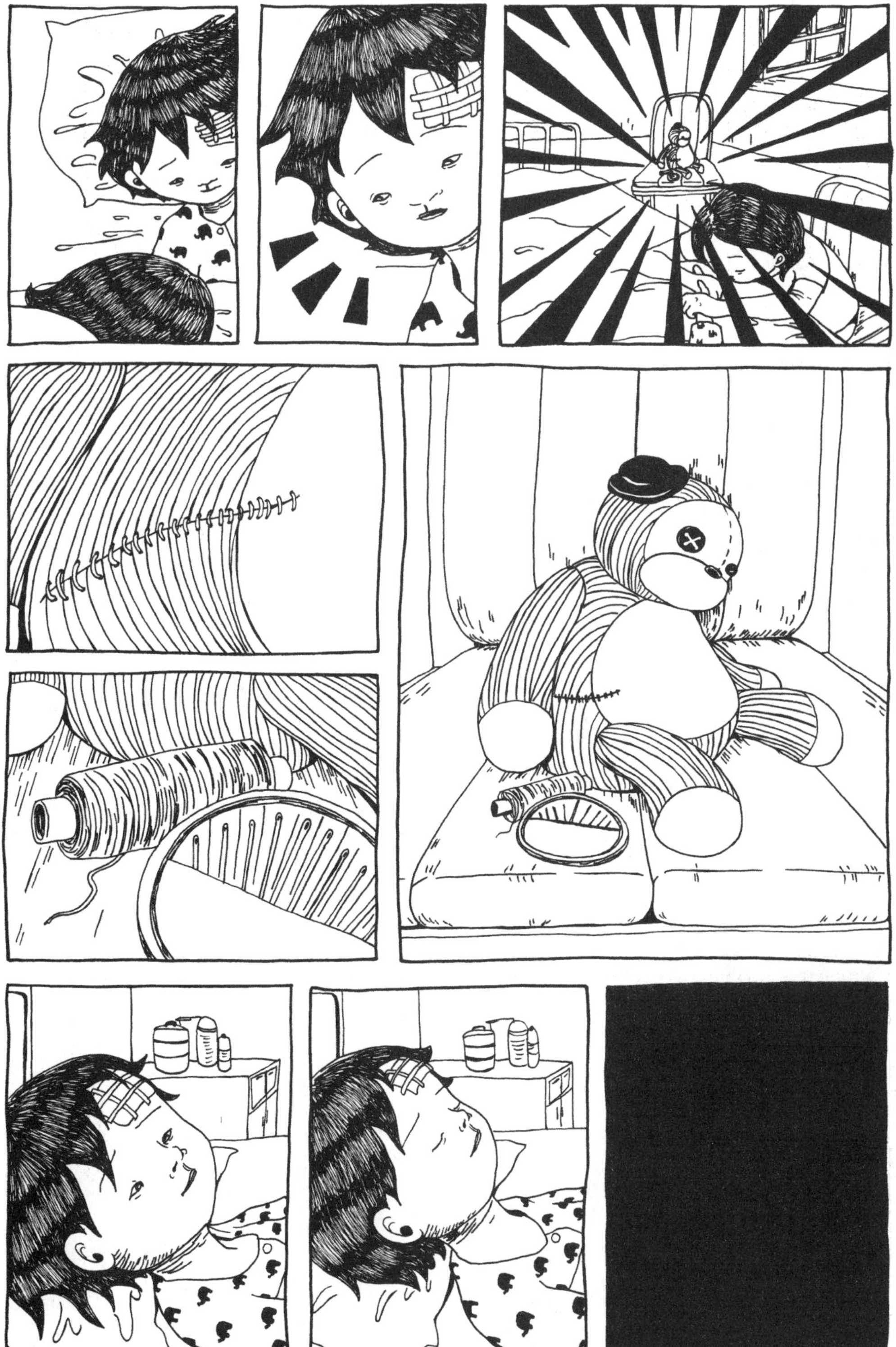

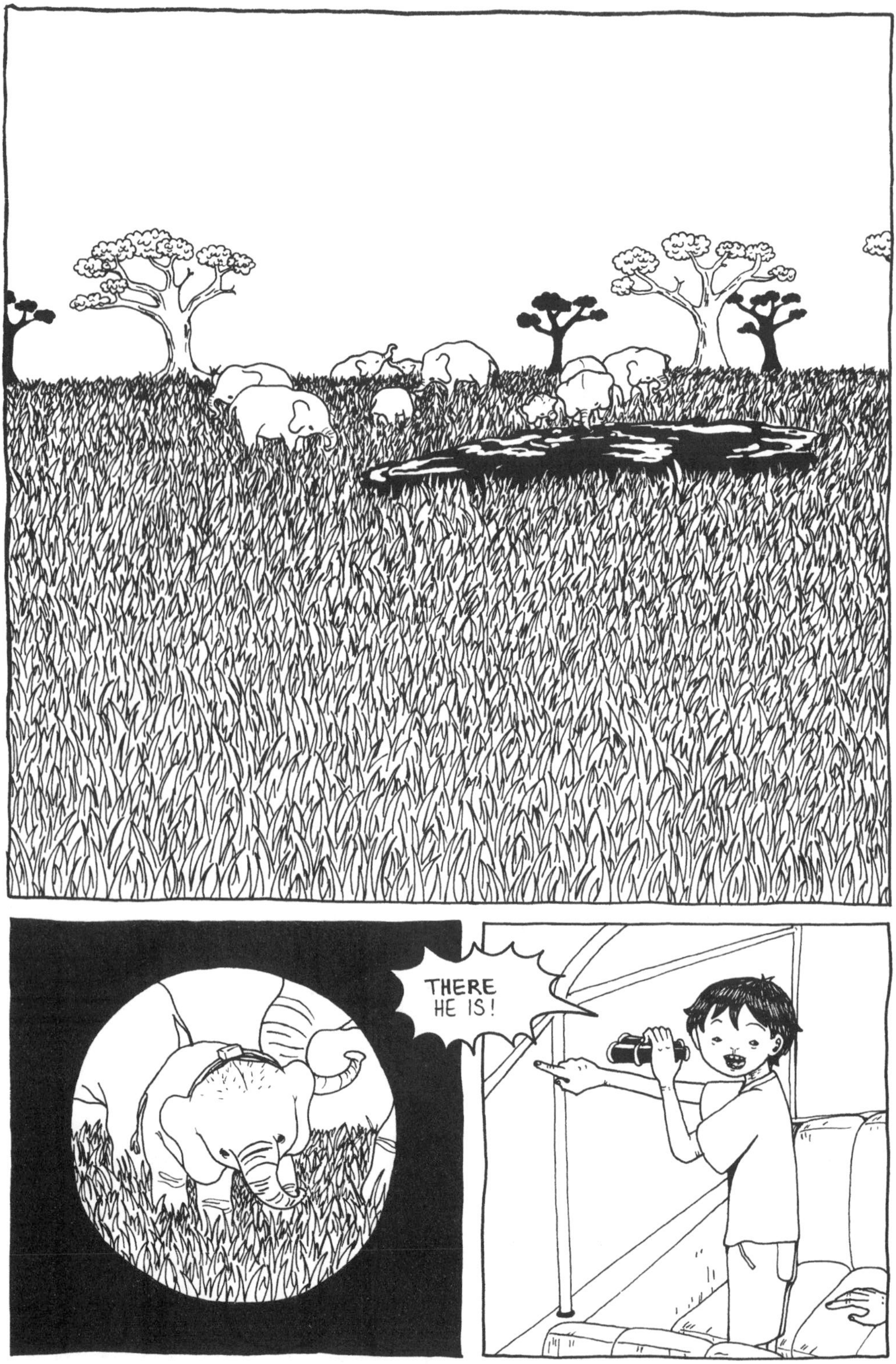
THERE
HE IS!

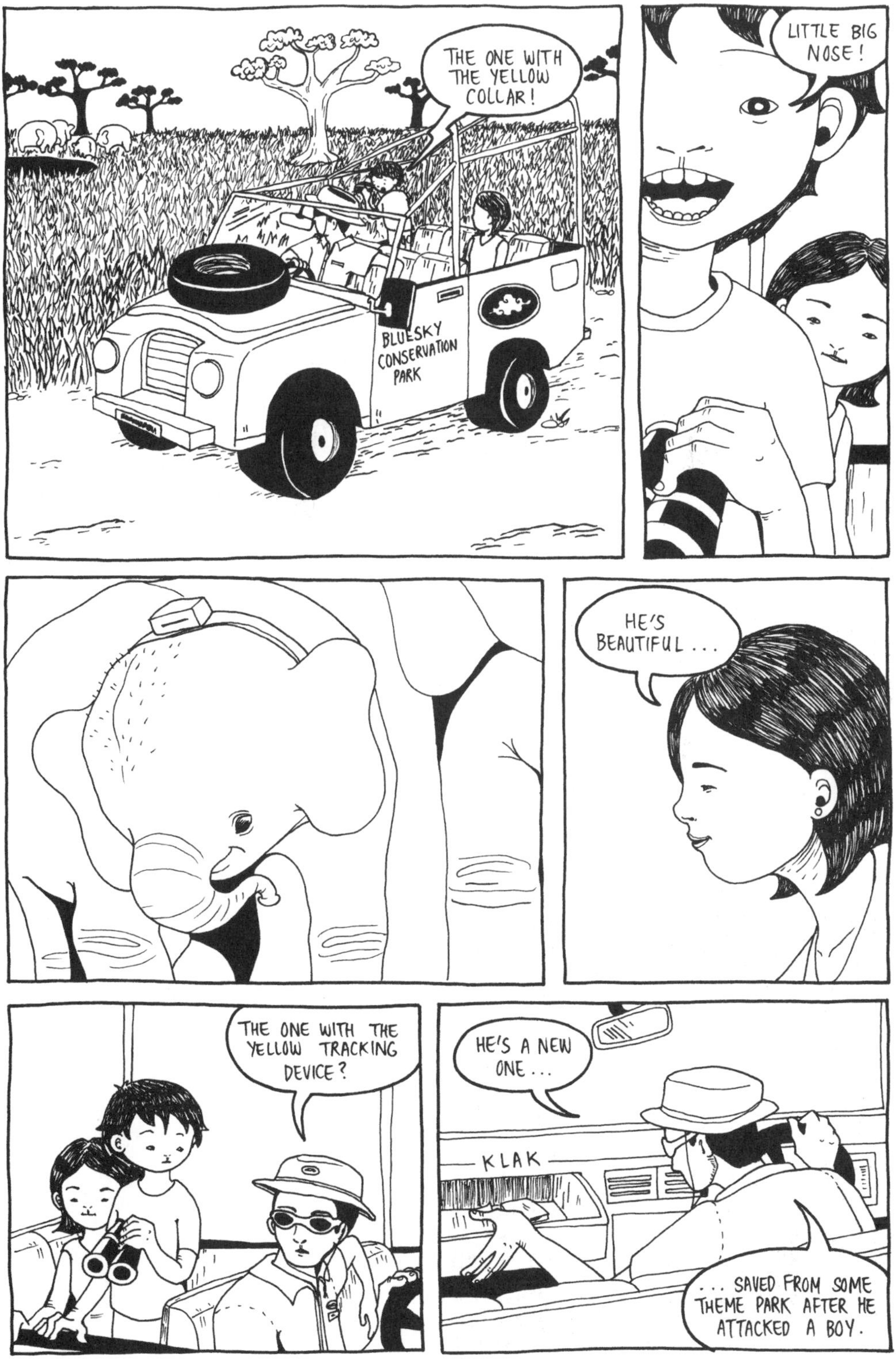
THE ONE WITH THE YELLOW COLLAR!
BLUESKY CONSERVATION PARK
LITTLE BIG NOSE!
HE'S BEAUTIFUL...
THE ONE WITH THE YELLOW TRACKING DEVICE?
HE'S A NEW ONE...
KLAK
...SAVED FROM SOME THEME PARK AFTER HE ATTACKED A BOY.

January 15, 2000

Violent theme park elephant sent to conservation park

HAPPY LAND

HERE. DID YOU READ THAT?

conservation

PY LAND

The elephant (above), had been in Happy Land for a day when the incident happened. An 8-year-old boy was injured but has since recovered.

boy victim says, "I saved Little Big Nose!"

to have been obtained by although the theme involvement.

The elephant is to be released into Blue Sky conservation Park in Thailand. Little Big Nose is scheduled to be flown to Thailand this Saturday to begin rehabilitation into the wild. Michael plans to visit Little His mother,

HEE HEE!

YES, WE'VE READ THIS. WE HAVE.

'TWAS PROBABLY A GOOD THING, EH?

MAYBE NOT FOR THE BOY VICTIM . . .

BUT THAT MADE THEM RETURN THE ELEPHANT TO THE WILD, WHERE IT BELONGS . . .

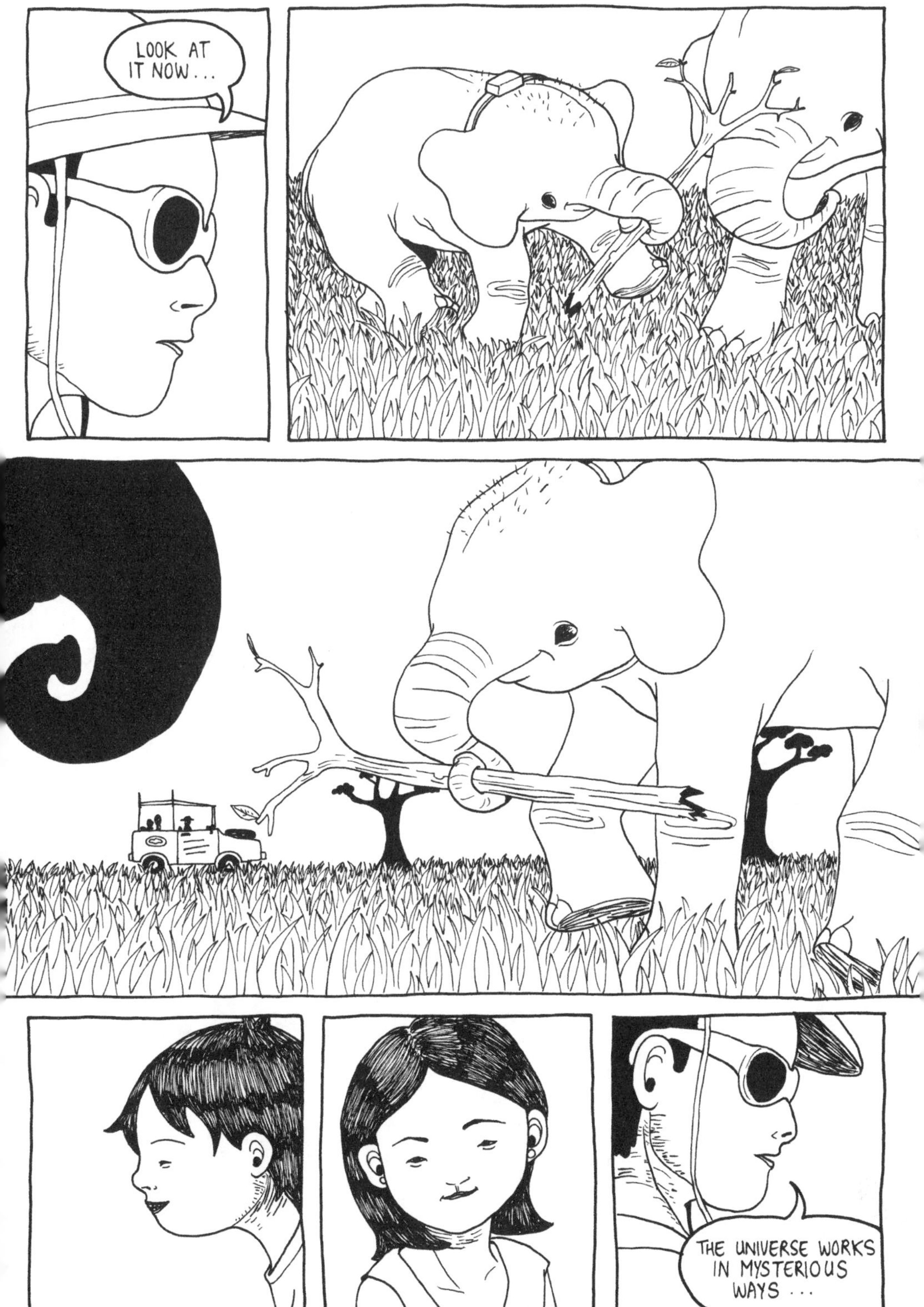
LOOK AT IT NOW...
THE UNIVERSE WORKS IN MYSTERIOUS WAYS...

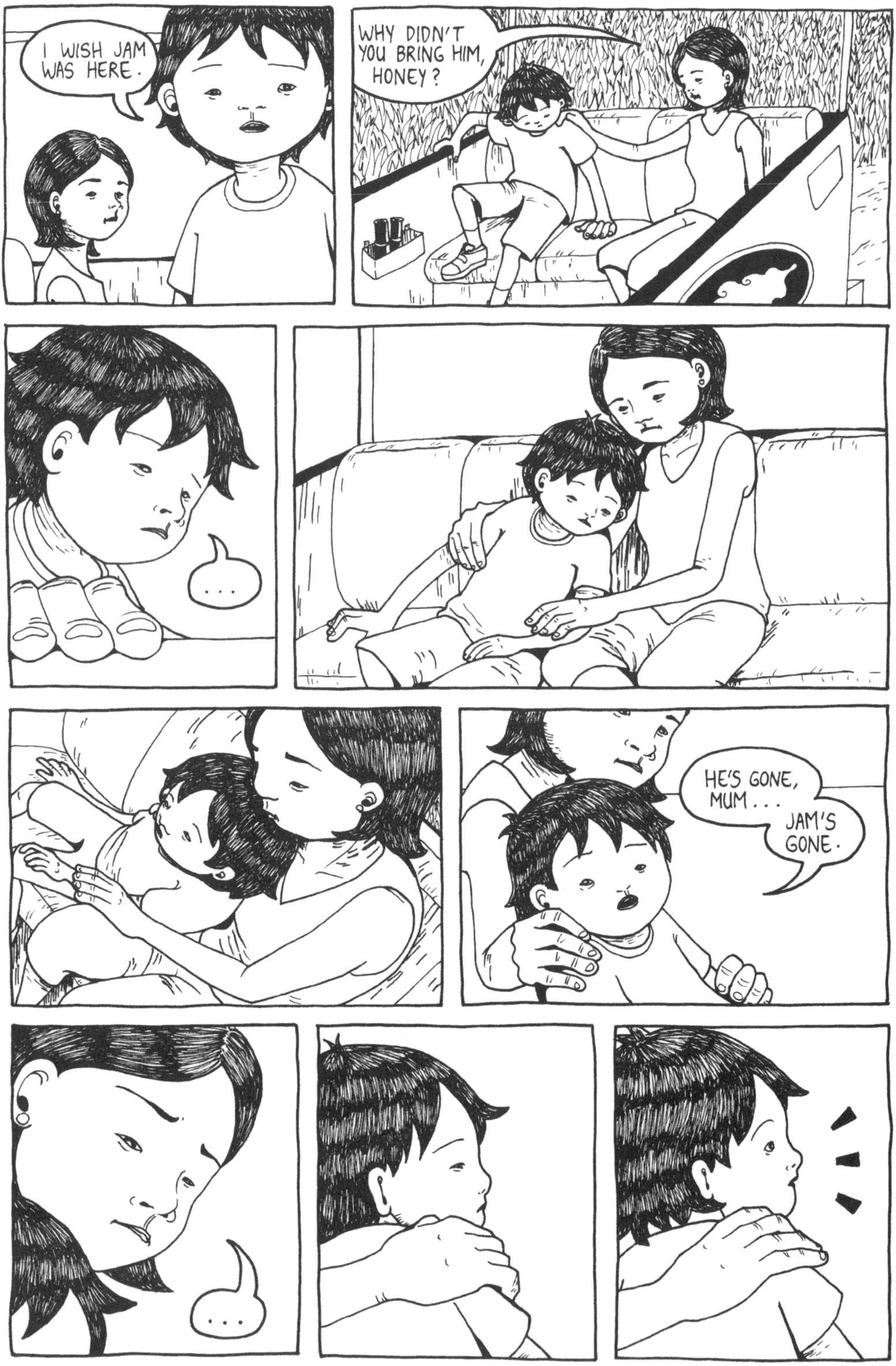
I WISH JAM WAS HERE.
WHY DIDN'T YOU BRING HIM, HONEY?
...
HE'S GONE, MUM...
JAM'S GONE.
...

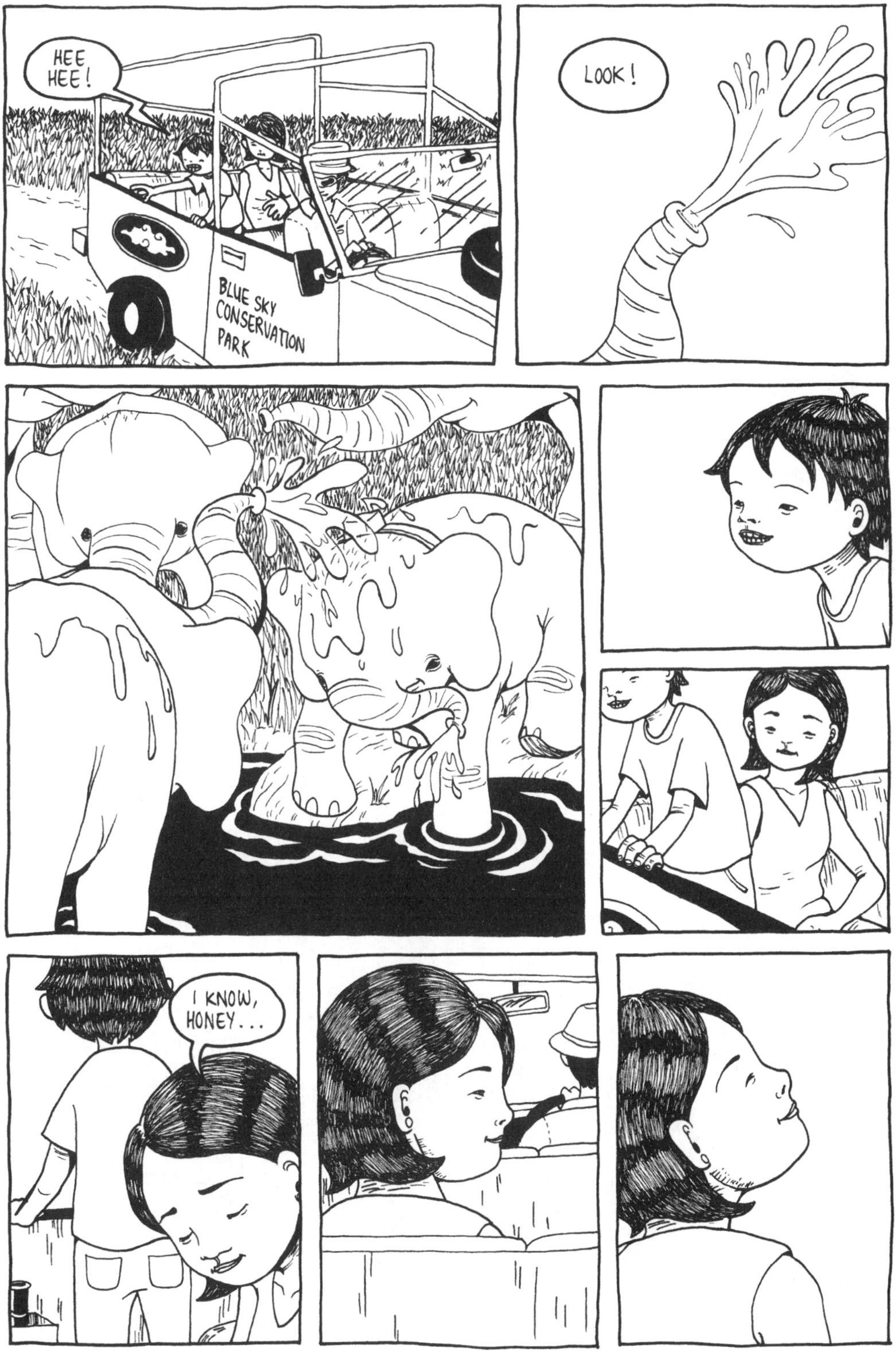
HEE HEE!
BLUE SKY CONSERVATION PARK
LOOK!
I KNOW, HONEY...

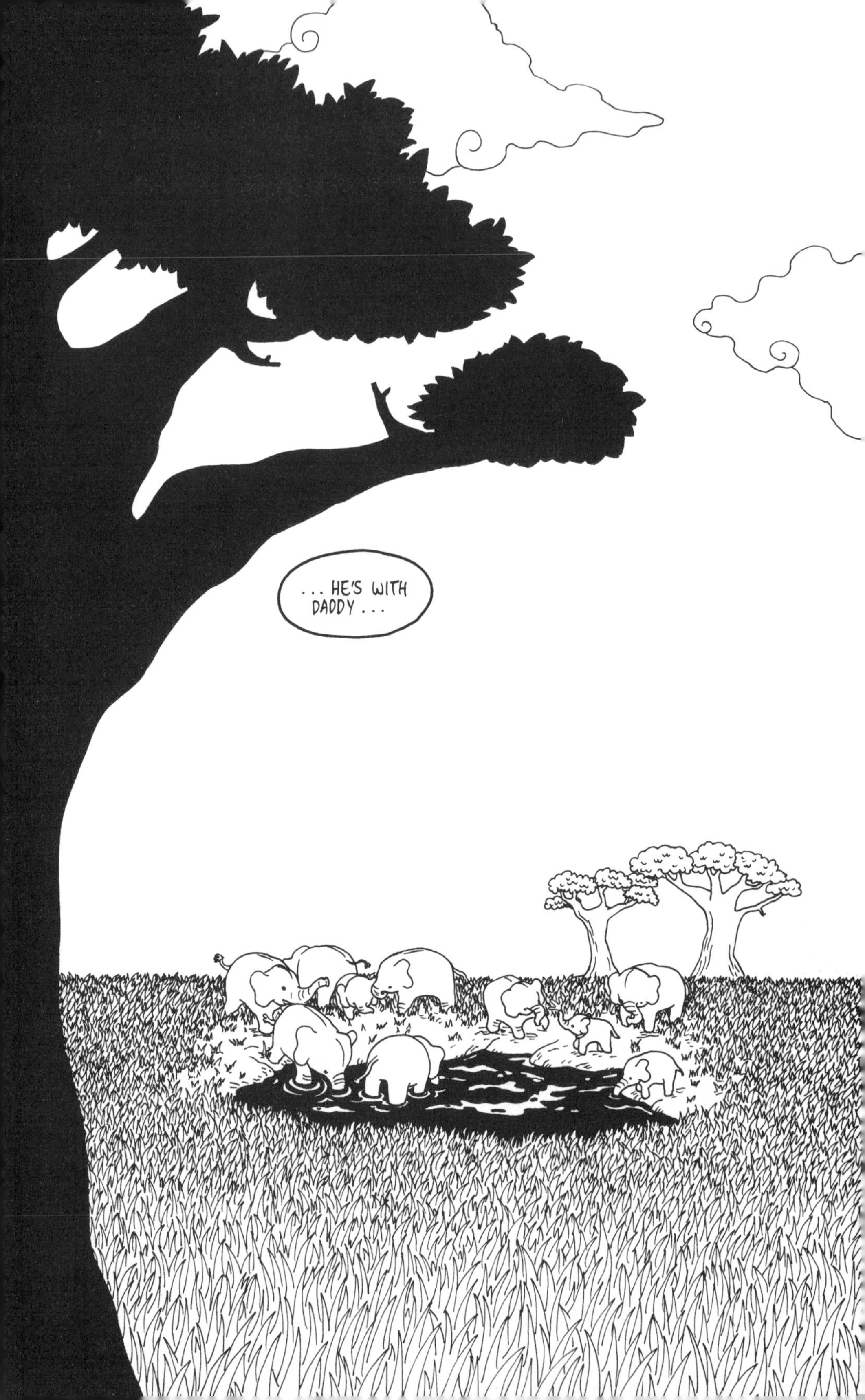
. . . HE'S WITH DADDY . . .

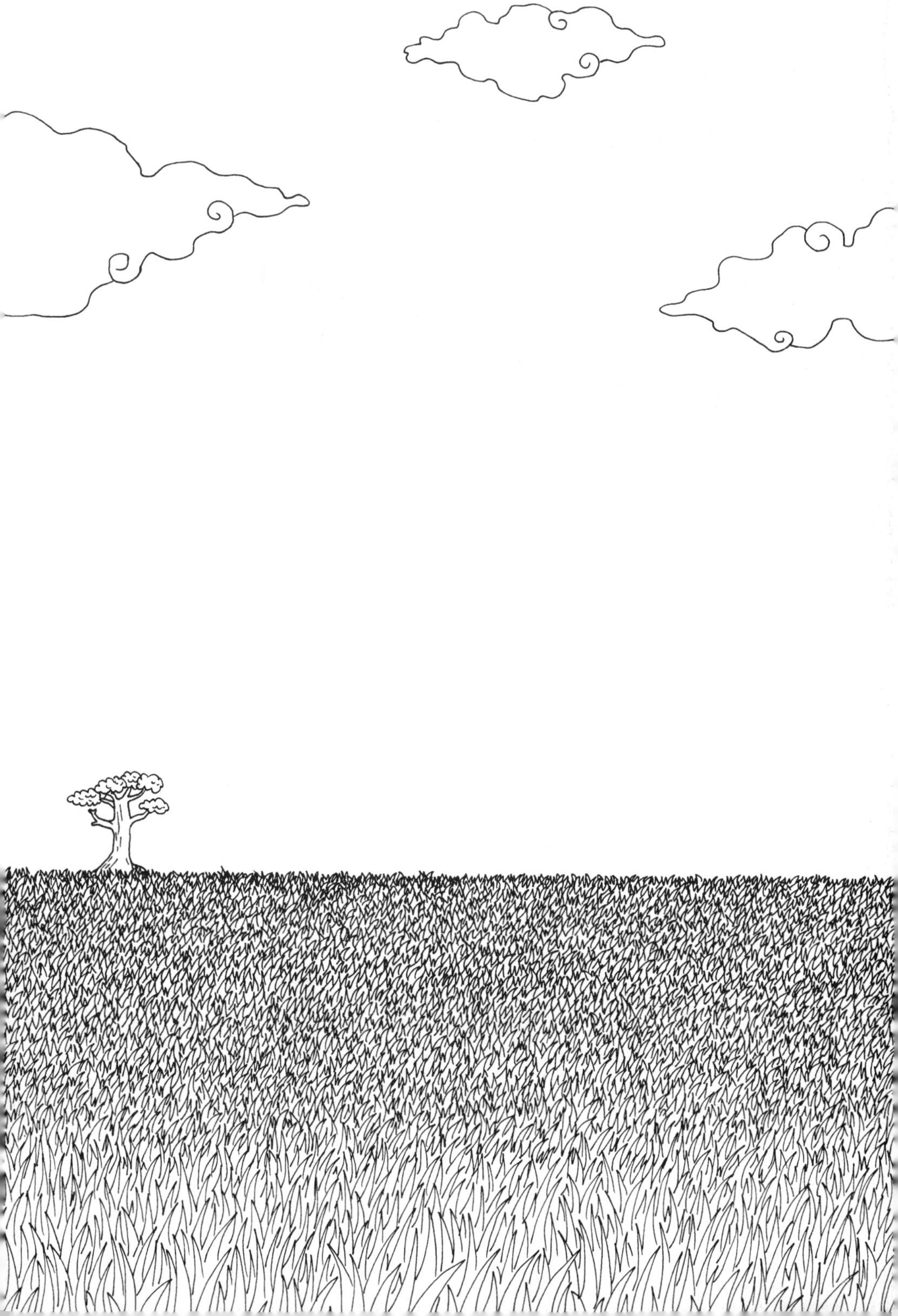

My Summer Vacation

by ~~Jam the Magnificent~~ Michael

It was a hot summer's day.

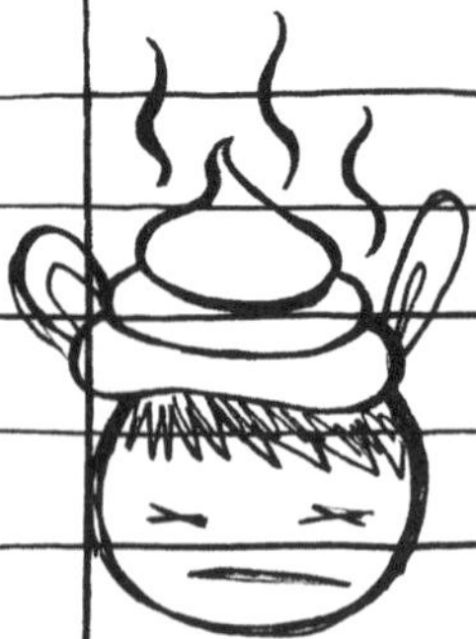

At this point, Captain Long Ears interrupted the flow of words from my pen and said, "That's STUPIDLY SUPERFLUOUS. All summer days are hot."

Clearly, he has forgotten The Cold Summer Day Fiasco (of yesterday). Caca-brain.

I threw the pen at him and he said, "You're an abysmal writer."

I said, "Then write your own essay."

He said, "I said those words with love and the highest of deference."

I said, "Thank you."

And then I sat at the desk for a looong time.

I have to admit: I'm not so good with the words. So I'm writing this essay in pictures. I know you've only asked for 500 words, but I'm giving you 1000 × $7\frac{1}{2}$ worth of words anyway.

turn over

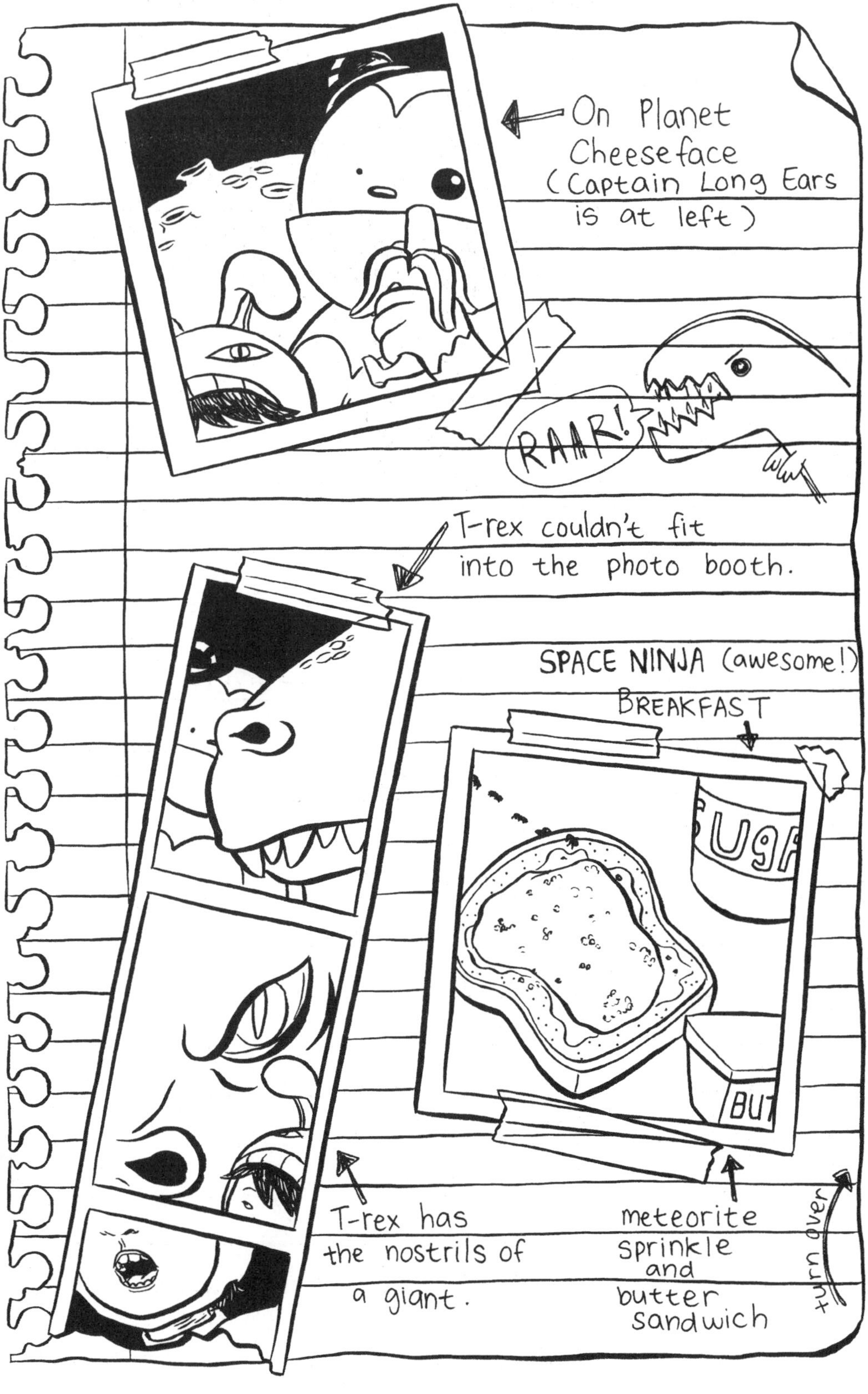

On Planet Cheeseface (Captain Long Ears is at left)
RAAR!
T-rex couldn't fit into the photo booth.
SPACE NINJA (awesome!) BREAKFAST
T-rex has the nostrils of a giant.
meteorite sprinkle and butter sandwich
turn over

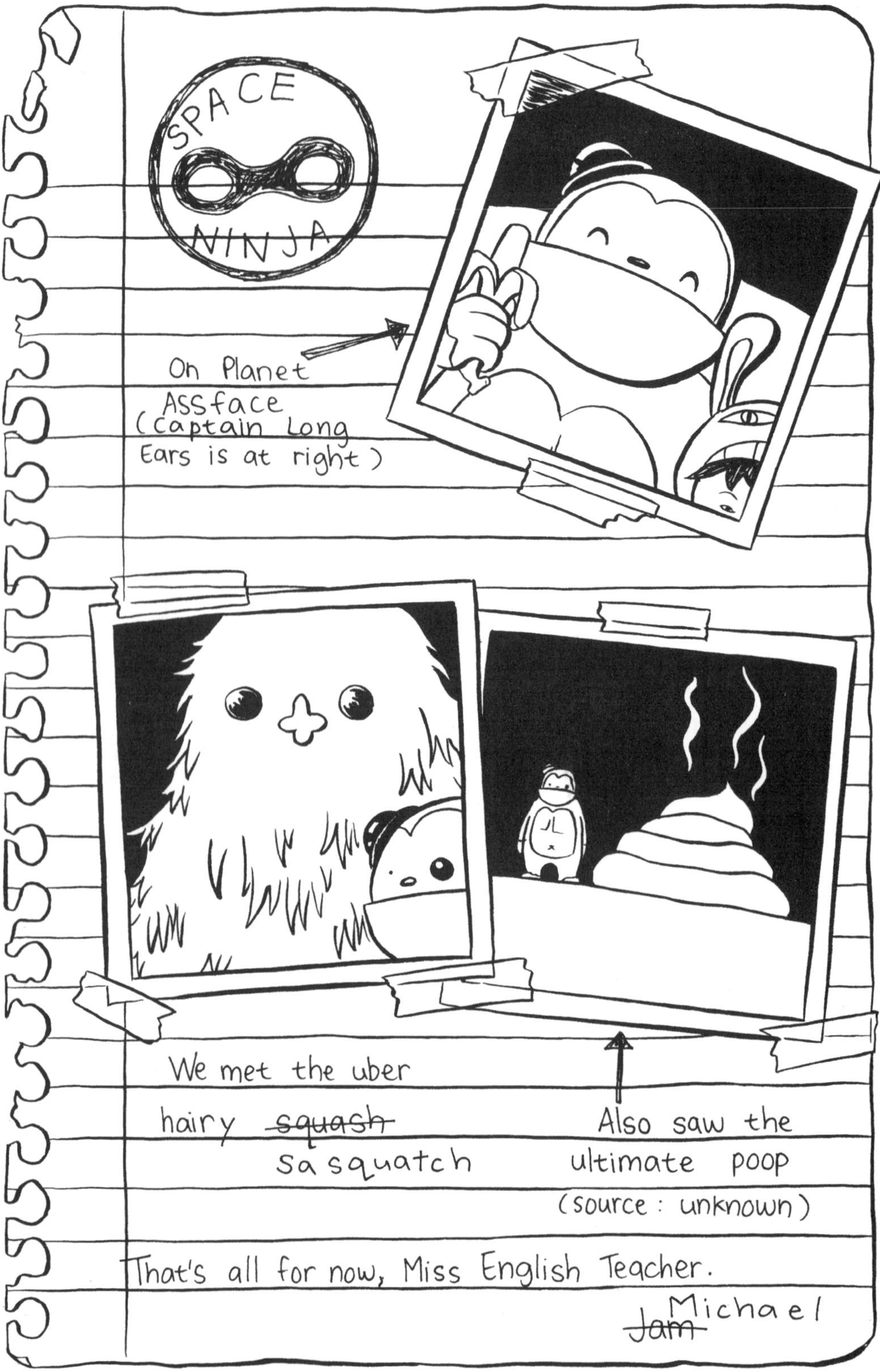
SPACE NINJA
On Planet ASSface (Captain Long Ears is at right)
We met the uber hairy ~~squash~~ sasquatch
Also saw the ultimate poop (source: unknown)
That's all for now, Miss English Teacher.
~~Jam~~ Michael